A WHISKY IN MONSTERVILLE

LOCH NESS: PEOPLE ARE DYING TO VISIT

Tom Morton

A Looderhorn Book
Northmavine, Shetland Isles

Copyright © 2013 Tom Morton
All rights reserved.
ISBN: 1484197518
ISBN 13: 9781484197516

The moral right of the author has been asserted
First published in 2013 by
Looderhorn Books, Northmavine Manse,
Hillswick, Shetland Isles, ZE2 9RW
www.looderhorn.co.uk

No part of this book may be reproduced or transmitted in any form or by any other means without the express permission of the publisher and/or author. Except by a reviewer who wishes to quote brief passages in a glowing and enthusiastic manner.

A WHISKY IN MONSTERVILLE

A note concerning the whiskies

Each chapter of *A Whisky in Monsterville* has been matched with a particular whisky, or whiskey. This makes the book interactive – if you can find the specific whisky to go with the chapter you happen to be reading. And this may prove somewhat difficult, depending on where in the world you happen to be. Instant downloads of books is one thing. Immediate availability of rare whiskies quite another.

However, substitution is permitted, if you cannot find or afford a Millburn 35 or an Ardbeg Galileo. Or the supermarket bottom shelf does not hold a TW Samuels. Close approximation is the name of this game. Or as close as possible.

The 'tasting notes' tend to vary. Some are personal observations, some are distillery or marketing descriptions. Many begin with the whisk(e)y's 'nose' or aroma, move on to the effect on the palate (mouthfeel) and then the finish, or the sensation of 're-breathing' the dram once swallowed. My rule is, add water to bring the strength of the whisky down to around 43 per cent alcohol.

Many additional whiskies are mentioned in the text – indeed, one may be crucial to the development of the events described. The contents page gives their names in italics. But consumption is of course optional. Specific ages, when not mentioned, should be whatever is available.

The book may be enjoyed without recourse to strong drink at all. After all, that's how it was written. If you do read-and-dram, please do it with... restraint.

Tom Morton

Contents

Midsummer, Loch Ness — *Balblair 1997* *1*

Five years earlier — *Macallan 10-year-old, cask strength* *5*

Southern shore — *Old Thompson American Blended Whiskey* *23*

Fisherman's blues — *The Famous Grouse* *25*

Ardbeg, Lagavulin, Bruichladdich, Laphroaig, Glenfiddich, Old Pulteney, Glen Moray

Souvenirs — *TW Samuels Kentucky Blended Whiskey* *41*

The official gaze — *Glenfiddich 12-year-old* *45*

Fishers of men — *Old Crow* *51*

Ice house — *Bulleit Bourbon Frontier Whiskey* *59*

Druids — *Loch Ness Single Highland Malt Whisky* *63*

Protect and enhance — *Ten High 'Bourbon blend'* *75*

Bruichladdich

Flaws — *Bruichladdich Octomore* *81*

A WHISKY IN MONSTERVILLE

Clynelish, Glenfarclas 105

Practical theology	*Glenfarclas 105*................................ 97
Rocks off	*Glenrothes Vintage 1991*................. 111
Down	*Abhainn Dearg (Red Rocks) three-year-old*................................ 123
Money	*Ardbeg Galileo*............................... 139
Lochside, Dores	*Yamazaki 18*.................................. 143

Clynelish 14, Lagavulin 16, Yamazaki 18, Yamazaki 12

Arrival	*The Notch, Nantucket Island Single Malt*................................... 157
Rest and Recreation	*Bushmills Black Bush* 169
Crown	*Millburn 35-year-old, Rare Malts Series* 177
A meeting in the air	*Redbreast 15-year-old*..................... 191
Killer app	*Tomatin 18-year-old*....................... 199
Queen of the Highland Fleshpots	*Clynelish 14-year-old* 207

Aberlour A'bunadh, 1978 Clynelish, Dallas Dhu, Talisker

The wrath of God	*Black Bottle*.................................. 215
Repentance	*Loch Dhu 10, 'The Black Whisky'* ... 227
Last supper	*Auchentoshan 1979 Oloroso*............ 251
Drumnadrochit time	*Dry Fly Port Finished Wheat Whiskey*............................. 261

Muckle Flugga, Springbank 10, Glen Scotia Distillery Select, Longrow 18, Highland Park 25, Famous Grouse

Students at private schools in Louisiana are being taught that the Loch Ness Monster is real – a claim that is then held as evidence disproving Charles Darwin's theory of evolution. Thousands of students across the state are eligible to receive publicly funded vouchers to allow them to attend private Christian schools where textbooks published by Accelerated Christian Education (ACE) claim the monster was actually a dinosaur that existed at the same time as man, an assertion which conflicts with the theory of evolution.

The Huffington Post, 25 June 2012

We will dwell altogether where none is oppressed,
Where no tyrant has power his legions to send;
And we never will part in the land of the blessed,
Where there's peace, love, and joy, without any end.

The Evils of War, or, The Ruined Family.
Broadside Ballad, c. 1856. National Library of Scotland.

And you know that's when I fall, I can't help myself at all
That's when I get whiskey bent and hellbound.

Hank Williams Jr. Copyright 1979 Bocephus Music/BMI

Midsummer, Loch Ness

Deep golden amber. An abundance of tropical fruits on the nose – bananas and pineapples, together with green apples, oranges and apricots. Hints of honey, vanilla and butterscotch can also be detected. Initially sweet on the palate, yet spicy and full-bodied. A long, spicy finish.

BALBLAIR 1997

A WHISKY IN MONSTERVILLE

On a fine night like this, everything seemed right with the world. It was the near-dark Highland dusk, the midsummer twilight that would last until it began to merge seamlessly with the dawn. A fingernail sliver of moon high above Abriachan. The dog star and its pack, pulsing.

The loch was still, rippled only by the occasional insect or the leap of a brown trout. Murricane sat on his plastic kayak, floating atop one of the greatest inland depths of water in Europe, gazing at the hulking ruin of Urquhart Castle, watching the car lights streak up and down the A82, halogen blue and cherrybomb red. The rattle of big diesels, the slow whine of tourist rentals. The screaming suicide runs of bikers along one of the most dangerous roads in the country.

The Great Glen. Loch Ness, Loch Oich, Loch Lochy, Loch Linnhe. Scotland east to west, the massive geological faultline splitting the country. Inverness at one end, Fort William at the other. Of immense strategic significance since the days of the Picts. The lochs linked by the Caledonian Canal, roads on either side, one busy, one little used. The hillsides, moors and forests along the Glen providing refuge for holidaymakers, runaways, downsizers, refugees from every past era that still had relatively intact human survivors. There were original, threadbare 1960s communes, moneyed new-age retreats, would-be artists and craftworkers galore. Candlemakers. There were always candlemakers. People doing pokerwork. And IT consultants complaining about their broadband connections.

There were eerily quiet men and women behind electrified fences who did not welcome visitors. Estates, aristocrats, gamekeepers and hunters. Cottages, caravans and would-be self-sufficient survivalists. The rich, the poor and the officially non-existent. Complete nutters and those only slightly, acceptably deranged. He wasn't quite sure of his own status, these days. Deranged, certainly. But acceptably?

At this moment, floating above immeasurable amounts of water, he felt more alive than he had for a long, long time.

A WHISKY IN MONSTERVILLE

The sodium orange glow to the north was the city of Inverness. Everything a tourist could want, from a decaf macchiato to a transvestite brothel. Or both in the same place, if you got a takeaway from the nearby Costa. It wasn't much of a transvestite brothel, so he'd heard. It was basically a motorcycle workshop with a sideline in bustiers and suspender belts. A bit of WD40 on the side. In some ways, it seemed like a natural outgrowth of the business, considering some of the bikers he'd known over the years. What the entrepreneurship gurus called 'economic convergence'. Adapting to the synchronicity. Lubricating the gears of finance.

He sipped at the bottle of Benleva Dark Ness stout he'd brought with him. These Ocean Kayak sit-on-tops were leisure and fishing craft, with built-in drinks and rod holders. The alloy paddle rested across his knees. He was wearing an old Umbro cotton tracksuit, a Polartec fleece on top. It was chilly on the loch at this time of night, getting on for 1.00am. Maybe the beer needed a chaser. He pulled out of his pocket a miniature of Balblair 97 he'd picked up during a visit to the distillery, north of Inverness, across the Black Isle. Whisky, they always said, was an outdoor spirit, originally made in mobile stills by a stream or a river, meant to be drunk as a medicine, a tonic, a guard against cold or a buffer against fear. The soft, fruity, maltiness of the spirit began to burn as it moved down his throat. American oak. He could taste the wood. He followed the heat with cooling, bitter beer, the combination working well. He felt the tingle of the liquor in his fingertips. Caught the dull glitter of a fish half-surfacing to his left. A brownie, maybe a pike. No rods tonight. The Ferox, the giant trout that lurked near the loch's murky bottom, they occupied his mind at times like this. Vicious cannibal creatures, the ultimate angling prize. He liked to help people catch them.

The pain in his leg was returning. The kayak was stable, but it was hard to get enough movement in his ankle to stop it seizing up. He swallowed the rest of the whisky, then the beer, stashed the bottles and prepared to head back towards the shore.

As he paddled slowly and steadily back towards the lights of Temple Pier and the opaque shadow that was the Cover, he thought about the reason so many flocked to Loch Ness, to gaze on its waters, crowd aboard the tour ships and barges, hire their own launches. Searching for the mystery.

The mystery. Suddenly he found himself giggling. Maybe it was the drink, but he was confident he hadn't taken enough to be a danger to himself. A danger? That was a laugh.

He slipped his feet out of the hollows in the hull moulded for them, and swung his legs over the kayak's sides and into the dark water. The relief was instantaneous. So was the shock of the cold. People loved to swim in Loch Ness at this time of year. Some of them died as a result. It was so deep, so well-fed with mountain snow melt, that it never really warmed up at all.

His feet were bare. He could see them, just, glimmering in the water.

"Come on," he muttered. Then shouted: "Come on, take a bite! Take a nibble, why don't you?"

At first he imagined himself talking to the Ferox, hundreds of metres down in the darkness. Then he thought of something else. Another creature.

"All right, here I am, if you want me. Come and take me, you old bitch." He stopped paddling, waited for a few moments. A bike thudded past on the lochside road, something hefty, a V-Twin, maybe a Ducati.

The ripples from his paddling ceased. The loch was absolutely still and undisturbed. The alcohol buzz departed and he felt alive in an utterly different way from before. He was part of the natural environment, integrated with it.

But he knew what he really was. He was an intruder. And he felt the thrilling terror of it, being human and in the presence of something alien and completely unfeeling, massive, ancient, indifferent.

And he felt the joy. The love.

Five years earlier

Red Mahogany. Dried fruits with chocolate, orange, vanilla and wood spice. Rich and smooth on the palate with fruit cake, vanilla and a hint of woodsmoke. A full and lingering finish, with dried fruits and spice.

MACALLAN 10-YEAR-OLD, CASK STRENGTH

A WHISKY IN MONSTERVILLE

They landed near the deserted ruin of a village about 10 clicks south of the old Al-Shabbala fort. The new millimetre-wave ground radar had guided them through the absolute darkness, made murkier by the vast amounts of dust Blackhawks were infamous for kicking up on landing. They were choking through the brownout as the helicopter lifted off and headed back towards the forward patrol base, their night-vision headsets turning everything into a primitive computer game as they stumbled north. *Tron*, the original version. But dirtier. Much dirtier.

Murricane had been forced to assemble the team even more quickly than usual, and in the end had kept it smaller than was ideal. Just three men. Foster and Miller, the Beer Twins, both SBS 'swimmer canoeists' like himself. And a Territorial SAS doctor called MacLachlan, inevitably 'Mac', whose part-time status merely reflected a terrifying capacity for what he himself called "varrr-iety": he was easily bored. Having a proper medic about was always handy. Having one as capable at killing as he was at healing was even better. At one time or another, they had all been part of Vulcan Squadron, the combined special forces group set up for anti-terrorist and hostage response. Elite of the elite. Now? Well, now they were scattered in various dark corners of Her Majesty's Armed Forces. They had been brought together for this by an authority which transcended regiment or service. Murricane was a captain in the Royal Marines, Foster and Miller warrant officer and sergeant respectively. Mac was probably a lieutenant. But official rank was irrelevant now. They were the best Murricane had been able to get.

They speed-marched across country, avoiding any tracks and roads except where necessary to cross steep canyons or the strange, unexpectedly fertile density of maize and poppy fields, some clearly using modern agricultural technology. They'd been warned about artesian wells, solar panels. There was occasional tinkling from the bell-carrying goats and the snores of their accompanying herders. They skirted around them or anything that moved, green and wavery, in their night-vision goggles. Murricane had seen detailed satellite surveillance of the territory and knew it should be virtually deserted. Hoped. Speed was essential. Dawn would break at 4.30am with the usual Afghan suddenness and they had to be in position on the rise overlooking Al-Shabbala half an hour before that. The American team would be hidden in the high corn to the north of the fort, a four-cornered mud and breeze block affair that looked like something out of *Beau Geste* but was actually the former lair of one of the country's opium barons. He had retreated to something more lavish and certainly safer in Kabul, hounded or bought out. Either by the international Islamic development organisation that was supposed to be operating here, or the Al-Qaeda cartels who wanted their poppy plantations back.

II

He had been drinking bad espresso in a Poole Starbucks, Macallan 10 cask strength from a pewter flask secretly giving it a sherry-cask kick, when the text came through: report to barracks. Back at Hamworthy he was met by the man he knew only as Percival, or Percy. Home Office, ostensibly, with what he called "a wider remit". Protection of state and citizenry 'regardless of context'. Which meant he could do bad stuff to anyone anywhere in the world, in the interests of Greater Britain. "Events at home or abroad that affect the homeland security situation." was how he'd put it once. The truth, Murricane thought, was that Percival could do anything. Or to be more accurate, could cause anything to be done.

He was a patrician figure, but small and compact. Hefty, like a bull. Calm, though, deliberate in his voice and movements, 50s, that dense grey hair that had spent most of its growing time under a beret or cap. Hair and emotion kept under an iron control. A face that would have been even more florid without the blood pressure pills, Murricane thought. His briefings were often somewhat oblique. This time, he seemed admirably concentrated. Concerned even. Though the tried and tested diffidence was in place. Mostly.

"Muslims. Sunni and Shia. Al-Qaeda, all Sunni. Afghanistan, mostly Sunni. And then you've got the Aga Khan."

"The Nizari Ismailis, Subset of the Shias. yes I..."

"All right, Murricane. Now, we like the Aga Khan. He's among the world's richest men, and he runs one of the most important development organisations in the world, the Aga Khan Development Network. He is also an absolutely crucial ally of the UK Government, an alliance reaching back into our military history. Or to be precise, an ally of the British Crown. He is a prince. He races horses. Our Royal Family like to keep on the correct side of princes, mainly, most of the time. It is, shall we say, an old school alliance."

"Kidnapped?"

"Don't be stupid. Nobody lays a finger on the Aga Khan. But the thing is, the Aga Khan doesn't really matter very much, politically. What we want is a sort of Sunni Aga Khan. Somebody we like. Who likes us. And who we can use to stop Al-Qaeda trying to wipe out the western world."

"There's nothing like the broad brush approach, I always think."

"Indeed. Anyway." Percival sighed, paused. That red face grew redder, the voice quieter, calmer. "The AKDN set up aid projects here, there, everywhere. Wonderful for winning wallets, hearts and minds. If these people have wallets."

"Purses, more like. And Swiss Bank Accounts."

"Thank you. Grooming a Sunni equivalent has been a long and cautious process, and not entirely... successful. In that the candidate for the post was assassinated. In fact, two candidates were. Sunni Islam is less... personality orientated, perhaps."

"There are still Sheikhs. Warlords. Leaders. Osama. Maybe we could have... just been a little less stupid and patronising."

"Well, we – and in this case, the 'we' involves the Americans as well as our own dear countrymen and women – learn by our mistakes. As for Osama, if it could have been tried, it would have been. Maybe it was. But with renegade Saudi billionaires like him, it's hard to find a means of persuasion. Not to mention Americans wishing him thoroughly dead at any cost." He

A WHISKY IN MONSTERVILLE

tapped the ends of his fingers together sharply. The skin was hard, Murricane noticed. They clicked. Maybe he was a gardener. Or a guitarist. Perhaps Percival liked to play Hendrix riffs to himself to alleviate the tension. Murricane could feel the remnants of the whisky, a miasma of smoke in his brain. The flask was next to his heart. "A decision was taken on high, on both sides of the Great Atlantic, to develop a more... general strategy. Large, even colossal amounts ploughed into a new Islamic development charity, run by sympathetic Sunnis. ICAGD. The Islamic Centre for Agricultural Growth and Development. Sympathetic Sunnis as far as we could tell. Well paid too. Projects, aimed at developing agriculture."

"Not opium."

"Aimed at developing agriculture that did not involve opium. Hearts and minds, hearts and minds."

"Bet that worked a treat."

"Well, it has not been, shall we say, easy. There has been constant attention by both private enterprise keen on growing poppies and attacks by Al-Qaeda wishing everyone involved dead. So they can get people to grow poppies. Sunni people. Their people. But there was a shining light, a glorious success. We all thought. In the countryside, out in our neck of the desert. Helmand Province. Something to do with maize, I believe. Solar power. Wells. Pumps. Making the desert bloom. Even the Taliban have realised they need to talk. They've even made mild noises of approval. I mean, solar power! Sun shining on the Sunnis! Hopeful signs, hopeful signs.

"Anyway, a British agronomist was recently seconded to this particular business by Her Majesty's Government, and he appears to have wandered just a tad off the, ah, reservation. And so now what we have is a hostage situation involving a UK citizen and some kind of aid executive from the US. The ICAGD has, on the whole, managed to avoid this kind of thing so far. Arrangements with local warlords of one kind or another, you know the drill. But these two seemed to be somewhat bereft of the requisite protection at the crucial, err... moment."

"What?" Murricane frowned. "So, reading between the bullshit. You mean there was a spook off on a little bit of a recce, accompanied by or at the behest of some CIA numpty?"

"They had taken some locally-sourced protection. ICAGD approved. But not properly screened."

Murricane snorted with derision. He knew what that meant in the Big A. Infiltration of native forces had been the name of the rebellious game in Afghanistan and environs since the 18th century.

"Yes, it looks like a set-up. Most of their protection magically melted away, they were attacked by what both the so-called Afghan government and less equivocal sources are saying is a quote renegade unquote Al-Qaeda grouping. Our chap and the American were spirited off."

"*Renegade* Al-Qaeda? Dear God, is that even possible? Extremely very *very* nasty?"

"We think so. A loose grouping of extreme super-Sunni Islamists, obviously very well informed, trying to expose the ICAGD as a western conspiracy against the pure and wondrous truth of pure Islam. Embarrass us. Drive the proverbial wedge. You see, obviously the ICAGD people on the ground are mostly true of heart and thought and word and deed, and doing the Lord's work. They weren't to know that their agronomist had any other function other than to explain how to water bloody plants. This could threaten the whole enterprise's neutrality, invulnerability, and good relations with Sunnis who know they could probably make more money growing opium and blowing up bits of Paris and London. Though not at the same time. D'you see?"

Murricane grunted.

"So, if the International Bribe the Sunnis Until They Smile Sweetly Organisation didn't know they were spooks, how did this off-the-charts group of headbangers?" But Percival shook his head.

"Our information is that the rabid lot, the kidnappers, have been applying their ideology to heroin production. Destroy western society through rendering it addicted, that old notion. Get rid of the nasty maize and linen, the olives and anything else.

Turn those fields over to our lovely drugs. They've already made a start. And the evil do-goody western-allied, pseudo-Islamists get it in the neck too. Imperialist lackeys, etcetera. You can kind of see their point. Or at least their strategy."

"So?"

"So, bottom line. American is called Lindsay Keating. He's ostensibly, what is it, head of global assessment or some such, for an American aid organisation, something independent but incredibly well connected, industrially connected, governmentally connected. Wealthy beyond the dreams of avarice, or has access to wealth. Money to spend. And spend and spend. The *Gardener's World* fellow is a Bill Connell. Bill Connell is, well, he's..."

"Agent or asset?"

"Oh, bit of both, bit of both. Cover as career, career as cover. He's a real agronomist, knows his stuff when it comes to organic fertilisers, and how to make bombs out of it if necessary. You must have met the type. Intellectual with dirt under his nails and rugby muscles. Our type of chap. The Afghan Government, bless their corrupt little cotton socks, are aghast. We've even been contacted by certain Taliban intermediaries to say it wasn't them, officer. By dint of their own greed, fanaticism, stupidity and sheer bloody-minded arrogance, this particular bunch of Al-Qaeda are now beyond the pale of their co-religionists. Slightly and briefly. Which gives us a window of opportunity." He folded his ample arms. "We need Connell back. We don't think the fuckers who have him quite know his full value, not yet. But if they carry out their usual forms of interrogation, they will find out. He's only human."

"Only a gardener, really."

"Indeed. And we can't risk him falling into the hands of perhaps more perceptive mujahideen than those he is with now, who are basically very good, very committed footsoldiers, as mad as brushes. We need to stop him moving along the line. Up the chain of command. D'you see?"

Murricane said nothing.

"Apart from that, we've been handed a political opportunity here. Even the Taliban are washing their hands of this lot. We can advance the cause of, well, let's call it *conversation* in Afghanistan by years. If we get things right. Redeem the agri projects. But we need the hostages back alive. And we need it done quickly. We think the Al-Qaeda capture team will be jittery. They know by now how isolated they are, but they won't want to talk and they won't want to compromise."

"So?"

"So here we go: it's a joint op, American and British, very small teams. We know where they are, we know how many. Satellites and local intel courtesy of... people who've been talking to people. Speed and silence is everything. No Apache rocket attacks, no warning. Quietly in and out. Slightest hint of ear-bursting slam-bang shit and those hostages are finished. So the ah, deal is this: Lear Jet to Kabul, Chinook to Bastion. Briefing with the US, then Blackhawks out and a Chinook over the horizon to get everyone out. Alive. I'll say that again. Alive." He swallowed carefully, as if his Adam's Apple was threatening to escape. Murricane stared at him.

"Can I ask one question? Well, two. Maybe three."

"Yes, of course you may. I do like to see you betraying ignorance."

"Are you serious? Where are the drone reports? Have we got grid reference guides? How many people is a small team? This should be about 30 people, and take months to plan."

"Here's who you have access to as of now, handy for Brize Norton at dawn tomorrow." Percival handed over an iPhone. A word-processing app Murricane didn't recognise was open. Some secure shit. He glanced at it, feeling the familiar lurch in his stomach, the sour taste of nerves. Or maybe it was just the remnant of that espresso. Percival's story had all the convincing detail of truth. He knew it was at least partly bullshit. He thumbed the screen, skimming the short list of names. Then he handed the iPhone back. "Foster, Miller, MacLachlan," he said.

And that was just about that. Percival took back the iPhone and sniffed loudly. He spoke in a ludicrously convincing Ulster accent. "Let me smell your breath, son!" And then back to his stilted form of received pronunciation. "As the Reverend Doctor

A WHISKY IN MONSTERVILLE

Ian Paisley said to a young Royal Ulster Constabulary officer who tried to stop him marching somewhere in an intimidatingly Protestant manner. A man among the myrtle trees! No whisky in Afghanistan, Murricane. Can you cope?"

Murricane blinked.

"It's a hobby, not an occupation," he replied. "The whisky. I'll look forward to a dram on my return." As he spoke he felt the metal flask in his breast pocket cool and cling.

III

They met at Brize Norton, in one of the anonymous Portakabins well away from the main buildings. Nods, muttered greetings. None of that American *Generation Kill* half-hug shoulder-bump stuff.

Civilian dress. Casual wasn't in it. Neither was smart. Hoodies, trainers, Goretex, a scuffed leather jacket in Mac's case. All three of them looked as if they'd come straight from looting a bad branch of Primark. They would kit up properly in the Big A. Personal weapons were another matter. On-call special forces, like armed customs officers, kept essential hardware at home. Or the hardware they particularly wanted to keep away from barracks thieves or prying eyes. People had their quirks. With Mac he knew it was a taste for obscure Japanese ceramic knives, illegal in the UK. Foster and Miller had small backpacks with them. He was guessing they both had odd guns, something Russian, maybe, like Makarovs or Yarygins. Ammunition was never a problem. Not with the fluid borders of the 21st century. Though the last time he'd worked with Miller, he was using an Ingram. It was a matter of taste, of self-expression. MacLachlan had his knives. Foster had his little hobby, making and using silent gas-power guns. Surprisingly useful. And Miller had his thing for *shuriken*, throwing stars, Ninja wheels, as in Bruce Lee and also completely illegal in the UK. He was always practising, much to the fury of a succession of RSMs. And he had used them to deadly effect, to Murricane's certain knowledge, during an embassy incident in Belize. Little boys loved them, especially the 'hand-hidden sword', the *hira shuriken*. And they were all little boys, weren't they? Very dangerous ones.

For Murricane it had always been more important being up to speed with the standard, unromantic weapons available to the marine or squaddie. Plus anything else you were likely to come across. Lying handily on the ground, so to speak. If it was there, he could use it. Having said that, he had always been fond of the little 1937 Walther PPK he had been gifted by a former East German Volksmarine commander he had helped evacuate out of Somalia. "The very one Hitler shot himself with," the man had whispered. "My father passed it to me." So many questions he could have asked. Should have asked. Like, 'exactly how mad and drunk are you, mein herr?' It was all nonsense, but a lovely little gun. And if it had been good enough for both Hitler and James Bond, it would do for him. An indulgence. But it worked. Most of the time.

The chartered Lear was white, bore no obvious markings and was flown by two American civilian pilots. No stewardess. No alcohol. A coffee machine and some RAF officer's mess sandwiches. No ham. Religious sensitivities. Big A here we come. Bastion ya bastard. He'd necked a Tramadol and was feeling its rosy euphoria, softening the edges of desire for alcohol. Not need. Desire. He was a feckin' connoisseur, wasn't he? Not for him the rough supermarket blends. Single malts all the way. Just not on this trip.

He had completed one tour of duty doing close protection for diplomatic staff and visiting politicians in Kabul. It had been, for once, uneventful. One jaunt out into the badlands courtesy of an old mate, a straightforward intel convoy through a couple of Taliban-tainted villages. No Improvised Explosive Devices, though the tedious and incredibly time-consuming checks for them had been frustrating for him, a mere observer. More than anything else, he'd been bored, always with the ticking awareness in the background of the risks that boredom represented. He'd had access to some illicit Glenfiddich which had eased things a bit. A week after he'd flown back to Britain, the old mate, a Parachute Regiment captain called Oates, had become a double amputee above the knee thanks to a nasty little DIY landmine placed overnight on the way to a temporary camp latrine. Clever.

Wait for a need to make someone careless. Take advantage. Even the shites could be fatal in Afghan. And as the old joke went, at least the Taliban were mostly Sunnis. Captain Oates. No more going for a walk. Even a short one.

The American team was five-strong, led by a lean, slow-motion and so almost ludicrously typecast Rangers colonel called Everard. Three of his men were also Rangers, two were not. Everard introduced these in a Virginian drawl as "our corporate cousins." Murricane had one of them pegged as a bog-standard freelancer from the off. Too much steroid muscle, a matt black Glock and a big, fuck-off knife strapped to the calf. Neck tattoo reading 'Born Toulouse'. Imitation Foreign Legion stuff. The other one was some kind of contractor too, but less showy. Smaller, more compact. An oddity about his eyes. Inwardly focussed on something that seemed amusing. He gave Murricane the creeps. There was the usual handshaking, nodding, muttered introductions. Suspicion. Shrugged off for the sake of concentration on the job in hand. But lurking in the background.

The teams were given a full geo briefing from a monotone US intel officer. He used satellite profiles which were then downloaded into the GPS and video systems they would take with them. Dawn was breaking by the time they finished. They would have to sleep as best they could through the day, kit up and be ready to chopper out at midnight. The Yanks were to be 'nominally' in command, Percival had said. "Nominally'. As it was so it would ever be.

IV

He grabbed an iced can of Coke from the inevitable machine and found Everard at his side.

"I know what you're thinking," the Ranger said. "Well, I know what I'm thinking. My guys are cool. Really sound. Been through a lot together. The two contractors are in because there's an insurance element."

"A what?"

"An insurance element. Keating and Connell, right? You've got Connell. I've got Keating, essentially." Eeeeseeeyunshallleee. "You know Keating works for the Global Repentance and Redemption Trust?"

"What, a religious group?"

"They don't say they are. Redemption in this case is about renewing the spirit of the people, investing in the, uh, redemption of their way of life. It's all very groovy and ecumenical and multicultural. Allow the truth of Sunni Islam and the glory of Jesus Christ to walk hand in hand, that kinda bullshit. But it's a trust funded by a company called KokVan. Founded by a guy called Cochrane Vance."

"With a 'K'? As in Kock with a 'K'?"

"No. Yeah, funny. KokVan don't appreciate no jokes. Originally oilfield equipment, now everything – electronics, defence, you name it. They really have juice. I mean serious juice. And they also own Solidity With Service Security.

"That's who these guys work for? SWS? Jesus. Did you know our own SAS took legal action to make them change their name from Solidity AND Service? Wankers, both. Jesus Christ."

"Yeah. I note your use of Our Dear Lord's name. Well, they don't work directly for Jesus. Just SWS. And via them for Vance, or KokVan himself. He kind of personifies all of this. He's like, not quite God, not quite Jesus, but with a hotline to both. Howard Hughes with a modem built in, sorta. Weird but word is law. He wanted his guys on board. And what he wants, he gets."

"Are they up to it? One looks like a gym rat with good steroid connections and money for hardware. The other one looks like he got dropped on his head. And quite recently."

"They got references. But it's above my pay grade. One's called Phillips, he's the bulked out roid abuser. Ex-Navy SEALS, so you and he should be OK if we have to go swimming. Jenks is the other one. Don't know much. One of my buddies in Iraq remembers him working the Green Zone as protection, and being a little over-enthusiastic. That's how he put. A little over-enthusiastic." Everard no longer seemed casual and good-ole-boy tentative. He seemed to be growing tenser the more he talked. "But hey, they're my problem. Don't worry. It'll be cool." He sighed. "Look, I need to get some sleep. Want some Ambien?" Murricane knew about Ambien. An American sleeping pill, it had become a cult in special ops. He'd tried it once, and been left feeling wrung out and slimy like an old chamois leather.

"No, thanks. Just stick to the speed, I think." It was a joke. Amphetamines didn't work for him either. And he didn't know if Tramadol was a brand Everard would recognise But the Ranger just nodded sagely.

Now Murricane was looking at his men and wondered what their secret substances were. For him, in the absence of whisky it was Trammies and coffee; he'd loaded up with a small steel thermos of the bitterest brew he could find in Bastion, heavily sugared. He noticed that Foster seemed to have a Mars Bar fetish. Work, Rest and Play. God knows what that did to your teeth.

V

The satellite radio bleeped in his earpiece. Everard's voice, compressed and phased by being bounced off a lump of space junk. "Ghostdog One in position. Confirm, 30 seconds, go. Repeat, 30 seconds."

"Roger, Ghostdog One. Ghostdog Two copy and in position. Confirm big go in..." he counted from the digital timer in the corner of his goggles. "20,19,18,17,16, 15 seconds." He turned to his team, their bodies lumpy with equipment, so close he could smell them: sweat, piss, old shit, fear. Fuck it. It would soon be dawn. "Time."

Silence apart from the thud of footfall and the soft squeak and rub of gear. All rattles carefully dulled, all the chink and clatter of weaponry muffled. Breathing though, heavy breathing. Someone sounded as if they could do with fewer cigarettes. They'd been told no mines. They'd been assured no mines. There was no time to think about it. The south gate. Sentries. Wavery thermal images. Two of them, seated and drowsy if not actively asleep. No, he smelt tobacco smoke. A glowing green hotspot that would be of burning ash. "Foster. Miller."

A WHISKY IN MONSTERVILLE

He felt, rather than saw Miller stop, momentarily, and shove his night-vision set aside. The mild, whirling whistle of the *shuriken* and the soft squelch as it took the smoking sentry just below the red cigarette-stub target, in the throat. By that time Foster had fired his home-adapted carbon dioxide pistol at the other figure. The darts contained minute explosive charges in their tips. Enough to comprehensively shatter someone's skull.

All these forts had two entrances, north and south. No sound from the other side, which meant, presumably, that Ghostdog One had either given up and gone home or successfully secured the entrance without using the usual American approach of tactical nukes and Especially Loud Noises. The old worn wood of the south door was studded with rusted metal, but it moved smoothly on oiled hinges. Murricane pushed and was through, throwing himself immediately prone on the ground.

Two tents, as they'd been told, as the satpics had shown. Army tents, probably Russian. Like scout marquees, about 20 metres apart. Dim lights from within, hurricane lanterns, candles, something natural and flickery.

Movement from the north. His earpiece whirred: "Ghostdog One to Ghostdog Two. Compound penetrated. Repeat. Penetrated. Confirm status. Over."

"Confirm, Ghostdog Two to Ghostdog One. In compound. West canvas yours, east canvas ours."

From this point on, noise was not the issue. Foster had two armed M84 stun grenades in his extraordinarily large right hand. Mac, using that sharper-than-razor-sharp ceramic knife, sliced a long downward opening in the tent wall, then another across it, the cross-shape opening four neat flaps. Foster armed the grenades, threw them in and jerked back, hands automatically cupping his already-headsetted ears. A pulse. A very loud noise. Miller stepped through the opening he'd made, his Ingram gangbanger machine pistol in hand. There was a series of short bursts, only the high frequencies audible, the bark, clink and chatter of that murderous little weapon.

Shooting seemed to erupt all around the compound, muzzle flash bursting like low stars from figures Murricane couldn't see.

A WHISKY IN MONSTERVILLE

Let the Yanks do their job. Concentrate. Mac went into the tent after Miller. Murricane waited for the shooting to end, then moved round to the tent's entrance, which had been loosely tied shut from within; he ripped it open with his own knife, a replica Smith and Wesson stiletto. Thermal imaging off. Naked eye stuff from now on. Inside the tent, in the guttering oil light, nothing moved. Two bound figures, hooded, propped against jute-wrapped bales of what he could smell was raw opium. What the fuck? Mac was standing over a thrashing huddle of robes, methodically cutting throats. Miller was covering him with the little Ingram that had almost certainly already killed the three guards. They were careful, these boys. Belt and braces stuff. Murricane went to the bound figures, carefully sliced first one hood off, then the other. They were recognisable. Connell and Keating. Battered and unconscious. If they were breathing, it was not easily. Where were the Americans? What was happening? He tried again.

"Ghostdog Two to Ghostdog One. We have hostages. We have hostages." Nothing.

Were Connell and Keating alive? He had to know.

"Mac! Life signs, check. Life signs check." Then he pressed the sat radio button once more.

"Ghostdog One, Ghostdog One, this is Ghostdog Two." There was no reply.

"They're alive," said Mac, slaughterer and resident medic. "Shot full of junk I think. Barely breathing. I'll bang in some adrenalin to get them moving."

"Will they survive if you don't?"

"God knows what kind of state their brains are in at the moment, but yes, they'll survive. If you'd rather just carry them, then..."

"Fuck it, Chinook should be in its way." The 'operation go' message was the signal for the over-horizon extraction helicopter to start making its swing into the fort. "Leave them comatose. Bastion can kiss them and make them better. What the fuck's going in the other tent?" He realised they were all shouting. The flashbangs had partially deafened them.

Then the screaming began. Strange, throaty, muffled. More firing, much closer. He turned to see the steroid-abusing ex-navy

SEAL called Phillips, a Heckler and Koch MP7 on short bursts, five or six bullets at a time. But five or six was all it needed to cut Miller and Mac in half. Uranium or tungsten shells, Murricane realised, diving to his left, reaching for the little Walther he kept strapped across his chest in a quick release clip, Prince Harry style. HRH, on his brief infantry sojourn in A, had copied that from a magazine, he'd been told. *Big Boy Soldiers* or somesuch. Phillips was swinging the H&K when the first of Murricane's three shots took him just below the Adam's Apple. Lucky. No body armour there, and the other shots all missed. But then old, small handguns were like that. Really, he would need to upgrade. James Bond and Hitler were long past their sell-by dates.

Where was Foster? No sign of him. The two hostages still leaned against the bales of heroin. But they were bloodied messes of flesh and bone, now, like Miller and Mac. Insurance? Hell's teeth. What had Phillips been trying to do? Murricane threw himself through the cross-shaped tear Mac had made in the tent, it seemed like hours ago. Clutching the Walther, safety off. It had a fierce trigger pull, no risk of accidental discharge. It felt puny in his hand. A toy.

"Everard," he shouted. There was no reply. The screaming had become a horrible low, wet grunting now. Someone in terrible agony. A gasping, thudding noise, too. Chinook, thank Christ. This was a total and utter fuck-up. Nothing made any sense. He raised himself to a crouch and ran for the other tent. Its doors flapped open. Inside, more paraffin lamps. Two men in Afghan tribal dress, dead. A table of satellite and computer equipment, trashed. Three of the Americans, inert. One lying on his back with his chest moving in and out, in and out, faster and further than any chest he'd ever seen. That was where the screaming had been. Where the groaning was coming from now.

It was Everard. Two gaping, bubbling holes, armoured vest rendered irrelevant by the MP7 and those witchy bullets, and Murricane could see instantly that the wounds were going to be fatal. But there was something odd about the Ranger captain's head. No helmet, no goggles. And no right ear. It wasn't a blast wound, either. It looked as if it had been severed deliberately.

A WHISKY IN MONSTERVILLE

Murricane's hearing was almost back to normal, so he heard the rustle of clothing and the click as the grenade pin was removed. He turned, everything suddenly in slow motion. A figure at the door, arm raised to throw. Jenks. The other contractor. Jesus Christ. He felt so, so sluggish as he began to raise his pistol, diving ruthlessly behind Everard's prone, gasping body. But suddenly a figure loomed behind Jenks. A scuffle, a scrabble of movement and shouting. There was an enormous thudding of rotor blades, then a ragged blast, louder and somehow more serious than the M84s. A jagged pain and then nothing at all.

Blackness. Oblivion. Peace.

Southern shore

Brownish gold with amber overtones. A thinness of body. Lemony notes, dried herbs, grit and stones. Edge, spicy, with a hot pear drops note at the slightly burning finish.

OLD THOMPSON AMERICAN BLENDED WHISKEY

This one struggled.

She'd run, first, through the midnight twilight of the trees, blindly following the path he would have dragged her down anyway. Then the solid, clunking collision with one of the lochside's old oaks, and he was on her. One heavy punch, two, and she was unconscious. Dead to the world, he thought, dead to the world. But not properly. Not quite yet. *Dead to the world*: just words.

The real killing didn't take long. The rest took a bit more time, but eventually he was done with it, though the smell of burnt meat hung around him. Sweet. He sniffed, sucked in the aroma. It took him back to a village, a house, a family. Stored petrol and a phosphorous grenade.
Good times.

His first trophy of this contract, and he was pleased. Neatly severed from the body, sealed using that sterile plastic sealant you got in aerosols. Incredible stuff. It was sold here under the tradename HoldFast. He liked that. Couple of blasts in an alloy field cup, then inhale, and he was pleasantly, cracklingly spaced. Headache, yeah, but gone in a flash. Like a drunken binge and hangover combined, all over in a second.

And he'd found the perfect place for his trophies, the ideal retreat. Somewhere he could rest, meditate, look upon his works, the achievements of his hands, and wonder. Rejoice. Take comfort. Be at peace.

There would be more, he thought happily There always was. This was just a beginning.

Fisherman's blues

Light and crisp. A florist's shop and the caramel sweetness of a confectionary store. Balanced on the palate with spice, grain, toffee and smoke. Sweet to finish. Treacle.

THE FAMOUS GROUSE

A WHISKY IN MONSTERVILLE

Murricane felt the loch working its magic on him, repairing the self-inflicted damage of the night before. Brilliant speckles of icy water flicked into his face as the old Orkney Longliner droned across Urquhart Bay, the ridiculously picture-perfect castle rising out of the morning mist like some Brigadoon fantasy.

It was going to be a glorious Highland day. The water had the smoky sheen that came from a warm and windless night, and the sun was already melting away the patchy special-effects fog. The breeze created by the boat's movement had begun to ease the throbbing behind his eyes, and the spray was cooling the whisky heat in his face. How many had it been? Why had he let Jan tempt him with those cask-strength Islay bottlings? Ardbeg, Lagavulin, Bruichladdich, Laphroaig. The names themselves sounded like small skulls crunching beneath jackboots.

His head. He'd gone to the bar looking for any signs of Rebecca, heard that she'd checked out first thing in the morning, heading into Inverness, Inversnecky, The Big Sneck. So then he stayed at the Piper's Rest for a beer. Just the one, probably. Not downcast, exactly. He and Becca had, he thought, enjoyed their three nights together. On the face of it, it was one of what Jan called his monster shags. Maybe.

Rebecca the lovely Israeli tourist with an interest in cryptozoology. Divorced, 40s, athletic. Staying at Piper's for a couple of nights, taking the Castle Cruises boat trip, checking out the rival visitor centres. Looking. Gazing out at that vast puddle, Britain's biggest greatest volume of fresh water. Monsters. The monster. Of course, her mind was open, but still. Loch Ness had the most famous unexplained lake-creature in the world. Had he seen it? Nessie, the Beastie? Well, he didn't really like to talk about it, not in public. But if she fancied a walk to his lochside abode, maybe she'd be interested in seeing some of his pictures, maybe a late night snack... yes, a boat. He lived on a sort of a boat. You'd love to see it? Excellent.

You could tell what the women were like by how they reacted to the walk. It was no ordinary night-time stroll. You had to cut through the protected woodland called the Cover, several acres of ash, alder, wild cherry and wychwood that was unique for its exposed root systems and the waterlogged ground they grew in. Protected: for Murricane, it was protection. The narrowboat *Gloria II*, veteran of middle England canal holidays, caught out by the treacherous winter tides of Loch Ness, had been abandoned here, after a storm had thrust most of her length deep into this strange miniature Everglades. He had lived aboard for a year and a half, squatting really, some blind eyes turned, an insurance company sweet talked into agreeing 'seasonal custodianship'. But approaching *Gloria* through the Cover was almost impossible, unless you knew how. Unless you were Murricane. Unless you were with him. While there were paths, they were tortuous and shifting, treacherous and tending to encourage many reassuring grips of the elbow, hand and shoulder.

Some women, sober, grew stiff and frightened. Some, drunk, laughed hysterically. Some demanded to be taken back to their hotel; Rebecca had said nothing. Just kept her balance, watched his footsteps, followed where he led.

Little ceremony, no ritual hunter-gatherer cooking to impress, no seared scallops with crowdie and garlic, no viewing of the pictures in his scrapbook – all the usual scams, the Surgeon's Photograph, the hay bales draped in tarpaulin, the hippo ashtray footprints, plus one or two strange ripples he'd snapped himself. No laughing over the old cassettes he used for music, the hissing analogue echoes of dead or dying bands. That had waited until the morning. They had taken each other with practised ease and what felt like mutual gratitude. He hadn't asked about her scars. She hadn't asked about his. But they'd traced each other's old wounds gently. He'd wondered who she really was, stayed awake most of that first night, watching her, tempted to check out the rucksack. But knowing from her shallow breathing that she was awake too, waiting for him to do just that. He'd slept, in the end. He wasn't sure if she had.

Maybe she had gone through his things. Maybe she was some kind of recruiter. Maybe she was, finally, his nemesis. God knew he'd given enough people adequate reason to erase his existence. But he'd fallen asleep anyway. Next morning he was still alive and she was still there. Sex, coffee, monster pictures, more sex. How come you live on a boat? It's a barge, he said, as he always did. And it's stuck, immovable, grounded for ever. Like me. She had nodded at that, gazing at him with those peaty brown eyes. Eyes like good, old Islay whisky. Three nights. Then, before dawn, without waking Murricane, which was unprecedented, she was dressed and departed; gone. She hadn't needed guiding back through the Cover. She was good, whoever she was. Afterwards, he'd checked his meagre belongings. He kept no computer, no phone, no files on the barge. No digital camera. Just books, his lure-making tools and materials, the battered, worn scrapbook. No ID. Stuff had been moved, though. And she hadn't woken him. She was very good.

*** *** ***

"Try this Ardbeg *Mairead's Breath* 18-year-old," Jan had said, as if for all the world he was introducing a particularly attractive young courtesan, one who exuded lovely oral odours. And for hours they were off to that little west coast island, inhaling the seaweed and bog aromas, numbing the palate with alcohol, dulling brain, heart and memory.

Somehow he'd got back to the *Gloria*, somehow he'd clambered aboard and slept until Ferg had woken him at 7.00am, his dinghy bumping against the hull, scratching onto the deck, then banging on the roof above his cabin, all of this accompanied by muffled bellowing.

"Murricane, ya bastard! Ye promised me a hand with they English tourists, after the Ferox, ken! An I need the voodoo, those stupid red fish magnets. Get oot yer scratcher!"

And now he was on Ferg's Longliner, the *Happy Adventure*, gradually reviving, the cheerful bellow of a Wolverhampton accent in his ear, as one of the anglers offered him a coffee from his stainless steel flask.

"There you go, mate! Looks like you're needing it."

"Cheers. I should be making you one."

"Nah, never fear. Hotel kitchen made us up flasks and sandwiches. Ferg says you're the man for the Ferox. Says you make those special lures?"

The dark, rippling ache behind his eyes began to retreat. Murricane shrugged off the PacSafe daypack he was wearing and unzipped it. There was a small aluminium case inside. He handed it over. The man, round, cheerful, in his 50s, took it and half turned to the stern of the boat, where his companion sat.

"Hey, Gerry, here's the bloody motherlode! The magic bullets for them killer trout!"

Gerry, small, thin and looking queasy, wiped a nervous hand through a few strands of sandy hair.

"Aw, go on, Fred, I'm fine. Don't think that bird agreed with me last night. Grouse, was it? Bloody wasn't famous, that's for sure."

"Bloody wimp! What else we goin' to eat? This is grouse country! Either that or a bit of the old Bambi, eh? Mind you, been better if it'd been hung for a week or two, but needs must. Spit out the lead shot and swallow, I say. As the bishop said to the actress. Ha! Fancy a wee dram, pal? That's what you Jocks call it, ain't that right? A wee dram. And this grouse IS famous."

A hip flask was being offered across. Murricane could smell the grain-cut oak and peat of the blend called Famous Grouse, Scotland's favourite whisky, as easy to identify in the clear loch air as petrol or creosote. For a moment he was tempted. But then his gut lurched unpleasantly. He reached for the box of lures.

"No thanks. Actually, I'm from Carlisle. Cumbria. English as you, mate."

"Maybe no' quite that English," muttered Ferg, standing at the wheel, blipping the throttle back, "thank fuck. Go and make sure they Canadian tools of destruction are set, Murricane, eh, pal. Old boy. Old *chap*?"

Ferg was chewing on a wet roll-up. He'd been told by the doctor not to smoke, so now he masticated his way through Golden Virginia rollies, staining his lips and white moustache a deeper and deeper brown. He was somewhere between 40 and 60, a former estate ghillie who'd fallen in love with the demon fish of the loch, the elusive predators. Pike and Ferox Trout. Somehow, he and Murricane had forged a kind of wary alliance, one centred on the Ferox, the massive and mysterious mutation of the brown trout that, at some point in its youth, switched from feasting on insect larvae and vegetable matter to other fish. Mainly the Arctic Char that inhabited the vast depths of Loch Ness – up to 800 feet in places, the sonar readings said. And sometimes, Ferox turned cannibal and turned on other trout. It was a big-game fish, one of the most ferocious fighters in any of the world's waters. Ferox. Fierce.

And it was in Loch Ness, not in great numbers, but there. Ferg knew where they were. Ferg knew them. Would have liked to know them better. Would have liked to know them intimately. In a purely platonic, put-a-hook-through-the-mouth-and-haul sort of way.

Some became enormous. Vast. Up to 34 pounds. And most of the time, they were down so deep they could only be caught by trolling with high-tensile American lines and eight-to-10-pound weights on downriggers, clever winches that dragged the fishing line down to the depth you wanted, far deeper than any weighted line could normally go. Bait, you could use bait, of course, but artificial lures had become Ferg's obsession. Finding the right combination of colour and density, of delicacy and crudity. It was black magic. These were talismen, ritual objects.

Murricane had begun making them on those first long winter nights aboard *Gloria*, carving them from old commercial fishing floats, feed containers, basins, buckets. Just for the hell of it, he'd shown one to Ferg. "Aye, ye smartass English bastard, think ye're clever eh?" It had been a weird yellow and red thing, cut from a discarded beach ball, roughly in the shape of cartoon fish. White glued-in fake pearl eyes, chopped feathers for a tail. Bits of tape, paint. The effects of too much Macallan. He was still heavily into Speysides then.

Ferg had taken Murricane out on the first legal day of the fishing season, set his two Canadian downriggers, developed for catching Chinook salmon in the North Western Territories, clipped in the lines from three rods, two with his normal lures, one with Murricane's. It was a rattly day, choppy with a cold northerly. They crept slowly down the loch, off Inverfarigaig. And it had been Murricane's that the fish called Rarity had struck. Magic.

A WHISKY IN MONSTERVILLE

"Old Rarity, 35 pounds if he's an ounce," said Ferg. "Fatter than a conger, and more vicious too. I ken him well. I've kent him since he was only a bairn. Strange markings, a ring on his back, under the slime. Catch him maybe once a season, maybe. Off Urquhart Castle, in the deeps, 100 foot of line. Always a battler, a merry battler."

That was true enough. The fish yanking the line out of the downrigger quick release, and then the palm-ripping, shoulder-straining fight to bring him to the surface.

They'd netted Old Rarity, brought him aboard and released him, Ferg removing his filthy John Deere baseball cap in a gesture of respect.

"Yon's the biggest Ferox in Scottish waters, I doubt," he said.

"A monster," Murricane had joked. Provoking in Ferg a stony look and a single shake of the head.

"Nah. Nah, nothing monstrous there. How long have you been in our shores now, Murry, eh? A year? Two? Ever seen herself?"

Herself. The Beastie. The creature of legend, myth, fakery and the bringer of the big bucks, the tourist millions. Nessie. You didn't talk about the Beastie. She was too precious, too big an issue. You didn't make jokes about her. It was near blasphemy. If you lived on or near Loch Ness, you were careful when it came to the creature. It was like being in a church, a cathedral, where jokes about God were off limits, where respect was expected. And of course you found yourself looking, looking, always. The odd ripples, the floating logs that caught at your breath and heartbeat. The tricks of the light. The hoaxes, clever and stupid, goodnatured and devious. Murricane had been aware from his first weeks by the loch that locals who made their living by its shores all believed there was indeed something deeply strange, and very much alive in the loch. The creature. Herself. Not that anyone talked about it. Her. Ferg never had until now, with Old Rarity heading deep, deep into the cold and opaque depths.

"Herself? Well, there's a question. Have you?" Ferg looked at him, seemed to catch some unspoken knowledge, and nodded.

31

A WHISKY IN MONSTERVILLE

"And if you haven't already, you will. If you're here long enough. You will meet the creature. And then you'll know about what is and isn't monstrous. Monster-us."

"Oh, I believe in monsters, Ferg. Don't you worry about that. I've seen them.

I've conversed with them. I've smelt their breath."

*** *** ***

Since then, he had crewed for Ferg when he could, when Ferg wanted company, when there were English anglers aboard Ferg didn't like. Murricane was the fender, the used tyre that prevented the usually harmless hail-fellow-well-met southerners sparking anger, fanning historical resentment into fury. He'd heard Ferg launch into furious diatribes in the past, mainly in the Piper's Rest when grating English accents grew too much for his proud self-loathing to bear.

"Aye, you come here wi' your colonial manners and your money, and act the feckin' master to us kow-towing serfs, and we're happy to slaver on your feckin' Gore-Tex boots and yer Barbour jackets, ya superior bastards..." Jan and Murricane more often than not manhandling Ferg out into the car park, convincing Matt, the very Yorkshire taxi driver ("Bloody 'ell, nor' again!"), to take Ferg home to Abriachan before he remembered his old Toyota pick-up was parked out by the Green, and tried to drive it home.

Ferg let the *Happy Adventure* drift as Murricane prepared the three rods. Two set for deep trolling, the downriggers taking the line into the loch's unthinkable depths. More water than all the lakes of England and Wales combined. Murky sediment down there, then a smooth, almost sterile bottom of clay. Below that, the shattered granite of the Great Glen Fault, the rock called moine schist. Deeper than history. Beyond human reach.

Downriggers. Not playing fair, some said. But in reality, the only way to truly tackle the Ferox. Blunt, businesslike things at each stern corner of the boat, running wherever the fishfinder said the shoals of Arctic Char were. Today, about 100 feet. That cannonball of lead. Gerry and Fred watched fascinated as Murricane prepared the rods, knotting on the lures – 'Glenfiddich' and 'Old Pulteney' he'd dubbed these two. One pale and nearly translucent, a laminating of Tupperware – the other brownish, with green speckles of Golden Wonder crisp packet, cheese and onion flavour. They were ambling out past Strone Point now, the castle's Braveheart outline clearing through the mist, the sun beginning to send slivers of warmth down into the shadowed cutting that was the Great Glen.

"Want to do some casting?" Involve the clients – 'the bastards' as Ferg called them, sometimes to their faces – see how they did with the rods. See if they'd need help, these two, if and when the fish struck. All that sucking at the whisky flask might not matter if the muscle memory was there, if there were some practised skills and some strength beneath the camouflage fishing gear. "No tangling, mind you!"

Gerry stood up, his face flushed a little from spirit and, Murricane could see, irritation.

"Been casting longer than you've been patronising hapless tourists, Carlisle lad," he said, reaching for a rod.

And they weren't bad. After half an hour of casting, they had the lines about 75 feet behind the boat, and Murricane attached them to the downrigger quick releases.

"How deep, Ferg?"

"Eighty feet to start."

Murricane threw the switches and the weights began to hum down, taking the lines with them. He took the third rod and cast it from the centre of the stern, locking it into its socket and thinking, you know, maybe a wee Grouse would go down quite well. *Te Bheag*, as they said in Gaelic, not that many folk spoke it around here. Other than the children being trained up for jobs in Gaelic development or the media. Or he could go into the cabin and fry up some of the bacon Ferg always kept in his battered coolbox, along with some shallow water bait and tins of Carlsberg Special. He looked towards what he always thought of as one of the loch's real monstrosities, the enormous white and blue industrial shell of the Foyers hydro-electric generation station, the turbine hall that brought brainless industrial un-design to the southern shore.

A WHISKY IN MONSTERVILLE

Now there were plans for Foyers, always the tourist underdog to Drum, hard to reach on the loch's undeveloped side, suffused with legends about Aleister Crowley and Jimmy Page's magical antics in the village's Boleskine House; it was still there, still a place of pilgrimage for the deranged, the disturbed, and the sad, innocent would-be re-enactors of Page's section of the Zeppelin movie *The Song Remains The Same*. Page himself was long gone, vanished back to London and a life dreaming of tour excess long past, that black mane of hair snowy white, the double chins dropping. At least he was still alive.

There had been a fuss in the *Courier* about a planning application for a kind of new visitor centre, something Nessie-orientated, to do with an American group, some weirdos up at the old shooting lodge Creag Dhearg, Monster hunters, Monster believers. Something like that. It had divided the south shore folk. Some were all for cashing in on the idea of economic development, growth, jobs, and giving the tourist traps of Fort Augustus and Drum a couple of bloody financial noses. A motley group of environmentalists were objecting, of course. As always.

"Carlsberg Special!" Ferg was in ruminative mood. "They brewed it up specially, invented it for Winston Churchill's visit to Sweden, ye ken. If it was good enough for Winnie, it's good enough for me." At nine per cent alcohol, it was a drinking session in a can. Maybe later, thought Murricane. Maybe never.

They trolled the lines slowly towards Foyers, Murricane fiddling with Ferg's ancient Trangia camping stove, the smell of its methylated spirit fuel taking him back to dozens of outdoor brew-ups, fry-ups, narrow escapes from that worst of all enemies, hunger. Bacon on a boat in the morning, as the Loch Ness mist cleared and the two noisy, half-drunk, half-sick tourist anglers remained, thankfully, silent. The smell of crisped, smoked meat wafted through the cabin and out. Has anyone done any research on the use of cooking smells in attracting fish, Murricane wondered. He checked the packet of bread rolls in the fridge: Stiffening, but edible. Lift the tiny frying pan, douse the flame.

"Murry, ya bastard, get a move one wi' them bacon butties!" Ferg sounding energised at the thought of hot dead pig, thinly sliced.

"Coming, Ferg. Just a minute."

And then all kinds of hellery broke loose.

First there was the howl of a reel releasing line, then a shout from Gerry.

"Christ, I've got something! Fish on!"

"Let it run, boy! Let it run!" They were approaching Foyers Bay. Ferg moved them further out into the loch's centre, gently increasing the revs. "Don't panic him! Don't snag him! Nice and easy!"

Now it was just boat, man, rod and fish, the downrigger's huge weight having done its work, taken the lure down into the peaty depths. The fish was running, aware that potential doom had sliced into its predatory mouth. Murricane felt a pang of jealousy, then rested his hand on Gerry's shoulder. He could feel the muscles quivering.

"Just take it easy, mate," he said. He wondered how long it would be before he panicked and snapped the line, despite its enormous breaking strain. He hated the thought of that great fish, trailing monofilament behind it until it was caught and hopefully released, or died of old age, or tangled itself in one of the wrecks that lay on the loch's bottom. Fishing boats, yachts, crashed World War Two bombers... poor old fish. Fred had socketed his own rod and was busy unscrewing the top of his whisky flask.

"Jesus," he said, "better get the water of life ready, boys, eh!"

Then Murricane grew conscious of another whine, a kind of lower harmony to the sound coming from Gerry's reel, a much slower buzz from the rod he'd set for shallow trolling in the centre of the *Happy Adventure's* stern. Midships. The words, the proper naval words were never far away. Sounded like it was caught on something static or slow moving. A log, maybe, or a piece of junk someone had abandoned to the water. He declutched the reel and gingerly felt for resistance against the spool. Too heavy. A strange feeling, a soft tugging.

"Ferg, stop the engine!" The line went slack. And at that moment he saw Gerry brace his body and haul hard, far too hard at his rod. Right hand wrestling with the reel. There was a report like an arrow being fired from a bow, a harsh twanging noise, and Gerry flew backwards towards the cabin door. Ferg, who had turned from the wheel to watch what was happening, neatly stepped aside.

"Ach, the smell of Murry's bacon butties will have that effect," he muttered. Gerry had cannoned into the cabin, narrowly missing the stove. "Pity about that lure, though, one of Murry's best. Compensation will be the order of the day. Careless, careless."

"Astern, Ferg," said Murricane. "Reverse, slowly." A bad feeling was beginning to grip his gut, and this time it had nothing to do with the previous night's drink. He'd glimpsed something behind the boat, something ugly. Something horribly familiar. Something monstrous.

*** *** ***

Ferg's radio, as usual, wasn't working, but Fred, who had once again been sick, had a mobile offering a wobbly two bars of reception, and he managed to get through to the police in Inverness. They were told to stay where they were. Within half an hour, Britain's only official inland lifeboat was hurtling towards them, the big orange RIB based at Temple. Fred by now was on his second bacon roll, his eyes wide and staring, face white as he chewed and chewed. It was an odd reaction, but by no means the strangest Murricane had seen. Ferg had helped himself to the supply of Glen Moray whisky he kept in the cabin, washing it down with Carlsberg. A fearful combination. Murricane was sober, his mind far away. Suddenly he saw the monster. Shit. Nessie. That was all they needed.

In fact, what he was seeing was a plesiosaur-dragon cross, or the front half of what a boat-building company in Buckie thought one might have looked like. It was bright green, halfway between a cartoon viking longboat prow and all the traditional Nessie caricatures. The Surgeon's Photograph, the infamous 1933 snap it had taken the sceptics half a century to actually prove had been a hoax. It had taken that long mainly because nobody wanted to disbelieve. Like religion, Murricane thought.

The Buckie-built imitation monster had been bolted to the bow of the gigantic hotel vessel the *Nessotora Regina*, built to the absolute maximum breadth, length and draught to get through

A WHISKY IN MONSTERVILLE

the Caledonian Canal's 29 locks, over four aqueducts, under 10 bridges. It was operated from Fort William by Nessotora Ltd, slept 50 paying passengers, and took a week to get from one end of Thomas Telford's 200-year old waterway to the other. Most of the passengers were probably still asleep, but a couple of dozen or so were leaning over the rails, focussing their digital SLRS on the approaching bow wave of the RNLI RIB.

Archie McMinnican and Kevin Bernardine were the RNLI volunteers aboard the RIB, resplendent in survival suits and lifejackets. The Drum cop was a world-weary 37-year-old called Seoras MacTaggart, an Islay man with whom Murricane occasionally shared a malt; they tended to regard each other with a cordial suspicion. It was possible he'd been told to watch out for Murricane. In the sense of both 'beware of' and 'make sure he doesn't get into any trouble'. There was probably a file. There was definitely a file. A red sticker. The Cover was no real protection against officialdom.

Seoras was a classic Highland policeman, recruited from the islands, taken out of his context, as they tended to do with coppers: never let them loose on their home patch. There had probably been plans to set him loose on the mean streets of Glasgow or Edinburgh, huckling psychotic football supporters into vomit-stained Black Marias. Or were they white, these days, the cop vans? But Seoras had settled in Drum, had resisted the attempts at transfer. And that old-beyond-his-years experience had been bred into him by the constant encounters with death in all its various brutalities.

Because Drumnadrochit was the road accident capital of the Highlands. The A82 along Loch Ness, twisty and deceptive, a main route along the Great Glen between Fort Bill and Sneck, west and east, was a killer on a monumental scale. Tiny side roads, people in a hurry, huge lorries, tourists driving on the wrong wide of the road, fleets of suicidal motorcyclists, mad pedal cyclists, pedestrians... it had everything. They all died, in dribs, drabs and sometimes multitudes. Even Murricane had been shocked by the mini bus full of SAGA pensioners that had been hit by a cattle truck just outside of Lewiston. Fourteen dead at the scene. Another dozen later, apparently. Some of those tough old bodies taking a long time to die.

"Ferg. Murry." The lilting Islay tones irresistibly took Murricane back to another lifetime: a pier by Port Charlotte, another fast inflatable, a case of rare Bruichladdich. Crazy days.

"What have we here then?" MacDixon of Glendochgreen.

"A body, Seoras."

"Aye, it is that." The bottle of Glen Moray – the 10, thought Murricane, not a great whisky, a supermarket favourite – was heading for half-full, two empty Carlsberg cans swilled about in the bottom of the *Happy Adventure*, and Ferg was slurring his words even more than usual. "Certainly, a body of water. A fine body of water. Hides a multitude of sins, the loch, a multitude, ye ken. Sin. And we all know about sin, don't we?"

Seoras turned his quizzical gaze on Murricane, raised an eyebrow. He was wearing his police uniform, no lifejacket. Maybe he had that islander's fatalism, thought Murricane: can't swim, won't learn, might as well drown quickly.

"A body," said Murricane. "Definitely human."

"I see. Lose a tourist, did you, Ferg? No reports of anyone missing from the *Deepscan or Nessie Hunter*."

"Not lost," said Murricane. "Not mislaid." He had secured the corpse, loosely mooring it to the side of the boat by a piece of blue nylon line. He had turned it with a boat hook first. "Definitely placed here. Definitely... killed. Nothing accidental, Seoras." The images flashed before his eyes. It was all far too familiar. Iraq. Afghanistan. Northern Ireland.

"Bound, naked, headless. Burnt."

There was a silence, broken by the regular chewing of Fred, a choking sound from Gerry, the clink and swirl of whisky being swallowed, the mutter of boat engines.

"Sounds like it might have been deliberate then," said Archie McMinnican, known universally as Crunchie due to an incident one Hogmanay when he'd eaten seventeen of the honecomb chocolate bars for a bet.

"Definitely non-accidental," said Murricane. "Definitely not drowned."

"Unless someone's set up a portable crematorium, and there's been an accident. Maybe tried to put the fire out and, eh, lost the heid." Kevin Bernardine, would-be stand-up comedian.

"Shut up, Kevin." Seoras sighed, raised his portable radio. "Ach well, better call it in. I'm afraid your fishing trip will have to be curtailed, gentlemen." He nodded at Gerry and Fred.

"Catch of the day," said Kevin.

And that was when Ferg hit him with his empty bottle of whisky. A moment caught by at least a dozen cameras aboard the *Nessatora Regina,* which had motored inquisitively closer, the lurid green dragon-cum-dinosaur head at her bow seeming to Murricane like a leering, laughing mirror image of himself. Too late, he realised he should have covered his face.

Souvenirs

※

Burnt caramel, nuts, disinfectant. Butyric acid and chilli pepper. Diesel oil and cloves.

TW S<small>AMUELS</small> K<small>ENTUCKY</small> B<small>LENDED</small> W<small>HISKEY</small>

A WHISKY IN MONSTERVILLE

He had loaded the headless, naked body, the meat, into the Hi-Lux and taken it to the little clearing in the woods below Bein a Bhataich. There was a clear pathway in from the track. Plenty of kindling, and he'd used some petrol but not a great deal. A cupful. An American cup. The cookery measure. Some people might find that funny, he supposed. Make it look natural. Leave something for them to find, though.

But don't make it too obvious. They had to put two and two together, act like detectives, like police. So he'd extinguished the flames with the Toyota's fire blanket, and after letting everything cool down, hauled the remains, still pleasantly warm though the blanket's protective asbestos, or whatever the modern healthy alternative was, to the truck, carefully leaving scrapings of flesh on the altar. He'd hidden and watched them, the pagans, druids, whatever they were, at their stupid rituals, cooking chickens and rabbits, scampering embarrassed in their nakedness. It was the right place.

The smell didn't bother him. Barbecued flesh was barbecued flesh, animal was animal. He believed in the unity of species. He was merely one of a vast number of predators in the world, fulfilling the function he'd been born for.

The collecting was something else. It was a kind of reassurance, a way of establishing his presence in a new territory. Well, it always began as that. Afterwards, it grew, in a manner of speaking, legs. He smiled. Legs were a bit awkward. He preferred smaller objects.

It had started in Iraq, back in the 90s, and had led to his dismissal, eventually, from the uniformed ranks of the army. Nothing sexual. He despised sex, the supposed need for it, something that had so weakened many of his comrades. He believed in purity, of mind, of purpose. The body was just meat, to be used up, to be strengthened and deployed. To be destroyed when necessary.

He had not been entirely forgotten. He had skills, after all, very particular ones. Specialised abilities. And when these were required, his habits – his, what was that word? His predilections… they were indulged. He was reliable, in a very specific kind of way.

A WHISKY IN MONSTERVILLE

It was that part of the Scottish Highland night when everything began to move inexorably towards morning. Maybe 4.00am. His Luminox confirmed the time he had always been able to hold in his head. Better get moving. People would be up and about soon. He drove down the track to the lochside road, originally built by some ancient general, he'd read, to subdue the wild local rebels. It was a narrow road, not much used nowadays except by tourists and forestry workers. He'd looked at the map earlier, what the Brits called Ordnance Survey, some kind of military thing there, surveying for ordnance. He'd double-checked on GPS, and parked in a lay-by below the rocky slope of Creag a Ghiubhais. The sky above the loch was lightening fast, now. He levered the bundle out of the truck bed, over the low wall and onto the small strip of shingle beach. Leave it on the beach, he'd been told, where it'll be found. We need traceability. We need to point the finger. And that's when it all began to go wrong.

He left the body, deciding to take the blanket with him. He'd reached the truck and was looking back at the shore when he noticed, in the rapidly increasing dawn, that the water's edge was no longer a good two feet from the meat. And as he watched, incredulous, it lapped around the bundle of human animal, seemed to embrace it and pull it out into the loch. A loch that wasn't tidal. Jesus, this wasn't the fucking sea. And tides didn't act like that, like some living creature, insisting on its prey.

He felt a shocked chill gather in his body, creep along his back, up to his neck. The small hairs there crinkled and flexed. It was not a sensation he was accustomed to.

No tides in the loch. This shouldn't be happening. But the stories. He'd heard them, all of course. The loch was famous, right across the world. A strange place. A mysterious beast, a monster. Had something pulled the meat into the depths? He felt vaguely pleased and excited, but anxious too, and annoyed that he had failed to meet the requirements he'd been set. Had not fulfilled his orders.

Later, he discovered that there had been some kind of sporting event on television. European soccer, a game involving the Scottish national team. Somewhere with a weird time difference,

43

maybe America. Anyway, it was half time, teatime, kettles being boiled right across the country. More electricity was needed than was available on the grid.

And just down the loch, in the village of Foyers, the pumped storage generation station came to life. Over 3500 cubic feet of water per second began thundering down from Loch Mhor, two miles and 600 feet above, high on the heights of the Great Glen. Giant turbines, the biggest in Europe with blades of almost 16 feet across, began turning. Within two minutes, 300 megawatts of power was hitting the grid, millions of gallons of water had entered Loch Ness. Further along the loch, nearer Fort Augustus, another, smaller hydro scheme at Glen Doe was also bursting into life. And the loch was rising.

The water level could be raised or lowered by several feet, by releasing the stored water in the mountain lochs or by pumping from Loch Ness up into them. There were outflow valves at the south-western end of the loch, but they were inefficient and inadequate. When electricity demand was low and power was cheap, water inched its way up tunnels and pipes and the level of Loch Ness lowered. That, it turned out, was why he'd been given this timescale. The pumps should have been on, moving water up into the mountains: more beach, not less.

But who would have guessed about the soccer? This local obsession with something that wasn't football, not what he thought of as football.

So the meat disappeared. Maybe it wouldn't be found, or not soon enough. Maybe he'd have to obtain another human target, or be provided with one. Trophies. There were always more to find, to collect, to have, to hold close. He started the Toyota, heard the engine rattle and clatter into life. This was an old truck, leaking diesel, reeking of oil, smoke and stressed metal.

He inhaled deeply. He couldn't actually smell the vehicle at all. All he could smell was burnt meat. It made him hungry.

The official gaze

Distinctive fresh pear, creamy with subtle oak flavours. A long, smooth and mellow finish.

GLENFIDDICH 12-YEAR-OLD

A WHISKY IN MONSTERVILLE

It had been mayhem at the pier. Or to be precise, at the marina adjoining Temple Pier, known as Loch Ness Harbour. Two ambulances, two police cars, and a van, two tour buses crammed with holidaymakers expecting trips on the tour boats Nessie Hunter and *Deepscan*; the operators of said boats, one incandescent with rage, the other calmly surveying the scene through his beard. They were eventually persuaded that tours would have to be cancelled for the morning, and the buses returned to Drumnadrochit's two competing Loch Ness Monster visitor centres, there to be recompensed with small furry models of the beastie-as-dinosaur, audio visual experiences, and every conceivable souvenir of Scotland made in the sweatshops of Hong Kong and Vietnam. It was impossible to make anything but the highest-end souvenirs, hand-made craftworks, in Scotland itself. That was far too expensive.

The RNLI building had been requisitioned for interviews. Ferg's aim with the empty bottle of whisky had been poor, and Kevin had suffered no more than what Seoras informed the inspector from Inverness was 'a minor clunk'. A bruised cheekbone. Ferg would, however, be charged with assault. Inevitable, thought Murricane, as he'd carried out the attack in front of a serving police officer. Fred was remarkably cheerful about the whole thing, probably imagining the stories he and Gerry would tell back in Wolverhampton. Mad Scots, the one that got away, dead bodies in Loch Ness, probably the monster responsible. A paramedic had checked the pair out and pronounced them 'unsaveably English'. Inverness specialised in sarcastic paramedics.

There was an inspector and a sergeant from the Raigmore HQ of the Scottish National Constabulary's (known as Scottish Police, like something from a bad movie) Highland Division. Murricane found himself staring into a beer-red, rumpled face in its 40s.

"I'm Sergeant Macalamine," said the mouth, opening barely enough to give a glimpse of bad, blackened, very Scottish teeth. There was a whiff of oral decay. "Can you give me your details please. Name and address? Occupation?" A small black imitation

A WHISKY IN MONSTERVILLE

Moleskine notebook and an iPhone lay open on the cheap laminate table. Murricane sighed.

"Murricane," he said. "Retired. No fixed abode. Living on a boat down... here. Quietly."

"First and middle names?"

Murricane said nothing at first. Then he sighed and said: "Do you, by any chance, happen to know an Inspector Flaws? Of Inverness. Late of your force, back in the days of the Highland constabulary, before you became part of Greater Scottish Centralised policing?"

"I fail to understand, sir, how a retired police officer I may or may not know, and whose reputation may or may not be inspiring or even edifying, can be of any interest to me or help to you. Now, please: your full name."

Murricane reached over and picked up the iPhone. There was a signal booster at the RNLI station, combating Drum's notoriously bad reception. His fingers flicked at the screen. This guy was on O2. Good. Macalamine seemed frozen. His personal digital space had been invaded.

"No security, sergeant? No password? That's not very good. That's neither inspiring nor edifying. Man in your position."

"Put that down sir, please. That's my personal property. I'm going to have to insist."

Murricane punched in the number from memory, lifted it to his ear, listened for a moment, and said, "Murricane. Weir of Hermiston page 145." There was a brief pause, and then he added: "Serpentine." He handed the iPhone to Macalamine.

"Just tell the lady who you are, and she'll tell you who she is," he said.

Macalamine slowly took the phone from him, and muttered "Hello?" He had an Aberdeenshire brogue, thought Murricane. North Eastern boy, over among the savages. He watched the colour slowly drain from his face in patches.

There was a brief huddled conversation between Macalamine and the inspector, whose name was Peyronie. He was 30-ish, clad by Slater Menswear, crisp in luminous shirt and razor-edge grey silk tie. He looked at Murricane with an expression that combined anxiety and disgust. *Christ, not on my patch.* Murricane remembered something Flaws had told him about a young constable he'd worked with called Peyronie. Dick Peyronie, that had been the name. Richard. Someone had found out that Peyronie's Disease was a scarring that caused the penis to distort, bend and shorten, and ever since then he'd been known as Erectile Dysfunction, 'or Eric for short', Flaws had laughed. He'd come up in the world, had Eric, thought Murricane.

Peyronie walked over to the plastic chair Murricane had allowed himself to slump into. Letting your body relax, adaptation to discomfort: that was the first lesson of dealing with interrogation, and he'd unconsciously slipped into captive mode.

"You're free to go, Mr Murricane," the inspector said, arms folded against the implicit threat represented by the figure before him: A large figure in stained jeans and a worn Fair Isle V-neck jumper, worn over a black t-shirt. Ragged blond beard, long greying fair hair. Just another escapee to the Highlands, hiding out from the forces of civilisation. There were hundreds of them, scattered throughout the forests and moors from Aviemore to Caithness, surviving in cheap accommodation and watchful for the inevitable pursuers. Murricane was just another one with some kind of official sanction. "Your get-out-of-jail-free card appears to work. Works wonders, in fact. But it's probably best if you try to steer clear of the official gaze. Don't you think?"

"The official gaze," said Murricane. He matched his accent to the Inspector's: Posh Glasgow, or nearby: Milngavie, Kelvinside, Bearsden. A high flyer on the way up and up and up. "I'll bear it in mind. Eric." He shouldn't have enjoyed the flash of anger and confusion that erupted on Peyronie's face at the use of his nickname. But he did.

He walked up the steep hill to the main A82 road and tramped along the verge into the village, lorries, vans, buses and cars teeming past him at high speed. He could have headed to the *Gloria* or cut through the Cover to Drum, but he didn't want any nosy, dysfunctional policemen watching him retreat into his private lair. It was almost noon, clear and hot. He pulled off the old Shetland jumper, feeling sweaty and old. And hungry.

A WHISKY IN MONSTERVILLE

At the Piper's Rest, he pulled a clean t-shirt and a towel from the rucksack Jan let him keep in the staff changing room, then showered and changed. The lunchtime tourist trade was beginning to rev up but he managed to grab one of the small tables, and ordered Cullen Skink with bread made that morning by Jan's wife Claire. Mineral water, Highland Spring. The soup was perfect, smoked and fresh haddock poached in milk with onions, potatoes and a separate jug of double cream in the classic east-coast style. It was, he thought, one of the greatest restorative substances in the world.

Afterwards, Murricane had an espresso and a small Glenfiddich 12 (hardly a whisky at all, more of an ice cream soda) and pretended to read some of the holiday brochures and leaflets every catering establishment in the Great Glen was so copiously supplied with. Here was Scottish industry: craft workshops, glass blowers, dozens of candlemakers and woodcarvers. Unaffordably expensive products. They came with redundancy packages and internet skills from the south of England, and began living a fantasy hobbit lifestyle. Digital Bilbo Bagginses, though many morphed into Gollums, ending up embittered, bored, smoking vast quantities of dope, drinking whisky and watching porn on their computers, their tablets, their smartphones. Some of them. Some of them didn't do very well at all.

Like him, he thought. Wasting away on an old boat, nursing grievances, fingering old wounds. Fucking passing women who seemed dangerously enigmatic, shaking off the smell, the memory of burnt headless bodies that just happened to float into his life. Waiting for the past to catch up with him. He drained his coffee, shouted to Wiola the Polish waitress to put the bill on his account. He felt tired. Time for a nap, maybe. Time to flirt with the bad dreams. He cut across the fields behind the pub, heading for the Cover and the *Gloria*. Home.

Fishers of men

Sweetcorn, dry straw, the whiff of spirit. Digestive biscuit in the mouth and some peppery spice, toffee, apple pie and burnt earth.

OLD CROW

A WHISKY IN MONSTERVILLE

The worship meeting was well underway, and entering the period Coldstream called 'The Quiet Embrace of the Christ Child's Spirit'. The main hall of the shooting lodge called Creag Dhearg, Red Crag, after the cliff face it nestled into, was flooded with light reflected off Loch Duntelchaig, a basin hidden in the hills just south of Loch Ness. One whole wall of this Victorian room was windows, facing west. There were three other small lochs close by – Loch Ruthven, Loch Ceo Glais and, even further into the mountains which would eventually become Cairngorm, Loch a Choire. They were famous for their pike and trout, the four lochs of Creag Dhearg. But for Fletcher F Coldstream, the 'F' standing for Fotheringay, some English folk group his hippy mother had been into, the fishing he was interested in was spiritual. Maybe some cynics might claim he was keen mainly on trawling for money. But he knew in his heart that was only a means to an end. And that end was God. The Omega. The Alpha and the Omega. Start, finish and everything in between.

"Fishers of men! That's what we are! Men... and women, of course. There is no gender in Christ! We are one. We must all be one. We must draw all men... and women to Him, and to us, as we await His return in glory!"

Coldstream's voice was southern TV honey, all Georgian sweetness modified with proper consonants and the lilt of what sounded like expensive education. It was truly amazing what a proper Hollywood acting coach could teach you. He had recommended one particular studio in Santa Monica to some of his more senior disciples, back when he was developing the Sanctified Truth of the Christ Child in History ministry in LA out of its storefront origins and into the massive, soaring edifice in Anaheim they were calling *Christworld*. That was a slang name, a kind of insult, but secretly, Coldstream didn't mind it. Christworld. The world for Christ. The Christ Child, pure and innocent, the child-man of holiness, dead and resurrected, reborn and fresh-minted, taking the world to himself. There was a great and powerful truth there. And the Church of the Sanctified Truth of the Christ Child in

History was, he had to admit, just a little clumsy tripping off the average English-speaking tongue.

He gazed at the 20 – no, 19 – people before him. They were fine examples of Christian humanity, most of them, Christian American humanity. Sister Melliflua, of course, was an exception. Somewhat wizened. But useful. Not all the rest were blond and blue-eyed. There were a couple of brunettes. He had soft spot for the Mediterranean heritage. After all, hadn't Our Lord been, let's admit it, brothers (and sisters), of that line himself? Italian, though, that was a look. Sophia Loren as Mary Magdalene. Young Avril had been that way. What a shame. What an unholy shame. The Lord did work in mysterious ways, His wonders to perform. And sometimes He needed a little help. Practical help.

He ran his fingers back through the white wings of hair on either side of his head. It was luxuriant and flowed a good few inches over his neck, curling slightly at the end. It was a real pity he was bald on top, had begun receding at the front when he was only in his twenties. And yet he'd never sought to disguise that. A noble forehead. He had a noble forehead that had just got bigger. And bigger. More and more noble. And besides, there were aspects of the sensual flesh he liked to feel on his naked scalp. Ah, the thought!

"Brothers and sisters, we are here for a purpose. Not the enslaved puppeteering purpose the heretic Calvin preached – free will is the essence of our faith, the freedom to act – but our purpose, our motivation, our Divine reason, is to fulfil the responsibilities, the duty of freedom, to provide freedom for others, to share the love of the Christ Child. My children, my brothers, my sisters, let us share that love. In a manner commensurate with our holiness and our mutual respect."

They were dressed in blue robes, his people. He imagined what they were wearing underneath. That was his privilege. No, his duty. Naked, he hoped, as was laid out in his book *The Pursuit of Holy Communication*. Some, he knew, did not, would not ever attain that higher state of spiritual nudity. Shorts, underwear, even vests – but the shedding of clothes and underwear was a progression for them, a movement toward the ultimate goal. He himself, his spare white body hairless, shaved, wore a white linen kaftan, one of several he'd had run up in Nashville by Morrie's Ecclesiastical Apparel. It was organic material too, soft and cooling in almost every circumstance. And, he thought, quite fetching.

He pressed a button on the oak pulpit, one of three portable units he'd had made in California, and flown over specifically for the project, this mission. Music burst from the two Bose speakers at either side of the room. Electronic and dreamy, woozy and new age. He watched as the congregation began to embrace, holding each other, male on female, male on male. There was a 70-30 gender split in favour of the men, the way he liked. it. He felt himself becoming aroused. They would feel it too. But it had to be within limits. It was simply a method of raising excitement, mutual dependency, commitment. Hitler had known how do it better than anyone. A man with only one testicle.

Enough. As the music played, he stepped behind the pulpit to hide his erection – a common enough ploy among preachers, so he'd been taught back in his Bible School days, that coarse little rural college in Indiana – and held his hands up in a crucifixion gesture, though in fact he was pointing at the two great pictures adorning the walls to either side of him. They were very high quality computer generated impressions of plesiosaurs.

"We are here to express our love for the Christ Child, and to spread that love," he said directly into the microphone, his favourite, thoroughly American Shure SM58 microphone, mounted on a flexible steel stem. He loved the way he could caress it with his lips, like a rock star, bringing out the bass in his voice, turning it into a sonic weapon. "We are here to establish a community, a community of vision, of truth, or purity and witness for the world. And we are here to say, crucially, that God created the earth in six days! That on the seventh day he rested! There is no negotiation on this, no liberal humming and hawing. The Christ Child is pure, the Christ Child is our salvation, but he and his Godhood are rooted in history. The true history of the universe.

"And brothers, sisters, the proof is here. Right here in Scotland. The proof that the great evil of evolution that has dominated our culture, our world for so long, is on the verge of extinction. Because we are in the location on this planet with proof that man walks, still walks with dinosaurs." His fingers flicked towards the two massive pictures.

" No monster this, that stalks these waters
but our sons, our wives and daughters
with abandon will rejoice
when, with one, united voice
we cry: they did not die, they live!
Creator God, thou hast displayed
the truth of what thy hands hath made!"

"Amen!" Cried a loud, male voice, to Coldstream's sensitive ears, slightly over-enthusiastically. There was a fake sincerity to it. He could always tell. The tall one was still holding the hand of a rather too-plump young blonde from Michigan – Sally, he thought she was called. There was something about their gestures towards each other, the body language, that caught his attention. A familiarity. Too much familiarity. Arousal in worship was meant to be mutual and non-specific, certainly not leading to any kind of pairing off without his express permission. He'd have them both up to his room later for further instruction. In detail. It was his onerous task to dictate partnerships. To impose sexual conditions on their discipleship. And only his.

"We are here to bear witness, and soon we will have the opportunity to reveal to the world, to this Scotland that was once a holy place, and will be again, the great plan that the Lord has placed in our hearts and minds. Until then we must prepare ourselves. Purify our hearts, our minds, our bodies, our very souls." Amen, a more unified cry, now, a sense of the entire room becoming one. He liked that.

"People have called us Creationists, Nessatorean Creationists. But in truth we are more, much more than that. Let us worship now, in the words of our revelatory testament, of scripture." He closed his eyes. He knew this off by heart. He dipped towards the microphone, let his vowels expand, his consonants roll.

"*And God said, let the earth bring forth the living creature after his kind, cattle, and creeping thing, and beast of the earth after his kind, and it was so.*" His enunciation of those verses from Genesis was, he thought, velvety, loving, full of wonder and conviction.

Irresistible. He let some more Georgia sugar flow into his tone. "And God made the beasts of the earth after his kind, and cattle after his kind, and everything that creepeth upon the earth after his kind. And God saw that it was good." He stopped, opened his eyes. The young people, the Sanctified, were gazing at him rapt, more of them now holding hands, reaching for each other, becoming one entity, one being. *"And God said, Let us make man in our image, after our likeness, and let them have dominion over the fish of the sea and over the fowl of the air, and over the cattle and over all of the earth and over every creeping thing that creepeth upon the earth. Dominion."* His voice still soft, but gaining in strength and volume. "Dominion. Dominion. Dominion! DOMINION!"

And the voices of these divine youngsters, these hopes for the future, these bastions of purity and power and truth, erotically charged in each other's presence, and maybe with one or two in need of corrective measures. They gathered with him, louder and louder:

"DOMINION! DOMINION!"

Afterwards, as usual, he felt that great infusion of adrenalin and relief, tiredness and exaltation, that desperation for a fuck. He could hardly be bothered with Jenks, but he had already decided what to do, and that Jenks should do it. That was why he was here, after all. Partly. To do his will, the will of Coldstream.

When the two young people came to his room, the round tower room facing west, just catching from its heights the sliver of Loch Ness below the nearby shimmer of Loch Duntelchaig, he was feeling both benevolent and, despite his usual post-preaching self-pleasing, in need of physical relief.

The two knew what was expected of them. Both fine specimens of God's creation, and enthusiastic, he thought. Was the boy a little less than forthcoming? All he asked was a massage while the girl pleasured him with her holy mouth. She seemed thankful for the opportunity. The boy grew physically excited, as one might have expected. Frustrated too. Angry. It was important for them all to learn these lessons of dominance, of submission. Of true discipleship.

A fine result. A worshipful result for all concerned, in the end. The boy in tears, crestfallen, broken. After it was over he asked them to put their robes back on and they knelt together on the floor, the afternoon light playing on their robes, as he brought himself to climax again in front of them. Blue and white, blue and white. Sky and clouds, water and waves.

"Attraction is a wondrous thing," Coldstream said, after he had finished. "And it is necessary for the maintenance of effective breeding and the alleviation of physical impulses." He gazed from one to the other. Sally, it was. And Liam. Some Irish, Celtic influence? His hair verging on red. There was no Biblical bias against red hair, but still. He thought of the Kennedy line and grimaced, despite himself. "Among we Sanctified, though, the necessity of unity behoves us to avoid personal entanglement. Without my blessing. My permission. Exclusivity is no part of our internal theology, unless gifted by the anointed leader." Their eyes were downcast, though he caught a sidelong glance from Liam. Something wounded there. Festering.

"There is a demon here, a demon which divides. And it must be driven out." He raised both hands above his head.

"Oh Lord, we thank thee for this expression of our holy mutuality, our essential and pure love. We thank thee for our togetherness, or sense of purpose, our adherence to the true discipline of Biblical community. Send us now to do your purpose in faithfulness and in obedience. In absolute obedience. And abnegation of self. " He lowered his arms, reaching for the hands of the couple before him. Then he let Liam's go. "Remain with me, Sally. I have a word from the Christ Child to share with you. Liam, you may go." And the young man – that hair, definitely too red for comfort, and slightly too long in the fringe, floppy and verging on the fashionable – got up and opened the door. Coldstream could hear his bare feet, on the sandstone spiral stair. Followed seconds later by another set of almost inaudible footsteps.

Jenks. He'd been, as instructed, stationed in the unused privy next to the doorway at the top of the stairwell. Unnecessary for toiletry purposes since the installation of a luxurious bathroom suite, fashionably open to the bed, desk and leather lounge chairs they'd so recently been making use of. Jenks was nimble, no doubt about it. Obedient, yes, and effective, most of the time.

There were issues there. He'd known about them from the beginning of this endeavour, this project. But Jenks was useful. Indeed, he was essential. And if he overheard the sounds of physical communion, well. Coldstream liked an audience.

He got up, went over to the extra-large tub, and switched on the hot water.

"Sally," he said. "Let me introduce you to the techniques of ministering through partial immersion." Immersion. That was what they were waiting for. The day of immersion, proper, public baptism. Collective and uncompromising.

Her accent had veered into the midwestern. Indiana wants me, Lord... He caught his own native twang coming through the much-practised public tones.

"Immersion... the baptism, the great baptism... will it be soon, Brother Coldstream? Brother... Fletcher?" Brother. Momentary irritation at the incestuous overtone. And the familiarity, the possessiveness. And then he thought, why not? They were all one.

"Soon, Sister Sally," he replied, his Hollywood southern accent back in place. "Soon and very soon. Meanwhile, a taster, a precursor. Only with the unguent oils of the east. And soap." She smiled.

Jesus, he thought, she was easy meat. He wondered if there was still a bottle of Old Crow hidden in the desk. For special occasions.

Ice house

Uses a unique rye recipe and Kentucky limestone-filtered water from the Salt River, this small batch bourbon is aged around six years and provides a distinctive smoky smooth taste. The bottles were used as props in Deadwood.

BULLEIT BOURBON FRONTIER WHISKEY

A WHISKY IN MONSTERVILLE

On his way to the old ice house, early in the mission, Jenks had surprised a sika hind grazing on some green, mineral-rich moss at the foot of a birch tree. He'd had plenty of deer, in the past. Hunting had been a childhood obsession, fuelled by his beloved dad, before the accident. Up in those foggy, rain-drenched Washington forests, clad in fluorescent vests and limited, supposedly to just the one moose per licence per season. Worshipping, *worshipping* his dad as they stalked the beasts, killing... how many? Five, six sometimes in that week's break. Fuck the rangers, fuck the rules, his dad had said. Just killing and leaving the bodies, maybe carving a little meat off for a campfire roast. Leaving the trophy heads. "Got enough at home," his dad would grumble. "The hunt's the thing. Eat what we need, leave the rest." They didn't eat much. Scavengers took what was left, or the inevitable decay. Sometimes he looked longingly at the carcases as they left them, wishing for something to remember them by.

Sika. Japanese deer. Smaller, spotted, unlike the native Scottish red. Though apparently they bred together all the time, according to the leaflet he'd picked up in the tourist office. The Sika had been imported by landlords as parkland ornaments. Inevitably, they'd escaped and bred like wildfire. The big shooting estates made strenuous efforts to keep their red deer stocks away from little Japanese interlopers, but what the hell, Jenks thought, animals. Animals were animals. Let them interbreed. Let the genetic line become polluted. In the end it would make for stronger, more adaptable deer. The toughest would survive.

Anyway, he'd geared himself up for serious hunting: crossbow, camouflage clothing, the lot; he'd dug himself in clear sight of the moss and waited. One whole night, if you could call it a night in these latitudes. Put up with the insects, those miniature mosquitoes they called midges, and then, in the first pearly dulling of morning, not a hind this time but a stag, like a miniature elk, good head of antlers too.

The crossbow was British, though it pained him to admit it. His old Stryker was back in the States, and besides, he liked the way you could fire ball bearings with this Talon Raptor. Almost

A WHISKY IN MONSTERVILLE

400 feet per second, all the power, at middling ranges, of a rifle, and no licence or bullshit like that. Especially handy when you were in an alien land.

He'd paced the distance out, 100 feet, set up the Barnet scope, sighted the dots on the lower neck of the deer. Carotid artery. How far would the beast get once he'd been hit? Jenks's heartbeat, that abnormally slow thunk, hadn't increased from its normal rate but was loud in his ears. The noise as he pulled the trigger was just like in those Robin Hood movies. A twanging hiss. Put the bow down, draw back the steel string, another ball was ready in his breast pocket. The deer had barely moved. Head drooping a tad, maybe. Focus. Fire. It tottered two, three steps, then fell. The crash and rustle of undergrowth. Then all he could hear was his heart.

Gralloching. They called it gralloching. The leaflet on Scottish field sports was really informative. Pronounced Gra-loch, as in Loch Ness. Bleed the thing as quickly as you could. Gut it. Hang it somewhere cool. The ice house was perfect for that. It had once been Creag Dhearg's primitive refrigerator, was clean and dry and almost completely overgrown. He'd come up on it by accident, setting up perimeters, checking for avenues of incursion. An ancient oak door in surprisingly good condition. A new padlock, some candles, and it was his. Some hooks, too, the kind you used for heavy coats.

So he'd hung the deer, throat dripping blood, over a bucket. Gralloching was preparation for eventual eating, but he was content to leave the deer there, unbutchered. Possessing it, seeing it, sometimes caressing it – that was a kind of healing, he supposed. Like art. Like great art. And you could hang venison for weeks, months before eating it. Some said the swarming of maggots was a good way of tenderising the meat.

Later, he'd brought the woman's head to the ice house. Now, that was a trophy. A really, classic hunter's trophy. He remembered that elk head in his mom and dad's house, his mother's grim determination there should be no more. The dozens of dead elk left on the mountainsides and forests as a result. And in the end, coming home to the aftermath of one of those thousands of arguments to find his mom's severed head neatly placed on the kitchen table, the rest of her in the garage, next to his dad's body, head blown off Hemingway style, shotgun in the mouth, bare toe through the trigger guard.

Meat.

The plastic aerosol sealant had been an idea he'd picked up during some of those early black ops in Iraq, when it was used as quick and dirty solution to stop bodies rotting before they were shipped home. Worked a treat, too, for up to maybe a week in hot conditions. Here, with the summer weather so variable, he thought he might get three weeks. The female's head was still looking good. Waxy but good.

Now he trailed the red haired boy, the Irishman. Ginger. Liam, whatever. He'd been told to make him disappear. No messing around, no deceptive trails of burnt flesh, no weird stuff. Just a problem that needed to go away. Though frankly, he thought this might be a bit of a whim from Coldstream, a bit personal. A bit kind of stupid, actually. Coldstream was seriously odd. Yet it was his oddness that provided cover for what was going down here, he supposed. And he'd been instructed to do his bidding.

Sometimes you just had accept that you'd be working with weird people.

So he made Liam disappear.

Most of him.

Druids

Star fruit and parma violet candy on the nose, followed by toast, digestive biscuits and fresh cut grass. Finishing with dry hay and a hint of smoke seeping through.

LOCH NESS SINGLE HIGHLAND MALT WHISKY

A WHISKY IN MONSTERVILLE

It was hot. A still, dry sunny Highland afternoon. Rare. So rare that Murricane wondered if he might be dreaming, might have hallucinated the oddness of the morning. He ran a hand over his face, blinked a few times. It was still hot. He was still in the Highlands. That headless, half-burnt body had been real. Ah well.

He traced his way through the dappled afternoon shade of the Cover, hardly glancing at the discreet penknife blazes that indicated his route home.

Home. A grounded barge in the Great Glen, on the faultline that divides Scotland diagonally in two. All the accoutrements of his life could be bundled into a couple of rucksacks, probably. There was no family, few friends, the occasional passing woman. Bad memories, bad history. Maybe he should count his blessings.

The Great Glen was a north-east/south-west highway, navigable by water and road. The Caledonian Canal linked the lochs between Inverness and Fort William. Yachts, fishing boats, drug smugglers, tourists aboard hired cruisers. They all wallowed their way, well or badly, from sea to shining sea. North Sea to Atlantic. Aboard the *Gloria*, he felt their wakes as they passed. Occasionally, when he was out in his kayak, they waved. He usually waved back. Human contact. Not that he craved it. It just seemed the right thing to do. Etiquette was everything. You just had to learn the right set of manners for the circumstances you found yourself in.

Once, in the little Ocean Rider sit-on-top, he hadn't waved and a sensitive Yorkshireman – hard to believe such a thing existed, but there you were – aboard half a million's worth of Sunseeker had shouted, deliberately and sarcastically moving his great fat arm back and forth, "We're WAAAAVING!"

He hadn't been able to restrain himself from replying to the effect that the skipper concerned should fuck right off back to Leeds and suck Geoffrey Boycott's dick, whereupon the bastard had swung round and tried to ram him, or at least swamp him and provide a good soaking. Which he had. It had all been seen by another of the Loch's casual kayakers, the legend that was

A WHISKY IN MONSTERVILLE

Davie the Druid. He'd needed no help getting back aboard the Ocean Rider, but Davie had been a friendly presence at the time.

Murricane had taken his old Land Rover that night, and headed for Lochend, where he found the Sunseeker tied up, waiting to go through the locks into Muirtown and beyond, out into the firth and then, proper waterworld in all its salt, squelchy glory. The boat was called *Mistress of the Universe.* Maybe the sensitive Yorkshireman was planning to turn around and sail back to the west coast. Murricane didn't care. Just waited until the party – two couples – had noisily climbed into a taxi and headed for the delights of Inverness. Then he'd broken into the boat, checked it for abandoned pets, budgerigars or children, and blown it up. Black powder tube bombs, improvised explosive devices, very crude ones. Bit risky. Switching on the Sunseeker's elaborate gas stove, cheap mobile phone fuse. Walk away, ring the number and bang. Glass fibre burned extremely well. Afterwards, he'd felt annoyed with himself. But he'd managed to get over it.

He unlocked the *Gloria,* and began thinking about food. He thought about food a lot these days; too much, maybe. Like some bored mid-life-crisis moron with too much time on his hands. And too many sharp knives to play with.

He checked the little 12-volt fridge, powered from a bank of batteries in the barge's engine room. He could charge them from the old diesel motor, which still functioned, but a tiny and scarily efficient floating wave generator was enough, usually, to keep it functioning and to charge up the alkaline cells in his cassette machine.

He had some salmon, two steaks of poached grilse he'd obtained in a rare foray to another of Drum's pubs, the Columban, known as the Col. It was the home of industrial drinkers, smalltime drug deals and occasional transactions in kind. The unofficial economy. Fish for tobacco, venison for Ecstasy. Scallops, no. That would have been good. He was partial to scallops from the west coast, dived not trawled, but they could only be obtained from the fish van that stopped in the tourist office car park three times a week. What day was it? Monday. No van today anyway. Black pudding, though, and some chorizo sausage, sweating slightly. Blood. Animal blood.

Worked well with scallops, but with salmon? He could have done with some venison. He was in a meaty kind of mood.

He settled for poaching the salmon, which seemed appropriate given its illegal origins, letting it cool to lukewarm, then serving it on Arroz rice with a thick sauce of black pudding chunked up with chorizo. A quick forage found some fennel in one of the Cover's few clearings, and some ground elder, bitter and refreshing. There was plenty of wild rocket. He sloshed the salad with olive oil and sherry vinegar.

He tried to eat slowly, washing the food down with some watered Glenlivet 12, THE Glenlivet, a session whisky really, light and airy, all mountain streams, melted snow and big white skies. Pudding? He kept a supply of Mars Bars in the fridge for just that. Mars Bars and, whenever he could get it, some decent cheese. Who was it said that there was no finer pudding than a Mars Bar? Someone reputable? Some big name gourmand? He couldn't remember. Derek something? Cooper, that was it. Skye connections.

He felt pleasantly full. Coffee, maybe another dram? He made an Aeropress, that great disguiser of cheap coffee's origins, using Taylor's Espresso grind, which actually wasn't that cheap, and was all the Drum Co-op had. A nip of Duncan Taylor Loch Ness malt, the one with Nessie on the label. It didn't say, but Jan had told him it was actually a rather good Ben Nevis. It had that fruity zing. Another, and he was ready to enter the bow bedroom, lie down on the built-in double bed, inhale what was left of Rebecca's scent and…

He woke in the fading darkness to a light scuffling sound towards the

barge's stern. Someone was on board. Mostly, even with the drink, he retained the hair-trigger wakefulness instilled by years of training and on-the-job fear. It went bone deep. He knew of one old comrade, ex-SAS, a married man, family, children, all those terrible agonies and encumbrances, who used to go camping with them, but always slept alone, in a bivvy bag outside the family tent. He'd explained it to Murricane during a whirlwind night of drinking when they'd met by sheer accident in Glasgow. Both of them eventually concluding it had been an accidental encounter, and neither had been sent to recruit or kill each other.

"Eh just can never trust myself." He was from Dundee, his speech inflected with the strange guttural lilting of Scotland's third city. Dun-Dee. Equal weight to both syllables. How many times had he said that? "Sleep in a separate bed from the wife, too. Was a single room for a while when eh first came oot the regiment. Slightest noise, waking up ready to kill whatever caused it. Reaching for them, for it or him or whatever. Glock under the bed. Illegal to have one nowadays, noo eh'm oot the ermy, but what the fuck? What do they expect? Maybe... maybe it'll pass."

Murricane thought of Rebecca, the way she'd slipped out of his bed and left without disturbing him. Maybe he was getting old. Soft and useless. Slow and dull. There was a soft tapping at the saloon door. He swung out of bed, bare feet on oak boards. The skylight above him was oiled and opened noiselessly. He knew his shoulders could get through diagonally, just, and the rest of him would follow. Naked, he emerged into the tree-shaded halfnight, hearing the high clatter of birdsong, padding around the side of the raised deck to the stern. The figure huddled in the steering well, tapping at the saloon hatch, was small, wiry, hooded. Murricane pivoted himself around and behind it, balancing on the handrail at the corner of the cabin and landing with soft thump. Unthinking, clear, balanced. He half-closed the fingers of his right hand and punched whoever it was in the left kidney. The figure fell backwards with a gasp, the fleece hoodie falling away to reveal an agonised face Murricane knew well. It was Davie the Druid.

"I'm no' a druid at all," Davie said, once he had seated himself at the saloon table, a restorative glass of Murricane's Glenlivet in hand. "You ken that fine. I'm a pre-Celtic Revival pagan." Murricane was drinking water. He knew Davie's capacities and the Glenlivet he had left wouldn't last long. There was the Loch Ness, but he was going to have to replenish his whisky stocks soon. Davie drained his glass. "I wouldnae be a feckin' Druid. Unity with nature, that's oor thing. Equality with nature. And feckin' sacrifice? Only if it's deid already, roadkill n'that. Mostly it's feckin' fruit and veg, oot o'date cauliflowers from Tesco. Maybe a wee hind that's tangled wi' a lorry, sure, or a rabbit or a pine marten. That's just recyclin' the energies of the universe, man. But Jesus Christ, this is pure crap. Pure feckin' crap. There was no need to belt me like that, by the way."

Jesus was an interesting name to come up in a pre-Celtic pagan's vocabulary, Murricane thought. But then, who was he to judge? What was he, anyway? A post-secret warfare husk? A remnant? An embarrassment?

"Sorry about that. Best start at the beginning, Davie." He was dressed now, in sweatpants and t-shirt. Davie, in his 50s, Invernessian, Sneck through and through, with tattoos on his knuckles that read 'Love' and, slightly crushed (the 'C' and the 'l' both on his first finger) 'Clach'. Murricane had never been able to work out if that meant he loved Clachnacuddin FC or that they had been the all-consuming hatred in his life. Before Pre-Celtic paganism redeemed him to a life of releasing cauliflower from the bondage of multinational supermarkets.

Davie lived in a mouldering caravan, secreted away in the forest near Barnagarlin, on the south side of the loch, north of Foyers. He supplemented his dole money by growing mediocre cannabis in a variety of disused sheep fanks high above Loch Mhor. There were several shielings up there, summer settlements where crofting families had once spent the lighter months. Davie's trick was to cover sheep fanks with plastic sheeting and hothouse the plants in the spring and summer. In the autumn he'd gather and dry magic mushrooms. The rest of the time, he ran a coven. Or whatever the pre-Celtic pagan equivalent was.

"Used to be we'd call it a coven, all that sky-clad dancing and stuff. Matter of fact, we had to abandon the naked bit. Too cold in winter and in the summer the midges would leave you bitten to feck. Not to mention the clegs and the ticks. One of the lasses, fine caster o' spells when we did that sort of thing, she got feckin Lyme's disease off a tick bite, in a very embarrassing place. Tried to treat it wi' dock leaves and essence of feckin' frog. Roadkill frog. Nae cruelty. She was in Raigmore for a month. Best tae keep your clothes on, I think." He looked nervously at Murricane as he said this, clearly rattled at the thought of him rampaging about The Cover undressed in the dark.

"Anyway. No' a coven these days. Some of the witches left, warlocks mostly stayed and agreed that we should go the pagan route, get rid o' all that wicca stuff. Worshipping the Great Mother. Too much bloody female authority, swung too much gender-wise in the distaff direction, Murry, ken? Druids? Witches? Wicca? Fuck 'em."

Murricane had heard the stories. Davie had a small collection of drug buddies and dope customers who lived on the wilds of the south shore, traditionally just a wee bit more bohemian than the north. The ones who fancied themselves as the inheritors of the Crowley and Page tradition. Magick, mystery, mushrooms and marijuana. It was a potent mix. And there was the sex – all of Davie's spiritual hi-jinks had involved multiple partner swapping, almost entirely heterosexual. And despite what he'd said, the women seemed to exercise as much domination as the men. Indeed, generally more. It was an effective way of alleviating boredom for the under-employed stress refugees of the Highlands. If it came to a choice between that and the Free Kirk, Murricane thought he knew which way he'd jump. Or maybe not. Maybe God would have him in the end.

"So, anyway. Come to the bit, I heard from the Sneck that the polis are heading oot my way, wanting serious words, Murry, and I mean serious words. That floater you fished oot the loch yesterday? Mind? Headless I heard? Burnt? They're pinning that on me. Flamin' cheek!"

No pun intended, Murricane thought.

"Is that not awfully quick, Davie? Like, what is it, 36 hours or something?" In his experience, the Constabulary in the Highlands were practitioners of the dead-slow-stop-possibly-start-again-several-months-from-now approach to murder investigation.

"Feckin' forensics, all that, what do they call it, Miami Vice, CSI stuff. What I hear is, they matched samples from the body to burnt human flesh they found on the Rock of Sacrifice. It's just below Bein a' Batach, fine spot for it, track in most of the way. Secluded. Witches didnae mind takin' off their kit in there. Back when we did that sort o' thing, before we were pre-Celtic, like. Not my scene any more, man."

Murricane was still puzzled.

"How do you know all this Davie? No offence, but stuck in that caravan?"

"Aye well, we're no' all as bloody backwards as you are, Murry. Satellite wi-fi in there, telly, the lot." He reached underneath his hoody and produced an object Murricane gradually recognised as a waterproofed iPhone. "On a forum, like, private. Pre-Celtic Paganism dot feckin' org. Password protected discussions. Don't want any old feckin' Findhorn new age yuppie or whoever on there. And besides, the truth is that there's a Sneck polisman's wife who fancies herself as a bit o' a shamanistic princess, read a bit of Castaneda, wee bit confused on the witches and warlock front. Been kind o' helping her along the straight and narrow Pre-Celtic way." He raised his glass. "Good on ye, Mrs Peyronie!"

"Well, fine. Thanks for sharing and all that, Davie. But what exactly are you doing here? You know me. I make trout lures, I paddle about in my kayak. Just like you, occasionally have arguments with bastards from Yorkshire." Murricane uncorked the Glenlivet so he could give Davie a refill, began to move the bottle towards his glass, thought better, reversed it and saw it enveloped in Davie's surprisingly large right hand. Steady as a rock, he noticed, as Davie emptied the whisky into his glass, eyeing him shrewdly. A ferrety face, stringy goatee, all Catweazle pose. It was easy to underestimate him.

"That polisman's wife? He's quite senior. Access to files and all that. Apparently there's one on you. Full o' blanks, secret stuff, he told her. You're a bit o' a joke, a bit o' a scary monster. Keep an eye out, all that. Been around, done things. bad things, good things, who knows? Fact is, I like you, despite you being English."

"Carlisle," said Murricane, with no idea why he was suddenly revealing this. "Borderlands. Hardly English. This accent..." he wrapped his tongue around a sudden twist into broad Invernessian, that weird collision between Highland whine and guttural Somerset drawl that came, allegedly, from the city's Cromwellian occupation in the 17th century. "Raaaaiiiiit Enaaafff, it's a wee bit chaaaangeable. Anyway." He switched back to his normal, middle class English elocution school neutrality. "What do you want, Davie? They'll track you through that phone, you know, if you use it."

"No, they cannae keep jumping on new SIM cards, and I've got dozens. Well, a dozen. You're underestimating the world of illegal substance dealing, my friend. Cutting edge of feckin' technology. Pornography and drugs, we lead the charge up the digital superfeckin' highway. Not that I'm into pornography. Though there was a time when we were witchin' and warlockin' all over the place when I thought... anyway, never mind." He leaned across the table. "Here's the thing Murry. The body, that burnt woman. They know who it is. Ken they weirdo Yanks up at Creag Dhearg? Ah'm ontae them. And they feckin' hate me. This is aw about this feckin' Monster Centre. Nessieville or whatever it's called. This thing they want to build at Foyers. Ruin the whole feckin' south shore of the loch."

Murricane remembered dimly that there had been several official objections to a planning application for the new tourist centre, including one from what Jan had referred to as 'hippies and tree huggers' that had had provoked some amusement in the Piper's Rest.

"What, you're standing in their way, Davie, are you? Davie the Druid, the Sting of Foyers, battling the evil Forces of Cartoon Nessie? Come on. Pull the other one."

"Coalition of alternative lifestyles, we ca'd it. Me trying to keep as quiet as possible, but I pulled a few strings, had a word with a few smokers, ken." Jesus, Murricane could imagine. Davie supplied dope to some unlikely figures. And this was the Highlands. Even the most established laird or industrial entrepreneur could have several dozen skeletons rattling in their closet. Was likely to. Crazed children. Criminal grandparents. Witchy wife. A dope habit.

"Official objection. A few meetings, bit o' activism. Christ, they're talking about a massive new pier, out into deep water, reopening some of the old Alcan hydro tunnels for more bloody hydro power. What do you think Crowley would have made of all that?"

Aleister Crowley. The wickedest man in the world, the Beast of Boleskine, and the chief Satanist of the Edwardian era, allegedly.

Boleskine House, purchased by him because of its 'south facing aspect' as an experimental machine for various arcane satanist experiments, and later bought by Jimmy Page of Led Zeppelin. Nowhere looked less sinister, Murricane had always thought, a kind of pretty, low Edwardian bungalow with Georgian pretensions and a friendly aspect. The parties thrown there, both during Page's occasional residence and when it was just the caretaking staff, were legendary. Crowley himself, thought Murricane, was just a bored, brilliant boy from a strange religious background – the fundamentalist Plymouth Brethren – who had tried everything he could think of in a very restricted culture, from edge-of-the-envelope mountaineering to extreme sexual experimentation, drugs and so-called magick. In the end, according to what he'd read, it was all about looking for love. But then, it usually was.

Crowley was often credited with inventing environmentalist activism, objecting to the original aluminium smelter at Foyers. Protesting. He was a posh Davie the Druid, with money and better taste in clothes. All the pictures showed him in silk kaftans or Harris Tweed.

"Tell you the timescale, Murry. There's no accident here. Planning application goes in, what, six weeks ago? Being rushed through. I'm telling you, like a feckin' express train, and you know what those wankers up at Highland Council are like. Tortoise crossed with a snail. Public meeting called for a week on Friday, then the following Thursday the council planning committee meets to decide. Full Council to rubber stamp it. And then it'll be goodbye feckin' Foyers, farewell tae the whole south shore of the loch. Never mind the pine martens and the swans, and the sea eagles, the red kites..."

"Spare me the propaganda, Davie. What the hell do you expect me to do about it?"

The little man raised his whisky glass. It was empty. So was the bottle.

"You're bored shitless here, Murry. Admit it. What is this crap? Fishing? Making Ferox lures? I mean, it's not even tying flies, is it? It's not complicated. It's just carving up bits of plastic to look roughly like feckin' fish. You're trading in bullshit and magic same

A WHISKY IN MONSTERVILLE

as... anyway. And whisky, eh, which incidentally is OK, this stuff. Maybe a bit bland. But listen, when you came around behind me on the boat there like feckin' Ghost Dog, like some Ninja bastard, that was the first time you'd been alive properly the whole time you've been here. That and when you blew up yon bastard's boat at Lochend." Murricane had spent a lifetime not revealing anything on his face. He didn't think even an eyelid flickered.

"Aye. Amazing the things people see." He reached one gnarled hand across to Murricane's.

"Just make an effort, Murry. Ye ken I'm not sacrificing feckin' American tourists. And I don't think you really want Foyers turned intae feckin' Disneyworld, do ye? Even if you're in with all these Drum bastards. What if it was the Cover? Eh? Tell me that? You think they'd let a Site of bloody Scientific Interest stand in their way? These pricks?"

Davie stopped talking. It was almost light, now, and the sound of waterfowl clacking and small birds chittering and clicking filled the silence. Murricane was thinking about coffee. He rose to light the gas beneath the kettle. There was enough water in it.

"Where will you go? You can't stay here."

"What, you think I'm stupid?"

Belatedly: "How did you get here anyway?"

"Paddled over. Still flat calm oot there. Ye ken the wee kayak, sit-on-top like yours, keep it in a creek below Balnagarlin. Right noo, it's out of sight from the loch, in where you keep yon fishing kayak. I'm... I'm gonnie be heading off, best you don't know where. There are people around who'll keep me safe."

"The Prince in the Heather, eh?" Infra-red helicopter tracking, dogs, electronic surveillance, satellites... Murricane knew that if anyone could give the forces of law and order the slip, it was Davie, in this part of the Highlands. He'd paddle as far up the loch as Abriachan, probably, then slip through the trees up in the network of glens – Affric, Strathglass, Cannich – on the north side of the loch. Maybe it wasn't as forested, secret and pregnant with oddness as the south shore, but there were several strange communities up there, one or two throwbacks to the sixties and beyond. Places where no law held sway, and probably never had. But he'd be best doing it at night.

"You'll need to stay here until dark, Davie. If they are looking for you, they'll know about the kayak soon enough, despite your bloody witchy pagan Druid policeman's wife. Or because of. After that you're on your own."

Davie nodded. "Dark? Have you no' heard of the Druid's Great Cloak of Invisibility?" He winked. "But ye ken, I'm no' a druid any more. So I'll just have to trust in luck, or the Great Goddess. Or the fella who's gonnie be down at Temple Pier wi a van in about –" he glanced around the *Gloria*'s saloon for a clock, then at Murricane's empty wrist "– about half an hour."

"That another of your Post-Celtic gifts, Davie? Divining the time?"

"Aye. Or it could be he's already there, and you've got time to find me another whisky. Maybe something wi' a bit more heft. Any Laphroaig? Dinna want any o' that Loch Ness stuff. Supposed to be Ben Nevis, but I dinna believe it."

Divination. There was a sample of very rare Bruichladdich, Murricane remembered, hidden away in the bilges. One of the extra-phenolic expressions they'd been working with a few years previously.

"Or anything peaty. I'm dying for a taste of Islay."

Protect and enhance

Spirit, a touch of ammonia. Caramel, ashes and tree bark.

TEN HIGH 'BOURBON BLEND'

"**Y**ou've really been a trifle inefficient, Mr Jenks," said Coldstream, who was purposefully dressed in Columbus outdoor gear, khaki ripstop trousers and dark blue denim shirt. He flicked his wings of white hair back. Fifty-seven. He was 57 years old, and trim enough, he thought to pass for late 40s. But what did that mean? You could be an obese monstrosity in your late 40s? What was age? Look at Jenks. Indeterminate. Could be 30s, 40s, 50s... and lethal. Utterly lethal.

But complicated. That's what he'd been told back in California. Lethal, but complicated. He remembered the smile, the private joke. *He's a collector.* What did that mean? *A collector. That could be a good thing. Useful. I'm a collector, too.* Well, he would have to work with the tools in the box, that was all there was to it. Jenks was kind of... non-negotiable.

Now the project was beginning to come together, everything was set. Even their renegade female, their traitor, traitress, she had played into their hands. And that mistake by Jenks, or you could put it down to lack of information on the soccer-playing and tea-drinking habits of the Scottish nation, seemed as if it might work in their favour.

Coldstream was gearing up for a visit by the local police, had already fielded a phone call from them. They were on their way. Although the presence downstairs right now of a man, a so-called private detective called Alexander Flaws, was slightly discomfiting. Perhaps he was just some freelancer offering his services. Scavenging for business.

The official Church of the Sanctified Truth of the Christ Child in History (Missionary Outpost Number One) office was cheaply, Swedishly sleek and a floor above the Sanctuary, one below Coldstream's private office. They were sitting on copies of Marcel Breur's infamously uncomfortable Bauhaus chair, only chromed and IKEA-ised. Coldstream felt as if he was undergoing some sado-masochistic rite. And while that may have been enjoyable, it made concentration difficult. Jenks looked as if the chair had become part of his body. Was slowly being absorbed into it.

A WHISKY IN MONSTERVILLE

"Mr Jenks." He brandished a copy of the *Inverness Courier*, out that day. "Tell me what you make of this headline." Jenks remained motionless, a smile fixed on his face. The eyes, as ever, unmoving, blank. He had plentiful hair, Coldstream had noted, not a sign of male pattern baldness, yet he kept it close shaven. A burr. Military thing, probably. Absence of baldness was a sign of stupidity, in his opinion. He thought of Henry Kissinger. Obviously, there had to be exceptions to every rule.

No reaction from Jenks. Coldstream read aloud:

"Monster attack scare: The headless and partly burnt body of a woman was recovered from Loch Ness off Urquhart Castle this week by a group of anglers... blah blah, *Gerald Northcote from Wolverhampton said...* blah blah... *police spokesman stated they were working on the theory that the death was suspicious...* Suspicious? Well, please... police sources indicate that victim may be an American tourist. Which means they know who she is, and in point of fact they are already on their way here. *Police sources added that a man is being sought as witness in the case. He is Mr David Lees, 45, believed to reside near Foyers and various other places. The public are warned not to approach him."* Coldstream put the paper down. "Your smearing of Mr Druidic pain-in-the-ass Lees, along with some luck, seems to have worked, Mr Jenks. These hapless fishermen snagged your elusive corpse and presented it, in a manner of speaking, to the police, who have drawn all the conclusions we wished, traced it to the correct source." There was even a picture, apparently taken from a passing cruise boat, of the fishing launch and some kind of altercation aboard it. A tall blonde man in a t-shirt was standing slightly apart, watching. "One question, however. Why no head?"

Jenks's smile never wavered.

"Perhaps the propeller of a passing boat, sir."

"Of which boat? The *Queen Mary*?"

"I believe one of the passenger vessels on the loch is called *The Jacobite Queen*, sir. Is that the one you mean?"

"Mr Jenks."

Coldstream placed his long, patrician – he thought of them as patrician now, though he had once seen them as thin and sticklike – fingers together and glared at the man. He was like a brick, solid, unyielding. And frightening. He felt a numbness in the tips of his fingers. Parkinson's disease, probably, or heart failure. He lived in terror of not being able to complete his work before one of the many maladies he feared carried him away. So much to do!

"You were recommended to me by my... associate, who will, in fact, be joining us here quite soon. He is known to you, I believe, as you are to him. I was, albeit enigmatically and tangentially, informed of your propensity to, how can I put this, collect things. I would remind you that we are not in some lawless war zone, but in a civilised country, albeit a virtually godless one." He paused. "Did you deal with... that other little matter for me?"

Jenks stood. He was dressed in a tracksuit and sneakers, and wore a silver whistle around his neck. He looked, Coldstream thought, like a particularly loathsome example of a PE instructor, which in point of fact, he was, officially. He took the boys and girls, the sisters and brothers for runs, for aerobics, or some perversely aggressive military version. Hence the whistle. There had to be some believable reason for him being around.

"I'm being extremely well rewarded to do your bidding, Mr Coldstream," Jenks said. The smile still on his face. "To protect and enhance, I was told. Protect and enhance the project. The fault as regards the temporarily mislaying of the woman's body was yours, sir, in that you appear to have no knowledge or concern for the national sport here. Or its effect on pump storage hydro-electric power schemes. I'd be obliged if you would ensure that such intelligence lacunae do not happen again. As for me I will assure you that I do take the notion of enhancing the operation and protecting it very seriously. You need have no concerns over any personal enthusiasm intruding. And as for your, ah, *associate*," Coldstream noted the careful syntax, the cool articulacy he'd never heard before from the man, "he is as well known to me as I am to him. I look forward to renewing our old acquaintance. We share certain... enthusiasms. And yes, the red-haired prick is dead, if that's what you're asking."

And all the time, that disturbing, terrifying smile never leaving his face.

"Fine. You can go. Use the back corridor. There are people downstairs and it would probably be better if you weren't to meet them." He looked at Jenks's face, at the strange, amused blankness. He had the terrible sensation of being assessed, of being weighed. Like meat. Like a piece of meat.

Flaws

'Sinewy and sublime, like the Sound of Islay. Deep, dangerous and hypnotic. Pulling you ever closer to the edge. A most exhilarating experience.' – Distillery tasting note.

BRUICHLADDICH OCTOMORE

A WHISKY IN MONSTERVILLE

Murricane had left Davie apparently asleep, clutching what was left of the Bruichladdich, a distillate quirkily dubbed *Last Gasp of Freerange Capitalism* by the wild, posh entrepreneurs who had once owned the place. One of the final expressions of Islay's most unpredictable and occasionally unpleasant malts prior to multinational takeover. He'd watched with a pang of regret as Davie started tackling the whisky, as it had been a gift from Jan and he hadn't tried it himself. Never mind. The ungrateful wee sod.

"It's no' Lagavulin. But it'll do. I can taste the west coast." It hadn't been peaty enough for the ex-Druid.

The day was cloudy, dull and humid. Midge weather. *Cullicoides Impunctatus,* the female biting midge, curse of the Scottish Highlands, was mustering her forces. Later in the day things would get worse, German tourists, warned and thoroughly prepared, would appear in full bee-keeping outfits, and the colossally expensive midge-eating machines would be switched on in an effort to free terraces and gardens from the bloodsucking infestation. Roll on autumn, thought Murricane, season of radiant foliage and 'nae beasties', as they said in Drum. Goodbye to the other bloodsuckers, the clegs and horseflies. No deer ticks, carrier of Lyme's Disease and horrendously easy to host in the groin area, as Davie's tale suggested. Sometimes the Highlands appeared as threatening as the Amazonian rain forest.

He traversed the Cover, heading east towards the so-called Loch Ness Harbour. Privately owned, whimsically run, it was still the only easy public access to the loch near Drumnadrochit, and even rivals in the tour boat business used it with little more than the occasional onset of bellowed insults. The RNLI station was deserted at this time in the morning. Next to it a dishevelled Ford Transit van, once red, was parked, with someone sporting dirty grey dreadlocks asleep, slumped over the steering wheel. Murricane didn't disturb him. Or her. Davie's lift presumably, to the netherlands of Cannich, Strathfarrar or the empty spaces further up, further in: a last refuge for all kinds of runaways.

A WHISKY IN MONSTERVILLE

A short, hazardous walk east along the main A82, there was an unmarked track leading uphill through the trees, away from the loch. Another, smaller path branched off, ending at the padlocked double doors of a former forestry shed. Murricane made a complete circuit of the building. There was no other way in except the front doors, though flattened grass and bracken showed that in the last week or so someone had tried to find one. Drumnadrochit neds? Backpackers on the Great Glen Way, the walking route between Inverness and Fort Bill? Or someone else?

The tiny scratches on the padlock suggested someone with a degree of determination and maybe skill. It was hard to tell if they'd managed to open the lock. Inside, the old Land Rover pickup seemed untouched, but the crinkled birch leaf he'd left between driver's door and pillar had drifted down to the floor. If you looked carefully, and he did, there were tiny signs of a sustained and careful search.

Rebecca? Rebecca.

Just checking? On what? His availability? His preparedness for attack? How had she found out about this place? Someone in the Piper's Rest, probably. Several people knew about the shed. Jan's pal Fingal had rented it to him: "Even though ah don't own it, ah've got squatter's rights," he'd said, exchanging the keys for a Ferox lure and a bundle of notes.

He released the handbrake and pushed the old vehicle about 18 inches backwards. Where the front offside wheel had been he dug away the packed dirt of the floor, revealing a whisky-bottle sized wooden box. It was whisky-bottle sized because it had once contained a particularly fine example of Clynelish. Inside, wrapped in waxed cotton, were several pieces of metal. He ignored them. The ziplock bag with the mobile phone was what he wanted.

It was a cheap, primitive mobile. It sent and received texts, made and received calls. In fact, it was time to throw it away and buy a replacement. But he had one call to make on the Nokia first. He attached it to the charger in the Landie, started the V8 engine, drove out of the shed, and locked up. He thumbed out a text and pressed send, knowing it wouldn't go until he hit one of the 02 reception areas on the way to Inverness. And then he headed sedately down to the main road. Sedately, he could get about 17 miles per gallon out of the Solihull-built beast. Driven in an extreme fashion, he could achieve perhaps two or three. For the moment, he was in a sedate mood. But still he wondered about Rebecca.

*** *** ***

Zander Flaws was contemplating the life of a Highland private detective, annotating its tedium and its trauma: collecting witness statements from wasted junkies in Dingwall. Spying on the cavorting of bored housewives, abandoned in their impassive red sandstone Crown mansions. Ah, those Range Rover odysseys to Sainsbury's, and then to Nairn's infamous dogging beach, accompanied by the tennis coach or the yoga instructor. The bairns safely at nursery, husband in his office, browsing through Zander's emailed pictures on his iPad.

And then, by way of contrast, there were burnt bodies in Loch Ness. A burnt body. Murricane involved, somehow, by accident it seemed. His photo flying out across cyberspace, courtesy of all those tourists on the *Nessotora Regina*. There were people who hadn't appreciated that at all. People who kept an eye out for the Murricanes of this world. Christ, to think there were more of them.

Flaws was a large man, policeman-sized, as that was what he had once been. Balding, expanding, frizzled grey hair, 50-ish and with the specks called whisky roses on his nose and cheeks. A generous retirement settlement was one of the benefits of former cophood, but he'd wanted to keep active, interested. And so he photographed cavorting mothers, mothers someone other than their husbands apparently liked to fuck, took statements, interviewed the moronic witnesses lawyers couldn't be arsed talking to, occasionally provided listless security advice for rock festivals and supermarkets. He drank at what was left of the old Phoenix bar, microbrews and malts, and felt himself slide deeper and deeper into contented irrelevance.

There were occasional requests, mainly from England or further afield, for him to find people. The lost, the escapees, the mad, the occasionally bad and dangerous. The one from America had come in six weeks ago. It seemed, at first glance, a familiar story. A young girl at college, drugs, rock'n'roll, a religious cult. She was in Scotland, according to the agency in Santa Monica. In the Highlands, something to do with Jesus and the Loch Ness Monster. Yeah, yeah. No, seriously. Very seriously, the neatly-suited man Skyping him had said. These people believe that the Loch Ness Monster shows that evolution is a lie, and it's on public school teaching programs, would you believe THAT? Sanctified Baptists, a, longer name – yeah, the Church of the Sanctified Truth of the Christ Child in History. Or something. You'll find them, there can't be many over there in bonny Scawtland. Bishop Fletcher F Coldstream, parents are worried it's all another Jonestown massacre kinda thing…

What, near Inverness? Near Supersneck? But Flaws knew about the madness around the Highlands and in particular around that strange cleft in the country, the Great Glen. The Crowleys, the Pages, the communes of new age millionaires and ancient hippy lairds.

So he'd called in some old police contacts when news broke about the burnt body, the monster victim. Call it a hunch. Teeth intact. Dental records? It just so happens. Those LA detective agencies covered all the angles. They were serious shit. Computer data flew back and forth across the Atlantic. Matches were made in seconds. It was her.

Yet what could he do? He was a hired hand, not an agent of the law, not any more. His job was to make the connection, send the invoice, maybe greet the mourning maw and paw when they flew in to retrieve the remains. No head. Christ, he hoped they found the head.

His iPhone bleeped. A text. He glanced around his office, which was up a stone stairway in a decaying tenement on Station Square, right in the centre of the city, a stumble along Academy Street from the Phoenix. It was a single room, high-ceilinged, previously used by a small specialist tour company catering for lovers of tartan. Everything was tartan. Carpet, wallpaper, even the metal desks, one for him one for his non-existent assistant. Only the computers and single filing cabinet were non-plaid. Anyone wearing a kilt who came here tended to disappear from the waist down.

A WHISKY IN MONSTERVILLE

He looked at his email. Nothing new from LA. Just more spam about Viagra and Nigerian banking scams. He could have blocked them, but somehow they fascinated him, the vast criminal enterprises which reaped rewards from the barely computer-literate. And one of those pieces of so-called spam was not what it seemed. It flagged up a secure message on the other computer. The one that was always on, but rarely used.

He picked up the iPhone. Murricane had texted him. Was on his way. He might have guessed.

*** *** ***

Murricane parked the Land Rover at the Heathmount Hotel in Crown, Inverness's Fulham, cut past the soaring walls of Porterfield Prison onto Ardconnel Street, a battlement of big houses overlooking the main bulk of the city below.

He liked Inverness. It had a proper river, a canal, docks, access to the sea and from most angles, a truly spectacular setting: if you swooped down the A9 from the south, Sneck lay beached on the firth, the miniature Golden Gate of the Kessock Bridge spanning the gap between it and the Black Isle. Ben Wyvis, vast and plateau-topped, lolled in the distance. From the Great Glen direction, Inverness just sort of gathered around you, house by hotel by supermarket, but this weird descent from the volcanic plug that Crown was built on always tickled him. Several sets of precipitous steps dropped you in unexpected parts of the High Street. He was tempted to go for a walk along the river, through the Narnia-like park of bridges and birch called the Ness Islands. But instead he veered onto Ardconnel Terrace, near where Flaws lived, and emerged where High Street became Eastgate, the concrete bulk of the deathstar Eastgate shopping mall towering above him.

In Inglis Street he collected two double-shot lattes to go from Costa, then headed across the road to Station Square, past the attractively crenellated bulk of the old Station Hotel, now desperately trying to move upmarket as the Royal Highland. It still possessed one of the great, old fashioned Victorian hotel lobbies, all hidden corners, aspidistras and pot plants. But these days there were too many strutting waiters in suits for his tastes. Flaws said it had once been a wonder of sordid liaisons and tiny, bathroomless boxrooms.

He went up the worn stone stairs and rapped on the frosted glass of the office door. It was beyond a cliché, really. But Flaws liked it that way, and who was he to argue? He was a cliché too. They were made for each other.

"Sight for sore eyes," said Flaws, bulkier than the last time they'd met, maybe three months ago. Old suit, open-necked shirt. Still a copper, really. "And just in the nick of time. Percy's been looking for you."

Percy. Percival. Just a name, casually mentioned. One that brought back a world of war, dust and injury. Fuck. He didn't want to stay in this strange, multicoloured office. It flayed his eyes.

"Reasonable day. Fancy a walk? You look as though you could do with some exercise."

"Too many damned curries and M&S cook-chill dinners," said Flaws, creaking out of his swivel chair. "Sure you don't want to use the computer first? You know Percy had one of his boys take a look at it last time he was up. Sorted it out. Works fine."

Sorted it out. Rendered it secure. From here he could converse with the bastards and know no-one was overhearing. It had been a condition of his being allowed to go what was called in the jargon of his trade 'semi-tethered'. Loose, but always recognised as reclaimable. An elastic rope around his neck. Semi-tethered: it made him think of a goat, tethered to a tree, left as a bait for marauding beasts.

"Walk first. Fancy a wee jaunt down to the Islands."

"Weird stuff down at the Islands these days, I've heard. Getting a bit wild since the council withdrew the park keeper funding. But listen, you and water, eh? Can't keep you away from each other." Flaws jangled a set of keys, reaching for one of the lattes as he headed towards the door. He was whistling between his teeth, tunefully enough for Murricane to recognise the Village People's *In the Navy*.

A WHISKY IN MONSTERVILLE

Flaws stopped momentarily as he headed for the door, retreated to his desk and pulled something from a drawer. Slipping it into one gaping jacket pocket.

"Smoking again, Zander?"

"Not yet. Not quite yet."

He'd met Flaws during a vicious and, in the end, explosively political operation, while moonlighting, in a semi-official capacity, from the Special Boat Service. Flaws had been a not-so-innocent Inverness policeman drunk in the present and dodgy in the past. Murricane had been a firepower-wielding undercover security specialist. People died, people disappeared. An ageing agent known as Serpentine sidled among them like the devil, then vanished. No-one was ever quite the same again. There was a girl. A woman. For Murricane and Flaws, it had been dislike at first sight. Somehow, since then, they had remained bound together. Tethered. Now Flaws was his cut-out, contact, interface. Friend.

At this time of year, Inverness was awash with tourists. They were of every age and nationality, but very much of a type, and easily recognisable by their common clothing: fleeces, nylon easy-dry hiking trousers, rough terrain sneakers and with Gore Tex waterproofing always to hand. It was like a uniform, Murricane thought, a bit like the leather shorts, linen shirts and backpacks carried before World War Two by the Wandervogel, those Hitlerian seekers of open air supremacy.

Nationalities could be discerned easily enough. There were fleece-wearer subsets, the Italians smarter, the Germans exuding a Vorsprung Durch Technik edge of quality. The Spanish women had hennaed hair, the men smoked and the English all had a look of panicked penny pinching. They gazed in shop windows or at restaurant menus in desperation. As if they could hardly believe that this Scottish tourist trap, this Highland honeypot, might soon slip into some kind of independence, charge them customs duty on their haggis and tartan.

Flaws and Murricane strolled along High Street down to the river, then turned left onto Castle Road, the ludicrously red sandstone version of a Brigadoon Highland keep towering above them. Inverness Castle. Actually Inverness Sheriff Court, forever surrounded by prison vans and flocks of narrow-faced neddish smokers with overnight bags. The triumph of expectation over hope. They walked along Haugh Road and Island Bank Road until the black standard lamps and cultivated forest of the Islands drew them in, over a rickety suspension bridge and onto this strange urban retreat. In the distance, Murricane could hear bagpipes. Nowhere was ever perfect.

They dumped their empty coffee cups and picked their way to one of the strangest aspects of this odd archipelago of a park, and Murricane's favourite: the pet cemetery. Most of the tiny gravestones were crushed and broken now, but names could still be discerned if you looked hard enough: *Yum-Yum, our very heart and soul; Hector. A Trusted And Loyal Friend.*

"Give a dog a bad name, eh?" Murricane said. "Give a dog a bad name and hang him. Never understood that. Why would you hang a dog?"

"Seen it done," said Flaws. "Not literally hanging, like with a rope. Strangling, though. Angry, demented old crofter up in Sutherland, back in the days. I was caa'in' the sheep with my folks and the rest of the crofters, caa'in' the sheep off the hill, the common grazings. Everybody mucked in. We separated the sheep later, worked out whose was whose. Anyway, this one sheepdog wouldn't do what he was told, so this prick just picked him up and strangled him in the fence. Spun round on two strands of wire. Dog just seemed... I don't know. Resigned to it. I was just... oh, 11 or 12 at the time."

"Explains everything."

"Huh. Hardly. But it does explain something."

"What's that?"

"How I've not got a dog."

Murricane looked beyond the lichen-covered gravestones to the river, which was languid and slow here.

"You OK? Getting by, what with being out of the cops? Making a living?"

"Pension covers most stuff. Retainers from one or two folk like... well." He glanced at Murricane, raised an eyebrow. "But yeah, just about getting by. In fact I've got something on the go that you're kind of connected with. That body in the loch? The

Monster Munch, they're calling it. Missing woman. The parents had been looking for her. Done a runner from the US of A with some mad Jim Jones religious wannabe."

Murricane thought about Davie the Druid, probably holed up in one of the scattered communes in the Cannich badlands.

"What, and now she turns up dead? Is this Jonesville person in the frame for it?"

"Jonestown, not Jonesville. My old mates at the copshop aren't saying. In fact, to be honest, I'm a wee bit ahead of them there. LA's finest detective agency seems to be a wee bit sharper than the Raigmore polis. And well, that's another thing…"

"What?"

"Aw, come on. Percy's call. It's linked to that as well. You know you were in those photographs? The ones of the body being recovered? The Nessotora lot, those tourists? You must be losing your touch, Lord Lucan. You've stirred up a few memories."

Murricane sighed. "Fuck."

"Indeed. That's if your presence in the vicinity of Nessie wasn't kind of a factor from the start. Maybe there's something you're not telling me, eh? Percy didn't say anything much to me, but I gather there's a bit of tension down in That London. Maybe it's just that you're meant to be the invisible man. He said there was a secure email message. Open and it will destroy itself, you know, the usual digital *Mission Impossible stuff.*"

"Fuck."

"Loquacious, too. Articulate. I do like that in a fella. Shall we go back?"

"One thing before we do." Murricane was never very sure about the so-called 'security' of Flaws's office. The London team who had rendered one of the computers suitable for 'tethered' comms. It could mean that everything said and done there was securely recorded and stored away on some southern hard disk. "This Jonestown character."

"Fletcher Coldstream. Sanctified Truth Baptist… Church of the Christ Child in Mystery, or something. They're also calling themselves Nessatorean Creationists."

"What?"

A WHISKY IN MONSTERVILLE

"Nessatorean Creationists. Like the name of the cruise boat. Except Ness-A-torean, not Ness-O. And obviously, the cruise operators are not creationists. At least I don't think so. Anyway, Coldstream and his acolytes believe that the existence of the Loch Ness Monster has been scientifically proven. They believe it to have been scientifically proven that said monster is a Plesiosaur, you know, like that great big model they've got in the car park in Drum. And therefore, the fossil record showing that dinosaurs disappeared before man arrived is wrong and so is evolution. Nessie is now part of Creationist theology."

"You're having me on."

"Nope. Mr and Mrs Anson's LA detective told me all about it. Looked it up on the net, and sure enough, there's an official curriculum for schools – public schools – in the States teaching exactly that. Texas and Louisiana, apparently."

"Jesus Christ."

"Yes, well, he figures very much in the whole thing too. Later on. I mean, later than the Plesiosaurs. But there's no suggestion that Our Lord was actually present at Loch Ness or that he and the Beastie have ever met."

"There's something I should tell you," said Murricane. "I kind of feel myself under a... a moral obligation to this poor soul, what was her name? Anson?"

"Avril Anson. Like the aeroplane. Not that Americans would know about the Avro Anson, Airfix kits and all that."

"Well anyway. Like I said. A moral obligation. Or to be honest, I've been kind of put under a moral obligation by... a friend."

Davie the Druid, a friend? A conniving, threatening wee shit, more like. And an ignorable one. The truth of the matter was that Murricane was interested. A body had floated into his vicinity. In his adopted home, on the water. And he was bored out of his brains. So what if there were photographs of him on the interweb? So what if Percy was angry at him, or had some kind of nefarious interest in this whole weird religious set-up? He needed an interest in life. He could feel an odd sparkle of adrenalin in his veins. It had been a long time.

There was a polite cough, an "eh-hem" behind them. They were leaning over the twisted railing that separated a small clearing from the remains of the pet cemetery. The voice that spoke was polite, badly-polished Sneckian. Flaws and Murricane looked round. An electronic flash momentarily blinded them.

"Say cheese, gentlemen! Oh yes, that'll do nicely. And another, just stay together, yes, as you were." The camera fired again.

Three figures were blocking the path out of the clearing. They were fairly large, thought Flaws. Overcoats, those hip-length gabardine ones, unbuttoned. Very neatly dressed. They could have been policemen – short hair, one with a shaved head. Two bigger than the one in the middle. Battered, bouncer material. They were the flankers. The muscle. But what was this? He'd heard the tales of murky goings on at the Islands, but paid little attention. Yes, the park had a bit of a reputation for dope smoking and illicit trysts, but it was a goddamned park, wasn't it? It was the middle of the day! The man in the middle had an intensity, a strange, febrile sense of threat. He smiled at them, revealing teeth that were almost green. And clearly his own.

"Gentlemen. Let me introduce myself. I am Pastor Malachi McGlone and these are my bothers in the true Christ, John and Peter."

"And on this rock shall I build my church," muttered Flaws. "Wait a minute. don't I know you from somewhere? McGlone, did you say?"

"Sir, I do not think so. We belong to a small congregation of concerned brothers and sisters here in Inverness, which as you may well, which as you probably *do* realise is a fallen city. A city gone astray. As is the whole country, indeed, a country judged under Satan. Consigned to the devil and his ways." McGlone took a step forward. "We are the Presbyterian Church of Pure Righteousness, and it has been revealed to us that our duty is lead away from the path of evil those who would indulge in sexual sin. Especially those males who take the path of beastliness, the way of unnatural relations. In broad daylight. In the open air, in a place frequented by innocent children."

"And pets," said Flaws. "Though these ones are dead."

"Jesus." Murricane had been gazing at the men in some confusion. "You think we're..." he turned to Flaws. "Do we look... I mean, how long have the Islands been a dogging destination, Zander? I knew the White Stone Hotel along the river was Inverness's only pickup joint for lonely swingers, but..."

"Oh, I don't know," said Flaws. "How long? How about, well... always. I didn't realise you were so prudish."

"Please do not take the Lord's name in vain," said McGlone. "Let me explain. We make it our business to dissuade sinful men, men who have been betrayed by the weakness of the flesh, from returning to this location. And we take a picture which we will post on our website – incidentally, it is optimised for mobile phones and other forms of portable hardware – which is called Highlandperverts dot com. I'm sure you do not wish to see that happen. And neither would your wives or employers. So we ask to you to leave this place and pay us an administration charge of, I would estimate, all the cash you have on you. Peter! John! Ah! Fuuuuuuuuck…"

But by the time he was shouting that last elongated swear word. Flaws had reached in his pocket, pulled out the Taser C2 he'd removed from his desk just before they left the office, and fired it at McGlone. The nitrogen canister sent the two small darts flying across the 15-foot gap between them remarkably slowly, Flaws thought. But the effect was reassuring. Fifty thousand volts seemed to reach into the little creep's soul, revealing its true nature. A real jerk. McGlone fell to the ground clutching his chest, twitching. Traces of foam bulged from his mouth.

By then Murricane had broken Peter's kneecap with a short downward kick. There was an audible snap and the denying but not necessarily deniable disciple went down like a sack of potatoes, moaning. John had grabbed Murricane from behind while this was happening, but slowly and lumberingly. Stiff bouncer's muscles. Murricane, slightly shorter than Jesus's beloved follower, snapped his head back hard into John's face, releasing a spray of blood from the man's nose. John's grip released, Murricane stamped on his instep and then turned to deliver a crude but highly effective knee in the testicles.

"That's enough," said Flaws.

"Bigots. Homophobes. Who the fuck do they think they are? I mean, we were just walking, talking, having a coffee. This is Inverness, for Christ's sake."

"And we're just good friends," said Flaws. "Or not even. I know. But listen, you heard the man. This is a fallen city. We're in a satanic nation. It must be cleansed. And if a struggling wee Presbyterian kirk can make some money doing it, well. Who can really blame them?" He drew one Loakes brogue back and kicked McGlone in the mouth. There was a grinding crunch. "Did you see his teeth? I'm doing him a favour. There's a real need here for some serious dental improvement." He kicked the man again. "All right Pastor? All right brothers?" John and Peter were stirring, but not in a threatening way. They were doing a reasonable imitation of unfairly fouled footballers. Only they were genuinely in pain. Flaws turned to Murricane.

"Shall we go? You have to check that message back at the office." He picked up the Canon McGlone had been using, removed the memory card, and threw the body of the camera into the river. The SD card he crushed between two fingers and flicked into the undergrowth.

They left the three figures on the ground, more or less recovering.

"What will you do, Zander? Going to call the real cops?"

"I don't think so. We probably won't have stopped them. These pricks'll see this as a testing by the forces of darkness, something they have to overcome. Next time they'll probably make sure they bring their own Tasers."

"Where did you get that anyway? Aren't they illegal?" Flaws just looked at him and shook his head. "And since when did mad religious vigilantes patrol the Ness Islands? What's happening to this place?" Flaws sighed.

"It's Inverness," he said. "Just... Inverness. Wish I could remember where I've seen that McGlone fellow before. Name's familiar too, kind of."

*** *** ***

Back at his office, Flaws unlocked the filing cabinet, reached inside the top drawer and removed a bottle of Glenfarclas 105.

"Wee treat for you. This and Aberlour A'Bunadh have to be the best value in whisky. Cask strength, oaked, sherried, meaty as hell. Just the job for a wee post-exertion dram." Murricane had noticed before that Flaws had a tendency to jabber, but given the situation he was prepared to put up with it. Glenfarclas 105, after all, was a very fine whisky. First sip neat, then a teardrop of water. And you were in Speyside, proper Old School Speyside, none of that American oak or stupid rum barrel finishes. Traditional Scotch whisky the way it ought to be. This was plummy, dark, full of honey and a sense of history. It was like drinking liquefied battlefield soil."

Murricane fired up the digitally disinfected and secured of Flaws's two computers, performed the combined keystrokes that took him to the security page, and logged in. Funny how you didn't forget some things. When you were told, when you were ordered to learn them. Two more security screens and he was at his inbox. There was just the one message. No title, no text. Just an attachment, a picture. He clicked it open.

Rebecca.

Practical theology

Deep peaty-gold. Complex, oaky, apples and pears, and a tempting dark toffee sweetness. Dry and assertive, develops quickly to reveal a rich spiciness, combined with a hint of oak and sherried fruit. Amazingly smooth for the strength; wonderfully warming and with a lingering smokiness, yet very rounded.

GLENFARCLAS 105

A WHISKY IN MONSTERVILLE

If Coldstream was surprised when two figures, one older and somewhat less dishevelled than the other, appeared in his office, he didn't show it. He'd been expecting just the one.

"Mr Flaws?" He looked inquiringly from one to the other. A greying, middle-aged man in a bad suit, too much red in his face, a whisky bloom. Running to seed. A worn leather shoulder bag. Ex-police. You could always tell. Coldstream prided himself on his ability to read people. The other one was vaguely familiar, sunburnt, fit, in jeans, t-shirt and a denim jacket. Younger, but not that young. Long hair but the appearance of somebody who had once been under discipline. It was in the movements, the squaring of the shoulders. A soldier. Damaged goods, probably. The Lord had dealt heavily with this one. With both of them.

"Mr Flaws?" He raised one eyebrow at the older of the two. "I wasn't expecting anyone else."

"This is Murricane," said Flaws. "He's an associate of mine. I believe my credentials have been emailed to you by my clients?"

"Indeed. Yes. I see." Both Murricane and Flaws had sat down without waiting to be asked.

"Man on the ground, if you like. He's, ah, local. In a manner of speaking."

"Wait a moment, please."

Coldstream reached for that week's *Inverness Courier* and looked at the picture on the front page. It was the same man, without a doubt. "Ah, I see." He looked directly at Murricane. "Do you make a habit of recovering bodies, then, Mr... Murricane? Some kind of salvage consultant? Mortuarial specialist?"

"I fish," said Murricane. "Sometimes I catch things." His voice sounded untraceably English, classless. Coldstream felt a vague shimmer of unease. He turned to Flaws.

"So, I understand you have been acting for the parents of poor Sister Avril. What a tragedy. We had been missing her for several days, you know. She was, how can I put this, a little fragile, and this, despite the tranquil, calming, and indeed gorgeous surroundings you find yourselves in, this is not an easy environment. We are fighting a battle, a great battle against the Evil One and the forces of ungodliness. It takes its toll." He sighed. "Even on me."

"That Satan seems to get about quite a bit," said Murricane. "All kinds of different churches seem quite happy to enlist him as an ally. Have you heard of the... what was it? The Presbyterian Church of Self-Righteousness Psychopaths? Have you heard of them?"

"And you had reported the fact that she was missing to the police," said Flaws, as if Murricane hadn't spoken, crossing his ankles and noticing that there was a distinct trace of blood on the left one.

"Of course. That was why they were able so quickly to contact me when the body... the remains... was found. Were found. Naturally we are all devastated." He nodded, his ample forehead crinkled with regret. "The police are on their way from Inverness even as we converse. I think an Inspector Peyronie is in charge of the case – do you know him?" Flaws nodded. "And he has indicated what we, tragically suspected. The forces of darkness, the forces of evil as physically represented by a small group of devil worshippers – pagans, they call themselves – are the most likely culprits. They aim to intimidate and destroy and inculcate fear. But they cannot intimidate the Lord! A man called David Lees, I understand, is being sought. And coincidentally, one of my... a member of the administration staff here seems to be able to identify him. Indeed, saw him dragging a heavy object towards the loch."

"Staff?" Flaws looked slightly perplexed. "Is that different from the, ah, sisterhood and brotherhood?"

"A fellow named Jenks," said Coldstream. "A kind of handyman."

"Jenks." Murricane spoke softly, not looking at Coldstrream, gazing instead out of the window, across the lawn to the trees and a glint of water beyond and below. "A handyman." Then: "You have a major... would you call it a construction project? At the planning stage? I understand that your proposal for Foyers is fairly far advanced. Monsterland, is it? Nessieworld?"

Coldstream tipped his head to one side and gazed quizzically at Murricane.

"Now, Mr Murricane, really. What we of the Church of the Sanctified Truth of the Christ Child in History, Mission Outpost Number One, commonly termed Nessatorean Creationists... what we are engaged in is not some tawdry cartoon of this Loch's most famous resident. We are, as I have said, engaged in a battle between good and evil. A war. And the Centre for Sanctified Creation Science Studies, as we call it, is at the very front line."

Flaws nodded.

"Aye. I hear you've been trying to buy old Crowley's house, too, the wickedest man in the world. Boleskine..."

"So far with no success. It is a piece of land that would be very useful to us and we would have the opportunity to redeem it from the evil uses to which it has been put over the centuries."

"I was there for a party, back in the day." said Flaws. "The fellow who used to be Jimmy Page's caretaker would have folk over. Sometimes it was handy to have an off-duty copper or two there." He winked at Coldstream. "You'd never believe it from my casual appearance, but I used to be a policeman. Would you credit it? You could still see Crowley's famous sandpit, where he used to summon up demons. It was weird. Page wasn't around, of course. He was too busy touring America with a giant snake and a million groupies. Or was that Alice Cooper? Anyway, it was a strange atmosphere, right enough. Some said the furniture used to move on its own. I just put that down to the amount of dope and magic mushrooms everyone had taken. Except me, of course. Even off duty."

"Well, I shall bow to your superior knowledge, Mr Flaws. I myself have only gazed at the place's exterior, and not without some sorrow. But no fear. No fear – the perfect love of God casts out all fear."

"Sorry," said Murricane. "But isn't there a public meeting in, what, a couple of days? At the Dores Hall? So that our thoroughly incorruptible and upstanding planning officials can gauge public feeling, listen to objectors, that sort of thing?"

"Yes, that is true. I will of course be there as the applicant for permission. But remember we are using a site adjoining the power station, part of which is a former aluminium smelter and, I'm sure you will agree, unsightly in the extreme. We will be harnessing the clean energy produced thanks to the work done on hydro-electric generation, we will be careful and considerate to our neighbours and our environment. They will see us, I hope, as representatives of heaven."

"Sorry," said Flaws, "but don't they see you as a bunch of weirdo monster believers with a religious agenda?"

"Is that how you see me, Mr Flaws? I can assure you our teaching materials are used widely in the United States education system – its *public* education system. And be that as it may, the Centre for Sanctified Creation Science Studies will employ a large number of people locally, irrespective of their religious affiliation. It will, of course, feature a major, interactive display about Loch Ness and its... creature, or creatures. It will become the pre-eminent visitor attraction in the Highlands, we believe, with a worldwide reach, using the latest digital technology, and always the shining light of spiritual truth emanating from it." Coldstream leaned forward. "This was once a Christian country. Scotland was the cradle of western Christianity, in fact. Columba, that great saint was one of the first to encounter the beast you call the Loch Ness Monster. Indeed, through the power of prayer, he prevented it harming one of his disciples."

"Or that could be, just possibly, no more than a useful legend," said Flaws.

"Useful to Columba's reputation? To spreading the power of the Gospel? Yes, perhaps. At any rate my point is this. Scotland was once a powerhouse of prayer, a battery of spiritual energy. And we aim to be part of a real reconversion. Our centre will be enjoyable, interesting, entertaining. We hope to have rides, rollercoasters, be at the cutting edge of what interactive digitisation can do. But it will also be a witness, and a very strong one." He opened one of the desk drawers. "Here. Let me show you."

The portfolio he took out of the drawer was leather, one of several dozen made up for distribution to press, councillors and other local movers and shakers. Coldstream opened it, displaying a double-spread artist's impression.

"Behold! *Ecce!* The Centre for Creation Science!" The pictures showed a rounded, organic building, its contours reflecting some out-of-scale mountains in the background. The loch, in blue, lapped, figuratively, right up to its entrance. It was not unlike Gehry's Museum of Modern Art in Galicia. But wooden.

"This is merely what we are calling the hub. The theme park will extend far beyond, of course. Rides such as Darwin's Doom and Hell Descender. But even there we will use all local materials and construction personnel. There will be an enormous employment dividend to the area. As you may be able to tell, the hub has been designed by that pre-eminent Christian architect, Folsom Nathaniel Bush."

"Relation to the ah, well-known American Bushes?" Murricane arched his eyebrows.

"A third or fourth cousin, I believe, of George Junior. A true believer and one who understands the use of natural materials to glorify God. We will of course have a chapel, where those who wish can worship in wonder at the glories of God's creation. God's virtually instantaneous creation."

Flaws leaned closer. The pictures were drawn from the perspective of someone afloat in the loch, and in the foreground was a strange object. Some kind of oddly shaped powercraft, with a truncated superstructure. "What's that?"

"What... oh, the vessel in the foreground! That, my friends, is a crucial part of our project. Courtesy of one of our major sponsors. Can't you guess what it is?"

"It's a submarine," said Murricane after a pause. "A passenger-carrying submarine. One of the new multi-use types. Fast on top of the water, capable of serious depths."

"Correct," said Coldstream. In fact, it's a tourist submarine, until recently used in the Sea of Marmaris to take a fortunate few on voyages to view some ancient ruins now covered by what we believe to be the flood of Noah. We have renamed her *The Baptist*."

"Wasn't the original Baptist a John? A male John, if you catch my drift," said Murricane. "Shouldn't boats be female?"

Coldstream smiled. "In Christ there is neither east nor west, male nor female."

Flaws stood up. "Mr Coldstream. I really came at the behest of the family of Ms Anson to intimate that your kind offer to take care of funeral arrangements will not be necessary. They have decided to bring the body, the, ah, remains, back to California for burial themselves. I believe they have already been in touch with local funeral directors."

"I see. That's understandable of course. I only thought they would appreciate my offer to oversee a full memorial service for poor Sister Avril. A communion service. To have her interred on the lochside, in our own consecrated ground, fully ready for the arrival from heaven of Our Lord and Saviour and her regeneration as one of the eternal. A celebration of her spirit. Our communions are unique. We do not use wine, we..."

"Let me ask you something, Mr Coldstream." Murricane had not moved from his seat. "At the supposed second coming of Christ, when as I understand it the dead in Christ are supposed to rise first... will that be like, *Dawn of the Dead, Zombie Apocalypse,* or what? They will rise from their graves like... what, rotted flesh? Skeletons? Like extras in some Michael Jackson video? Will poor Avril still be slightly scorched, and be missing her head?" Coldstream stiffened in his chair.

"I really think you're reading more into a terrible crime than is warranted, Mr Murricane. Yes, some disgusting form of ritual sacrifice was carried out on the poor girl, but I understood that her head had been removed by the action of a passing boat, some kind of sad and grisly accident. Doubtless it will be retrieved in due course." But Murricane was shaking his own head. He felt a curious sense of relief to find it still attached.

"I was there, Mr Coldstream. Her body was burnt, but not greatly, and it hadn't been in the water long. The burning took place after the decapitation. I assure you, I know what I'm talking about."

"Forgive me, but really? Are you experienced in decapitations and burnings, post or pre?"

"I believe he is, actually, Mr Coldstream," Flaws said quietly. "I believe he is."

Murricane was remembering the pile of bodies in Kandahar, the severed right hands, the heads. The children.

"To an extent, yes, I am," he said. "Sadly."

A WHISKY IN MONSTERVILLE

There was a silence. Something seemed to be working behind the ready glint in Coldstream's eyes. Calculating. Eventually he stood up.

"Yes," he said. "You were just going, I think."

"Just one more thing," said Flaws. "I understand that my erstwhile Constabulary colleagues will wish to examine Ms Anson's belongings. I would not wish to trespass on their or your good offices. But for the reassurance of her parents and to indicate what they can expect to receive, I wonder if we could simply have a sight of the material, the objects she has left behind here? I know it may seem irregular and Inspector Peyronie may have already asked you about them. But is there any way you can help me with that. Us?"

Coldstream tipped his head to one side and then upwards, as if consulting with an invisible, taller friend. Which, thought Murricane, he probably was.

"Well, that is somewhat irregular. But then, none of this is straightforward and within our normal purview, is it? I presume there may be forensic tests but I can see no problem if you do not touch anything." He picked up the modern multi-extension digital telephone and pressed a button.

"Sister Melliflua? I wonder if I may drop in on you for a moment? Can you ensure that the late Sister Avril's belongings are to hand? Are they? Excellent." He put down the receiver. "Let me take you to the house mother of our female contingent, Sister Melliflua. You may view Sister Avril's belongings and then, once the police have examined them, they or I can ensure that the various items are passed onto you and therefore to her family. We wish only to provide what love and reassurance we can, and indicate the availability of God's eternal mercy. I am sad that she will not be buried here. This is where she would have wanted to rest, until That Day."

"You said she was fragile?" All three of them were standing now. Flaws had half turned towards the door, while Murricane remained motionless, looking at Coldstream. Flaws stooping and fattening, Coldstream thin and willowy. Murricane poised, Flaws thought, like an animal about to strike.

A WHISKY IN MONSTERVILLE

"Fragile? Did I say that? But yes. She burned with belief. Do you know what I mean by... oh, that's an unfortunate description, given what... she was intense. She wandered alone, liked to spend time praying alone on the hillsides, on the mountaintops. Mountaintop experiences, like Moses with God. Those, after all, are things we all should seek. But they can be... draining."

"Did she have any particular... role within the group? Was she a cook, a nurse, did she..." Flaws was wondering if Murricane was all right. He knew that he used drink as a kind of pain killer, and maybe one or two other more pharmaceutical concoctions. He'd been through a lot. Sometimes he seemed... distracted. Or too intense. Like now.

"No. No, not really. Some of the women feel they do have a role in service to the male leadership, of course. That's understandable."

"What?" Murricane and Flaws spoke almost simultaneously. Coldstream smiled.

"Come, come gentlemen. These are liberal times and we are pursuers of the Sanctified Truth, not some frustrated set of cold, legalistic rules. We accept the body. And its demands and needs must be met. Some of the women in our group see that as their extremely valuable, valued function. And it is with grace that we men must accept that."

"You won't be accepting this body," said Flaws. He opened his leather shoulder bag, took out an iPad, unfolded the cover and began flicking through pages in a way that told Murricane he had hardly ever used the thing before. "You know, it's funny you should say that. About valued functions. Because Ms Anson's parents, Kevin and Samantha Anson, informed my colleagues in the United States that to their knowledge, Avril was recruited initially to your service as a result of her specialised skills. Skills that you indicated were needed as part of the process of preparing and planning the rather wonderful centre you've been telling us about. Valued skills, presumably."

"Monsterville," added Murricane, helpfully. "You could call it Monsterville. Or Monsterland, perhaps. Or maybe Nessieworld. Actually, there's already a Nessieworld, though not on the same scale you're proposing."

"She was a geologist," said Flaws. "I understand she was a geologist. Wasn't she? That was her specialised service. Not blow jobs for the boys."

There was the briefest of pauses, then a brilliant smile of agreement from Coldstream. "Indeed," he said. "Indeed, geology was supposed to be one of her skills. One of her many alleged skills." But his voice lacked its resonance, its normal timbre. There was an edge there, thought Murricane. Of stress, bringing back a tinge of hardcore midwestern Americanese, of anxiety. The ornate southern drawl, the cultivated charm, was waning.

"Why don't you show us her things?" said Flaws.

Creag Dhearg had originally been a shooting lodge, built to Edwardian tastes for architecture of the High Gothic Dracula school, but extended over the years to accommodate new roles. As, among other things, a boarding school, a drug rehabilitation unit, a backpackers' hostel and an 'outdoor adventure' centre. That had been its function immediately before Coldstream had taken it over, along with its extensive grounds, its sale hurried and bargain basement following a carbon monoxide gassing which had killed two youth leaders and a Pyrenean Mountain Dog called Trump. The dog had its own grave in the kitchen garden.

The two dozen members of the mission were accommodated in four-bunk rooms that resembled, Murricane thought, every barracks he'd ever inhabited, though marginally less tidy. No pictures on walls, as far as he could see. No pornography. It sounded as if there was plenty of that in Coldstream's head, however.

They were introduced to a small, thin, female figure with a pinched, middle-aged smoker's face. She had a single bedroom to herself, with a desk and computer, and she smiled with all the warmth of an emaciated alligator, revealing yellow teeth.

"Greetings, Sister Melliflua," said Coldstream.

"Greetings Brother Coldstream." She coughed, a racking, glutinous cough that combined the summer humidity of the Highlands with countless Marlboro or Lucky Strike. Born-again smokers, thought Murricane. Some things even God couldn't handle.

"These gentlemen are representatives of our late Sister Avril's parents. They have decided to have the body, that poor, sorry remnant, flown back to them for interment, and so she will not after all be buried here in great expectation of Our Lord's second coming."

Melliflua lowered her head. She gave a tiny, almost apologetic cough. Murricane wondered if she'd seen a doctor recently. "They require poor Avril's belongings. If you would be so kind." Coldstream was looking professionally sorrowful.

The woman already had a Banana Republic rucksack, a day bag really, on her desk. She pushed it towards Coldstream, who backed away.

"Ah, we should not really be touching... forensically speaking..." he said. "Ah well. I expect the outside of the bag has been much used by many hands, as they say."

"It's my bag, actually," said Melliflua, in a Bostonian voice cracked and battered by years of carbon inhalation. "She didn't seem to have one. Or maybe she took it, had it with her when she... there's just what was in there, in her locker. I thought I'd... for the sake of the parents, you know. A tidy package."

Flaws put on the disposable rubber gloves he kept in his bag. He unzipped the rucksack and looked inside. One by one he placed the contents on Melliflua's desk: a copy of the Bible, in the King James Version, leather-bound, heavily used. Katherine Stewart's *The Story of Loch Ness* in paperback. He flicked through it, noting that an early section had been heavily highlighted in yellow luminous pen.

"This is all?"

"Yeah, that's it," said Melliflua. "She travelled light, it seems."

"As must we all, in this world, if we are not to be weighed down by the unnecessary appurtenances of the suffering world, the decayed accruing of riches and so-called goods," added Coldstream.

"Toiletries? Notebooks? A diary – a journal you'd call it? What about her geological notes, assuming she was actually doing some work for you?" Flaws's voice betrayed a certain tetchiness.

Melliflua turned to Coldstream, who was smiling, his Georgian drawl now back confidently in place.

"Why, we follow a regime of natural cleanliness here, Mr Flaws. We have natural heather soap supplied in every bathroom, and so we become, in an olfactory sense, part of our environment. One with the location God has chosen us to inhabit. Such abhorrences as makeup and artificial perfume, we have no need of." Murricane wondered how Sister Melliflua's evident tobacco habit fitted in with this. "And as for poor Avril's geological notes... well." Regret creased his noble, patrician face. "It turned out that Avril was not as capable in that regard as she had led us to believe. Understandably anxious to be part of this mission, clearly she exaggerated her capabilities in that field. We ended up with no way of usefully deploying her, geologically speaking. Fortunately, we had specialist consultants flown in to carry out the work required."

"I see," said Flaws. "Well, thank you. Thank you both." He smiled at Melliflua. "Sister, may I ask? Were you on close terms with Avril? Do you have anything, any words or memories I can pass on to her parents, any comfort for them?"

Melliflua's face twisted into what was an initially alarming rictus that may have been meant as a sympathetic smile.

"She was... she was..."

All three men were looking at her now.

"She was clean. Clean living. She was pure."

"Thank you Sister. I know that will be of great reassurance and sustenance to her bereaved parents."

Coldstream ushered Murricane and Flaws towards the door. "Melliflua," he whispered. "Despite her, ah, flaws, Mr Flaws, she is a fine woman. Tempted by the fruits of the devilish tobacco plant. But we all have our temptations. She is overwhelmed, I think, with the loss. Overwhelmed. As are we all. As are we all."

A grey late-model BMW was pulling into the car park as Flaws was climbing into Murricane's old Land Rover. Too many aerials to be civilian. He stepped back down onto the gravel and watched Inspector Dick Peyronie uncoil himself from the unmarked BMW's passenger seat.

"Coming up in the world, Eric," he said. "Gone are the Vauxhall days, eh?"

"Think we clattered the sump coming out of Dores," said Peyronie. "And it's Richard."

"No, sir, not the sump. Probably the front lower spoiler," said his driver, Macalamine. Flaws remembered this florid, beefy man as having incredibly bad breath but also a preternatural understanding of, a connection, almost fusion with machinery. He was like McCruiskeen in *The Third Policeman* – only part car, not part bicycle.

"I heard from one of your old chums, one of those flatfoot greybeards they don't let out any more, that you were taking an interest in this business," said Peyronie. He eyed Murricane. "And your friend. He can't seem to keep away either. I hope he's not going to be interfering at all." He stared at Flaws. "Or yourself for that matter. Interfering."

Flaws nodded.

"Got your eye on Davie the Druid, then, or so I hear."

"Mr Lees? Maybe." Peyronie had stiffened like a salmon hit by a priest.

"He's not a Druid. He's a pre-Celtic pagan these days." Murricane slammed the Land Rover door. It made a hollow clanging sound, as if it was made of cheap aluminium. Which it was.

"Do you know where he is? Either of you? We have a witness, you know. Someone clocked him dragging an object towards the loch four nights ago. And the burning took place at his so-called pre-Celtic glade. The altar they have there. Cair Paravel, the locals call it. Blasphemy in my opinion."

Murricane and Flaws looked at each other, confused.

"Cair Paravel? CS Lewis? *The Lion, the Witch and the Wardrobe?*" Peyronie sighed. "It's a Christian allegory. Aslan, all that. Oh, never mind." He glared at Murricane. "You know the devilish wee shite, don't you? You would. Drinking companions? Light entertainment for tourists like you, Mr Murricane."

"Who, Aslan?" Murricane smiled. "Is he or she the lion, the witch or the wardrobe?"

"Davie must be a tremendously irritating practitioner of the devil's rituals to you and your Free Kirk sensibilities, Eric… Richard." Flaws smiled. "Come on, your pure appreciation of the divine Calvin never stopped you rolling up your trouser leg and hopping about the Mason's Lodge, did it? And as for that religious pervert in there," he jerked a thumb at the door to Creag

Dhearg. "You may find something in common with him, probably in terms of language. But I fear your sensitive morals would be even more outraged by how he uses his female followers. Unless Free Kirk blow jobs are part of the new enlightened theology of grace these days. Small 'g'. I don't mean someone actually called Grace. Although who knows? How is your lovely wife these days?"

"Come along Inspector Peyronie," said Sergeant Macalamine, the stumps of his teeth bared at Flaws. "Inspector Flaws was always one for a flyte. A bit of a wind-up merchant, he is. A stirrer."

"Flytie Flaws, they called me. But I'm not an inspector now," said Flaws cheerfully. "Just a detective. You should try it, Richard."

"What, the private sector?" Peyronie shook his head in disgust. "No, Eric. Being a detective."

Rocks off

'Enticing, open and refined, it is a lively and spicy dram on first meeting.

Followed by a fruity voluptuousness and creamy butterscotch flavours.'

GLENROTHES VINTAGE 1991

A WHISKY IN MONSTERVILLE

Murricane dropped Flaws off at Station Square, then played dodgems with the tourist traffic through the Inverness one-way system until, with some relief, he was left in a slow parade of caravans and campers heading west. First the glint of the canal, and then the wider expanse of the loch appeared on his left. By the time he had locked away the Landie and trudged back into Drum it was heading for 3.00pm and he was conscious of a great and unarguable hunger.

The Pie Shop, one of the village's greatest assets, nestled between the two rival Loch Ness Monster Centres like some kind of embassy for the state of normality. He bought a salmon slice and something the owner, Marie, called an Abriachan pastie ("Cornish, but with vegetarian haggis"). He detoured via the village tourist office, which adjoined the public toilets in the middle of one of the biggest car parks in the central Highlands, where he found and bought the book he was looking for. He picnicked in the fading sunshine, washing the pies down with a bottle of local Beastie beer, dangling his feet in the River Stinchar. A most inappropriate name, unless someone's septic tank had overflowed. Not today. The pies were delicious, flaky and light, the salmon delicately flavoured with coriander and lime, the haggis a gloriously sweet and pungent comment on the usual sheep-gut rankness. He dozed for a few minutes until the midges woke him up.

The Stinchar emptied itself into the loch through the Cover, so he followed the river down until he could trace a path back to the *Gloria* by the blazes he'd left on the trees. As the late afternoon began to chill down in its inevitable descent towards evening, the midges came out in force and he began wondering if he had any of the Avon Skin So Soft skin cream left on board. This Highland legend was a simple skin tonic, somehow discovered by a particularly grooming-conscious bunch of Norwegian Special Forces soldiers to be an effective weapon against summer Scandinavian mosquitoes. They brought it to the attention of commandos on exercise in Scotland, and soon it was being sold

A WHISKY IN MONSTERVILLE

in hiking boutiques from Oban to Acharacle. It actually worked, too. Nobody knew exactly how.

There was no sign of life from the *Gloria*. But the key to the saloon door was not in its usual place, where he'd told Davie to leave it – under one of two blue ceramic flower pots gifted to Murricane six months ago by a woman with designs on a romantic idyll as his live-aboard companion. They had originally contained flowers of some garden centre variety. Now they were covered in moss and lichen.

The cabin door was unlocked. Inside, all was tidy. Tidier than he had left it. Tidier by far than how he imagined Davie would ever have left it. An unopened bottle of Glenrothes Vintage '91 was on the table. Two glasses. A jug of water. Rebecca, wearing the old silk dragon dressing gown he'd bought himself in Thailand, sat cross-legged in a leather-upholstered corner. She looked up from the book she'd been reading.

"Hi," said Murricane, removing the slim volume he'd bought at the Tourist Centre from its brown paper bag. He tossed it towards her. Effortlessly, she caught it in her left hand. Now she held two paperbacks. They were identical.

"Katherine Stewart," said Murricane. "She used to live up at Abriachan. Knows the loch well."

"*The Story of Loch Ness*," said Rebecca. Her accent, Murricane remembered, was cultured southern English rather than the more common middle European lilt you got in Tel Aviv.

"You should check out page 15. 'Old Red Sandstone, Gneiss, Granite.' The chapter on geology."

"I have. Not written by Ms Stewart, as I recall, but in fact by the eminent Christine Matheson." Rebecca placed the two copies of the book neatly on the saloon table.

"Indeed. And of such interest to the late Avril Anson that it was heavily highlighted in the copy she had."

"I'm not surprised. She had no need to do that, of course. She was very highly trained indeed as an academic and field geologist."

"Sister Avril? Really, Sister Rebecca?"

"Yes, really, Mr Murricane. Very, very good at her job."

"That's not what Mr Coldstream, the sex guru of godliness, said. Can I ask how you know anything about her at all?"

Rebecca reached for the bottle of Glenrothes, which was squat and bell-shaped. Murricane knew the whisky as heavily sherried, old-fashioned and with an unexpected tartness that undercut its natural sweetness. It was a heavy whisky. A bedtime dram. That dressing gown fell open. His dressing gown. On her. There was nothing flirtatious about the gesture, but he suddenly felt sweat break out over the entire surface of his skin, forehead to toes.

"A colleague," she said, pouring two large drams. "Water?"

"This one, the way it comes." He reached for the glass, drank. Warming but not burning, balanced on the edge between sweet and pungent. A great Speyside from a distillery once lost to all but blenders. A stray midge whined next to his ear. He ignored it. "A colleague?"

"Geologists. We had a common interest in what they're calling political geology."

"You mean, like oil? Uranium? Usefully bomb-proof caves, impenetrable rocks, that sort of thing?"

"Yes, but our interests were a bit more specialised than that. I mean, we met occasionally at conferences, but mainly we ploughed our own furrows, so to speak."

"Who for? For whom?"

"Well, there's the thing. I was doing a Ph.D at Tel Aviv when I met her at a very small, very select conference. It was called something like Rare Earths and the Defence Dividend. She was there courtesy of the CIA. I was there as part of... well. A recruitment drive by our own dear Percival. You do know Percy. Doesn't like to take no for an answer."

"Indeed." He picked up the Stewart book.

"Page 15," she said. "Yes, it's pretty basic. For a popular audience. But check out the stuff about granite magma."

"Heat and deformation?"

"Secondary Abriachanite. Blue Crocidolite. Aegerine. Haematite."

"I do like it when you talk dirty. How come you never mentioned this before?"

"Well. I had to check you out, didn't I? Percy insisted."

"You were very good. Quiet. Careful."

"It was a pleasure."

He moved over, sat down next to her and slipped a hand around her waist. She put down her glass and the dressing gown slipped from one shoulder. He leaned in closer and kissed the corded muscle on her neck. She smelled of whisky, sweat and that Spanish soap, those grey cakes he remembered as a kind of street perfume on childhood Costa Brava holidays. She gripped his hair and pulled his face away from her, then brought their lips together, hard. Her mouth was full of Glenrothes single malt and as he opened his mouth to meet hers, the neat spirit flooded past his teeth and into his unsuspecting throat. In a paroxysm of coughing he broke away from her.

"Jesus Christ, Rebecca."

"What's the matter, Mr whisky expert? Don't you appreciate my choice in drams?"

She stood, unknotting the dressing gown and shrugging it off. Memories of that body came flooding back as Murricane tried to shake off his whisky-fuelled choking fit. What age was she? Forties, outdoor fit. He remembered the soles of her feet, hard and cool, the carelessly broken toenails, the unshaven leg and underarm hair. That musky aroma mixed with the soap. Maja. The name came back to him. The pint of water she kept by her bed. How it was always empty in the morning. Those scars, casually worn, distinctive. How they matched ones on his own body. No tattoos. Breasts, one marginally bigger than the other. No woman ever had symmetrical breasts, he remembered reading, unless they'd been worked on by some surgeon. Any of Rebecca's surgical procedures had been driven by necessity.

"Come on. Lightweight." She pulled his head up and his hands drifted down until he was able to grip her buttocks, pushing her upper body down onto the red leather of the bench seat. She parted her legs, laughed throatily. His fingers caressed her, found her.

"Are you ready for this, Mr Murricane? I know I am."

And he was. He certainly was.

Afterwards, he boiled some lentils, then fried them with butter and three cloves of Nairnshire-grown purple garlic, plus some wild garlic picked from the Cover. Chilli, mustard seed, cumin, ginger, cinnamon, garam masala. A tin of chopped tomatoes, another of sliced carrots plus some sorrel, and some quick chapatis kneaded up from chickpea flour and griddled. They ate naked, semi-entwined, slick with sweat and sometimes with food, drinking more of the whisky. And then they fucked again. Garlic, chilli and sex, their bodies were grainy with flour and sweat.

"That works," Rebecca said at last. "That works for me."

"Why shouldn't it? It did before," Murricane said. "When you were spying on me."

"Convenience, then," said Rebecca. "It's Rebecca Elmsworth, by the way. Not an Israeli name. Mother Jewish, maternal line, all that. But essentially I'm English. British."

"Working for Percival, you would be, maybe," said Murricane. "But then he always had strong Tel Aviv connections. Ever meet my friends David and Moshe? IDF, kind of."

"Is that a joke? Do you how many Davids there are? How many Moshes?"

"Yes. But I think that was kind of the point. You'd remember them. They were a kind of double act. Specialists in hostage extraction. Nominally Israeli Defence Force, but a couple of buccaneers. Helped me out once or twice. Back in the day."

"That was your thing, wasn't it? Hostages?" She felt his body go still. Caution, a kind of pulling back. "Sorry."

"Don't be. Yes. You get some out, you leave others behind. And when I started leaving too many, too many bodies, it was time to stop. Time to leave all of that behind. Job for younger men. And women." He reached for the whisky. They'd drunk about half. "This isn't really a session whisky, you know. I think there's beer cooling in the loch." She was gently caressing him, that patch of skin between scrotum and arsehole. Fucking hell. This was ridiculous. She used her left hand to grab his and placed it in her mouth. One by one, she began sucking his fingers. "I do like the smell of garlic on a man," she murmured. "How about one more time to cement our unity of purpose? I do believe you want to. I do believe you can."

"How can I refuse?"

The leather of the saloon seating, the long banquettes along the hull – were they called banquettes on a boat, or a barge? – was slippery beneath him as she pushed him down and took him inside her. She drew her knees up to his waist and began slowly twisting her hips from side to side, her hands – strong, hard, practical hands, he noticed for the first time – why had he never paid attention to that before? But then, they would be. Strong. Practical – pressing onto his shoulders, then moving to the sides of his head. One, the left now in his hair, holding, gripping, the other caressing the right side of his chin. Christ, he knew this move. One twist now, one very hard movement with all her muscular wiriness, and his neck could well break. He was vulnerable. He had made himself vulnerable. It was a classic assassin's sex trick. And he found he didn't much care what happened.

"Think you can do it?" he said.

"What's that?" Not out of breath, not consumed with panting passion. Measured, mildly excited.

"Now that you've had your pleasure, can you kill me? Like a praying mantis. Twist my head off. Snap, crackle pop."

Rebecca increased the movement of her hips.

"Who says... who says I've had my pleasure?" She moved one hand down her own body and began to caress herself.

"DIY. Sometimes it's the only way."

He sat up, trapping her hand between their bodies. It was difficult not to bump her head on the cupboards above the seat, but he managed to reverse their positions until he was on top of her, thrusting again and again until he came, or at least he thought he did. It was difficult to tell. Rebecca was silent. For about a minute there was nothing but the sound of their breathing. Then: "Murricane, fancy a cup of tea? I'll tell you a story."

Murricane had a block of Russian caravan tea, and he crumbled some into a metal pot. The kettle whistled its readiness and he switched off the gas ring, let the water stop bubbling, then poured it. "Three minutes to infuse," he said. "You might as well start."

It was dark now, a breeze getting up, almost midgeless, so he was able to open the hatches and let the cool loch air eddy around their bodies. There was the strange translucent Highland semi-darkness of late summer. The fading twilight that would eventually turn blue-black and then begin to lighten almost immediately. Rebecca pulled on his dressing gown. In response, he draped an old denim jacket around his shoulders. A kind of modesty.

"You look ridiculous," she said. "You're too old for denim jackets. Unless you're turning into a Status Quo fan."

"Not yet. Not quite deaf enough," he said. "So, you're one of Percival's little girlies, are you? As he calls them."

"Used to call them. Sex discrimination act and all that. After your time. Fully qualified survivor of those nasty courses you were involved in setting up. You and those SAS bastards."

"SBS does it…"

"…underwater. I know. Anyway, I am, genuinely, a geologist. Extremely relevant, these days. Well, it always was. Gold, silver, diamonds, oil. And now rare metals. Strategic metals. Rare earths."

He took off the denim jacket and carefully climbed over the stern. The water was about a metre deep here, the bottom silty, with the occasional gnarled branch and smooth rock. Cold. Mountain run-off cold. Snowmelt cold. Unless you were careful, even in summer there was a survival time here of barely an hour. He knew this part of the loch bed well, but still he was careful. The loch could be vindictive. Fatal. He felt out the safest sections with his feet. Then he held out his hands to her. Rebecca slipped out of the dressing gown. There was a little light glinting from the south side of the loch, and the spillage on the dark, rippling surface from Temple Pier's orange sodium lights. Her body glimmered and flickered. She swung her legs over the stern and he held her around the waist as she allowed herself to slip lightly into the water. She breathed in sharply, caught it, steadied.

"Just watch your feet. You can get caught on old roots, or stub your toes on the rocks."

"Let's swim before I die of exposure."

"We've got about half an hour before we need to worry."

"Actually, let's not swim just yet." And she wrapped her legs around his waist, pulling him under the water. He gasped as his head went under, feeling the icy ache and remembering, just, to close his mouth before it filled.

A WHISKY IN MONSTERVILLE

He held her tightly, and it became a battle of wills, of breath. There was no arousal. It was too cold. Instead, they tested each other, holding each other's body under the water, until he tapped her shoulder and she released him. When they burst through the surface, they were caught by a weak torchlight held by someone nearby. Blinking the water from his eyes, Murricane caught the shadow of a kayak. A voice.

"Aye, aye. Don't wish to disturb you in your general rituals of cavorting. Communicating wi' the water sprites n'that. But I just wanted a quick word."

"Davie," said Murricane. "I thought you were away up in the wilds of Glen Affric or beyond."

"They seek him there, they seek him here." Davie chuckled, and the torch went out. Murricane could smell his cigarette, though, and see the red dot of its tip. "Just wanted to make sure you were going to be in Dores for the public meeting tomorrow."

"The planning meeting?" Rebecca sounded relaxed, though Murricane could tell she was cold. There was the beginning of a tremor in her voice. "Oh, we'll be there. Won't we, darling?"

"Aye, well. Whoever the hell you may be, darling. There's obviously going to be problems if I turn up. Problems for me, that is. Polis are swarming around, issuing pictures. I hear they think they've got a witness, too."

"Someone called Jenks," said Murricane. "Convenient. He works for Coldstream."

"Very convenient," said Davie. "Still, there's more than one way of making your presence felt. I'll expect you to be there, anyway. Remember, Murry, boy. You promised no' to let me down."

"Where are you going now, Davie?"

"Aye, don't worry. I won't disturb you and your lady friend any further. Wasn't planning to cramp your style. And anyway, ye'll be getting a wee bit chilly. Best you don't know where I'm off to. The loch shore has lots of secrets, though. There are places even big things can hide. Monstrous things. You know that." And Davie's croaking, liquid smoker's cough echoed across the water, followed by the quiet splash of his paddle as he reversed away, out into the vastness of the loch.

"Davie the Druid," said Rebecca. "Lees of that ilk."

"Indeed. A man in trouble."

"Not as much trouble as we'll be in if we don't get dried. I can feel hypothermia creeping up my legs."

"That'll be the leeches."

Dried, in bed, they slept facing away from each other, barely touching. Both slept lightly, the accidental touch of flesh in the night bringing instant wakefulness. In the morning, there was enough hot water left in the solar shower for Murricane to offer its use to Rebecca, which she accepted.

"True gentlemen are so rare these days," she muttered, giving him a playful bite on the shoulder.

"Rare earths," he said. "You never finished telling me."

"I'll do better than that," she said. "Once I'm clean and you're less dirty, I'll show you. What time's this public meeting? It's in the evening, anyway, isn't it? Catch all the nine to five workers?"

"Yeah, about seven, I'd guess. Over in Dores, but we can take the Landie. You know about the Landie."

"The shed above Temple? Yes. We'll need some motorised transport, right enough. We can complete… your briefing, so to speak. But perhaps something a little more, well, speedy than that corrugated iron go-kart of yours."

Murricane sighed. "Sure, what with you and Davie the Druid, I'm well and truly recruited, I think. Hopefully not to mutually exclusive interests."

"He's the one the police think killed Avril."

"Yes. Don't pretend you don't already know that."

"Well, he didn't, obviously. But he's got something on you? Something local? Been up to some naughtiness? Getting a tad careless?"

"Something like that. Do you know, I'm surprised I haven't had a personal call from Percy, that he hasn't chosen to exert his authority over me. What passes for authority. Or tried to, at least. But I suppose I'll just have to place myself in your hands. I presume you're all geared up with mobile phones and computers and tablets and all that?"

"Ah, you want the horse's mouth, not just a fling with the rider. You could use my mobile. It's secure. After all, you just bury your throwaway mobiles under your Land Rover wheels and use poor old Flaws's cumbersome machinery when the spirit moves you, don't you? Of course you can have all of me, all of my technology. But in point of fact, we won't need it. Percival is meeting us this morning. It'll be quite a little reunion."

Murricane shook his head.

"Just when you think you've got out..."

"...they pull you back in. But you knew that, didn't you? You never really quit."

"Ever since I laid eyes on you for the first time, Ms Elmsworth."

"In the Piper's Rest? When I was an Israeli tourist?"

"No." Murricane smiled slightly. "When Percy showed me your file. So I'd know you when you came." There was a frozen moment and then he laughed. "I'm joking. Come on, let's get some breakfast in Drum."

"Actually, let's not. We need to get going. We have a bit of a trip ahead of us. And we'll leave your lovely Land Rover for the moment. I have transportation."

It was in the Piper's car park; a dusty blue Subaru WRX STi.

"That is a seriously ugly car," said Murricane. "The older ones were better, the Macrae saloons. They looked old fashioned but they really went like shit off a shovel."

"This one just goes like shit," said Rebecca. "I like it. It's like a hatchback on steroids. Hop in, as they say."

He hopped. Or to be precise, inserted himself through the low, vicious-looking car's pillarless door. He was in her hands.

Down

Malt, corn, burnt wood, spice and honey and ginger snap biscuits. Lots more honey and pepper on the tongue and in mouth. A bit oily. Ends with burnt toast and brown sugar.

ABHAINN DEARG (RED ROCKS) THREE-YEAR-OLD

A WHISKY IN MONSTERVILLE

They left Drumnadrochit at around 8.00am, just as the midweek tourist and business traffic was building. Murricane spent the first half-an-hour on the A82 alongside Loch Ness and then Loch Lochy practising panic control techniques he'd learnt for diving: deep, slow breaths, moderate holding, then a long release. It was meant to be heart-slowing, and it wasn't working. He kept finding his fists clenched unexpectedly tight.

The A82 was twisty and frustrating, rammed with caravans, motorbikes and trucks, with just enough open, not-quite-long-enough straights to encourage overtaking, overtaking that had to deal with goggle-eyed landscape spotters and the risk that someone would stop suddenly to take a snapshot. Or simply forget that they weren't in France, or Germany or Holland, and drive on the right, not the left.

Rebecca drove as if she was trying to outrun the devil. Not, Murricane pondered, as if she was on her way to meet him. Percival. Percy. A bad man. A powerful and bad man. Not that he saw it that way. Percival thought of himself as the country's conscience, a repository of Britain's best interests. And he had the authority, Murricane knew, to act on that. To cause others to act on his behalf. It wasn't a department, a section, though he supposed it was one of those little inheritances, fiefdoms, you could trace back to World War Two and the SOE, which had established several well-funded and highly secretive groups, all supposedly in service to Britannia, all with only nominal accountability. Percival – ageless, but probably no more than 60, so post-war in every sense – was simply, as he had once put it to Murricane, "an enabler and preventer". He worked out of the Home Office, so had links to MI5 and none of the activities he sanctioned actually took place abroad. Not officially. Not often. But they could. They had. They did.

He opened his eyes at Fort William, and shut them again as Rebecca slithered down a now-wet A82 south, turning right and halting at the queue of cars for the Corran Ferry. He watched the flat-bottomed floating platform approaching from the Ardgour side, the Subaru's engine off and ticking as it cooled.

A WHISKY IN MONSTERVILLE

The peninsula, reachable only across the Corran narrows if you were driving, was one of the most haunted and beautiful stretches of landscape in the Highlands. It contained Ardnamurchan Lighthouse, Britain's westernmost point. Lochaline, where you could catch a ferry to Mull. Morvern, Moidart. It was a repository of Scotland's most tragic and sometimes deranged history.

"Be a love," she said, smiling sweetly at him. "They do particularly nice kipper rolls at that wee seafood stall. Get us one. And a coffee."

"Do you promise to finish eating before you start driving again?"

"I consume quickly." He opened the door and stretched his cramped legs, levering himself out and up. He leaned back in. "Kipper rolls? Are you serious?"

"Absolutely. Try one. You'll thank me."

The stall was a crudely-adapted caravan, pungent with peat smoke and old fish. It was uninspiring. So was the mass of hair and tattoos gazing at Murricane from the serving hatch.

"Aye?"

"Err... kipper rolls? Two please."

"White or brown?"

"Are they not, sort of naturally brown? The kippers? You'd need to bleach them to make them white. Or are they those yellow boil-in-the-bag ones?" There was a brief and none-too-friendly silence.

"The rolls. White or brown? Our kippers are mildly smoked over old whisky barrels. Do you want the name of the boat that caught the herring?" The accent was Highland-moderated Scouse. An uneasy combination.

"Oh, I see. Well, might as well go for the healthy option. White."

By the time he got back to the car, balancing the rolls with two large lattes, from the look of them effectively caffeinated, the ferry was unloading its cargo of cars, and Rebecca was standing by the Subaru waiting for him.

"We're not stinking out the Scooby with smoked herring," she said. "If I can eat quickly, so can you."

The fish rolls, with melted butter soaked into the soft bread baps, burnt and crispy on the outside, were surprisingly delicious. Rebecca was prepared to allow coffee in the car. It did taste of fish, but mildly. By the time they reached Ardmore, Rebecca had finished hers. They stopped to bin the cups and then Murricane shut his eyes once more.

"I'm not that bad a driver," said Rebecca.

"No. But I am that bad a passenger. Wake me up when we get there. Wherever it is."

*** *** ***

Strontian was a huddle of houses, mostly painted white. An ultra-modern school, a shop, a hotel. The towering conical lump of Beinn Resipol grey and threatening, but the community itself surprisingly lush, with a curiously Anglified village green and some mature trees. Murricane awoke from a sleep crammed with dreams of movement, risk, danger, attack, discomfort.

Strontian. One of several planned settlements in the Highlands, he remembered. Ullapool for the fishing, this for lead miners. Rare earths. Of course.

"Ready for a walk?" Rebecca was wearing, he noticed, a pair of Merrill approach shoes. He had on a much-repaired pair of Brashers with commando soles. "Nothing too strenuous. How is the leg these days?"

"My leg? It's... fine." And it was, for the most part. After the Afghanistan debacle, the surgery, he had regained enough function in it to return to active duty. Enough for the crazy debacle that had allowed him to meet Flaws and discover the Highlands. Enough to bring him to the north. *The Further North You Go*. That was a song by someone, someone from the 80s, someone in a band that had a couple of hits. But who? Lost now, like so many pop music memories. His leg, though, that was a remembrance of things past. A proper one. A bad one. There was the occasional twinge, a creaky day or two of midwinter agony. Age was a factor too, though. Age and a deep, creeping sense of disgust with some of the things he'd done, the things he'd seen. Things he remembered. That was what had ended his active service. Or what had caused him to try and end it.

He'd been put on the so-called ARL – the Active Retirement List. Too much information in his head, apparently, to let him drift off unfettered, untethered towards the disgrace of ghostwriting lurid Special Forces potboilers. Sometimes the Official Secrets Act wasn't enough. Percy had demanded contact protocols. When he had drifted into Inverness and then Drumnadrochit there had been an insistence on the Flaws connection. The occasional call-in for what was euphemistically called 'consultation procedures'. And he had been warned, explicitly, that in some ways he would never be free, that there were people around, organisations who remembered if not his name, then his presence, his shape. Folk who most decidedly did not have his best interests at heart.

So he took precautions, armed himself, remained watchful. Yet the old skills were fading, slipping. The aggression, the hair-trigger psychopathy. Mellowing. Drink-dulled. Old. He was getting old. And the thing was, he liked it. Or had given up worrying about it.

Yet other people saw in him the demons and monsters he himself thought were dying, or sick, or sleeping. Davie the Druid, for example. Trying to threaten him. Or was it a threat? Was it just a ploy to awaken those ancient, viciously trained beasts within? To put him at his service? Management?

Maybe he was bored, Murricane thought. Maybe he was actually looking for trouble and tragedy. Perhaps he attracted it. Body in a loch? Headless and burnt? Sure, I'll haul it in. I'll make sure I'm out there with a bunch of drunks, waiting for Nemesis to come floating up from the depths.

Monsters. Monsters everywhere.

They walked. Through the section of Strontian called Scotstown, presumably because the lowland Scottish miners had been billeted there. At first the path was a parkland stroll, carefully tended and sprinkled with gravel. The trees were oak, and inheritors of ancient seed. There was something deeply strange about this woodland, almost magical.

"Ariundle," said Rebecca. "I don't know how to pronounce it in Gaelic. But it's... *Arrig Sundial*, or somesuch."

An information board allowed Murricane to show off some of the soft west coast vowel sounds he'd picked up from all those nights in the Piper's Rest, learning how to say *uisge beatha* properly. "*Airigh Fhionndail.* 'The shieling of the white meadow'. Part of the Sunart woods. And Strontian means 'the Point of the Fairies'. Well, there you go. Watch out for Tinkerbell in a kilt. I thought this would be all godless Norwegian spruce."

"Plenty of that still to come." On they went, the path changing, coarsening.

There were interpretation boards about Strontian's mining history, its place in mineralogy. Lead, zinc, silver, all the way back to 1722. Adair Crawford, Strontianite, French prisoners of war digging up lead for shot, and finding something strange. Then Sir Humphrey Davy, of miner's lamp fame, isolating Strontium. All the horror of that name. Strontium 90, in milk, the fear on his parents' faces. He remembered his childhood in Cumbria, stories of the Windscale fire, the dead fields, dead cows and sheep. Then, much later, a comic book character, a dog called Strontium, somehow associated in his mind with the ludicrously jocular, sinister Judge Dredd. *I Am The Law.*

Higher, into industrial forestry, identikit trees, alien species, plantations of toxic firs, nothing like the gnarled birch, ancient and twisted and mean, of the Loch Ness shoreline. Or the lovely, Hobbitesque Ariundle oak below them. The Forestry Commission had a lot to answer for. Patches of clear-felled debris and destruction, touches of green creeping up through the rotting stumps. Peering in under the evergreen canopy of still-growing spruce, it was all brown, dank and dead.

"Galena," said Rebecca, not even slightly out of breath after they came out above the treeline and began to see the raw stretches of worked landscape, the soaring peaks of Morvern in the distance. They were on the meandering shoulders of Beinn Resipol now. "Lead sulphide. That's what brought the big industrial concerns here in the first place. And now this." She swept a hand at the ravaged hillside. Modern earthmoving machinery, none of it actually moving, provided patches of yellow and orange. Portakabins and shipping containers leaned at crazy angles.

"Mud. Drilling mud. Or to be precise, Barite. Serving the great god petroleum, making the drillbits bite. At least they're not sinking crap mineshafts and killing miners anymore."

"Just ripping the surface of the mountains apart. God bless the miners, eh? All that noble suffering underground. The romance of labour. Until you die of it."

"Indeed." They left the path, and struck out over heather and bog, aiming for a corrie, a gap in the escarpment to the north. "That's... *Arji Vraggen*," said Rebecca. "Another half an hour or so."

"*Airdhe Bhraighan.*" He couldn't help himself. "Softer on the consonants. 'The song of the hunted man'. That's... slightly sinister."

They had met no-one so far, seen no sign of life, human or animal, save the omnipresent midges. Not even the deer that ravaged large tracts of Ardnamurchan, and no sheep. No woolly gods. As they entered a glowering canyon, the bracken slopes steep and shadowy, the atmosphere changed. It was if this little glen had its own weather system, its own phonics. There was no echo. Little wind. As they spoke to each other, they automatically lowered their voices, and the words died on their lips, dulled. Hushed. The fugitive's song, the ballad of the hunted man: silence. Silence was always best.

He was waiting for them in the least ruined bothy of three, formed in a protective triangle around a mine shaft that was like a half-healed wound someone had been unable to resist poking. It had been fenced off at some time in the past, strands of broken, rusted barbed wire still spiralling from weathered grey fenceposts. A cable or rope disappeared from one of them down into the shaft. Murricane didn't like the look of it. Even less than the look of the man who stood waiting for them, hands clasped behind his back. The man who owned his soul. Rebecca's soul too. Percival. This close, 'Percy' wasn't just inappropriate. It was nearly blasphemous.

"Murricane." A crisp nod, the grey hair hidden beneath a Fair Isle skullcap, the body-born-to-rule encased in birdwatcher's Gore-Tex. He was holding a shepherd's crook, wearing Hunter Wellington boots, the face reddened by weather, the voice as usual mild and military. No offer to shake hands. "Miss Elmsworth." He gestured at the hole, which Murricane could now see bore signs of recent human access. Broken bracken, trampled grass. "Have you told him?"

"Not quite."

"Rare earths," said Murricane. "Geology. Bits of rock, ancient volcanic eruptions, great lumps of stuff poking up through the earth's crust."

"Yes, yes. Always keen to show how bloody smart you are. But the question is, how do you get from lumps of dirt like the stuff all around us to the beloved technology of today? Weapons systems. Advanced communications. Laser sights. Satellite guidance. Computer. Computers. Computers. Faster and faster and faster bloody computers." Percival shook his head as if in despair.

"And smaller," said Rebecca. "Well, small as you can deal with, now, until they start inserting them into your head. Connecting up your limbs. Adding some robotics."

"Robocop," said Murricane. "Sometimes I think I could do with some of that technology. When I wake up in the morning aching from all the shit you and your governmental superiors have put me through."

"How do you know," said Percival, suddenly with a half grin on his face, "we haven't already done that? Maybe that's the only reason you're still functioning. If you can call it functioning. Perhaps you've been – what's the word – mechanised?"

"The only reason I'm still here is because after that last comprehensive fuck-up in Afghanistan, some paramedics managed to stabilise me before that murderous American bastard called Jenks could finish the job he started at that fucking compound. The murderous American bastard you refused to believe existed, once I was back at base and you, mysteriously, Percy," he spat the diminutive name, "turned up with as worried an expression as I'm ever likely to see on your fucking stiff upper lipped fizzog. With a lawyer, no less. A lawyer in uniform waving Official Secrets Act shit at me, as I lay there half way to fucking paradise on morphine. And guess what? There's someone called Jenks working with the slimy Reverend Coldstream. A handyman, no less.

Crucial witness to the so-called crimes of Davie Lees." There was a silence. Rebecca was looking into the distance, embarrassed.

"But we've looked after you, Murricane. A duty of care. We have remained in contact. We've pensioned you generously, or rather Her Majesty has, so you can afford to live that gloriously bohemian lifestyle of yours. Fishing. Gone fishing." Percival snorted with contempt. "And please mind your language. We are in female company."

"Oh, she knows all about fucking. Is that what you tasked her to do? Is it?"

Rebecca looked at him stonily. She said nothing.

"This is a payroll job, Murricane," said Percival. "For her and you. If you're interested. I'm not going to force you."

"Oh I'm interested. I'm FUCKING interested, as a matter of fact. I've been threatened with blackmail by a sneaky little sod who worships the Great Goddess or whatever divine entity he's found in the spiritual supermarket of Findhorn or Valhalla this weekend. I've had sex with Mata Hari here at truly tremendous cost to my own self-esteem and so, yes, I might as well get her Maj to pay me for whatever titanic trouble is going to be added to those sufferings. Because they're going to happen to me anyway, aren't they? The bad things?"

"I would imagine so. You tend to attract bad things, as you call them. And people. Believe it or not, those pigeons from that little jaunt in Afghanistan you seem to resent so much might finally be coming home to roost. Wouldn't that be nice? To deal with them once and for all? American bastards called Jenks included?"

"No. No it wouldn't be nice. It might have a certain circularity. It would certainly be informative to get some sort of explanation for what was going on there."

"You mean in Afghanistan generally? Over the past 200 years? There are books."

"You know what I mean." He could feel his anger dissipating. What the hell. He was in this thing. There was no way out. Percival shrugged. He knew he had him.

"First things first. There's a rope ladder attached to those fence posts." The older man knelt, and rummaged in the old Karrimor backpack at his feet, pulling out a blackened Optimus petrol stove and a state-of-the-art Petzl head torch. "Here's some illumination. Go down there with Miss Elmsworth and she will give you a quick briefing. She knows the way. I'll see you back here in half an hour." He tapped the old Optimus. "I'll make some tea. I trust Earl Grey will be acceptable?"

"Will you be all right here on your own? An old man, all alone?"

"What on earth makes you think I'm alone?" Percival knelt to light the stove. Murricane looked around at the empty landscape, feeling an involuntary twitch between his shoulders. Of course, they'd be here somewhere. More of the Percival stable.

It was a titanium chain-wire version of a rope ladder, light and strong, but not really capable of handling two people at the same time. So Murricane gallantly let Rebecca descend into the mineshaft first, her own backpack having produced a headtorch, Kevlar gloves and a climber's safety helmet.

"No health and safety concerns for me, then? What about my sensitive palms? My vulnerable head?" She looked up him bleakly, the torch's LEDs momentarily blinding. And then she disappeared from sight.

Helmetless and gloveless, Murricane wobbled down into the depths. The shaft was surprisingly smooth, the stone grey and slippery, but free of vegetation. Here and there were signs that it had been cleared fairly recently. After about 50 feet, the ladder ended, worryingly, before the bottom had been reached. The light from the entrance had vanished quickly and only the blue LEDs of Rebecca's Petzl assured him the mine wasn't in fact bottomless. He dropped about six feet onto a crackling pile of slaty rubble, peat and dying plants scraped off the shaft. There was a smell. A bad one.

"Can I hold your hand, darling?" She didn't reply. Two tunnels, both about seven feet high, led in opposite directions from the bottom of the shaft, both sloping slightly downhill. "Where does the water go? Surely they'd have had to pump these mines out all the time?"

"Yes, steam pumps back in the day, pony-power before that."

"Air?"

"Enough for our purposes."

She set off down one of the tunnels. Left or right? Murricane was disorientated and couldn't tell which direction they were going in. Did it matter? Probably not. He didn't like the sensation of ignorance, of being led. The smell grew worse and worse. After a while the tunnel widened slightly and he was able to squeeze alongside Rebecca when she stopped. In the ghostly light of their torches, reflected from the rock walls, which seemed to be impregnated with something granular and shiny, like Christmas glitter, he could see where they stink was coming from.

"Recognise them?"

"Well, not from their tone of voice, that's for sure. Should I?"

The two bodies, about a fortnight into decomposing, he estimated, were similarly clad in outdoor shop Gore-Tex. One was bigger than the other. They were a couple of metres away, lying on their faces where they had fallen, both clearly shot multiple times in the back. Large calibre handgun. The smell was sickly and overwhelming, the acidic tinge threatening to make him gag. It was an aroma he knew only too well. Still, he had to get nearer.

"The small one is a forensic geologist called Elizabeth Mainwaring. I knew her quite well. So did Avril. You didn't, so don't bother turning her over. I already have. Her nose has been... cut off. We'd worked together in Brazil and El Salvador. She had a rather a nice nose, you'll be happy to know. Audrey Hepburnish. The large one is someone you used to work with, I believe."

He moved, with difficulty, the stiffened lump that had once been living flesh. The face was blackened and bloated with damp. Rot and maggots were crawling where there had once been eyes.

"Johnny Foster. Still on retainer from Percy, eh, the bastard."

"As I understand it, he saved your life."

"Did he, indeed?"

The scuffle in that compound, just before the grenade exploded, and sending him into that dark, jagged tunnel. Darker than this one. No sparkling sediment on the walls. Just the sudden awakening, moments later, though it felt like hours, days, months. Medical team, fresh in off a helicopter. Foster. The Yank.

Jenks. He'd never seen either of them since that fuck-up deep inside Afghanistan.

"Foster was the one who..."

"Foster jumped Jenks, the American, just as he was about to throw the grenade. Probably wouldn't have, we reckon, if he'd known Jenks actually had a grenade, armed. Anyway it fell short. You were behind Everard, who took the brunt of the blast. Your shoulder and ankle got some shrapnel wounds, your knee a lump as well. Jenks was lucky too. He had his back to the blast, fighting off Foster. Took some superficial wounds to his back and legs, nothing permanent. Scratches. Foster was completely unscathed."

"Well, he isn't now. He could have come and said hello. During my long and painful convalescence."

"Percival had sent in a Super Puma chopper as an emergency backup once he realised the mess he was involved in. That was the only thing that saved you. The Chinook that was supposed to pick you up? Mysteriously recalled. A Polish medical team and two Australian SAS hoodlums. Didn't feel he could trust anyone else. They got everyone out. Everyone who was left alive. Three of you. No judgements, no more shooting. Foster had Jenks unconscious. Would have killed him if he hadn't been distracted by your condition. Back at Helmand, Jenks just disappeared. Or was disappeared. Percival was out there, had to sterilise the whole scene. He says nobody had any idea those two private contractors were going to be there until it was too late to call the whole thing off."

"Oh, come on. Somebody must have known. The heroin. The bodies. What happened..."

"Team went in within 12 hours. Everything had been wiped clean. Nothing."

"Return of the mysterious Chinook?"

"Or some speedy camels. Who knows?"

"Someone does."

"The American side of things was compromised. There was... let's just say there was private input. The Global Repentance and Redemption Trust. Influence brought to bear. The whole thing was so messy and threatening to our entire Afghanistan operation that it had to be hushed up."

"So. Percy gave Foster a job."

"Foster already had a job with Percy. And he was fitter than you were. He was able to carry out a few errands."

"Like protecting a geologist."

"Like failing to protect a geologist. Or himself."

"So who'd he run into?"

"He ran into the same guy he did before. The same one you ran into in Afghanistan. He ran into Jenks. At least, that's the name we have for him."

"So it's the same Jenks. He's here. Why the fuck would he be?"

"He's here. Why don't you have a look at Foster's right hand?"

"Do I have to?"

"You have to."

Murricane crouched down and lifted Foster's arm. The hand was missing. "That some sort of Zen thing? Look for the one hand missing?" But he was remembering the chaos of that tent back in Afghan, that Ranger captain dying, Everard, the terrible noise...

"Missing bits of bodies. Seen that before? A nose here, a hand there?"

"An ear. There were rumours in Iraq and in Afghan. There are always rumours like that." Murricane stood up, shook his head. He turned and started half walking half crawling back to the shaft.

The titanium ladder was easily within his reach, although Rebecca would have had to jump for it.

"I'll lift you," he said.

"Don't you want to know what they were doing here?"

There was a metallic taste in his mouth. Blood, maybe. Revulsion. He thought about the bodies back in the tunnel. "What's going to happen to them?"

"Percy has a closedown extraction team coming in tomorrow. Decent burials, tragic accidents, tearful relatives. It'll all be dealt with."

"So what were they doing here? Geology?"

"Geology." She nodded back down the tunnel. "Did you see that sparkling on the walls? The silvery granulation?"

"Yes".

"And you know that this is an area historically rich in rare earths, strange combinations of oxides, somewhere God laid his finger. Or if you prefer, where eruptions and seismic shit caused some strange chemical reactions to occur. Producing Strontium, Barites, lead, you name it?

"Well, since our little post-coital discussion, I do know something. I suppose."

"So, devoid as you are of any endorphins enabling you to absorb information comfortably, I'll keep it simple. The silvery sparkle is a mineral called Varlindium. It's a superconductor. It conducts electricity faster and with less loss than any other substance on earth. It's radically better at doing this than the other rare earth compounds, though it's chemically related to them. It's not quite as fast as the compounds that have to be cooled down or put under pressure to make them work. This is room temperature stuff. It's the holy grail. The Chinese have been able to extract only about a tonne of a related mineral, Zycindium, every year for the last decade. They have an absolute monopoly. It's about half as effective as this stuff is. For the manufacture of every form of miniature electronic gadget, this is like the industrial revolution. In a rock. In Scotland. It's safe, stable, light and it doesn't degrade easily.

"And nobody knew it was here."

"In the early 20th century, everybody knew there was something here that sparkled. But there was literally one surface deposit and the Galena was beyond that, so they tunnelled through it and just let it be. A man called Varley dug out the shiny stuff from curiosity and named it Varlindium. They weren't big on conductivity tests in those days, let's face it. This mine was closed up just before World War One when it became uneconomic as far as Galena was concerned."

"And?"

"Samples of Varlindium were held at Tonne-Tech University in the States, in California. Museum stock, bought up wholesale from the UK. Research student was carrying out some dumb luck tests. Or maybe not dumb luck. Maybe looking for it. For the grail. Some studentship funded by a tech company called... well, you can perhaps guess. Or maybe you don't remember? KokVan. Bingo. Superconductivity. The mine was re-opened last year and a survey done by something called Cellardyke AG, based in Luxembourg. They then bought this and all the surrounding mines at truly, pitifully tiny expense. And belatedly, the money got our attention. I mean, it was still several millions. Then we carried out a detailed search through the paperwork and digital shit, trying to find the real ownership of Cellardyke AG.

"And that would be..."

Rebecca reached up towards the weighted base of the ladder.

"If you can bear to touch me, give us a lift up, will you? Percy should have the tea ready by now. He can tell you the rest."

*** *** ***

Percival had the Earl Grey boiling away in a less than delicate manner.

"It needs to be strong, I think," he said. "Properly infused. The oil of bergamot has to set your palate a-tingle."

"A-tingle? I've never heard you use language like that," said Murricane. "It's always been more, 'kill them, blow that up, go there, don't come back, keep quiet'."

"Well, it's always worth adding to one's lexicon, I think."

"Here's some more words for you: 'Go away. Shut up. Never say a word. Forget it happened. You're finished in this organisation'."

"Ah, but you see..."

"'But you will keep in touch. Because you should never forget. I own your scrotum, sonny boy'. What a tingle that gave me. Percy. When you talk dirty."

Percival poured the tea, still boiling and very dark, into small aluminium cups.

"I do apologise for the lack of porcelain. These cups are guaranteed stable, so you should not absorb any oxides which could cause Alzheimers later. They have done studies you know. Aluminium hydroxide, as used to take the peat out of drinking water in these parts, is implicated in dementia."

"Live locally these days, do you, Percy?"

"Ah, humour. Informality. I suppose they have their place. Miss Elmsworth? you briefed him?"

"Up to a point, Sir.

"Which point?"

"He needs to know about KokVan."

"Does he, indeed?" He turned to Murricane. "So, you're up to speed with Jenks, with Varlindium. You just to need to join up the dots, really, don't you? Drink up."

Money

Raisins, seaweed, salt, followed by peat, heather, sherry and ozone. Tar, hot roads and whin flowers in the sun.

Ardbeg Galileo

A WHISKY IN MONSTERVILLE

Coldstream had offered to collect Cochrane Vance from Inverness Airport himself, or at least to be there with a small phalanx of disciples, a kind of welcoming committee. The prettier sisters at the front, obviously. A parade of possibilities. They could have hired a minibus and the Mission had a reasonably comfortable European saloon, some unpronounceable brand beginning with 'V'. Vauxhall, that was it. What was that all about? It sounded like some kind of Greek thing, an island or a deity. Anyway he had been told by the Dallas office of KokVan that Mr Vance would make his own way to Creag Dhearg.

"His own way?" he had queried into the Skype microphone. "What? He's going to hitch?"

"I believe you have Mr Jenks there," came the impossibly bland, measured reply, barely affected by the distance, the fibre-optic cables, the deer doubtless gnawing on badly-buried wire somewhere between Inverness and the house. "I think he has made arrangements to collect Mr Vance. They are... acquainted. They go back."

"I see." Coldstream snapped the connection closed. That figured. Jenks was a KokVan man, all the way. The sociopathic jerk. Back in California, he had tried to check Jenks out. One of the church members knew someone with Delta Force connections, or who at least drank in the same bars, had the right tattoos. Second, third, fourth-hand rumours. Jenks's taste for cruelty and more. Stories about him collecting things. Souvenirs. Physical souvenirs. It had got him thrown out of the military, or so it was said. Still, the Lord worked in mysterious ways, his wonders to perform. That aspect of Jenks had, if truth be told, appealed to Coldstream. Sin, proper sin, the bad, dark stuff. It had that frisson, didn't it? And if you couldn't feel it, how could you understand it? How could you forgive it? Anyway, if everything came together here, major and glorious wonders would take place. A few missing appendages would be neither here nor there.

Coldstream clicked the trackpad on his computer and called up the plans for The Centre. Nessieland. Monsterland, Monsterville, Nessieville. They'd need something short and snappy as well as the more sober, accurate description. It was a place that would draw thousands, millions from across the world. It would make money. What did they say in this godless country of Scotland? He'd heard a shopkeeper say it about some line of stock, something sweet and dentally damaging; that was another thing the Scots liked. Anything sweet, fatty and death-dealing. It had 'washed its face'. That was it. Monsterville – yes that would be better. Or Monsterland. That would play on the expectations and memories of those who had done the Disney thing. Monsterland or Monsterville would wash its face. And, if Cochrane Vance delivered his part of the bargain, he could see the Church of the Sanctified Truth of the Christ Child in History spreading worldwide, from its intellectual and theological centre: Mission Outpost Number One would become two, three, three hundred. Nessatoreanism would save the world. Or rule it. Or both.

He smiled at the ceiling, at God. Who had created the world in six days, resting of course on the seventh, 6500 years ago. Give or take a few hundred million. For his purposes, 6500 years would do. And God had left some goodies behind for godly men like himself to find and utilise too. To share with the deserving rich, those men with vision to see the truth and act upon it. "Thank you Lord," he murmured. "Thank you."

*** *** ***

Flaws was drinking coffee – bad coffee, an experiment with one of the so-called 'microground instant' varieties of expensive crap, all failed efforts at outdoing Nescafe – and sifting through a series of links sent to him from Percival's office in London. There had been a terse message saying only 'co-ordinate with mutual friend/interested parties' which he took to mean he should pass on the material to Murricane. The pretence of him working for Avril Anson's parents and their supposed American private detective agency had been dropped. As he'd suspected, the whole thing was one big pile of Percival-flavoured shit, and the brief email from London stating that Mr and Mrs Anson's affairs would henceforward be handled from there had been confirmation.

Apparently there was a Miss Elmsworth in the picture as well. One of Percival's people. An interested party.

He glanced at the winking clock in the corner of his screen. 4.00pm. He'd see Murricane at the planning meeting tonight. At Dores. He wondered if there was time to get a steak at the Dores Inn beforehand, and concluded there was. Pity he'd have to drive, as the venerable pub had some excellent ales on tap. Maybe just the one pint. The meeting was bound to go on for a couple of hours and he'd been told, back in his uniformed days, that a series of experiments in New Zealand showed that one unit of alcohol was expelled from the human system with every hour that passed. Add a couple of pisses to that and he'd be fine.

He began printing out the Wikipedia profile on the American company called KokVan and the separate one on its owner, founder and all round weird bastard, Cochrane Vance. Why Percy, or Percy's people, had asked him to do this escaped him. Until he clicked on another link and found himself looking at an embargoed news release, due for release that evening.

'KokVan founder proud to announce association with Church' read the headline. It was all there in the first couple of paragraphs, as per standard practice for some hack turned flak catcher

'Petroleum and microelectronics company KokVan, privately owned by Fresno, California native Cochrane Vance, is to invest in a major development in Scotland, on the shores of legendary Loch Ness. Mr Vance said the multi-million dollar plan to build a centre for Creationist Science represented his long-term commitment to the Sanctified Truth Baptist Church of the Christ Child in History, and their desire to spread the Good News of the Gospel throughout the world.

' "We have a chance to disprove Darwinism and pull out at the root the source of much atheistic and satanist evil in the world," he said. "What is money when such a great and golden opportunity is made available?"'

What was money when golden opportunities were available, thought Flaws? What indeed?

Lochside, Dores

Treacle, tar, caramel and stewed blackberries. Oak and liquified Jaffa Cakes coated with dark chocolate. November bonfires and old brandy casks laced with Christmas cake and golden syrup.

YAMAZAKI 18

A WHISKY IN MONSTERVILLE

Flaws arrived at the Dores Inn at 5.30pm to find it packed to the rafters with local journalists, politicians and the kind of Loch Ness shorelands humanity you didn't often see in the same place at the same time, and certainly not indoors.

Hunting, shooting, fishing aristos and would-bes, all Harris Tweeds and Drizabones. Gore-Texed mountain types, fleeced and toned, whip-thin and ready for Everest. Dreadlocks, grey, purple and white. Straggly beards and Barbour jackets. Tibetan yak wool jackets. The reek of old dope and nicotine, and frequent dives outside for smoking one or the other. Dozens were already planted at the outside picnic tables, smoking, eating, drinking and placating a variety of weans, ranging from Osh Kosh B'Gosh-clad little gods and goddesses to kids in hand-knitted pseudo-hippy wear, one of whom had a miniature pewter beer tankard chained to the belt of his holey jeans. He couldn't have been more than seven. It was the kind of gathering you used to find at the Scoraig Free Festivals and to a lesser extent at the early Belladrums. Highland culture in all its ungainly and bizarre variety.

He spotted Murricane and a watchfully beautiful woman, apparently of the Gore-Texed mountaineering school, sipping pints of what looked like Murphy's or Guinness at an outside table. It was a still night, and midges were out, but the Inn had a couple of Midgeater machines busily belching carbon dioxide and sucking in hapless *culicoides*. It was mass midgey murder. Flaws had heard of a business someone had started where midges were sealed in small blocks of clear plastic and sold as jewellery. It seemed too kind a fate for the little bastards, he thought.

"All right, Murricane? I don't think we've had the pleasure, Miss?"

"Elmsworth," said Murricane. "Rebecca Elmsworth. Servant of Her Majesty."

"Shut up," said Rebecca, glancing at the couple they were sharing the table with. They were in late middle age, sporting almost identical dreadlocked hair styles that appeared, to Flaws' suspicious eyes, to be moving. You weren't supposed to wash dreadlocks, he remembered, dimly. Not ever. God alone knew what was living in there.

"Excuse me, I wonder if I could squeeze in?" He addressed the couple, who regarded him with indifferent and rheumy eyes. Both were smoking rollups. He flashed an old warrant card he carried for just such occasions. "Perhaps it would be better if you moved elsewhere, in fact. I would hate to have to conduct strip searches in these circumstances. The midge machines' power only extend so far, you know."

"Fuckin' rozzers," said the man, in a broad Liverpudlian accent.

"Fuckeen' midche machine killing planet," said the woman, in guttural German tones.

"Very true," said Flaws, nodding. "Now piss off, Ulrika Meinhoff, and Stuart feckin' Sutcliffe, before I get one of the DS guys in the pub to come out and make your life a misery."

"Very good, Zander," said Murricane, after they had left. "Most impressive. You've never lost your hard-nosed bastard pig proclivities, have you?"

"Nope," said Flaws taking off his Belstaff jacket and spreading it on the now-empty space opposite the pair. "Put your bag here, Rebecca. Keep my hard-earned spot." He stood up. "Is that Guinness? Have you ordered any food?"

"No, it's Orkney Dragonhead," said Murricane. "Not bad. I've ordered pan-seared king scallops with black pudding, pork and honey sausages with mash."

"Same starter for me," said Rebecca, "but with fish pie to follow."

"Fish pie?" Flaws grinned at Rebecca. "My favourite. If only there wasn't steak on the menu. Which there always is. Worth travelling here for." When he smiled, the hunted, engraved look disappeared, and he looked 15 years younger. He swept back his receding hair with one heavy hand. "Good choices all round, I think. Cockburn's black pudding, or Charlie Barleys?"

"Cockburn's. As good as the Stornoway stuff, if not better. Zander, come on, you know either's fine."

Flaws shrugged. "Whatever. Long as it's made with real blood, not powdered."

"Real blood's better," Murricane wasn't smiling. "Always."

"Right, I'll away and order a bit of dead animal. Bloodier the better. Oh, and drinks? Same again?"

"Not for me, said Rebecca. "I'm driving."

"If you can call it driving." Murricane laughed. Rebecca just shook her head.

*** *** ***

The food, good, tasty and plentiful, came promptly. They ate quickly. Flaws handed over the printouts he'd made of the links sent to him from London. Murricane read them, and handed them to Rebecca.

"Publicly accessible stuff. Frame it if you want. I think we're all up to speed now. KokVan and Coldstream."

"And Jenks," said Murricane.

Flaws frowned. "Jenks?"

"Mad, bad and dangerous to know," said Murricane. "Best leave him to me." He went to the bar and returned with three whiskies and a small jug of water.

"Proper Glencairn tasting flutes," said Flaws. "Serious. But I'm driving."

"So am I," said Rebecca, reaching for the palest of the drams and sniffing deeply. "But these are single measures and we have at least three hours to go before we need to get behind the wheel again."

"Ah, the New Zealand argument. I've heard that from Zander a million times. And he's a policeman, or used to be. So you definitely shouldn't trust a word he says."

"This is Clynelish," said Rebecca, after swirling a small amount of the whisky around her mouth and spitting. "Death to the Duke of Sutherland and all that."

"Good," nodded Murricane, appreciatively. "I'm impressed. The distillery built as part of the clearance of crofters. Good history. Or bad, depending on how you look at it. Age?"

"Standard 14-year-old, probably. Didn't look like that huge a selection in the bar when I was in. A bit mainstream. Lots of Diageo action, and it's one of theirs, isn't it?"

A WHISKY IN MONSTERVILLE

Flaws raised an eyebrow at Murricane, who was holding up his hands and grinning.

"Absolutely on the money, Bec. Where did you..."

"Call me Rebecca. You don't know me well enough. Neither of you. And my dad was a member of the Scotch Malt Whisky Society, one of the first. Taught me all he knew, and then I set out to learn some more. Practice makes perfect. And whisky's the most portable of alcohols when you're travelling."

"OK." Murricane pushed over a malt the colour of island burn water. "Try this." She inhaled, sipped, and this time didn't spit.

"Mmm. Islay. That's Lagavulin, and I think you mostly get it at 16 years old these days. They have to let it age at least that much or it's utterly disgusting, so I've heard. Let the oak leech out the toxins. First female distillery manager too." She smiled. "They have it on optic. I noticed. Best bargain in malt whisky, this stuff. I hear Diageo lose money on every bottle."

"I'll need to write this down," said Flaws. "Very impressive. May I?" He sipped at the Lagavulin. "Like being face down in a peat bog. Marvellous. if you like being suffocated in rancid mud."

"Heathen," said Murricane, sipping the final dram, which was darker, a kind of ruby brown, almost black in the fading light. "This is how we should always drink whisky, you realise. Out of doors. It's a fresh air drink."

"Midge-free air, too, thanks to those machines." Rebecca reached for the glass. After a moment she handed it to Flaws. "Well?" he smelled it and sipped.

"I can feel it coating my teeth. God, that's lovely. Sweet, oaky, full of sherry. Tastes really old. Scotland in a glass."

"Japan in a glass," Murricane and Rebecca said at the same time. They both laughed.

"Yamazaki 12," she said. "Adorable, but definitely not Scottish."

"Actually, it's the 18-year-old." Murricane looked smug. "I happened to know Sue had a bottle hidden away. She only allows one dram per order."

Flaws took out a packet of Canary Islands cigarillos. "Something to take away that nasty taste." He offered one to Murricane, who declined. Rebecca made a point of reaching for one, then waved an embarrassed Flaws away.

"Sorry. Just doing that feminist thing for the girls." She leant her chin on one hand. "So. What about you, Alexander."

"Zander. With a Z." The combination of gruff voice and sing-song Highland lilt, was, in Flaws's experience, quite effective with women of a certain type. Rebecca was the type, but she seemed impervious. He couldn't quite work out the relationship with Murricane. Professional, but with a personal element that could be simmering sexual tension or plain unhappiness with each other. "What about me?"

"Have you seen the monster?"

"Everybody's seen the monster. Every time they look in the mirror." All three of them laughed.

"Murricane showed me the monster today. I was quite impressed."

"Really?"

"Really."

*** *** ***

They had stopped in a lay-by just north of Foyers on the Wade military road that hugged the loch on its southern side.

"I think it was near here they found the so-called burning site. That body," said Murricane. "Davie the Druid's famous altar. The... thing we found in the loch."

"Want to go and look for it? The altar, that is."

Murricane said nothing. He opened the passenger door of the Subaru and climbed out, stretching in the clear loch light. Then he leaned back into the car.

"No. Get out now, though, and I'll show you the monster."

Rebecca stood next to him and together they gazed out on the loch's mildly rippling waters. A heat shimmer prevented them seeing the opposite shore clearly.

"It's rubbish," Rebecca said. "Isn't it?"

"Rubbish? It's a story. It's a story millions of people want to believe. Without it thousands around here probably wouldn't have work, wouldn't have money. There would still be tourists, but they wouldn't spend as much or stop as long. They wouldn't buy so much shite. It's a story that sells. And it sells because there's nothing solid to prove or disprove it. In that way it's just like a religion. No body in the empty tomb. No proof or disproof. Just faith. Just belief. Just tourism. Just money." He turned and looked at her. "That story of Percy's. That has solid stuff. Proof. Dead bodies. Money. Very bad people. That tomb was fucking occupied, wasn't it? That's why you took me there."

"And you've seen the other body. You pulled that... her out of the loch. You pulled what was left of Avril from the water. You don't need faith. You've got the physical proof. Rocks. I showed you the rocks."

"And what have we got? A religious group, run by, I don't know, some Hollywood haircut fucker who has a sunbed tan and an itchy dick? Something, a company called KokVan, owned apparently by a nasty billionaire, as if there were any other kind. Buying up land and houses around Foyers, and mines at Strontian, and who you and Percy say is funding Coldstream and his cretinous church of the fucking poison mind. Dead bodies and rocks. Dead geologists and rocks."

"Rocks beyond price. Beyond gold and platinum and anything you can think of. And here's the thing: there's only very small amounts of Varlindium at Strontian. But a weird seam of this most precious of stuff stretches from that hole in the ground along the Great Glen Fault to Foyers, getting bigger all the time. Under the loch there's a massive outcrop of the stuff. Basically just sitting there. Snap it off and take it home. We've done an electromagnetic survey, and it's a hundred per cent. It's not hard to scan for the most conductive metal in the world, you know. Once you know what you're looking for. Basic magnetic pulses will show it up. There's a near-surface throbbing vein of the stuff at Foyers, under the loch. KokVan – Vance – wants it. Even the tiniest amounts are worth millions. Coldstream and his Centre for Creationist Bullshit – it's a cover. This is a very sensitive area, after all. environmentally. Christ, it's got a monster!"

"And what's our own esteemed government's role in all this?"

"We want... need Varlindium. And it's on British soil. Scottish. All part of the still-just-barely-united Kingdom. The American Government, defence establishment, whatever, is in deep with KokVan. So much so that they can turn a blind eye to

Vance's little... personal issues. They even help him out with them occasionally. Gave him Jenks. Support the Global Redemptionistic nonsense, use Solidity With Service Security. Come on, that's always been the way. Think of Northern Ireland, MI5 filming boys in the Glencora children's home with local politicians. If there's an edge, leverage, a perversion provides it. Intelligence has always used that kind of illicit muscle, going right back to Roman times.

"And there's the monster."

"What? Yes it is monstrous, but you'd have to be naive to think..."

"No. I mean, there it is. The monster. Right... there." He extended his arm and pointed at a ripple on the loch's surface, offshore, it was difficult to tell how far. Something dark extended maybe a foot above the surface. "Quick, camera, telephoto, shoot it, motordrive, again, again, again!" Mockery in his voice. The object seemed to dip its head into the water, then surface again. How big was it? Rebecca felt a coldness catch in her lungs, quite different from the tension she'd felt and hidden so successfully, she thought, down the mineshaft

"But it's... it's... what is it? It moved, it's moving. Did it? Did it move?"

Murricane put one arm around her. "Yeah, it's moving because the water is moving. Do you have binoculars in the car? She shook her head. "Then make them with your fingers. Like this." As a child would, he made two cylinders with his fingers and held them to his eyes. After a second or two she did the same.

"It's a tree. It's a floating tree. Jesus, I can see the branches."

"That's right. It's a tree. It's a tree now." He sighed. "Let's get back in the car."

Inside the Subaru, Rebecca switched on the radio, but didn't fully turn the ignition key. The sound of the Canadian band Arcade Fire billowed out of the speakers, suffused with static and interference.

"Bad reception," she said.

"Two stories," Murricane said. "Two more to add to the bunch we already have floating around. First one, I'm in Iraq, specialist retrieval unit, chasing some poor hapless hostage, some fucker from a telecoms company I think. Never got him back. Small village. Deserted. We have intel that it's hostile. That there are active Al-Qaeda units in there. Numbskull fanatics, kill a Brit go to heaven, that sort of thing. Anyway it doesn't look right. Feels funny. Wrong. We're in two Land Rovers. Snatch vehicles. Crap. No proper armour, Nothing. Anyway, small square houses, you know the kind, low wall on a flat roof. And I catch a glimpse of something. Something, someone maybe crouched behind the wall." He paused. "We have a sniper team with us. Rifle, shooter, spotter. I have binos, proper ones, not finger ones. Look again. There's somebody there all right. Definitely moving. A head, I can see reflections. Glass. Spotter Scope. Sniper team, they can pick a fly off a moving turd at a mile or something, I don't know. OK, I say, little lump, someone's head, take it out. They set up on the bonnet of a Land Rover. Takes forever, or seems to. That little lump's still there. Bang. Not a pop, by the way, a bang. A really loud bang. The lump's not there anymore." Another pause. "I'm hungry. We can get a decent meal at the Dores Inn, before the planning meeting."

"I've got some crisps. Tyrrell's."

"Not the parsnip?"

"No, sea-salt and vinegar. Potato." She reached into the cramped back seat, rummaged in her backpack. Handed him the packet. He opened it noisily and began eating. "Open the door and let the crumbs drop outside, will you? I don't like getting food on the seats." He opened up and swung his legs outside, putting his feet on the ground. He looked ungainly, she thought. For the first time since they'd met, he looked crumpled and twisted and uncoordinated. He finished the crisps quickly, crumpled the packet up and was about to throw it away when he reconsidered, folded it and put it in a pocket of his jeans. Then he swivelled back inside and closed the car door.

A WHISKY IN MONSTERVILLE

"It was a child, of course. A boy of about 11. And he did have a rifle, and he did have a spotter scope. But it was still a child." He looked in front of him, at the lay-by, the trees, the loch. "So I called it right. The right story. But the wrong story. The wrong fucking context. The story that boy had been told was powerful enough and big enough to convince him to do the bidding of a bunch of bastards with a hotline to their notion of God. That was his story. But mine was the right one and it killed him."

"And maybe saved your life. Others too."

"Maybe. Anyway, that's just one story. Here's the other. Every year, just prior to the main tourist season, someone sees the Loch Ness Monster. A local. It's become a joke. It might not even be a deliberate hoax. It's like, people need to see this, need to have that blurred image, that story to tell the new batch of tourists. Front page of the *Inverness Courier*, yet another ripple or wake or silhouette of a tree stump, a log. This year, about May, there's a fantastic picture of the monster. Local boatman claims to have snapped it. It gets checked out. No Photoshop, no fakery. Get this: he took it on a film camera, he says. Left the film lying about, and it was only when he developed it he saw this image. This... thing. People are saying, bloody hell, this is the most convincing photo since God knows when." He shook his head and smiled. "No wonder. He'd snapped it three years ago when a film crew was shooting some low budget horror flick, and they had a specially-made fibreglass monster which he was towing in his boat. He'd actually been hired by the film crew to tow this thing, this specially made dinosaur model, or the fins off its back. He just took a careful shot from a distance, odd angle, you couldn't tell what the object was properly. So there was doubt, there was uncertainty. There was a degree of faith needed. But unfortunately for him, someone still had the fibreglass monster, stored away, and they matched it up. Anything to drink?"

She reached into her bag and got him a bottle of mineral water. He unscrewed the cap and drank.

"And the moral of both stories is this: sometimes things aren't what they seem. And sometimes they're worse. But every story has an effect, whether it's true or false."

"Did the tourists still come? Even though the story wasn't true?"

"They come for the story, not the truth. That's what I've been trying to tell you."

She started the car in a guttural flurry of revs, the flat-four Subaru engine sounding like a Harley-Davidson motorbike, then settling to a low growl.

"Don't spill your water," she said.

*** *** ***

"So the monster thing," Rebecca said. They were taking the fuzziness off the beer and whisky with espresso now. There was still half an hour before they had to leave for the hall, although the bar and the tables outside it were beginning to empty.

"What do you mean, 'so'?" Flaws had stirred three sugars into his coffee and let it cool. Now he knocked it back in one, feeling the caffeine and glucose hit. "It's money, it's history, it's delusion, myth. It's you and me. It's the human soul reflected off the waters of the loch."

"Oh, poetic! Religion, in other words." Rebecca sounded angry. "And now we have Nessatoreans climbing on the bandwagon, trying to turn it into the bedrock, sorry, of belief. You have a surviving plesiosaur, you have no evolution, you have God created the earth in six days, you have an earth that's 6,000 years old, or something."

"Look," said Murricane. "Here's the potted history: 565 AD, Columba apparently drives away a 'water monster' who was pursuing one of his disciples, looking for an early lunch. Sea serpents, water monsters, kelpies – big part of all seafaring and lake cultures. Spooky thing that lives in the deeps, right? Nothing much from Columba on until tourism hits the Highlands. Get that? Tourism. Victorians, fishing, deer stalking. Pissed, probably, or off their heads on laudanum and too much tea. There are monsters everywhere – Loch Arkaig, Loch Morar – and the Duke of Portland gets all excited about 'a horrible great beastie in Loch Ness'. Doesn't see it himself, of course. Drunk ghillies tell him about it. Am I going too fast?" Rebecca shook her head.

"Don't forget the first hoax." Flaws wagged a finger. "Deception and tourism: those two frauds walk hand in hand."

"That would be 1868. Someone skinned a dolphin and threw it into the loch. Nice. Much excitement. A scared ghillie again in 1916, but there were a lot of old and scared people about then, their sons all gone away. Wars'll do that. A few folk start saying they've seen prehistoric monsters, dinosaurs, mainly because lots of them had read Arthur Conan Doyle's *The Lost World* or seen pictures of artists' models. Fossil record is coming into its own now, you see. Big date, 1933, new road along the north shore of Loch Ness, and from then on lots and lots of sightings. Some more convincing than others. Most of them talk about something like a whale or a big fish, though."

"So, what about the dinosaur stuff?"

"Starts to get help from big hoaxes. Weatherall in 1933, a hippo ashtray used to make fake footprints. Surgeon's Photograph, 1934 – that's the one everybody's seen, the one that Coldstream probably has tattooed across his heart. Do you know how long it took them to disprove that? The long neck out of the water? Sixty years. And everyone involved knew it was a fake from the start. Sixty years and still you'll find folk who say it's the real thing. Who'll base religions on it. That's how much folk want to believe in Nessie."

"And what about the locals? I've heard there are folk who just won't talk about it?"

"Unlike Murricane," said Flaws. "Who loves to talk. It's an Official Secrets Act thing. Anything that isn't covered, he can't stop yapping."

"Folk who won't talk about it now. You mean Father Gregory of Fort Augustus Abbey, when it was an abbey and not millionaire apartments? And his like? Most of them saw shapes. Big fish. Something. Like I showed you this afternoon. The loch can get to you, spook you. I met a journalist once, established, sober, relatively, local corr for a daily newspaper. He said that he drove the loch road, the A82, dozens of times every year, hundreds. And he lived in terror of seeing the monster. Because it would either destroy his reputation or mean he wouldn't be able to think about anything else. See that?" He pointed to a van parked near the pub, one that seemed to have taken root, and was surrounded by the signs of being a permanent fixture – tables, a small garden, decking. A steel chimney was silhouetted against the indigo sky.

"Cy's van," said Flaws. "Good guy."

"Yeah," said Murricane. "Twenty years Cy's been here. Waiting and watching. Clever guy, loves it here, part of the community. Makes models of the Beastie and sells them. Runs a website. Scourge of hoaxers, but he's a believer. He believes there's something here."

"Wait a minute." Rebecca was frowning. "TV. He made a TV film, years ago."

"That's him," said Murricane. "It was about coming here. Childhood obsession, all that. But he's probably done more for the monster's credibility than anyone, because he won't let any of the locals away with their wee scams, their attempts to keep the tourists goggle-eyed. He takes it very seriously. Very seriously indeed. And do you know how many times he's seen Nessie? Even something that he'd consider a credible, unexplained sighting?"

Silence.

"Never. Not once in 20 years. And then you've got folk like Professor Analine De Montfort, the man, probably the best on the whole subject, certainly he'll think so. He runs a department, a whole department at the University of the Highlands and Islands: 'Suppositional Cryptozoology'. Funding? No bother. It's sexy as hell. And he's got explanations. Most sightings can be explained as boats or their wakes, mirages, wind on the water, birds, rocks, logs or swimming deer. Or maybe a sturgeon. I like that idea. One sturgeon living for 150 years would explain most modern Beastie encounters. Maybe. But the funding comes from people's desire to believe. So he always inserts a little bit of mystery. A little bit of voodoo dust."

"God." Rebecca drained the last of her coffee. "You love this stuff, don't you? Come on, we better pay. And go."

"I paid when I ordered the coffees," said Flaws. "Police pension, don't worry about it." They got up to leave and he leaned close enough to Rebecca to whisper. "He believes in it, too, you know. It's what keeps him going, I think. He'd never say it was a religion. But it is. Theology."

"Sure," said Rebecca. "We're all Nessatoreans now."

Arrival

Strawberry tart with aerosol whipped cream. Floor polish and oak and white chocolate. Caramel and smoke to finish.

THE NOTCH, NANTUCKET ISLAND SINGLE MALT

A WHISKY IN MONSTERVILLE

When Cochrane Vance eventually arrived at Creag Dhearg, he was three hours later than expected and in a camper van. Jenks was driving, a dreamy, twisted grin on his face. In fact it was something a little more substantial than a camper van, Coldstream had to admit. Considerably more impressive than even the most extreme Winnebago he remembered from the likes of Daytona Beach or Burning Man, the great fleets of grizzled snow-birds gathering along the sunshine coasts, the cashed-in moneyed hippies dragging their unfortunate families towards some acid flashback tarmac nirvana. Why didn't they admit they were searching for God, his God, and park up near one of the outposts of the Sanctified Truth Baptist Church of the Christ Child in History? There was always free parking.

Vance emerged from the rear of the vehicle, which was British registered, the size of a rock band's tour bus and bristling with antennae. As soon as it came to a hissing, air-braked rest, and settled on its haunches like some crouching beast, motors began whining and dishes reared from their housings, searching the skies for celestial connection.

"Hey, Coldstream," Vance, stooped, six four, maybe five, sported a honed, expensive gym thinness and was paper white. No Californian tan, no sunlamp orangeness. He had an obsessive fear of getting skin cancer, he had once confided. But God could heal that, surely?

The obsession or the cancer, Coldstream had replied. Obviously, The Lord could heal both, but it was the particular direction of the prayer, psychological or kinetically physical healing, that had to be ascertained.

"Hey, God should be able to suss that out, man," Vance had said, fixing Coldstream with his piercing, but curiously blank gaze. "I mean, if he or she is really God, right?"

"Yes, but God works through his servants and through the requests of his children. There has to be an identification of need."

"Fuck that, man. I need God to be working in the background, like a program, like a virus, man, sniffing out the bad stuff, sorting it out. Can you manage that for me? Get God on my side?"

And Coldstream had said, in his most assured voice, that of course he could. That God was speaking to him, was enabling him. Giving a real discernment into Vance's problems. Issues. And after he'd supplied Vance with a few godly extras from his flock of willing adherents – Vance's tastes, at least initially, ran to a kind of ritual submission with religious overtones that had its roots, Coldstream thought, in his Pentecostal upbringing – they established quite a mutually supportive relationship. Sealed, of course, by the Loch Ness Monster. By Nessatoreanism. God had truly worked a miracle. Though as ever with miracles, there were snags. Like Jenks.

"Hey Coldstream, come and take a look inside the KokVanmobile. KokVanmobile numero seven, in fact. Got others in Canada, France, Italy, Germany and two in the US. Controlled environments for me and my little boxes, fine petite kitchen for me to cook my own grits in, exercise materials, pollen-free bed to my exact specifications... clinical standard air conditioning... I got my own environment wherever in the world I have to be!"

Coldstream advanced towards the spectral figure, extending a hand. As usual, Vance was wearing surgical gloves. They shook, the thin film of talcum on the rubber gloves feeling almost slimy. He peered inside the motorhome. The interior was part electronics lab, part hospital ward. There was, he noted quickly, a draped-off area presumably hiding the bed and various... accoutrements. He sighed. Who was left among the sisterhood in residence at Creag Dhearg, able, or persuadable, to meet Vance's stringent tastes? He would have to have a word with Melliflua, and see who was available. Who was most willing. Though they should all be willing, given what was at stake. They'd been chosen for their usefulness, their amenability, their capacity to provide pleasure, for himself and of course for Vance. They would surely and cheerfully accommodate most of what Vance wanted. It depended on what they'd heard, the stories. Some of his tastes were a little too extreme for comfort. That was why he and Jenks were close.

"Got my testing gear here, latest stuff. All kinds of connections to the labs and my infrastructure back in Cali. And it's clean, man. Stocked with all the food I like, all the good stuff. All that God can provide, I provide for me. God works that way, man, ain't that what you told me? Ain't that the truth, the *sanctified* truth? The gospel truth?"

"God works through our own wills, absolutely, Cochrane."

"Yeah, and my will works through Mr Jenks over there. He's my *extended* will! I hear he's been doing my will and God's will and your will all at the same time, and his own too. God, I love to see that boy work." Jenks appeared, wearing that same strange grin, and found himself enfolded in what passed, with Vance, for an embrace: a light, distant touch by two gloved hands.

"Damn, it's good to see you, Cairnduff!"

"Cairnduff?" All this time and Coldstream hadn't even thought to ask if Jenks had a first name. And what a name it was.

"Cairnduff," said Jenks, in that irritating low growl. "From my mother's side. Scottish. Why I was glad to come here. Part of the reason."

"Cairnduff Jenks. My man," said Vance fondly. "Now, Coldstream, you gonna show me what you got, and I'll tell you what I got in mind. What I got coming. How I got it coming! Show and tell, show and tell. And this is gonna blow your mind! A truly divine entrance! Signs and wonders! This is God at work in a big, big way! Will power, it's now or never! Grandiloquence! That's what we got here. Heading here. Grand. Ill. Oh. Quince!"

*** *** ***

The hall was more than packed, rumbling with conversation, humid and heavy with the skin-sweat of second-hand cigarette smoke, perfume, aftershave, soap and the lack of it. There were no seats left, so Murricane, Flaws and Rebecca squeezed in next to an upended pool table. Murricane ran his fingers over the green baize. It was damp and warm. Squashed flat against the rear wall next to them was a display bearing detailed drawings and computerised impressions of the proposed centre, along with photographs of the locations affected. The images of what the centre might look like were beautifully printed Cibachromes, glistening and alive with colour and promise. The location shots looked like someone had snapped them on an old Nokia. They were drab. They made Loch Ness look like a dull puddle surrounded by tedious trees.

Over a bobbing carpet of heads, bald, hairy, hatted and coloured all shades from grey to lurid vegetable pink, the platform party was visible, and nervous. A planning official and his convener, a well-known local slaughterhouse and meat processing factory owner who had retired to politics, sat facing the crowd, two flimsy card tables in front of them. The rest of the planning committee were in the front two rows of the audience. Two uniformed policemen, one of them Seoras Mactaggart, were positioned on either side of the stage. Trouble, of worse than the verbal variety, was clearly expected.

"They've been advertising. Offering the chance for objectors and supporters to speak," Flaws murmured in Murricane's ear. "Strictly limited to five minutes each, had to sign up on line. Take it you haven't?"

"Sure," Murricane replied. "Great idea. What would I be, objector or supporter?"

"I don't know. Whichever would cause most trouble, I expect." Flaws grinned. "Too late now. Maximum of 15 on each side. Bet there's far fewer supporters, though. And I bet they've fiddled the ones who actually get to speak. Ach well. Here we go."

The convener, a large florid man with a white goatee beard he probably thought made him youthful and attractive, in a Colonel Sanders sort of way, rose to his feet. There were three or four photographers crouched on the floor below him, and there was a flurry of electronic flashes. TV lights suddenly flooded the front of the hall. There were two video cameras on tripods, both apparently operated by teenagers. Another crouched figure held a large furry, tubular object, either a microphone or some sort of dead animal.

A WHISKY IN MONSTERVILLE

First the convener tapped the ancient PA microphone, producing a crackling boom from the hall's sound system. Then he blew into it, making a sound like ripping cardboard.

"One-two," he said. "One-two-three-four." There was a howl of feedback, "Is this working?"

"Naw," shouted someone with a strong Glasgow accent, "An' neither am I! Gie's a job! Ah want tae be a monster maaan!"

There was a roar of laughter, interrupted by the amplified clearing of the councillor's throat.

"Right then. Good evening, ladies and gentlemen, and thank you for coming. My name is James Macindoe, planning convener at the Highland Council, but I prefer Jimmy. Call me Jimmy. Anyway, we, myself and my committee colleagues, are here to, ah, hear you, to listen to your views on what is clearly a very important application, one which could have major implications, an application with implications. A major impact indeed on not just the immediate area of Foyers and the southern shores of Loch Ness, but on the entire Highlands of Scotland and indeed Scotland itself. Let us be clear about the importance of what we are engaged in. It is an application with impactful implications."

"Sounds like you've already decided, eh?" An Invernessian voice. "What's good for the butcher's good for the Highlands, eh? Meat is murder!"

Councillor Macindoe flinched as the crowd, or a large part of it, rustled and muttered like a forest in a gust of wind.

"Ladies... ladies and gents, please. We wish to listen to you, to hear you, but we need order in the way things are presented. Heckling... interruptions... intemperate and personal attacks... we cannot have that and the meeting will be adjourned, at my advisement, should things move in that, err... direction. Please. Let me ask Mr Smithwick here to continue."

The official glanced to the side of the platform, provoking a young woman in a wholly inappropriate but status-significant pinstripe business suit to rush towards him, a clipboard held firmly in one hand. He waved her away and stood up. He was small, trim, and disguising what looked like a small pot belly behind a Harris

Tweed waistcoat with a watch chain. Vain, thought Murricane, and pompous. What you kind of expected.

"Good evening. I am Ian Smithwick, the council's depute interim director of tourist infrastructure planning, a mere, ah, servant of the councillors. It is my responsibility to see that this meeting runs smoothly and to that end I wish to outline what we foresee happening tonight. You will have had a chance to view the display, I hope, now alas somewhat, ah, sidelined, or backlined, at the, ah, back of the hall. And in any case full publicity has officially – and unofficially – been given to what is proposed." He glanced at his own clipboard. "Which is, under Section 456 of the Town and Country Planning Act, Scotland, the erection of an educational, recreational and tourism development at various locations around Foyers and the south side of Loch Ness, as stipulated in the detailed drawing submitted by the applicant, Creation Science Developments Ltd, of Creag Dhearg House.

"We have the applicant, or the applicant's representative, or... ah yes, I see from my notes we will hear from the applicants themselves, who are, or soon will be here and will speak to the project, for it. So to speak. And several, ah, in fact five supporters wish to back their case, support their case as well. Also, we have 15 objectors and a waiting list should they not take up the full allotted time allowed." He glanced at his watch. "It is 8.00pm now, and we have the hall until 9.30pm." There was a clamour of disapproval.

"That whole 15 won't be heard, and you know that fine well." A local voice. "This is just a nonsense. A nonsense!"

"I am informed," said Smithwick, "that there is a legal obligation for all advisory meetings under the Town and Country Planning Act to finish by 9.30pm in order to provide for the potential fatigue of working people who are attending."

"And those that are nae working!" That same Glaswegian voice. Smithwick frowned. His attention was caught by movement at the door of the hall, which was to the left of where Murricane, Flaws and Rebecca were leaning. "Ah, Mr Coldstream. Reverend Coldstream, I should say. May I ask you to come to the lectern to my left and make your ah, submission?"

Coldstream was wearing white jeans and a white fleece over a button-down shirt and plain tie. It was clearly some kind of uniform, as he was followed by two other figures wearing the same outfit. One was immensely tall, stooped, thin but moving with a kind of bouncing energy that indicated general fitness. The other was shorter, heavily built, squat and had a shaved head. Murricane caught his eye as he entered the hall, and there was a flash of recognition on both sides.

"Jesus Christ," said Murricane, louder than he meant to. "Fucking hell, that's..."

"Your friend and mine," said Flaws, "the slightly Reverend Coldstream, and I think his partner in holiness and property development, not to mention monster theology and much more, the legendary Vance. And some form of bodyguard, I shouldn't wonder."

"No, you shouldn't. That's someone who knows about bodies. Definitely."

Rebecca leaned across Flaws and poked Murricane on the shoulder with an extended finger. It was surprisingly painful. But when he looked across at her she was gazing at the figures standing behind the lectern. He felt confused, angry. And yet unsurprised. Jenks and he were both part of this. Had always been part of it. He wondered just how much of his escape to Loch Ness had been controlled, manipulated, directed. Fuckers.

Coldstream, the consummate performer, the diviner of crowds' needs and desires, the saver of souls, was first to the microphone. He smiled, a beaming, televisual grin full of beautiful American teeth that caught the flashguns of the assembled press with their plastic glory.

"Convener. Councillors. Ladies and gentlemen, Her Majesty's press and anyone else I've missed! What a privilege it is to be here among you, to share with you my... our vision for the future, the glowing, the bright and economically buoyant future of Loch Ness-side." He grasped the edges of the lectern and slowly moved his gaze from side to side, to the back of the hall. It was like being licked by a giant slobbering St Bernard, Murricane thought. Nice but also disgusting.

"I know that some of you regard our presence here, the presence of the church, as an imposition. I'm sure you think of us as weirdos and me as the weirdo in chief!" There was a rustle of hesitant laughter. "Well, you know, if it's weird to want to provide maybe three dozen jobs – well-paid, secure jobs – if it's weird to want to attract thousands, tens of thousands of high-value tourists to the area... if it's weird to want to be part of this glorious, welcoming community, then, I have to say, meet the weirdo! Because he's here! I am that man!" This time the laughter was immediate, and warm. There was a smattering of applause, some shuffling, then a mild stamping of feet. That Glaswegian voice again.

"Jobs, big man. Ah don't care if it's a weird job, long as ma national insurance gets paid!"

"I think we can guarantee that we will meet all our necessary official requirements, financially and fiscally," said Coldstream. "Now, there have been some tragic and grisly developments, some genuinely sad things have happened over the past few weeks. We have lost people. And the constabulary," – he nodded to the uniformed policemen at either side of the small stage; Seoras remaining impassive, gazing, ear-pieced at the audience. Looking for someone, Murricane thought, in particular – "the constabulary have been indefatigable in searching for the culprits. And I have to tell you, that myself and my faithful, and my partners in the endeavour, we had our faith shaken. I am not ashamed to admit that. We feared. We felt the need to ask the Lord if we were in the right place, doing the right thing. To be frank, we doubted." He was interrupted by an amplified cough, Smithwick leaning into the microphone, their lips almost touching.

"Please, Mr Coldstream. This is an official planning meeting for consultation. You are restricted timeously and in content. I would ask you not to proselytise."

"I do apologise, Mr, ah... Mr... Smith. Smith...Wick. I do not have much more to say. The plans are there. The economic impact assessment has been carried out. We can provide jobs and our visitors will bring goodwill and money. And we bring an offer of forgiveness. No matter who may have been responsible for trying to scare us away. I am here to say we will not be. Now, I would like, if possible to introduce…"

"Only if you are introducing another certified witness to the committee, one who has been agreed aforehand," intoned Smithwick.

"Indeed. His name has been submitted. He has come from America to be here and his is a name that will be familiar to some of you. Ladies and gentlemen, councillors, the legendary figure behind the mighty concern known worldwide as KokVan, Mr Cochrane Vance!"

The tall figure loped onto the stage and approached the lectern. He and Coldstream exchanged artificially whitened grins but did not shake hands. Those closest might have noticed the now flesh-coloured surgical gloves Vance was wearing, but they were easy to miss. There was a stutter of flashguns, and then a high American voice. Murricane couldn't take his eyes off the squat, uniformed figure that now stood below Vance, arms folded, brutal and brick-like. Some kind of thuggish avatar. Jenks.

"Welcome, Mr Vance," said Smithwick. "You are recognised to speak."

"I am recognised! Why thank you."

Murricane dragged his gaze away from Jenks. There was a wolfish appearance to Vance. Murricane could see not just the avarice but a real physical threat. He looked hungry. Consumed by hunger. Rebecca was whispering in his ear, tugging at his arm. "He's a predator. Not just in business either. He's a predator and a collector."

"I am here to stand in solidarity with my friend and my brother Coldstream. I am here to pledge my allegiance to this cause and to say that no attack, no attempt to intimidate will succeed. No, sir. And I pray that you will reward our commitment with your support."

"How can we know if you are truly of The Lord?" An Invernessian voice, from the middle of the hall. With a shock, Murricane noticed McGlone, the would-be blackmailer of the Ness Islands. It was turning into a real gathering of religious oddities.

Vance leaned close into the microphone so that when he spoke it was in a booming, hugely loud whisper.

"All I can say is this: in three days, look to the skies. Look to the skies and you will see signs and wonders. You will believe. All will believe."

"Enough, Mr Vance, Enough," said Smithwick. "I believe we must progress the meeting more speedily. Next witness."

After that it was predictable tedium, for the most part. Local business folk liked Nessieville. Or Monsterville. Coldstream seemed to use the terms interchangeably. Local residents who worked in local businesses supported the plan. Those who had moved to Loch Ness from elsewhere – white settlers, some called them – were opposed. Davie the Druid's much-vaunted coalition of opposition seemed disparate and bedraggled. Among them were environmentalists who claimed that the almost undeveloped south side of the loch would be forever besmirched. Notwithstanding the massive bauxite processing and power station developments of the past and present, thought Murricane. There were neatly turned out retirees, commuters to Inverness, and hippie throwbacks or their descendants.

And then from nowhere, came Davie the Druid.

It was like magic. Voodoo. Druidism. If there had been a puff of smoke, Murricane wouldn't have been surprised. Especially if it smelt pungently of prime Black Isle weed. As it was, all that happened was that the outside door to the packed hall opened, and there he was, dressed in his usual army surplus, dreadlocked hair instantly identifiable, a wireless microphone matching the ones at the front of the hall in his hand. Nice move, thought Murricane.

At the lectern was the constantly-interrupting Glaswegian, now revealed, oddly, as a rotund and red-faced man in Pringle golf sweater and neatly-pressed chinos.

"Davie!" he cried, on seeing the figure. Coldstream and Vance had managed to obtain seats from somewhere, and were perched just behind the internally opening door, Jenks, standing, was blindsided behind it.

"I'm here to tell you, it wisnae me," said Davie, speaking slowly, his voice electronically loud and deliberate, dominant. Every head in the room was turned in his direction, or trying to. "It wisnae me, and you shouldnae believe these bastards. The old gods'll hae their justice! The old gods'll hae their justice!" And with that he threw the microphone at the platform party, all of whom ducked as if they were facing a grenade attack, and was gone. Seoras and his beleaguered colleague were trying to fight their way through towards the door in pursuit, but were making heavy weather of it. Most of the crowd were on their feet and at least some were jostling and attempting to trip the two cops. Murricane glimpsed Peyronie, grim-faced, arms folded, watching from among the platform party. Trapped by council officialdom. Coldstream, Vance and Jenks were wrestling with the open door which blocked their way out, trying to push their way around it. There was a loud swell of conversation, and above it came Coldstream's voice. "That man is a murderer. Arrest the pagan! Arrest the satanist pagan!"

"Arrest the pagan! Arrest the satanist!" An Invernessian voice, one Murricane recognised. The bastard from the Ness Islands. McGlone. Malachi McGlone. And then the lights went out.

Chaos reigned for about ten minutes, with Smithwick pleading for calm, his voice reedy without the PA, hoarsening quickly.

"Stay still," said Flaws, "and hold hands." Chairs were falling, there were shouts and a few screams. The crowd was shifting and moving like an uneasy sea. "This could get ugly."

"Get ugly?" Rebecca's voice. "Somebody could get killed."

"Several people already have," said Murricane. And then the lights came back on, amid a huge thump from the PA amplifier and a howl of feedback.

"This meeting is adjourned," came Smithwick's voice, rasping thinly like Tiny Tim on a Tom Waits bender. "This meeting is hereby... adjourned."

"To the pub, I think," said Flaws.

"Yes," said Rebecca. "Follow that pagan, quick!"

"Be great if Davie was at the Dores Inn, just waiting, a pint in hand, wouldn't it?" Murricane laughed. "Well. Let's go and see. And then we'll wait three days and look at the sky for a bit."

"Three days," said Flaws. "A lot can happen in three days, religiously speaking. There's a precedent."

Rest and Recreation

Ripe bananas. Fruit salad – mangos and pineapples, with melon and some kiwi fruit, plus ginger beer, liquorice, lemon and pepper.

BUSHMILLS BLACK BUSH

A WHISKY IN MONSTERVILLE

The squirrel moved like some kind of stop-motion animation, and it was a pale, lovely red, almost a pinky brown, with a white blaze on its chest. It made Jenks's heart accelerate with pleasure, looking at it. Thinking what he would do with it. Those tufty ears. It's hands, claws, paws, like a baby's. A human baby.

Next to him, he felt a twitch, a rustle. Excitement. Vance's long, thin body, like his own, was encased in camouflage gear and half-buried in dried pine needles. He even had on a pair of khaki-green surgical gloves and a camouflaged gauze mouth-mask. Apparently custom made. He felt a moment of annoyance at this strange creature, but it passed instantly. He owed Vance a great deal. He'd given him a job when the military – reluctantly, they'd claimed – gave him an honourable discharge and a pension that wouldn't have bought him a bed in some downtown LA hobo hostel. Vance had sought him out. Heard about him, he said. Checked him out. Mutual advantages.

It turned out – or clearly, Vance had discovered – that they'd been members of the same internet forums, deep, darknet stuff with titles like *Personal Memento* and *Souvenirs To Savour*. Their tastes matched. Jenks was in a position to help Vance assuage his needs. *Asssuuajje*. Ass-wage. Funny. Vance had taught him that word.

And being on the payroll. Solidity With Service, one or two jobs there, then to KokVan itself as security consultant. That trip back to Afghanistan had been an emergency, a dire emergency Vance had said. Retrieval and removal. Another arm of his business empire, and one of the most profitable. 'The organics division,' Vance called it. The Global Repentance and Redemption Trust. Smack Team, a few brave insiders joked. Except it had gone badly wrong at the end. Brits. They should never have been involved, but as with so much in the Big A, co-operation between the allies involved was shit. It all fell to bits, panic set in among The Powers That Weren't. And some kind of half-assed cover-up began. Yeah, he could see why they'd want to, protecting themselves, protect Vance, their deals with KokVan. But it meant he'd never been able to get in and finish the job properly there, take the English bastards out, the only two left. One of them had got lucky. Leave the scene clean. Vance had said it didn't matter, in the end. They'd got the heroin out, re-established the route of supply. All the technology stocks in the world didn't count for nothing compared to what you could get, the power you could wield, with raw materials, Vance said. Vance said. *Vance* said...And then, down that mine here in Scotland, there he was, one of them. Small country. Coincidence? Huh. He'd taken that lucky bastard Brit out. A souvenir to prove it, too. Just the one. Just the one left.

Vance said: "It's all about materials. Source, transport, process. Supply. Profit, profit, profit. Everything else flows from that." And so it had proved. And here they were.

He'd heard that Vance had started as some technogeek small-town drug dealer in Omaha or somesuch, then realised that he could move up and along the supply chain bit by bit, until he had everything under his control. Oil. Oil extraction gear. Digital. Drugs. And now rocks. Everything falling into his lap. Governments at his beck and call.

Now Vance was whispering in his ear. They were both using Leitz field glasses, electronically stabilised, the best of the best. Like certain weapons, they made him feel at ease, a kind of pleasured lassitude, when he touched them. Things that did exactly what they were supposed to. He lowered the binoculars carefully.

"Hey Cairnduff," too loud. He put a finger to his lips, gave the minutest shake of the head. Vance was gazing at him, eyes brimming with excitement. "Hey, Cairnduff." Quieter. "Good call. Can we? Can we?" The guy was like a child. Jenks felt a certain warmth in his gut, a sense of fatherhood and almost, well, love for this strange elongated creature to whom he owed so much. He nodded, once.

The Daystate Ranger .22 air rifle was beside him. He'd carefully camouflaged it to match his own clothing, smearing the Beamshot laser sight with black and green face paints. Now he rested the gun carefully on a piece of rotten log he'd positioned earlier, focussing in on the jerking, near-epileptic head of the squirrel.

Sciurus vulgaris, it was called in Latin. Rare, these days, or getting rarer everywhere but here, in the Highlands. They were saying that Loch Ness and the surrounding woodlands would one day be more famous as a place to come and see the red squirrel than the monster, the so-called monster. Nessie. He had no illusions about Vance's so-called belief in it. Vance believed in money. He believed in God only if he thought there was a usefulness there, if God would do something for him. Heal his imaginary heart disease, maybe, his allergies, provide a cure for cancer. But in the end it was money. Money would cure his ailments, real or fake. Some clinic in Switzerland, that place where they supposedly exchanged all of Keith Richards' bodily fluids, pumped him dry, filled him up again, living embalming. How else could you explain the fact that the Rolling Stones were still going, that Keith was still alive, at least officially?

Jenks had loaded the Daystate with stainless steel feathered darts. He wanted as clean a kill as he could, and the power of this rifle over – what was it, maybe 20 yards – was such that the animal should be left intact if he hit at just the right point. Which in this case was the neck, just below that lovely head. He wanted the head as it was. Half rodent, half teddy bear. Lovely. something to keep and treasure. Steady. Breathe in. The squirrel froze, as if it knew, sensed something was about to happen. He fired.

*** *** ***

They cooked the squirrel meat, the saddle, using a little MSR Pocket Rocket stove, crouched outside the Ice House. Vance had been anxious, almost petulant in his desire to see inside, but Jenks had made him wait while he carefully removed the squirrel's head, paws and tail, then skinned, gutted and filleted it. He fried the saddle meat, two small thin steaks, in butter, added some fennel and wild garlic from the forest. It tasted good. It tasted like the forest did, gamy and smoky and earthy. Better than grey squirrel. Where was the fun in killing those? They were an invasive species and there was even a bounty on the things. This was like eating lion, or Zebra or something magical and potent from Africa. Vance had his eyes shut, and chewed like a gourmand, slowly, occasionally licking his lips. Jenks could smell the rubber from his gloves.

"Hey, we could have done with something to drink with this, Cairnduff Jenks, my man. Maybe some Chateau Musar from Lebanon. How cool would that be? Squirrel and Lebanese war-wine? Seems kinda, I don't know, appropriate? And Biblical! Though I think it was cedars that came from Lebanon. Jesus's wine was probably Palestinian." He opened his eyes. "Do they make wine in Afghanistan? "

"Islam," said Jenks. "Not big on wine."

"But hey, Lebanon, that's Islamic Muslims too, ain't it?"

"Not all of it. That was kinda the point about Lebanon, boss. Why they fought. Christians against Muslims thing. Afghanistan's a whole different kettle of dust. Hey, come on. You're foolin' with me."

"Yeah, they just do the hard drugs there, man, don't they? But then, you know about that. You were there."

"I was there on your behalf, sir."

"Not entirely successfully, Cairnduff. Not entirely successfully. Shit, this squirrel sure is good. Any more? No? Ah well."

"We retrieved your, ah, supplies, sir. In Afghanistan. Production and lines of distribution secured. Can I ask, is there some reason you're bringing this up now? Because I have to say sir, at that goddamned meeting, that planning meeting where you announced the second coming of Christ, I saw a face I kinda knew. From that fucked up time in Afghanistan. Someone I never thought I'd see again. And not here, not in the godless mosquito infested jungle of Scotchland. Not when I'd just dealt with another member of his fucking team, down that fucking mine. I got a good memory for faces. I like to remember faces. Never know when you see one you want to... keep. And your words, sir? 'He's just freelance security, Cairnduff, just like you, hired help'. Now this guy turns up. Seems like too much of a coincidence. More freelance security? More hired help?" All of this was said in his usual monotone.

"Well, now. Well then, there now. You been thinkin', Cairnduff! You know I warned you about that! What did you imagine, you were going to be allowed to cut a swathe through the geologists and half-assed spooks of the United Kingdom without anyone asking a few questions, my friend? Without running across some faces from your past? As it happens, I have a few connections in the, uh, how can I put this, the commercially aware sections of Britain's defence establishment. Ones who wouldn't mind making some kind of deal with me once we've managed to get our hands on the good old rocks of the Highlands. Highland rock, man! Loch Ness *rawks*!" He laughed, a rasping giggle that shook his frame.

"And yes, as it happens, your companion in arms from Talibanland is in the vicinity and I'd guess he's in play. More involved than you can imagine or I would like. Seems he was on the boat that picked that... poor unfortunate burns victim out of the lake here, and then managed to get himself photographed by about 200 Japanese tourists who just happened to be passing. Hey, this place! World attraction! Like Bigfoot with fins! Some of my contacts have his facial data on a recognition software package, and bang, up he pops. Name, rank serial number. Murricane. Marine captain, retired. Ties in with all that activity over in the mines at Strontian, Strontium, whatever. Trespassers and spies will be dealt with by my man Cairnduff. And they sure were. A warning shot to these Brit bastards. Leave me and my Godly boys and girls alone! But they don't appear to be listenin'."

Jenks slowly shook his head.

"Anyways, your paths have nearly crossed a few times already. Captain Murricane's a piece of work, though he's something of a... how can I put this? A lost soul these days. Demon drink's got its hooks in him. I have a few sad details. He has companions, too. Maybe more than one. I expect you'll enjoy dealing with them. But remember..." Vance stood, straightened his bent spine, and was suddenly an authoritative figure. In control. "Remember, there are allowances being made for the sake of my connections. My potential, beneficial associations. Allowances for you. for what you may have to do. Murricane's linked to a kinda semi-official intel agency my Brit contacts wouldn't mind seeing... disappear. So we got some kind of cover. But the gap, the period of opportunity is shrinking, and you need to be circumspect, my friend. A little more circumspect. If people gonna disappear, from now on they need to disappear. Of course, one or two, what shall we say, remembrances, souvenirs are of no great import, if you catch my drift. Between you and me and the Ice House."

Jenks said nothing. The man talked. Oh how he talked. It was the usual intelligence multi-agency fuck-up. Murricane was being played, Vance was probably being played. Well. He'd chosen his side. He wiped the pans and field plates with leaves, gathered the head, paws and tail of the squirrel in a ZipLoc bag and said:

"Shall we?" He gestured at the closed door of the ice house. He thought for a moment Vance was going to soil himself.

"Oh, man. Oh Lord. Oh yes."

Crown

A golden Highland malt with an initial peppery aroma leading to a full, mature mouthfeel. Rich and sweet, with a spicy, dry finish.

MILLBURN 35-YEAR-OLD, RARE MALTS SERIES

A WHISKY IN MONSTERVILLE

Flaws lived in a tall, narrow terraced house on Ardconnel Street, part of the escarpment that gave Crown, Inverness's most desirable residential area, its name. Ardconnel Street and the adjoining Ardconnel Terrace looped around the cliff-like walls of Porterfield Prison, one of Scotland's toughest and most secure jails. Flaws loved the way houses seemed to huddle into the jail, like a shanty town around some medieval keep. There were big houses, and tiny cottages, one-room affairs that had become unexpectedly trendy. His side of Ardconnel Street was somehow separate from the prison, teetering on the very edge of a steep slope down into the very centre of the city. There were four floors, with the basement a self-contained flat rented out to a French couple who ran an artisan bakery in Nairn. He slept in the top, attic room, his bed positioned so he could look out over the city, out to the Kessock Bridge, the Black Isle and beyond, to the great flat-topped mass of Ben Wyvis, to the frequent Landseer skies and promise of the Far Northlands.

He loved Inverness. It was a strange place, with its nasal, whining, rolling accent. A small, tightly-knit city, a town really, stretching itself culturally courtesy of the youthful University of the Highlands and Islands, and economically via its new high-tech industries and perpetual housebuilding. There were chunks of the outer suburbs, whole roads, housing developments, supermarkets, cinemas and churches – that you could only reach by car. Some of it was like a cross between Milton Keynes and Los Angeles.

And some of it was contained and gorgeous. The Ness Islands, the parks, the river; that wonderful river. Sure there was horrible 70s architecture, but there were hidden corners, strange outposts of the past. A tweed merchant here, a private gamekeepers' club there. Lost, locked medieval cemeteries. The churches, still impressive in their variety, the result of innumerable Free Kirk schisms and simple fallings-out. But as a social force, Christianity was shrunken, no longer a power over the citizenry. Once, they said, the only traffic jam in Inverness was on Sunday after kirk. Now that was one of the quieter times.

A WHISKY IN MONSTERVILLE

The real God now was tourism. All year round, Inverness swarmed with visitors, in buses, on foot, in cars, motorcycles, bicycles and in guided flocks led by umbrella-wielding tour guides. They came for Scotland, the Highlands, the kilts and the heather and the hills. And they came for Nessie, just down the road. They came for the monster. Of course they did.

He stretched at the window, the warm golden light of the fading summer warming his ageing bones. How long had it been since someone had shared this bed, this oversized double from IKEA, bought more in hope than expectation? A long time. A woman he'd met in Tesco, late light shopping, that classic collision of trolleys. Both buying ingredients to make meals for one, bottles of good wine. They'd laughed at the cliché, pooled their purchases, your place or mine? His, in the end, and so they'd cooked and drank and fucked and never seen each other again, He wasn't quite sure why. They'd exchanged numbers, email addresses. But neither of them had made the effort. She was single, she was sure, not some temporarily abandoned wife. How long was it, anyway? Two months? Three? Maybe he'd... but really, it was up to her. Wasn't it?

He thought about the meal they'd shared. Two main courses, but one, hers, could be a generous starter. You do the main course, she said. I'll kick off. He'd shown her around his kitchen. You cook! You actually cook? I do, he answered. Always. And she was quick, precise. Not exactly hard. Maybe a touch brittle. So, anyway: spaghetti carbonara; pancetta, not bacon, proper pancetta. The new big Tesco was pretty good for stuff like that. Fried in olive oil. Egg yolks, double cream, Parmesan cheese, a decent wedge of Parmiggiano. So easy. More Parmesan, black pepper, parsley. A bottle of Pinot Grigio, cold, bought from the chiller cabinet, actually, and shoved in his freezer for ten minutes. Cooked, served, eaten. He'd put on some music, something utterly inappropriate, Johnny Cash or whatever, country whining and grunting, and jokingly, drunkenly – Jesus, half a bottle of white wine – they'd danced, stripped each other, fucked on the carpet, all friction rash and desperation. Strange new flesh, unprepared clothes, not stuff you'd wear for seduction. Odd socks in his case, voluminous

A WHISKY IN MONSTERVILLE

knickers in hers. Her body, soft, fighting a battle against age via the gym and running; she'd said she liked to run.

Somehow, no real embarrassment. Second course, let's see what you can do then, she'd said. What was her name? Mairhi? Lisa? She was from the west coast, couldn't speak Gaelic, though her mother had it, had been from one of the islands. And then it was his turn to cook.

He'd bought salmon, organic Shetland salmon, pale, the palest of pinks. The pack held enough for two, and really, his dish was easy, easier than her carbonara... olive oil, fried skin side to the pan, until just about done, not quite, then wrap in foil and in the oven. Shit, he'd forgotten the lentils, But that was OK, they were a bit of a faff, anyway. Keep it simple, stupid. One of those plastic bags of pre-washed rocket, some balsamic vinegar and olive oil, into a bowl. Wee packet of North Sea prawns, peeled and cooked, two cloves of garlic. Fry down the garlic in the same pan he'd used for the salmon, toss the prawns for 30 seconds, unwrap the salmon, serve together with... with... Hellman's mayonnaise. She'd laughed and laughed. But it was good, it tasted great. Bottle of Chilean Cab Sauv with that, a good one, too robust for the fish, but what the hell. Coffee, stovetop Bialetti espresso, large Aberfeldy 18 year-old each. Another. Thank God, she was a whisky drinker. And so to bed.

In the morning, she was gone.

*** *** ***

This morning, he rolled out of the too-big bed, stretched his getting-flabby body (pyjamas; not a good sign), stood at the window and gazed out over Inverness. Still there. It looked like a too-warm, muggy day, the fading heat of the Highland summer using itself up. He kneaded his protruding belly and sighed. Time to go for a run.

But on the way downstairs, tracksuited and trainered, he felt his knees creak and crack. Age, he thought was a terrible thing. He was in his fifties, feeling it, letting it get to him. Look at Murricane, maybe 10 years younger, living that outlandish outdoors lifestyle, on a boat, for God's sake. Fit, despite all those injuries. But then he had been special forces, fitter than a dozen fleas. Fitter than the fittest flea that had ever flown. Or jumped or whatever fleas did.

So, to preserve his knees, he decided to go for a ride on his bike. An old Trek mountain bike, cluttering up the hall. He hadn't used it for ages, and the tyres needed pumped up. Probably the chain needed oiled as well. Then he thought, fuck it, I'll just run up and down the stairs a few times. But by the time he got to the top floor, he was puffed out, sick and peckish. So he showered, changed and got ready to walk to the office. After all, wasn't walking the best exercise of all? He could take a detour, extend the route a bit. Maybe wander down the Ness Islands, just as long as those vigilante pricks weren't there. Hadn't they been at the Dores Hall meeting as well? Fuckers.

Finally, dressed in jeans, a corduroy sports jacket saved from Oxfam, brogues and a loose Pinks shirt, he was ready to leave. Coffee. They did good coffee at McDonalds. Murricane laughed at him for drinking it, but it was fine, proper cappuccino, from decently roasted beans. So he walked to the Market Brae car park and cut down the long, curving flight of stone steps to the corner of Castle Street and Church Street, and the biggest McDonalds in the Highlands.

That meaty, fatty smell. Half ferociously appetising, half vomit-inducing. He knew he couldn't eat there, couldn't sit there with the junkies and the children, the hungover alkies and the desperately, wilfully obese. So ordered his coffee to go. And then asked for a Double Sausage and Egg McMuffin. Make it a meal? Oh, why not. Large? Uh huh. Sup with the devil, get a takeaway.

When he emerged the sun was shining more strongly, determined to prove that summer wasn't quite over. He clutched his brown paper bag in one hand and headed down to the river. Maybe not the Islands today. Not that he was frightened of some wankers with a yen to beat up gays. Not that he was gay. Not that... oh shut up. He crossed the river by the road bridge and turned left down Ness Walk. In five minutes he was outside St Andrew's Cathedral and he was able to find a bench. Enough exercise. He opened his brown bag and inhaled. It all smelt so much better out of doors. Coffee and fat. Could there be a better way to begin the day?

The sound of singing woke him up. What was happening to him? He was turning into some kind of elderly down-and-out. There wasn't enough action in his life. Even that trip out with Murricane and his woman, what was she called, Rebecca, seemed to have exhausted him. And then he heard it again, faintly. Singing, definitely.

The Cathedral, he thought, some service or other. A mass. A choral evensong or whatever they called it. Except in the morning. Morningsong. But the noise grew louder, and as he looked to his right, coming along the riverside was a column of people, all dressed alike in white, singing to a bad guitar accompaniment. The same song, over and over. The same words. A jumble at first, but clearer and clearer:

Oh, creator God
Oh creator Love
Six days, six days, six days to make the mountains
Six days, six days, six days to make the sea
Six days to make you, six days to make me
Six days from sin to set us free.

The theology was more bizarre than the music, he thought, which was half way between early Donovan and *Watch with Mother*. Six days for creating the earth, fine. But the timing was all wrong. Sin didn't enter the Garden of Eden, which was presumably what they were singing about, until the following... week, was it? Month? Decade? Century? Millennium? Temptation of Eve and all that. Snake action. So there was no sin until that point, and the setting free part couldn't happen until after the Fall, which was later still. And the setting free was presumably... ah, but wait. There was another verse.

Oh, the saving God
Oh, the saving Love
One day, one day, one day crucified

A WHISKY IN MONSTERVILLE

One day, one day, one day the Saviour died
Three days, three days, three days he was alive
And the day came when from death he set us free

He was lost, now, and not just spiritually. He was just completely puzzled. Unless... the story of creation was surely meant to be part of the great Divine plan to retrieve the world from sin, brought to completion in the sacrifice of Christ! That must be it. But then he looked closer at the group of about 15 young people, and noticed they were all wearing white t-shirts and matching nylon jackets bearing a stylised picture of what looked like a Plesiosaur. The Loch Ness Monster. They were Nessatoreans. And they had decided to invade Inverness.

The group began to break up into couples. He noticed bundles of leaflets being handed out, and then a pair of them, males, were approaching him, smiling, terrible smiles. Oh, for fuck's sake. It was that tosser from the Islands. The religious gay bashing vigilante, and one of his confederates. What was it? McGlinchy. Bastard McGlinchy. McGlone. Some strange first name. Malachi. Malach-ee! Why did he think he knew him? Not Malachi, some other name?

McGlone stopped in front of him, a frown of recognition on his face, which bore the fading marks of Flaws's previous attentions. His teeth appeared to have had attention from a dentist with imagination rather than skill. They were gapped, bent and crooked. But they were the originals. The changes added, thought Flaws, character.

"Ah, I believe we have..."

"Fuck off, you creepy homophobic little shite."

"Don't get shirty, sir. I merely wish to..."

Flaws sighed and stood up. He felt both sickened and energised by the coffee-and-industrial-sludge-breakfast he had consumed. "I'm surprised you can actually still walk," he said. "My friend and I must be losing our touch. Or touches."

"I merely wished... we merely wished to hand you one of our communications," said McGlone. "And to say that while I, while we retain our commitment to the purity of the heterosexual act, I have now aligned our church with Brother Coldstream's Sanctified Truth Baptist Church of the Christ Child in History, err... Alliance, and am proud to walk with him towards the triumph of true Creationist thought. And the first step on that road is forgiveness." He pushed one of the leaflets forwards. It flickered glossily in the warm breeze from the river.

"Really," said Flaws. He took a step towards the squat shape of the man. McGlone's companion moved closer. "We about to have a prayer meeting? A group hug? I'll take your fucking leaflet, but why don't I give you something in return?" He grabbed the crumpled, greasy McDonalds' bag and thrust it into McGlone's chest. "Take this, you revolting holy scumbag. Dispose of it thoughtfully."

There was a low rumble of anger from McGlone's sidekick, whose face was particularly battered and whom he now remembered was called Peter. Then Flaws was conscious of another presence. Darker, no white jacket or t-shirt. Taller. Smelling of fire and brimstone. The devil, probably. No, it was worse. Peyronie. Erectile Dysfunction himself.

"Ah, former Inspector Flaws. Having a spiritually stimulating discussion? Mr McGlone! Pastor! The conversion to Sanctification and Nessatoreanism is holding, I hope? No longer do we have to worry about your activities in less, shall we say elevated areas of entertainment?"

"Mr McGlone and his friend do appear to have embraced a second stage of religiosity, and merged their own church with a higher authority, as you say," said Flaws. "Namely Fletcher Coldstream and his American monster hunters."

"'Monster' is such a negative term, Mr Flaws, don't you think? I'm certain Mr McGlone would agree. After all, it was once applied to himself, back in the days when he was the owner of that fine repository of holiness, the Dog Pit."

The Dog Pit. A pub and night club complex more formally known as the Excelsior out in Dingwall, which had been notorious a decade previously, before it had mysteriously burnt to the ground one winter's night. It was called the Dog Pit because of the occasional after-hours dog fights that took place in its basement. He remembered McGlone now. Murdo McGlone, known as Murder. His memory was fucked. Lack of exercise, probably. Murder got two years in Porterfield for that fire. After they found the burnt bodies of what a vet had said were Staffordshire Bull Terrier-American Pit Bull crosses.

"Born again in prison, was Mr... should I say Pastor McGlone. Turned over a new leaf. New name. St Malachi of Farthingall, patron saint of... well, dogfights, actually. I believe."

"I've seen his turning over at first hand," said Flaws.

"I am proud to say that I have given up my pastorhood," said McGlone. "I and my fellow worshippers, like Peter here, have been subsumed by the Sanctified Truth Baptist Church of the Christ Child in History and we stand now against evolution and for the beginning of the creationist revival. Have a leaflet, Inspector Peyronie."

"Thanks. And you were just leaving, I think, Murder, weren't you? Have a not very nice day. And put that burger bag in a bin, don't just chuck it on the ground. Otherwise I might have to arrest you."

Peyronie sat down on the bench and gestured to Flaws that he should do the same.

"Well, Zander. Still tangling with the wankers and the pricks?"

"Not if I can help it, Eric. You?"

"That's what police work is about, isn't it? Scum and lowlife. Even if they have their eyes on a higher power, or say they have. What's Murder McGlone to you, anyway?"

"You worked that case, didn't you? I should have realised I knew him from somewhere. Did you know he and his pals were cruising the Islands looking for blackmail victims?"

"Yes. Didn't know you swung that way, though? You and your spook pal Murricane caught in a clinch, were you?"

"Aye, sure. Let's just say that Murricane and myself had a little contretemps with Murder and his accompanying twosome. There may have been some bruises. And by the way, I don't think he was ever a proper spook. He was a sailor. Royal Navy. Marines. Jolly Jack Tar and all that."

"Well, you would say that, wouldn't you? As for Murder, now he's thrown in his lot with Coldstream and the rest of those

A WHISKY IN MONSTERVILLE

weirdos out at Loch Ness, maybe some of his more socially unacceptable behaviour will be modified. Not that it's very reassuring, him being part of that bunch. Unless it's a headless McGlone corpse we get next. Here's hoping." Peyronie sighed heavily and uncrumpled the leaflet he'd been given. "Jesus. Look at this."

There was a picture of the same plesiosaur-like creature that adorned the Nessatoreans' t-shirts and jackets. A web address, and the words: WATCH THE SKIES.

"'We believe that Christ will return in Glory,'" Peyronie read aloud, "'and His Saints, those who believe in Him and have accepted His Salvation, will meet Him in the Air.' Lots of capital letters. 'Signs and Wonders will precede this Event, however, many of them the result of our Sanctified efforts to praise Him. One such will take place above Loch Ness, in the vicinity of Foyers, on Thursday of this week. You are cordially invited to Bear Witness.'"

"They're not saying that Our Lord is coming back to visit Loch Ness, are they? Aleister Crowley'll be spinning his grave!"

"Well, the Great Beast certainly wouldn't be joining the Saviour for a trip to heaven, that's for sure," said Peyronie. "Are you going to come clean with me about Coldstream, Zander? I know you and Murricane are joined at the hip, and there are all kinds of stories about your connections with the higher echelons of spookdom. But that poor wee lass, Avril Anson? Come on, the policeman in you surely wants to see justice done. Is yon Davie fellow part of your... your web of deceit?"

"Justice?" Flaws laughed. "Deceit? Or maybe just to satisfy your curiosity, Eric?"

"Don't call me Eric."

"Why the fuck not? I saw you at that meeting in Dores. Looked like you were to all intents and purposes there to see no harm came to Mr Coldstream and his ugly American friend... Vance, isn't it? How's your wife?"

"You know fine well it's Vance. Ach well. Orders, as they say. You wouldn't know about that, being freelance and fancy-free. Or is it just a matter of sucking up to the big shots who pay the bills, eh?" And with that Peyronie turned on his heel and walked off, balling up the Nessatorean leaflet and throwing it on the pavement.

"Litter lout," muttered Flaws under his breath. He folded his own copy carefully and put it in an inside pocket.

*** *** ***

The door to his office was unlocked. Inside was Percival, neatly dressed in seersucker jacket and linen trousers, occupying the threadbare sofa that took up one wall, drinking something from a Costa cup and reading *The Highland News,* the tabloid sister publication to *The Inverness Courier.* Flaws always read Margaret Chrystall's music columns in both papers, usually about new local bands or acts he'd heard on the radio which were coming to Inverness's Ironworks venue. He hadn't been to a gig in a decade.

"Ah, Flaws, good man," said Percival. A straw hat sat beside him on the settee. It was as if he'd just come from a hot summer's day at Lord's. "Nice to read a newspaper for a change. Something printed on the residue of trees, I mean."

"That's the populist version," said Flaws. "You'd probably be more at home with its close relation, *The Inverness Courier.* It's still an old-school broadsheet, it carries lengthy reviews of local Gilbert and Sullivan productions and you can, if you buy two, sleep under it quite comfortably on a summer's night."

"Indeed? My, ah, kind of newspaper, then. Now…" he folded *The Highland News* carefully into a number-plate sized rectangle. The headline read 'LOOK UP! Nessie cult seeks sign in sky'. "This business of, ah, something arriving by air… one presumes that Messrs Vance and Coldstream have something quite definite in mind? Specific. Not some spiritual visitation."

"I would have thought you were in a much better position than me to gauge Mr Vance's activities, Mr Percival."

"It's Sir Alex actually, but Sandy will do, thank you, Mr Flaws. I do prefer my informality to be one-sided. Well, to be truthful I am in a slightly invidious position, with regard to my, ah… those to whom I must, alas, account. It would seem that Mr Vance has connections within the American hierarchy – I would not go so far as to call it an actual government – that in turn interface, if that is the correct word, with interests in the British... shall I call it establishment? The structures that enforce government, shall we say."

"And that includes you?"

"That includes all of us, Flaws. As the subjects of said enforcement. But of course, in a democracy there is always scope for disagreement. Would you agree?"

"Possibly. So, can you be clear about how things stand with..."

"Now what was the name again? I think we were, quite informally, calling the activity surrounding Mr Coldstream, the mine at Strontian, Murricane and yourself... what was it? Operation..."

"Operation Monsterville." A look of mild distaste crossed Percival's face.

"Yes, quite. That. Well, there have been, as you know, several unfortunate deaths associated with said event or events. And an agreement has been reached by my... by my..."

"By your accountants?"

"By those to whom I report. To whom I am accountable. They have come to an agreement with those, who have been, shall I call it, *engineering* Mr Vance's activities? Permitting? Encouraging? Looking to take advantage of. Anyway, it has been decided that the mortality will ease, or hopefully cease, and the project shall go ahead to the benefit of, ahem, tourism in the Loch Ness area, the profits of Mr Vance's company, the spiritual health of Mr Coldstream's church, and the wealth and power of the British and American governments. It's a win-win situation, I believe that's what you call it."

"Technically, you're saying it's a win-win-win-win-win-win situation," said Flaws, deadpan.

"Indeed."

"So, let me see if I'm – here's a nice piece of jargon – up to speed. Vance and the American government get access to a vein of rare minerals crucial to the defence – or perhaps that should be offence industries. Britain gets its share. Coldstream gets to build his Monster Centre and attract both hapless tourists and brain-dead co-religionists. All without scaring the horses, or with just a little local planning difficulty which can be, probably already has been, ironed out. Is that it?"

"Well, that is one way of putting it, I suppose. A very specific way."

"And what about Vance and Coldstream's utter disregard for human life? What about their mad fuckwitted religion and rampant disregard for legality? More especially what about Jenks?"

Percival blinked twice. Something that could have been mild amusement sparked in his white-blue eyes.

"Do you know, I rarely feel guilt over my actions, Mr Flaws. I have without compunction sent men, and, increasingly, women, to die. Or with the merest hint of regret, perhaps, on occasion. It's a question of value. Of returns. Of doing what I perceive to be the right thing. But there was an operation involving Mr Murricane that I have a degree of, I'll be honest, irritation about. And yes, regret. Because, in many ways I was misled and consequently I misled those most intimately involved. Some of them to the detriment of their, ah, lives." He sat up, grasped his straw hat and began to idly trace the ribbon's edge with one long finger. "Such an operation involved Mr Murricane encountering the man you know as Mr Jenks for the first time. In the course of which, it was discovered that Mr Vance, whose importance to the American defence establishment was and is regarded as sacrosanct across the Atlantic, was involved not only in expressing his extremely unfortunate personal tastes for human destruction, but also in profiting from the importation of opiates into the USA."

"Not that the American intelligence agencies have entirely clean hands in that regard, of course."

"Of course not. *Realpolitik.* Going back to Vietnam. Thence to Colonel North, Irangate et al. And, ah, others. But after the Afghan thing Vance began making his presence, shall we say, felt. On my, as it were, patch. And now, since the association with Scotland and Mr Coldstream, the mines, the minerals, and indeed, Murricane, others have died, and Vance's presence is impinging even more strongly on my sense of..."

"Annoyance?"

"Shame, actually, Mr Flaws. Shame. Which is why I am telling you this, as Mr Murricane's de facto handler, in the sincere hope that you will not tell him anything of our conversation whatsoever. I, meanwhile, will make sure that Rebecca Elmsworth also remains in ignorance of what has happened at a higher, err... remove. For the time being."

"And?"

"And so," said Percival, getting to his feet in one easy movement, a kind of languid lope, "I shall, essentially, unleash the dogs of war, and hope that Murricane fucks the whole thing up sideways. He used to be good at that, and frankly he deserves a chance to prove it once again. He has not fared well since that business in Afghanistan."

"And presumably this would also clear up some, shall we say, issues in the hierarchies you work within. And without. I'm guessing at least some powers that be have hinted that it might be an idea to take Vance down." Percival said nothing. He examined his fingernails. "So what do you want me to do?"

"Well, Mr Flaws, in your personal case, I would suggest a break. A small tour of somewhere out of the way."

"But not the Highlands?"

"Not the Highlands, no. Perhaps Southern Scotland would be best, or even England. Do you golf?"

"I don't. Not yet. An old man's game."

"Pity. I could have introduced you as a guest at Royal St George's down at Sandwich. Anyway. I'm sure you'll find somewhere to take yourself off to. I shall make myself scarce too, and we shall await developments."

"Hands off, no comebacks, from your accountants, or should that be superiors? I always rather saw you as not having any superiors, Sir... Sandy."

"So did I, Mr Flaws. But the truth is, we all do. Even if it's only a particular idea of God. Or Gods."

"Or monsters."

"Gods and monsters, gods and monsters. Yes. I wonder though: is there really any difference?"

A meeting in the air

Candy floss, oak and copper, some sherry and a lot of general fruitiness. Some cake and slightly burnt pastry on the aftertaste.

REDBREAST 15-YEAR-OLD

A WHISKY IN MONSTERVILLE

The *Happy Adventure* was drifting slowly off Urquhart Castle, Ferg blipping the boat's engine and side thrusters back and forth to keep her steady while Murricane helped their client with the novel technique, for her, of downrigging. Rebecca had insisted on paying Ferg in advance for the charter.

"Fuck it, I might as well have some fun at the office's expense before I'm hauled back to dear old London town." Apparently, Percival and his irregulars these days all had official credit cards to which they could charge any expenses incurred in their nefarious activities, assuming said costs were payable with plastic. In Murricane's experience, there were some things, notably second-hand weaponry and drugs, that were hard to obtain with anything but used bank notes, gold, silver or transfers to and from Swiss bank accounts, but Ferg simply scanned the card with his iPhone, grunted something incomprehensible, handed the phone back to Rebecca for her to punch in her pin, and they were off.

"I can't leave this hanging," Murricane had said, when Rebecca announced her recall. "I've got Davie the Druid to think about, after all. Local responsibilities."

"Come on, it's time to shake off this hippy bullshit and get back to work." Rebecca and he had spent two frenzied nights aboard the *Gloria*, fuelled by some west coast hand-dived scallops (it was fish van day), some fresh farmed trout and an 18-year-old Smith's Glenlivet. She had gone back to the Piper's Rest to check emails and texts, and returned changed, a creature under orders. A London look in her eyes, Murricane thought.

"I'm going. But I'm not leaving before whatever's due to happen on Friday happens," she told Murricane. "And besides, you promised to take me fishing. For Ferox. For the big boys. The big bastards." But there was something else in her face, in her posture. He reached for her, felt an unexpected coldness on her skin, in her entire attitude. She shrugged him off. Fishing yes. In the morning. The day of the supposed arrival. The Great Coming. Could he fix it up?

So he had arranged the early trip with Ferg. She'd meet him at Temple Pier. Everything already over between them, he thought. She'd stay at the Piper's Rest. Wanted time to pack, to sort things out. Probably best.

And now they were fishing, nobody's mind properly on the job, nothing biting, nothing showing on the sonar. Waiting. Looking at the sky. There were a lot of boats on the water, which was utterly calm, oily, metallic. There was no wind. The day was humid, cloudy, what the locals called close. And finally Murricane started the electric motors that hauled in the heavy fishing rigs, socketed the rods and told Ferg to head for Foyers.

"That's why we're here, after all. That's why all these bastards are here." He swept a hand at the yachts and dinghies, a couple of the tourist barges that waddled up and down the Caledonian Canal. The big cruise boats were out too, crammed with camera-wielding tourists.

"Speak for yourself," said Rebecca. "I'm here for the fish, and… God. I thought I heard a choir there. Some sort of…"

"Angels, probably. Shut off the engines, Ferg."

The big motors grumbled to a halt, and the sounds of the loch overwhelmed them: lapping water, buzzing two-stroke outboards, the clatter of cable against mast. Shouts and laughter from other boats. And somewhere, singing. Confident voices, quite a lot of them, singing together. Ferg had his binoculars out.

"There's a whole heap of folk on the pier, in front of the power station," he said. "I think that's where the singing's coming from. Doesn't sound like any psalm

I've ever heard."

Murricane sighed. "All right. Start them up and let's get over there."

In minutes they were idling with an assortment of craft outside a series of bright orange, brand new buoys, marking off an area extending about 50 metres from the pier. Notices had been attached to every second one stating that this was a 'restricted zone'. There was a windsock hanging flaccid from a flagpole on the pier. Murricane couldn't remember having seen it before. The Loch Ness Lifeboat RIB burbled along quietly, patrolling in a meaningful and watchful manner. He spotted Archie and Kevin, none the worse for Ferg's bottling and holding no grudge. They waved at each other. And there was the choir, all in white, a uniform white, he saw when he borrowed Ferg's binoculars. Bomber jackets and jeans for the men, floaty dresses for the women. He saw Melliflua there, focussed on her face. She looked happy. She looked illuminated in some way, from within. He strained to catch the lyrics of what was being sung, the same choruses over and over and over.

Oh, creator God
Oh, creator Love
Six days, six days, six days to make the mountains
Six days, six days, six days to make the sea
Six days to make you, six days to make me
Six days from sin to set us free...

And then he heard something else.

It was faint, as yet, but he knew it would soon be loud, louder than hell, louder than bombs. Earsplitting. Helicopters always were. It was a noise both familiar and strange, terrifying and reassuring. Helicopters. Choppers. Helicopters to save, helicopters to kill. He'd waited for both in his time. It seemed several were approaching, he thought. But there was something odd about the engine notes. They were synchronised. Their clattering, virtually unsilenced bass rhythms were coming, he could now tell, from the east, were beating as one, constantly being tuned to each other. Like a couple of twin-rotor Chinooks, maybe. But... what the hell...

"Jesus," said Ferg, pointing up the loch towards the eastern entrance, to the grey and glowering sky. "What the fuck is that?"

The noise grew louder and louder. But there was no *Apocalypse Now* fleet of choppers approaching. Just a single object. Or rather, a single massive shape, like some kind of glittering cloud, rounded, bulbous, with another, harder, sleeker object dangling beneath it.

"Appropriately enough," said Rebecca, "seeing as Jimmy Page used to own Boleskine House, which we can just about see over there, that looks like a Zeppelin."

"It's a hybrid," said Murricane. "Helicopter-cum-airship. People have been working on them for years, Boeing were involved in something like this. With a Canadian company. Some stupid name. Idea was to use the blimp for basic lift, sort of like the main rotor of a big chopper, and then several smaller rotors to lift really, really heavy stuff."

"It's called a Skyhook," said Rebecca, nearly strangling Murricane as she grabbed the glasses from him, its strap still around his neck. "Vance bought the prototype. It's in production now, but I think there are only about five in the world. It's technically the world's biggest helicopter. And it will carry almost anything, almost anywhere. It's 300 feet long, it's got like four normal chopper rotors as well as helium in the bag. Brilliant idea for things like logging."

"How do you even know this?" Ferg was gazing at Rebecca with a confused expression on his face.

"Research. You can find anything on the interweb these days." She shrugged. "I'm a researcher. Didn't Murricane say?"

"Ideal for supplying any kind of industrial development in remote locations, presumably," said Murricane. "And to terrify the shit out of the natives."

"What's it carrying?" said Ferg. "That's surely some kind of luxury speedboat, some cigarette boat or something? Sharp end, no'-so-sharp end? What's the point of lifting it in, for goodness' sake? They could have sailed it through the canal."

"Not that thing," said Rebecca." She sounded oddly ebullient, as if her sense of preoccupation, which she'd carried like a shroud ever since news of her recall had come through, was lifting. "Not that. I've never seen one before, but that's what serious billionaires like to play with most these days. That's the ultimate playboy toy. Though I imagine Vance has something more serious in mind for it."

The giant machine and its burden was close, now, slowing and about 200 feet above the loch. In giant letters on its side was emblazoned the word 'Glory'. The noise was deafening, the loch's surface ruffled and torn by the downwash. The object below it did, in fact, look like a sleek, modern power yacht. Except for the strangely deep hull and the series of oval portholes that seemed to be beneath its waterline. Its superstructure too, was weirdly rounded, and the whole design seemed to be the reverse of a normal boat, with what was evidently the bow rounded and the stern, if the shrouded propeller was anything to go by, long and pointed.

"I know what that is," said Murricane, remembering the drawings in Coldstream's office. "It's called, what was it, *Baptist*. How literal do these people have to be? Is the airship called *Glory*? They stole my barge's name."

"It's a floating gin palace," said Ferg. "What, it's maybe 20 metres? Plenty of stuff like that on the west coast. Like a Sunseeker. You've seen a Sunseeker, Murry, eh? Seen them coming through the canal, drunk bastards for the most part. In fact didn't one of them go up in flames..." He glanced at Murricane and became suddenly silent.

"It's a submarine, Ferg," said Murricane. "Coldstream had a picture. Never mentioned it at that Dores meeting, but this is what Vance was mouthing off about I guess. I remember we assessed these subs on paper back at Portsmouth. They're used by Navy SEALS, I think. Built as rich men's toys or for tourist trips, but they're serious, things. They can go to amazing depths"

"Roman Abramovitch?" Rebecca had full possession of the binos now and had them fixed on the vessel. "Do you know who he is? Russian oligarch? Owns Chelsea Football Club. He's got a sub, allegedly. Some hack asked him about it, and he said, "if you can find it, you can keep it". Paul Allen from Microsoft. He's got one. And Vance, of course. This isn't his only one. This is just a tiddler. He's got one with a gym and a swimming pool. Basically a kind of underwater yacht. Imagine, a swimming pool underwater. This is called a Nomad. It'll go to 300 metres. Think of it, 300 metres! Massive range too. Fantastic!"

"God, you really love this stuff." Murricane was amused. "And you've done the research. You knew about this, didn't you? You knew this what they were planning."

A WHISKY IN MONSTERVILLE

Rebecca lowered her voice. "Had a team tracking Vance's chartered cargo vessel ever since it left Alabama. They got to Invergordon, deepwater port just north of Inverness, in case you didn't know, three days ago. And they've been working on this stunt ever since, unloading, inflating."

"And you're heading south? You just wanted to see this?"

"Ah. Well, orders is orders, as they say. Apparently we're all on the same side, now." She glanced from Ferg to Murricane. "Maybe."

The singing was reaching a crescendo:

Glory, Glory and hosanna
Comes the seeker for the Lord
We will search in love
For the creature who will prove
The glory of our great Creator God

The tune was familiar, Murricane thought. It was like *In-a-Gadda-Da-Vida* by Iron Butterfly, a band from long, long before his time. How had it stuck in his brain? Some incessant whistler on a desert mission somewhere. An incessant whistler who had stopped whistling all too suddenly. For good. *In-a-Gadda-Da-Vida*. He felt numb.

"All on the same side? All on the same side as Coldstream? Vance? Jenks?"

"Above Percival's head. The Americans need what KokVan can bring. What they need they demand, what they want they're going to have. We need the Americans."

Like some magical trick on a vast scale, the gigantic Skyhook gently settled its dangling cargo in the water within the no-sail zone around the pier. The noise was utterly deafening, the water whipped and flicked by the rotors' downthrust. And then it was floating, the cables went slack and suddenly there was the kind of aching, vast silence you get when a constant and disruptive noise suddenly ceases.

"They've switched off the rotors," said Ferg. "They've switched the bastards off. And look it's just... it's sitting there."

There was a series of barks as explosive releases let the cables drop in the water. Figures began to appear from within the

Nomad as the *Glory* began to move, and the envelope of the blimp slowly dipped closer to the surface of the Loch. And then a booming amplified voice from the pier.

"Oh God, Oh Lord, we thank thee! We thank thee for thy mercy, thy great and glorious deliverance to us of the instruments of your knowledge, of proving the knowledge of thy true salvation! We thank thee for the means of discovering the creature of goodness and truth. The creature of certainty, of the creature of disproving the antichrist Darwin! Of proclaiming your mighty truths to the world!"

Coldstream's voice. And then another, a rumble and crackle as somebody seemed to seize the microphone.

"Ain't she beautiful? Meet the *Glory*. And meet the *Baptist*. *Glory* has delivered the Baptist right here, right on time. There's your sign, folks! Monsterville is on its way. This is my gift to you folks, to the people of Scotland! The first passenger-carrying submarine on Loch Ness. We will find her. We will seek and with God's help we will find!"

"Amen!" Coldstream's voice again. And then the earsplitting, shattering rumble of the Skyhook's rotors kicking once more into life and the vast object beginning, so slowly, to rear into the air.

"Oh, the humanity," said Murricane.

"It's not on fire," Rebecca pointed out. "Helium doesn't burn."

"No, it just makes you speak in a really stupid high voice, doesn't it?" Murricane shook his head. "Christ, What will Davie the Druid make of this?"

Killer app

Oak and seaweed, salt, beaches drying in the sun. Wedding cake and stewed tea, with some autumn leaves and a dab of sulphur – volcanoes in the distance!

TOMATIN 18-YEAR-OLD

"Very impressive." James Macindoe, convener of the Highland Council planning committee, was a man used to boats. He had been a share fisherman out of Nairn in the days when that seaside resort had its own small whitefish fleet. Before turning from fish to meat, from catching to slaughtering. It was the same thing, he argued. He was enjoying the thrumming sway beneath his feet. "Does it have a name, this… this craft?"

"*Baptist*," said Coldstream. A small buffet had been mounted for the senior planning committee members invited out to Foyers to witness the arrival of the submarine, and Coldstream had to admit, the whole show had worked like a charm. The first proper tourist submarine on Loch Ness: a massive, multi-million dollar investment. And what an arrival! Nobody could do anything but agree that the Nessatoreans were serious and would bring untold tourist income to the area. It was a no-brainer, surely, that Monsterville would get planning permission? But, Vance took no chances. The millions involved in transporting the sub and that massive airship thing from the US, the sheer cost and hassle of flying the submarine in… it was impressive. For such a queasily perverted dolt. Still, he had his uses. It surely was the case that these activities would speed up the process of Christ's coming? He thought so. After all, weren't they all about paving the way, easing His passage into the world? Proclaiming the truth?

And now an immaculate little reception for councillors and media aboard the *Baptist*, this strange cross between luxury speedboat and commercial sub. He was astonished at how easy it had been obtaining permission to bring the vessel onto the loch. In that they hadn't had to ask for permission at all. If they only knew what other little tricks Vance had built into the thing.

The waitress smoothly removed an empty champagne glass from Convener Macindoe's hand and substituted a full one. Cristal, Vance had specified. Women servers, dressed as mermaids. He had even supplied the costumes, which were alarmingly convincing. So tight at the feet, where a fan of cloth splayed into facsimile of a tail, that the girls had to shuffle like traditional Geishas. Actually, one or two had a look of availability about them. They'd be better off with him than Vance and his gruesome servant Jenks. He wondered what they got up to on their little trips to the forest. Their camping sprees, Vance called them, provoking a thin grin from Jenks, who was like a faithful, cruel, one-owner dog.

"Of course, naebody's gonnie see much at 300 metres, if this thing'll really go down that far, and if the Loch really is that deep, ur they?" The speaker was a corpulent hack in a Drizabone coat, his red-meets-purple face bearing the signs of incipient heart failure. He had muscled his way between Coldstream and Macindoe and was holding a notebook, pen and half-drunk glass of champagne in one hand. In the other he had a pewter whisky flask, from which he took the occasional swig. Coldstream assumed this was typical of Scotland's journalistic drinking culture: grape, grain and grilling some hapless politician. Drunkenly.

"Want a drop of the hard stuff, the cratur, Reverend? Decent drop, local, Tomatin 18. No, you're not drinking, I see. What about you Convener Jimmy? Naebody to tell, My editor's miles away." The councillor shook his head.

"Ach no, Gary, always removes the enamel from my teeth, that supermarket guff you carry about with you."

"And… you are?" Coldstream could hardly believe that in this recession-hit, obsessively sober day and age, fat journalists with whisky flasks were still permitted to function.

"Gary MacKerrachan, freelance, on assignment for that paragon of press freedom and investigative complacency… is that right word? Competency, *The Highland Mercury*. Online and in your pocket. I mean, in your pocket in the sense of, like, smartphones and that. We're web only. But also, ah mean tae say, we're not for sale, not our souls, not our, emm…enthusiasm, Mr Coldstream. Without fear or favour, that's us. Of course, I know who you are. The Jim Jones of the Highlands, they're calling you. How do you react to that kind of label?"

Suddenly, Coldstream noticed a winking light coming from behind the whisky flask. An iPhone. "Are you… recording this?"

"Och, ma memory's a shocker these days, it really is. Yeah, video and audio, for the website. And we can sell stuff on, sometimes to the nationals, such as they are, such as they pay, which is paltry, bloody paltry. Anyway, Jim Jones of the Highlands? Maybe we shouldnae be drinking your champers, eh? Case you've poisoned it."

"The Jonestown Massacre was the work of a deranged, power-crazed lunatic, and I can assure you that our beliefs do not even begin to coincide. We are a mainstream Christian group who simply wish to proclaim the truth of creationism, and we are here in your fine country because we believe the creature that lives in Loch Ness is prime, physical proof that God made this earth in six days, praise His Name! That man and dinosaur walked this earth together. That the so-called fossil record is a trick of Satan."

"Aye, fair enough, fair enough. Monstrous suggestion, eh? Eh? What about that, Jimmy? You happy to have the political process suborned by religious mania and free alcohol? And a submarine as bribery?"

"We are above being influenced by hospitality such as this, which is merely a gesture," said Macindoe. "We will make our decision without regard for anything but the effect on the local community."

"No' been handing out any wee gifts, then Mr Coldstream? Or Mr Vance, nice to see you, by the way. This must have all cost a pretty cent, eh? Where'd you get the heliship, or the aircopter or whatever it's called? Not to mention this drag racer of a submarine? Dive, dive, dive! Heil Hitler! Graf Von Spee! Royal Oak ya bas!"

Vance had appeared, dressed in the same white outfit the other Nessatoreans were wearing. They looked like hospital orderlies from an American TV show. Jenks, his perpetual shadow, was also in white, Coldstream noticed. Suddenly, he found it difficult to breathe. He swallowed his cranberry juice carefully, but it just seemed to make the dryness in his throat worse. Together, Vance and Jenks exuded a kind of lascivious threat. And he was a man who knew about being lascivious.

"Well, a gentleman, a gentleman of the press! Her Majesty's press, I have no doubt. The Skyhook's just a fabulous, fabulous tool for major mineral extraction and lifting…"

"That's not something you're planning for here, Mr Vance? I hear stories…" MacKerrachan slipped in and out of his broad

Scots twang with ease. One minute he was Billy Connolly, the next he was Lord Thurso.

"Why, no, absolutely not. This is a site of special emotional and spiritual importance for me, sir! The Reverend Coldstream drew me to the Lord and I am committed to his fine mission, to the spreading of the gospel, to the second coming of our Lord and the proclamation of His glorious name."

"And your submarine, this fine vessel. Won't be able to see a thing once you're awa' doon in the depths of Loch Ness, will ye? Tourists won't see anything. Strapped into their nice leather seats." MacKerrachan gestured round the luxurious main cabin. "Holds 26, your press release says. I thought it would be more. But you're no' gonnie have dances doon here. What if they can't see anything oot the portholes?"

"We have side sonar and high definition screens," said Vance smoothly. "There will be much to see and the sheer sensation of being in Nessie's actual lair will, I'm sure, be a huge draw. Now if you'll excuse me, I must have a word with the Reverend Coldstream in private. Mr Jenks? I wonder if you'd show our journalist friend and the esteemed convener back to the bus for Inverness." It was like consigning two fat sheep to a particularly vicious wolf-bear cross, thought Coldstream. "You be nice to them, y'hear? I truly believe Mr, ah, Her Majesty's Press will do us proud. Given our advertising budget in the coming months. Ain't that so, sir?" He eyed MacKerrachan in a glinting parody of friendliness. "Freelances got no security, that's the peril of their lives. But we're always in need of PR help. Always."

MacKerrachan took a swig from his flask and coughed wetly. "Aye, well. We serve the community, obviously. Act in its... best interests."

"There's a bar on the bus and a couple of the mermaids are travellin' with you gents. Enjoy!" Vance gripped Coldstream's elbow and guided him towards the front of the cabin.

"You see the piece de resistance, Rev? The killer app?" A bank of TV and computer screens surrounded a curved window of armoured Plexiglas, through which only the opaque muddy green of the loch could be seen. And this was at a depth of oh, eight feet, thought Coldstream gloomily. He sat in the left-hand control seat, while Vance squirmed into the right, and began playing with the various controls, which resembled nothing more than a domestic computer games console. Suddenly two bright lights in halogen blue burst through the murky water they were floating in. Like the eye of God, thought Coldstream. The two eyes of God. If they were halogen. They went out, and then the *Baptist*'s own powerful lights picked out the vague shadow of something else floating about a yard or so in front of her.

"Where's the, the err... captain?" Coldstream had met the two taciturn men who had flown in with the *Baptist*. They had fussed around her like mother hens, checking and tightening and securing, and then, when the VIPs and press came aboard, they had vanished.

"Oh, they're ashore. There's a truckload of ancillary stuff on the dock at the moment, and they're checking through it. This little baby arrived in a pod attached to the hull, though. Released as soon after splashdown as possible."

Using a remote joystick, Vance moved the object even closer, until it was just a few inches from the submarine's bow. It looked, for all the world, like a small mobile generator, Coldstream thought, though with what appeared to be claw-tipped arms stretching out in front.

"Meet *Mary*," said Vance. "*Mary Magdalene*. Servant of the Lord! She's an ROV, Remotely Operated Vehicle. A Seabotix LBV950, adapted by my guys for mineral extraction."

"Mineral extraction? I thought we were at an experimental stage? During the construction phase, surely that's when..."

"Well, samples. It has a small drill attached as well as a grab and secure containment. Our surveys indicate that Varlindium is present below the surface here in quantities big enough to buy and sell this goshdarned country, Reverend! And the building of your Creation Science Monsterland Nessieworld Centre will provide me with the perfect opportunity to extract it. And only me. But clearly, we need to extract some samples initially. Something to show the clients."

"Clients?"

"Oh, you know! One or two minor league governments. My own, this colonial outpost we call the United Kingdom. I am the perfect front man for them. Because I am so, so imperfect. They think they can control me, buy and sell me, provide for my little predilections. And they never appear to have anything to do with the actual extraction of my lovely mineral. KokVan does their dirty work. I do, you do, and at any given moment they can wash their hands of me. Destroy me. And through me, you. Threaten us. So they think. So they think."

"But... they can't! Well, God is on our side. We are dealing with higher powers." Coldstream could hear the querulous note in his usually orotund voice.

"I own this shoreline, Reverend. Or KokVan does. Through a network of blind companies. I own a stake in the energy company that runs the power station, owns the pier. I own you. I own the people that matter in Defence in Washington and London and Edinburgh. I own part of God, probably. Your part, for sure." He laughed. *"Mary Magdalene! Baptist.* Fabulous! Thing is, you really believe this crap about the Loch Ness Monster, don't you? Or you've convinced yourself you do. Well, it doesn't matter. You'll get your Monstertown. Your state-of-the-art Creation Science Study Centre, or whatever it's called this week. It'll be a wondrous addition to the local tourist infrastructure. Maybe it will hasten the return of Christ." He made a small movement with his right hand, and the ROV disappeared into the murk of Loch Ness. "But only with my permission."

Queen of the Highland Fleshpots

A delicate, perfumed nose, spicy and with floral overtones. There is a hint of the sea and a lemony aspect, with the leathery spiciness cutting with tannin and old wood.

CLYNELISH 14-YEAR-OLD

A WHISKY IN MONSTERVILLE

Murricane was in the upstairs lounge of the Market Bar in Inverness, drinking quickly so he didn't have to listen to a local three-piece midlife-crisis electric blues band called The Deid Grateful Gardener soundcheck. With their equipment, they took up fully half of the space in the tiny room. The minuscule stage wasn't big enough for the drum kit, let alone the band's massive Marshall amplifiers. Not to mention the large, balding, beer-gutted band members

"Let's get out of here," he said to Flaws. "We have a booking at the Prebble for 7.30 anyway." There was an enormous, air-moving thump and then a hum; the guitarist had switched on his amplifier. Flaws nodded. And then the guitarist played a chord. Murricane felt the central organs in his body move slightly.

"These fuckers'll be audible from space," shouted Flaws into Murricane's ear as the guitarist continued to lumber through an early Soundgarden song. Murricane nodded. He hadn't made out a word. They stumbled through the sparse crowd of early evening drinkers, wives, roadies and scared-looking tourists to the crumbling staircase that led to the outside world. In the cobbled lane, blinking in the evening light, they stood momentarily with the small group of aged smokers, refugees from the smokeless zone that was the downstairs bar.

"God's waiting room," said Flaws. "You wouldn't believe that Connolly and the Proclaimers had played here, would you? All right Jethro?" One of the elderly men, his face a curious yellowy brown, nodded at him, then deliberately turned away. "Jethro Henderson, former sheep rustler. Used to be part of a team dealing with wholesale butchers in Northumberland. They'd get a lorry, tour the Highlands until it was full of sheep, head south and sell them."

"Sounds like a scheme," said Murricane. He felt slightly light-headed. Double 60-per-cent alcohol Aberlour A'bunadhs would do that. Especially chased with bottles of Duvel beer. Eight per cent alcohol. Those Belgians.

"Oh, it was. Worked for years. Until they crashed the lorry into the central barrier of the Kessock Bridge, and one of them panicked when the traffic cops pulled up. Dived over into the Kessock Narrows. Dead as a fucking doornail. It's like concrete, the water, from that height. The rest were so shaken they made a clean breast of it. Five years each. Jethro and two others."

"What happened to the sheep?"

"Couldn't identify the owners. Ear clips and tags had been obliterated or removed. All prime lambs, good sized. Sent them to the Jimmy Mac's slaughterhouse, money went to the Northern Constabulary Benevolent Fund. And all of us on the investigating team got a sheep to ourselves. Each."

"As a pet?"

"No, as a sexual partner, what the hell do you think? As a carcase for the freezer, jointed, bagged, the lot. And very tasty it was too."

"Perks of the job, eh?"

"Aye. And speaking of which, I'm getting hungry. Let's get a jildy on."

*** *** ***

The Prebble Hotel's Patrick Sellar Lounge was an exercise in failed irony. It was where knowing parody became grand kitsch. The public areas of the hotel were themed on the Highland Clearances, the great 19th century movement of smallholders from clan lands to make way for sheep. It was the period when former clan chiefs transformed themselves into aristocratic landowners and began treating their former clan members, their tribes, as commodities. In Highland and especially Gaelic culture, it had enormous historical resonance. It had given rise to a mythology of self-conscious guilt and suffering, of victimhood, and the Prebble Hotel systematically tried to take the piss out of that. Unsuccessfully.

John Prebble was an English author who had written a series of books on Highland history, now largely regarded as romantically inaccurate. The Sutherland Suite was named after the Duke of said county, a monstrous figure who was often portrayed as having deported half of Scotland to America. Patrick Sellar was his factor, Heinrich Himmler to the Duke's Hitler. There were imitation thatched cottages for bars, tables made of stuffed sheep, even a half-size plastic copy of the infamous Croik Church, where herded crofters waiting for ships to the New World had supposedly scratched their names on the windows. The whole thing had proved wildly popular with Inverness's self-nominated hipsters. And of course, with American tourists.

The hotel was a straggle of Victorian houses on the riverside beneath the pseudo-castle, knocked together and joined by extensions ranging in age from the early 1960s to a glittering steel and glass concoction from the 1980s. It had been bought a decade previously by a local boy made accidentally quite good, a failed rock star who had suddenly become excessively rich when one of his neglected songs featured in an internationally successful movie about talking dinosaurs. Since then he had renovated, renewed and indulged himself in stocking the Patrick Sellar Lounge with some of the most expensive whiskies known to man. He had brought in a top chef and begun chasing a Michelin Star, so far without success. On a nightly basis, he sought very expensive insensibility, based on an attempt to drink his way through Scotland from south to north, navigating by distillery. His name was Gorham Sheldon, and Flaws had known him since their school days at Inverness Royal Academy.

Murricane and Flaws sat at the bar and ordered the Perdition – a half-and-a-half combo of 1978 Clynelish, the distillery set up by the Duke of Sutherland after the Clearances – and half-pints of Die in Agony Ya Bastard, a micro-ale from a small brewery in Brora. It was a light IPA and quite delicious.

"Last time I was here, Gor was asleep at the bar," said Murricane. "There were two waiters kind of pecking around him, not knowing if they should try and wake him, pick him up and carry him to a room, call a taxi."

"Yeah, and guess what they did? They called me." Flaws shrugged. "I was at the pictures, believe it or not. Some French shite about Jonny Hallyday on a train. Hadn't switched off the phone, of course.

I told them to drag him outside, leave him on the ground and call a taxi."

"Well they didn't do that. But they did haul him off his stool and take him somewhere. I was trying to impress that wee Polish barmaid from the Piper's, so I didn't take too much of an interest."

"Did it work? Impressing the barmaid, I mean?"

"Up to a point." Murricane shook his head. "Foreign women, they don't judge you as harshly as Britchicks. Not initially."

"Why? Different culture?"

"No. Different language. Even if they're fluent in English, they don't catch on to your tragic boringness for maybe weeks. Or they put down their boredom to their poor English rather than your poor personality."

"Women, eh?"

"Yes. Women."

"And... Rebecca?"

"Rebecca was... well you know what she was. Just business. Still..."

"Did you see her off?"

"I beg your pardon"

"I mean, did you see her to the airport, or the train or however she was..."

"She was driving."

"Really? What, that wee Subaru hooligan thing?"

"Yes, the car she had at Dores. Mad, fast as fuck. Blue. Dirty. Like her." Flaws was frowning. "Why?"

"When did she go? Yesterday?"

"Yeah. Didn't want any goodbyes, she said."

They had been looking at the menu. Ballotine of marinated foie gras. Kyle of Tongue Oyster with bacon foam. Celeriac and white truffle puree. Flaws wasn't really a fan of foam, in any form. Especially not on a dinner plate. If he wanted spit on his plate, he said, he'd do the spitting.

"Funny thing," said Flaws. "Sure I saw a car like that yesterday. It was in the Tesco's car park. The one next to the station. I was in there getting some... something for tea. something that didn't have foam in it."

"She was probably just getting some supplies for the trip. I wouldn't worry about it."

"She wouldn't have parked it and got the train? No, not in the Tesco car park."

"What, and leave her car? Probably one of Percy's pool vehicles. Nothing too good for the spooks, eh?"

"Aye. Probably you're right. Come on, we're here now. I know you'd rather be at McDonald's. But this is my treat, so eat and forget. She's gone, you're out of this. Let the dead bury their dead and the mad religious fucker do his deal with the devil."

"And Percival can go to hell."

"If he's not already there."

And so they ate. Flaws kept it simple, and it was delicious food, no question: dressed west coast crab and slow cooked and roasted fillet of Speyside beef. The Dauphinoise potatoes were fine, but he could have done with plain roast. Murricane went for the seared razor clams, known locally as spoots, and the rack-and-braised shoulder of lamb. They split a bottle of Les Ormes de Pez 2001, shared an ungenerous cheese plate of Lanark Blue, Mull Cheddar and Sandstinger from Shetland, and finished with espresso and large Dallas Dhus, drams from a dead distillery. They spoke little. Until eventually, dribbling a tiny amount of water into the cask strength Speyside whisky, Flaws said:

"How're you getting back to Drum?"

"I got the bus in. Thought I might crash at yours, if that's OK."

Flaws glanced at his watch, and heaved a sigh. "Fine. Let's pay and head back via Tesco's. We can pick up some beers and maybe some whisky. I'm running low on good stuff and I think there's a deal going on Talisker."

"And see if the Subaru's still there. That's bothering you, isn't it?"

"Just something Percy said. Yes. Yes it is bothering me. He still thinks you're his evil right hand, his hooded claw, you know."

"Thinks he can manipulate me?"

"Yes."

"Maybe he's right."

A WHISKY IN MONSTERVILLE

*** *** ***

It was raining now, a drenching late summer Invernessian downpour carrying the breath of winter. The River Ness glittered to their left as they headed into the city centre, sheltering under a golf umbrella Murricane had casually stolen from the hotel while they were leaving. "Twenty quid tip," he muttered to a tutting Flaws. "Gor's always good for umbrellas. Now, into the dripping armpits of the Queen of the Highland Fleshpots!" It was a phrase he'd picked up from an old *Scotsman* column about the city. Whoever coined it didn't like Inverness much. Or maybe liked the place too much.

Despite the rain, Church Street was busy, the tourist shops open late in an effort to capitalise on the final dregs of the season. They cut through behind the Royal Highland, the former Station Hotel, and into the 24-hour Tesco car park. Three rows in from the boundary with the station was a blue Subaru. Murricane knew immediately that it was Rebecca's. He tried the driver's door. It had been left unlocked. The keys were in the ignition.

"Honest men and bonnie lasses," muttered Flaws, peering in behind him.

"That's Ayr, not Inverness. It's a fucking miracle it's still sitting here."

"24-hour supermarket, secure car park, the permanent threat of God's wrath. This is the Highlands of Scotland, after all." And then Flaws' mobile began to click and trill. The opening section to Pink Floyd's *Money*.

The wrath of God

A blast of peat smoke, fading fast to American Cream Soda and honey, with heather and biscuit. A roar of alcohol and smokiness to fade. Firewater.

BLACK BOTTLE

"**E**asy." Flaws was speaking through clenched teeth. The Subaru's flat-four turbo howled briefly as all four wheels left the ground, and then they were over the canal bridge in a screech of wet rubber and Torvean Golf Club was a damp green blur on their left.

Murricane said nothing. He had been silent since Flaws relayed the call from Percival: Rebecca had been due in London the previous evening. She had not arrived. Operational rules meant she had to check in every three hours while travelling on the UK mainland. She had not done so. There was a satellite tracker in her phone. It was not functioning. It was possible that her identity and movements had become known to Vance, had been made known in fact, probably at levels senior to him. He was no longer confident of his organisation's security and was calling to warn Flaws and Murricane that some kind of laundering of assets may be in train. Including them. Especially Murricane.

"Laundered all to fuck. Laundered with extreme prejudice. The stakes are just too high, and the players too powerful, even for Percival," said Flaws. "That's what he's saying, anyway. That we should go to ground. That you should get out of the way of all this, make yourself scarce. Either that or he's trying to set you on the pricks. Like a suicide bomber."

*** *** ***

They were doing 120 mph as they passed Kilreoch Wood and what had once been the main Highland psychiatric hospital at Craig Dunain. Its grim main building had been converted into luxury flats and executive villas littered the grounds, symbols of brash, moneyed sanity.

"Where are we... you are so pished, my friend. I mean, you're driving well for a drunk man, but you do realise there are traffic cameras back at Kenneth Street and all the way through Inverness? You went down Glenurquhart Road like some kind of mad wee Vauxhall Nova fucker on sulphate. How over the limit must you be? Jesus, I couldn't even... "

"More police after us the better." Murricane's voice sounded rusty, choked, phlegm-ridden. He coughed. "Call your mate, that prick Peyronie. Get him to send a team out to Coldstream's place at Creag Dhearg." The Subaru was electronically constrained from utilising the full potential of its rally-bred flat four engine; Murricane was banging the rev limiter off its bumpers as they howled down towards Loch Dochfour, the wooded basin before Loch Ness proper. The rain had eased, but there was still a lot of standing water and the road was greasy. Flaws jabbed at his mobile, trying to keep it steady as they reached 150 mph, the turbo howling as they rocketed past a timber lorry heading for the Fort William pulp mill. "No signal," he grunted. "Christ, does this thing have suspension? Everything's going sideways, but there's no fucking... up and... down." There was a scraping noise and the brief firework smell of burning metal as the car hit a deep pothole. "Hell's teeth, Murricane, you drunken fucking bastard."

"Four wheel drive, Flaws, old chap. Old... pal. Low centre of gravity. Lower still with you in the passenger seat, you fat old prick."

This stretch of the A82 was particularly notorious. Blind bends, unsighted rises, doddering pensioners in Kias, tourists on the wrong side of the road, crazed crofters in pickups. It had everything, and it was wet and getting darker and darker. But Murricane seemed blessed, touched by the hand of Colin Macrae's ghost. He threaded his way past and inside laggards, slid inside lorries, thrashed the WRX towards Drumnadrochit almost, but not quite as fast as a young man called Erasmus MacGillnain from Beauly had done it, a year previously, as part of the highly illegal and desperately unofficial Monster Belladrum Challenge. This was a timed run from Inverness to Drumnadrochit, over the hill road to Kiltarlity and the Belladrum Estate on the shores of the Beauly Firth, scene of the annual festival, then back along the firth to Inverness. Erasmus had been driving a Nissan Skyline, tuned to produce 900 horsepower. A stalwart of the Dingwall Young Farmers Club, Erasmus - Moose to his friends - was now dead, the result of that perennial cause of Highland fatalities, a drunken, depressed encounter with the wrong end of a shotgun. He'd sawed the barrels off his dad's lovely old Holland and Holland first, just so he could pull the trigger with his thumb. What was wrong with using the big toe, like everyone else did? Flaws remembered one of the uniforms who attended joking about doing it the Hemingway way.

Just before Temple, Murricane slid the car brutally to the right, and they were immediately enveloped in dust as they rattled up the track which led to his garage. The silence when he switched off the engine was shocking, alleviated only by the tick and sizzle as the car started to cool.

"Come on."

Murricane was inside the garage by the time Flaws had the Subaru's passenger door open. "COME *on*." It was dark among the trees, but the Land Rover's interior light flashed on, and Flaws could see Murricane pushing against the door pillar, moving the vehicle backwards. He added his weight to the task, and as the heavy old truck gently rolled into the back wall, he saw Murricane sink to his knees and begin to dig where the Landie's front offside wheel had been.

"Take where the rear nearside was, Zander. There's a steel ammo box about three inches down. Soft earth, hard packed. Fingers'll do it."

Flaws began clawing at the floor of the garage. Soon his fingers hit something solid and within a few seconds he was hauling out a small ammunition box sealed with Gaffa tape.

"Open it. We won't have time later. Full armoury check, now." Flaws wondered at Murricane's powers of recovery. He wondered at his own. Apart from a dry throat and headache, he felt sober enough. But for what? He used his Swiss Army Knife to slice the tape. Inside the box was an oil cloth and waxed paper bundle. He unwrapped it. Two dismantled weapons. One Flaws recognised as a variant of the infamous MAC-10 machine pistol beloved by American gangbangers. This looked like the smaller M-11, using .380 ammunition and so quiet when the suppressor was mounted you could hear the bolt clicking and clicking and clicking and clicking. He fitted the bulky silencer. It looked naked and odd without its magazine.

"Ammunition separate." That's what Murricane had been digging up. He threw two magazines to Flaws one after the other. "You know what you're doing with these, right?" Flaws sighed.

"Firearms training may have been a while ago, but they've been making these things for a long time, haven't they?" His tongue felt swollen. All that rich food. Car sickness. Any minute now he was going to vomit. No. No way. Not a Prebble Hotel meal. He slotted one magazine into place, and put the other in his pocket. "I take it you want the Sig?"

"Blackwater Tactical Version. This is the one made for mercenaries." Murricane crouched beside Flaws and reached into the box. He slotted in one magazine. "Twenty shots per magazine. Came new with five mags. Parabellum. Not bad. Made for numpties. Shoot until you can't shoot no more. Right. Did you get hold of Peyronie and the boys in blue?"

"No. He's quote, unavailable, unquote. Emergency operator has the address, said she'd pass it on. Clearly thought I was drunk and mad. Which I am. Listen mate. Listen to me. We're both more than half-pished. How you got us here without totalling the car is a tribute to all those fucking SBS driving skills courses, and that's fine. But we should..."

"'Should' nothing. I'm sick of this. It's time to go and seriously fuck these bastards up."

"Is this all about Rebecca? Because there's something you should..."

"What? Don't tell me you were in there too? Nah. That doesn't make sense for one thing. No time. No opportunity."

"You're being played here. We both are. Percival... Percival spoke to me, in person, came to the office. You know I've been on a kind of, well, a retainer. I'm the cutout if they want to get hold of you. You know that. And we're friends." Christ, he could hear the wheedling drink in his voice, feel the clouds of lumpy illogicality, the rubbish that came from alcohol. Sober my arse.

"What do you mean, played? What does it matter? Come on, we don't have time for this, Zander!"

"OK. here's how I read it..." Flaws reflexively checked the safety on the M11. "Percival's position is... kind of... how can I put this?"

"Shadowy. Amorphous. Deniable."

"All that."

"That's the point of what he does. What he does is run a... a talent pool. Across the services, outside them. He gets things done people don't want to say they want done."

"Well, I think he's found himself, if not out of his depth, at least in the middle of a gigantic fuck-up. A rotting, toxic bomb of... well. A fucking bomb, right? A mine! One with the potential to explode in his face, the Government's face, and all laid by some of those psychos in the MOD and Civil Service. The ones that railroaded the Iraq weapons of mass destruction crap through. The ones that made Ollie North such a hero and then a fall guy in the States."

"That's decades apart. You think it's all Varlindium?"

"Are you serious? Of course it is. What? You thought it was about the Loch Ness Monster? About appeasing a bunch of religious loonies with friends in high places? Vance is a monstrous fuckwit, but he has access to the single most valuable mineral on earth, and it's on British soil, under British water. It could also seal British and American relations for decades to come. Or months, or weeks, I don't know." Murricane was staring at him. Flaws noticed his eyes were bloodshot.

"The play is this, probably: Percival has been told to let the Vance thing run. To let the bodies disappear. Factions. He's been playing factions against one another. Somebody was keen to protect British interests and stop the psychotic American bastards. Too many burnt bodies. Too much of your pal Jenks running amok. But then somebody else saw mileage in us all playing happy mad-as-hell families together. Pin all the bodies on Davie the Druid, track him down and kill him before he can start mouthing off in court. Or let him just disappear, if he's willing to. All too very convenient. A little local difficulty. I'm guessing that the mad-as-hell-families-faction won the day. Percival's been told to play the appeasement card. Except..."

"What?"

"Except part of that might have been a deal to give you to Vance. Or more precisely, to Jenks."

"What, Vance would jeopardise something as major as what you're talking about for little old me?"

Silence. The sound of an owl hooting somewhere. Breathing. Flaws sighing.

"No. Not quite, Murricane. I don't think anyone saw you as capable of jeopardising anything. I think they saw you as what you are. A half-crippled drunk on retirement who does occasional fetch and carry errands. I think that's what Rebecca told Percival. And I think Vance and Jenks asked for you as part of the deal. A little extra sweetener. A souvenir. You, maybe, and Rebecca."

Murricane said nothing. There was the oily snick of a Sig-Sauer magazine being removed and reinserted.

"Of course, the other possibility is that Percival still rates your possibility of causing absolute and utter mayhem, and the game he's playing is to rid himself and the Government of this entire toxic scam. Fuck Varlindium, fuck Vance, and fuck Coldstream's plans for Creationism to run rampant across the earth, along with the Loch Ness Monster and all sorts of little Coldstream babies. No doubt there's a breeding programme secreted away somewhere in that Fantasy Island mind of his. Oh, and fuck Percy's enemies within the British, what would you call it? Establishment? Government? Something undemocratic anyway."

More silence. Then: "Keep talking, Butch. That's what you're good at." Another pause. "You finished?"

"I am. Perhaps we both are."

"You still know how to use that little M11?"

"I think so."

"Then let's go and play out Percival's game. They'll probably be using Rebecca as bait. That's the bottom line. They're stupid enough. And we're not entirely alone in our dispensability and stupidity." He opened the driver's door of the Land Rover, scrabbled under the front seat and pulled out a small rucksack package. "Here. More goodies. Red Bull, fully sugared."

"That's not going to sharpen you up too much, Ace. What, is this some kind of soft drinks advert now?"

"I also have the trusty American soldier's standby, Adderall. 'Instant Release' and 'Extra Release'. Take one of each. Four amphetamines for the price of one. Eradicates drunkenness and tiredness. Popped an IR back in Inverness. Time for XR. Hangover's exponentially worse, but what the doo-dah." He held out two capsules. "What do you say? Shall we?"

"Oh, go on." Flaws took the pills. "Ambassador, you are spoiling us. You drive, I'll scream."

*** *** ***

The only road bridges across the River Ness were in Inverness itself, and Murricane's chemically-enhanced drive back to the city was a screeching jumble of impressions for Flaws. The Adderall had begun to kick in almost immediately, accelerating his heart beat and eradicating whatever alcoholic fuzziness remained. Instead, everything seemed to be crystal clear, being recorded in painstaking, high definition detail. The terrified expression on a motorhome driver's face caught in their headlights as the Subaru screamed past an ageing Jaguar XJ on the Dochfour straight. The pattern of the filaments in sodium streetlamps. The dark-blue flicker of dying light on the clouds over Ben Wyvis as the twilight slipped completely into inky night.

They didn't seem to be going that quickly, now. Both their brains had been enhanced past the capabilities of the car. There was only the sliding, thumping sensations, the clatter and thump of rough road surfaces, and those visual impressions. Recording, recording: faces, astonished, frightened. No sirens. No police. Why not? The way they were driving? Calling again, still no Peyronie, trying the 999 operator, getting a curiously terse response. Warned off, Flaws wondered?

They crossed the Ness on the main A82; Murricane threw the car onto the A9 at the Kessock Bridge roundabout and floored it up past the winter snowline to Daviot and on to Scatraig. After that it was the black moorland emptiness of the B851 until forestry erased all glimmer of moon and stars and they were corkscrewing past the small lochs of Bunchaton and Dunfichty. Murricane slowed. It had taken them no more than 25 minutes to get from Drumnadrochit. There were various shooting lodges and estate houses with drives leading off the road. They had looped right around Inverness and then approached Loch Ness from the southeast.

The entrance to Creag Dhearg was marked by a ruined keeper's gatehouse. Murricane turned slowly into the drive, and then slid the Subaru into a gap behind the ruined gatehouse and the forbidding mass of old pines.

"How far to the main house? Can you remember?" Flaws nodded. His memory seemed to have been boosted. Electrified.

"Short drive. About 100 metres or so. Couple of bends, blind. Thereabouts." His jaw felt sore. Clamped. He could have done with some gum. Murricane reached into the back seat, scrabbling in a rucksack. His pistol was in there. Flaws noted dispassionately that he had been clutching the fully loaded M11 throughout the journey. His fingers were stiff. Murricane had something else in his hands now.

"Summit SNBVG 7s. Infra-red night goggles. Amazingly, I have two sets." They were like cyclops eyes, a single lens with two eye cups. "We won't need them if we follow the road and I don't think there'll be any guards here. Closer to the house maybe. Don't switch them on just now." He demonstrated the lens-side switch, large and rubber-coated for gloved fingers. "Arms check?"

Flaws felt for the two spare M11 mags and once more checked the safety on the sub machine gun. "Fine. Two mags and one in the hole."

"Check. I'm carrying the Sig and five mags. I also have three M84 flashbangs, one of which I hereby give to you." He handed Flaws one of the tubular black stun grenades as if it was made of solid gold. "Pull round pin. Check target. Pull triangular ring, throw immediately. Fall to floor with fingers in ears and eyes shut. I don't have any earplugs unfortunately. Stupid... anyway, we good?"

"Good. Err... what's the overall strategy?"

"The strategy? What do you mean strategy? IIDFTU. Know what that stands for?"

"No. Wait a minute... no."

"If In Doubt, Fuck Things Up. That's the whole of American foreign policy in a nutshell."

"What about Rebecca?"

"If she's alive, she's alive. If she's dead, and if they're sensible she will be, then she's dead."

"So the aim is to fuck things up anyway."

"I have an odd feeling we're not dealing with sensible people here. I'm kind of hoping not. I'm not feeling very sensible. Let's go."

*** *** ***

Flaws was acutely conscious of the way he was dressed. For a casual summer's night out in Inverness. Light North Face anorak in orange, the better to be spotted by a rescuing helicopter should he fall off a mountain. Not that he was prone to falling off mountains. Or climbing them. Jeans, black, dark blue shirt. Fine. He took off the jacket, shivering in the cooling air. The night-vision goggles dangled around his neck. Everything smelt of pine resin. Or did it? There was something else, something more pungent, dirtier. Burning plastic in one of the Creag Dhearg fireplaces? Murricane was in dark walking trousers and sweatshirt, wearing trainers. Fuck it. He followed the loping figure down the track, staying behind Murricane, ready to dive off into the verge if anyone made their presence felt. There was a glow ahead of them through the trees. Flickering. And that smell. Stronger now. Something was burning. A bonfire? A celebration? And then there was a muffled explosion, the whump! of gas or petrol, and even at a distance he could feel the change in temperature.

In the car park, a large motorhome had all but burned itself to a blackened chassis. The explosions they'd heard, petrol or cooking gas, had scattered shards of burning material into the woods and onto several parked cars. A Toyota pickup stood battered and impervious. Like the old stone house it had shrugged off the flaming fallout. Not so the body, dressed in white robes, that lay between the camper and the porch. It was smouldering.

The lights were on inside Craig Dhearg lodge itself. Every window was illuminated. But there was no movement. Just the sound of quiet singing. A lone female voice. Flaws strained to make out the words, but couldn't. He was very conscious of the gun in his hands.

Murricane was bending over the body, pistol in hand. He made no attempt to pat out the burning ashes that threatened to set the robe alight.

"Dead?"

"What do you think? Shot in the back, running away."

"Some kind of argument? Lovers' tiff? Theological dispute?"

"Something. Take a look. Recognise him?"

The man's face was orange and chimney red in the dying flames from the camper, and creamy in the light spillage from the lodge. It was the would-be blackmailer from the islands, the Pastor. McGlone. Murdo Murder Malachi McGlone.

"No more vigilante shite from him, anyway. Murder McGlone. Living up to his name." Flaws wondered about names. How you lived up to them. Or down. Names like his own.

"Guess he made the wrong spiritual choice. Should have stayed with his own hotline to God. Maybe he's in heaven?"

"Fuckin' hope not. What now?"

"Inside. Cover each other. I'll go first."

They tag-teamed their way into the porch and the hallway beyond. No more bodies. Nobody at all. All the lights on, though, and still the singing, louder now.

And we are walking through the valley
And we are walking o'er the plain
Over the mountains and the hillsides
Until we rest with you again

The singer turned out to be Sister Melliflua. She was wearing a white robe, the same kind that adorned the body of Murder in the car park. She was strumming what looked like an expensive guitar, a deep reddish brown one. 'Gibson', it said on the headstock. Just with her thumb, amateurishly down-strumming what might have been a C chord. She had a cigarette clamped in its neck, like one of those old blues guitarists from the 1960s. The smell of American tobacco mingled with the chemical combustion fumes from outside.

And we are walking through the valley
And we are walking o'er the plain...

Her voice was strong. There was a glottal rasp from the cigarettes, but still, thought Flaws, she could sing.

When she saw them watching her, guns drawn, heads distorted by the night-vision sets, she stopped singing, and casually plucked the cigarette from the guitar, sucking it red in a great inhalation which looked full of desperate relief. She blew the smoke out in a great gout, out over the dozens of bodies, all in once-white robes, that lay on the floor or slumped together on conference chairs. Behind her, the great pictures of Nessie in Plesiosaur guise frowned solemnly down. There was nothing pure or virginal about the scene. The robes were stained with urine and shit. The smell, tinged somehow with whisky, was appalling. They had all soiled themselves as they died.

"Welcome," she said. "Ah, it's the detective and his friend. The searchers after truth and enlightenment. For Miss Anson and her elusive remains. Her smoking remains. *Smokin'*! Smokin' like me. Well, here we are. Here we all are. Here you are. Here I am." She coughed, a hacking, spluttering, wet cough. "Me, I'm going to die anyway. I was going to die anyway. Full of self-inflicted shit, full of emphysema and probably cancer and years and years of abuse. But it was me fought to stay alive. Fooled them. Fooled the Reverend. Fooled God." Melliflua's laughter was terrible to hear, like tearing, rotten cloth.

Repentance

❦

'Patiently rested in charred sweet oak casks to create a whisky as black as night, with a rich velvety taste. Savour the smooth, intense flavour and discover hidden complexities in this unique black whisky. A bottle of Loch Dhu would make a fantastic and unusual present...' Dealer advertisement.

LOCH DHU 10, 'THE BLACK WHISKY'

A WHISKY IN MONSTERVILLE

Coldstream had been feeling the hand of God on him less and less. He had, he realised, begun depending on the fleshly will of man, the old urges: money, power, sex. He had been flattered by Vance into this... this collaboration. This unequal yoking. Vance had claimed discipleship, seemed to be willing to follow him. Had believed, so he said, in the power of the returning Christ and the crucial importance of the Loch Ness creature in defining creationism, in accelerating that return.

So often over the years, God had spoken to him, guided him in acts that had reaped their own rewards, led him in different paths. Back in childhood, the funerals he had held for roadkill, and then the animals he had killed himself. Rats, cats, dogs. The healing services, the snake handling, though that had been mostly for show and a very short phase following the accident and that terrible week in the Santa Cressida toxicology unit. And later, the burning of the Qur'an, before it had been taken up by every hick string-tied cowboy evangelical from Texas to Alaska. The condemnation of Bruce Springsteen for the alleged wearing of a hairpiece, which had led to legal action and a subsequent cease-and-desist order, accepted quietly, but a learning experience nevertheless. The abortion clinic protests, again usurped by others, copyists, plagiarists. The building of that grand edifice in California, so fraught with debt and accusations, one of the reasons it had been useful to get out of the US for a while. But God had shown him that it was his task to pioneer these things, to lead and inspire.

Nessatoreanism had seemed like a pathway he could take on his own, gradually bringing disciples on to the way with him, the pilgrimage, the journey. And then the Texas school system had adopted the Loch Ness anomaly as crucial to its Creationist teaching, and he had attracted the interest of Vance. So flattering. So enriching, fiscally. The debts gone. It had led to this glorious settlement on the shores of Loch Ness, itself, the prospect of the Centre for Creationist Studies, the triumph of Nessatoreanism. Sanctity! True Sanctity! And Vance was working for the US

Government, really! It was for the good of God and America! The very rocks cried out!

But then Jenks had been foisted upon him. Vance's requests had become orders. The bad things had started to happen. And not even the undoubtedly soothing sexual favours of his chosen ones had been able to alleviate the sense of drift. Away from the Lord. Away from His will. Into the hands of... well. There was no shirking it. Of Evil.

And there was no other way of describing what he'd found in the old ice house. He had watched Jenks disappear down the path through the woods too many times without questioning what he might be up to. Well, he had assumed it was harmless hunting, his collection of crossbows and other weaponry well known to the brethren and sistern. And then the disappearance of Sister Anson and that red-headed renegade... well. They could be justified. He had justified them. After all, wasn't everything under God's control in the end? God willed everything. Everything that happened was God's will. Even the bad things were done for His greater glory. Except, the enactment and allowance of evil was... had to be... in some way...

Wrong.

The ice house had been a vision of hell. The heads, that rotting deer carcase, the smell, despite the evident use of some chemical preservative, the presence of lime and curiously, a dozen or so bottles of Paco Rabanne eau de cologne. Human and animal heads. Fingers and hands. Paws, claws, tails. All carefully positioned around the walls of the old stone and earth vault. Sister Anson. That lascivious bastard. Sightless eyes, staring, accusing. Worst of all, that ginger haired boy, what was it? Liam. Killed on his whim, his instructions. Made to disappear. Maybe Jenks reconsidered. He had been dismembered and reassembled, wrongly, left arm for right, head backwards. Six battery lanterns in the centre of the floor, their lenses facing outwards, set in a circle around a stained tartan travel rug. Plenty of space for two. Vance and Jenks. A relationship beyond unnatural. How could God's will contain this, allow this? Even a will that permitted evil in order for good to conquer? Sister Anson's head. Shrivelled and bloated, both together, and a slow pulse of movement that almost caused him to drop dead in terror. But it was only maggots. He felt as if they were eating at his brain too.

He had gone back to the lodge, to his study. Reached into that bottom drawer and picked out the Colt single-action Peacemaker revolver he had bought all those years ago for the great anti-gun control marches in California, when the visible display of weapons, not against the law, was such a statement of holiness, of the glory that was the Second Amendment. Its pearl inlays always reminded him of George Patton. For he too was a general, a general of souls, a commander of the spirit. There was a box of old .45 slugs in another drawer. The gun was from the 1930s, but was faithful to the original Samuel Colt design, the pistol that had tamed the wild west. Established civilisation in America.

But as he held the loaded weapon to his temple, felt the cool imprint of its barrel and the wild longing for release, for entrance to God's kingdom, forgiven, if somewhat stained, he thought of his disciples, his flock. The Sanctified, among them the one or two new converts or recruits, the 'local fraternity', he called them. McGlone and his adherents. More coming, too, more attracted by the Great Call, the wondrous message. Didn't they deserve his leadership? His knowledge? His blessing? Didn't they all need to know what he had discovered, and to share his journey to a greater light and understanding?

Communion. This was a time for communion. It had become so much holier, communion, for the Sanctified Church of the Christ Child In History, since they had started using the whisky instead of non-alcoholic wine. What a revelation that had been, and what an uplifting of spirits had resulted! The purchase online of the Loch Dhu had been God's work. Such a rare whisky, so black and bloodlike. Congealed blood, yes, but blood nevertheless. And from the darkness came forth such glorious, blinding purity! He pressed the intercom that allowed his voice to be heard on speakers throughout the building and the grounds. His disciples would be praying, cultivating the market garden they were so proud of. And the jewellery workshop, where they cast those little images of the Creature. He fingered the gold-plated inch-long version he wore around his neck on a chain. He remembered the processes. How the plating involved careful use of potassium cyanide. The fume cabinets they'd had to install.

Some of the flock were meditating. Some were in Inverness, witnessing. Some were at the Foyers pier, part of the regular parties that scanned the loch looking for signs of the creature. Some were aboard the *Baptist*, receiving technical instruction from the crew.

They could wait. They would know, they would see the sign he had left them and know what to do. And Vance's precious, sterile motorhome? That would be a fiery symbol too.

*** *** ***

"Where's Coldstream?" They had taken Melliflua into the porch, after she had warned them about the spilt whisky on the floor, the plastic cups, the crusts of bread, stained black.

"Cyanide. He got that idea from Jones. Jim Jones. You know, the Guyana massacre? The People's Temple?" She sighed, lit another cigarette. The flames from the camper van were dying now. Flaws kept expecting to hear sirens, approaching help. But there was nothing. He had tried using his mobile, but there was no signal.

"Potassium cyanide. I remember ordering it for the jewellery workshop. The Creature pendants." She fingered the gold plesiosaur that hung around her neck. "Plating with gold. Gold over base metal. Story of my life. Story of this... this fucking place." No tears. Just a grim dry-eyed fury. And disgust. "He didn't take it. Oh no. At the altar, presiding, singing his bastard hymns. He wrote them himself, you know. Had plans to sell the records. Make money. Make money. It was all about money. And power. It always is.

"He had a gun. That Scotch guy, the guy from Inverness. He realised what was happening, saw the people start to slump. He didn't drink the... stuff. Neither did I. I hate it. Whisky. Black whisky. Foul stuff. Too sweet. Terrible for the teeth. Bad memories, too. College, Jack Daniels. Black Jack. But not as black as this stuff. God told him, he said, not wine, whisky. Black whisky. Christ, I could do with a proper drink. I'd love a vodka. Something pure."

"Just tell us where Coldstream is," said Murricane. "And Vance and Jenks. And if you're good we'll buy you some Grey Goose."

"He shot the Scotch fella, and the rest of them just... it was as if they were hypnotised or something. But then we were. We were all hypnotised."

"And why not you? What made you refuse?"

She grinned. It was a twist of the mouth, nothing more. Showing the classic sign of an American with money lurking somewhere in the background: beautiful teeth.

"Vanity. Maybe history too. I'd been on the fringes of the Guyana thing. Heard about it. Knew people who might have been there, but weren't. Nine hundred people died there, you know. Fuck it. Fuck religion. I knew once Avril... after that began, the killings. After Liam. Jenks. Maybe he went to the ice house. Coldstream might have gone there."

"The ice house"

"Yeah, an old stone, kind of a stone-lined pit, about half a mile downhill through the woods. Always locked. Jenks's lair. His den. I've never been in there, but it smells bad. In every way. You'll know it. You'll know it by the smell."

*** *** ***

They were virtually on top of the ice house before they realised, their senses swayed and dislocated by the night-vision goggles they were both now using. Everything swam in ghostly green and puce, marginally delayed. It was like being in a swimming pool. A swimming pool filled with trees. And it was indeed the smell that told them where they were. A dreadful combination of familiar aromas. After-shave lotion, lime, rotting flesh. It was a warzone smell. A warzone in a fruitmarket, next to a pharmacy.

No conversation. Murricane's finger was at his lips. They were in a clearing, on top of a short slope, a clear drop of about eight feet in front of them. He signalled to Flaws that they should circle to opposite sides of the clearing and descend. He was feeling slightly ill, he realised. The drugs and the alcohol, the Prebble food, the stress. There was, in the end, no drug like adrenaline.

Adrenaline was winning the battle for his body. It was the Arnold Schwarzenegger of drugs. He had a silencer for the Sig in one pocket. He felt weighed down, not dressed for this. He missed his old Walther. Civilian clothes. Stupid. Magazines here, there. Tight against cloth and flesh. No battle rattle. He hugged the treeline, watched Flaws doing the same, his body moving against the green and black of the forest. Crouched low, everything green. And then the shards of light from what had to be the front of the ice house. A door, ill-fitting. Warmth and light behind it. Something in there. The smell, now overwhelming.

Jenks. That night in the Big A. All that heroin. The truth was, Percy must have known that's what it was all about. It was all about Vance, even then appeasing Vance. keeping the bastard sweet, the Americans sweeter. Global Redemption. Jenks. Suddenly Murricane felt sorry for him. The poor sod didn't realise just how disposable he was. Like Ollie Fucking North, when his usefulness was used up or his cover blown. Then he'd be fed to the wolves or worse. In chunks.

Or fed to someone like him. Was that what was going on? He signalled to Flaws: left, back, down, stay. Cover me. All fingers and arms. A thumbs up from Flaws. Now he was at the door. He switched off the Summits, closed his eyes and waited for them to adjust to reality. A heartbeat. Two. Then it was just, breathe, movement, muscle memory and an utter lack of thought. All training, no anger, no fear. Reflex. The drink, the drugs, the injuries, the wasted time, the running away... nights on the loch, fucking, waiting, thinking, dreaming. It all came down to this in the end. This was what he did. Who he was.

Time stopped. Time stretched. He was in front of the door, had a flashbang in his hand: yank one pin, open the door, – no lock – why? – pull the other – get it right, round first, then the triangle. Throw it in, close the door, down, fingers in ears. A concussion of noise and explosive spillage of light. And then he was in the room, the cellar, pit, whatever you'd call it, a weird circle of halogen from lamps set in the middle. A figure there, lying on its side, jerking convulsively, howling like a wounded dog. And around the walls...

A WHISKY IN MONSTERVILLE

Around the walls was... a cartoon. A horror comic. Hell on earth. A circle of hell. A joke. This was Monsterville.

A joke. He realised he was right. This was what passed for a sense of humour when it came to Jenks. It was a hidden part of any soldier's make-up, what no-one had ever got about the torture scandals at Abu Ghraib. It was a joke, it was the only way of coping, of fighting off the horror. Of defusing it. Jenks had just taken it to a different level. To penetrate his blunted pathology, it had just needed to be more extreme. And safer, maybe, too. More under control. Other people arranged live bodies in piles, made prisoners simulate having sex. He used the bits of bodies. Set them out.

Jerking in the shadows cast by the circle of lights, deafened and blinded by the stun grenade, Coldstream was smeared with dirt, snot and tears. Charisma had deserted him. A long pistol, an old Colt, lay on the floor. As he began to recover, his hands scrabbled for it. Murricane stepped forward and kicked it to one side. Coldstream was trying to say something now. Amid the moans there was a word. He leaned towards the quivering flesh on the floor. He had only a mild tinnitus from the grenade's shock wave, like having been at loud rock concert. Death metal. Something unpleasant like Necrophagist or Behemoth.

"Lock... locked. Locked... Can't..."

Another noise behind him. He turned, saw the door opening and the shadow of a gun barrel wavering across the horror show along the walls. The figure holding the actual gun uncoiled from the stooping position necessary to get in. It was still bent. Still hunched. But bulked out. Flak vest. It was Vance, holding a tactical shotgun of some kind, probably a Mossberg 590. Perfect for this kind of situation. He was smiling. What the fuck? His hands. His hands were strange. White. Fleshless. Dead. Gloves. This was a man who played hardball with governments, and now... but the flash of thought was over in a millisecond. It was no time for conversation, at least not a verbal one. Murricane dropped prone, holding the Sig's trigger down and firing five shots before rolling and firing another three. Vance was thrown bodily back against the door jamb, the shotgun exploding into the ice house roof.

And then there was a tinny mechanical chatter from outside. A suppressed M11 machine pistol. Fuck. He should have told Flaws to get rid of the silencer. Less impact, less accuracy, and this was a rough-and-tumble firefight. With shotguns, for God's sake.

His pistol shooting had been wild. Only three bullets had actually hit Vance. Two in the centre of his Crye precision armour. The best. But then it would be. And one expanding soft shell in the unprotected upper arm. Which had been severed almost completely. Vance was still smiling, a rictus grin, in shock. Arterial blood was pumping out. The brachial artery. It was a body armourer's black joke. Aim for the upper arm. They'll bleed out in minutes. Murricane pressed hard, held the flow. Left hand, right hand still holding the Sig, safety off. Remember. Remember.

"You can leave your arm for Jenks's collection, Mr Vance. What the fuck are you doing? You could have had a whole private army in here, doing your dirty work."

"Cairnduff said..." the voice was oddly conversational, almost contented. "Jenks said... it would just be target practice. Said you were just a gift from the... powers that be." More chattering from outside. *Chinkachinkachinkchinka*. Christ, he hoped Flaws wasn't just wasting bullets. Jenks was a harder target than this amateur game-playing piece of shit.

"A gift?" There was the sound of soft giggling. Or gurgling. A kind of pleasure.

"Yeah, a present. Unarmed. To him. And from him to me. Grateful... he was grateful..."

"Maybe it was. But Jenks was playing you, Mr Vance. Protecting himself. That's all he's ever done, I think. He pleases himself, and it gets harder and harder to find anything that actually gives him pleasure. Maybe you thought you were in the same league. The same tastes. You're not even kindergarten sadistic. But maybe you'll enjoy this." He removed his hand, wiped the blood off it on the front of Vance's vest. "You've got maybe three minutes to live unless you hold this artery closed. And I don't think you can. Can you? Consider it a test. I don't think you can."

A loud mechanical click. Jesus. Silence. No giggling from Vance. Murricane twisted round to see Coldstream pointing the old Colt at him. He threw himself to one side as the gun went off in a cloud of smoke and flame and with a huge, old-school bang. He found himself covered in blood, bone and pieces of brain tissue. The Colt's huge, lumbering shell had hit Vance neatly in the head, causing it virtually to explode. So much for holding down an artery. Coldstream was struggling with the revolver's action. Murricane shot him twice in the lower abdomen. Big target. Maybe he'd take some time to bleed to death. He hoped so. Then he threw himself out of the door, face down in the leaf mould and pine needles, as that moneychanger's clink from Flaws's M11 sounded again in a long sustained bursts. No jamming. Good gun.

"Jenks!" The shout echoed off the pines, that strange echo you got in forests. "Jenks, you there?" Nothing. "Flaws?" His voice sounded hoarse and rusty and strange.

A pause.

"I'm here. Someone was covering the one who came in after you. I don't know if I hit him."

"Where are you? Stay hidden if you can. Don't come out."

"Other side of the clearing." A range of about 30 feet. He'd probably missed. But you never knew.

"Will he head back to the house? Is he still around?"

"Unless he's got a vehicle stashed down towards Loch Ruthven, then that's his only way out. But I'm not sure he wants to just get away."

"No," came another voice. "He doesn't." There was movement in the trees. A figure emerged, hands held up, palms out. Full camouflage gear, tactical vest. No visible weapons. But there was only the light leaking from the ice house doorway to tell. Rebecca was probably armed to the teeth. "He thought you'd be unarmed. I was supposed to deal with all the little toys you had stored away above Temple, the one buried oh-so-smartly underneath the Land Rover, buried in your little caches. No Walther PPK, though. Your favourite lucky charm gun. Lost that in Afghanistan, didn't you?"

"There are no lucky charms," said Murricane. "There is no luck."

"The car and Percy. Lured you out here, supposedly at their mercy. Idea was to change your bullets for blanks, all that. Couldn't really do anything about the flashbangs, but what the hell. As it was, I consulted with Percy, and we – he – decided to leave things as they were. Nice, eh? Ensuring a fair fight. That's why Jenks sent in Vance. He wasn't sure. Vance thought you were just some drunk, deranged with grief at the kidnapping of his beloved slut. I knew you better, though Murricane. Didn't I? So did Percy. And so did Jenks. Though I have to say I did lose confidence in you. For a while. Monsters, indeed!"

"Is he here? Maybe you're still playing games. Is he waiting for you to draw us out, finish us off?"

"No, no more games. Or just the one. Get him. He's heading up to the house. I think his idea is to disable the vehicles, then hunt you down. Possibly me as well, now. He'll know that I betrayed him. He's very good at hunting people down, Jenks is. You know he likes his souvenirs. You've seen them. As you've discovered. I rather think he fancied a souvenir of me, but I had an official capacity, you see. Seconded to the same team, so to speak. But temporarily."

"Are you armed?"

"What do you think?"

"I can shoot her," said Flaws, his voice sounding thoughtful, somehow, considered. "Should I?"

"Probably not a great idea," said Rebecca. She sounded amused, thought Murricane. "The truth, such as it is, being that Percival had a degree of faith in you, Murricane. Even though you are a crocked up piece of spent white trash, and a drunk. All that whisky! Jesus, I thought I was going to throw up half the time I was with you. Thank fuck for Adderall, right? You should be thankful to Percy. He was walking a fine line, doing what he was told, feeding you to the American wolves, making sure that the Varlindium extraction went ahead, easing the way for the horrible Vance and the worse Jenks. But he's so *British*, Percy, isn't he? In the end of the day, it's public school fair play and give a bloke a fair go. Or rather, he saw his best interests possibly, just possibly being aligned with the complete and utter destruction of the Vance project. And you were just the kind of faulty weapon to do the damage."

"IIDFIU," said Murricane. "One way or another, it would turn out?"

"If In Doubt, Fuck It Up *Totally*. You forgot the 'T'. Percy had his preferences. Unleash the puppies of conflict, all that sort of thing."

"But we're not finished yet," said Flaws.

"No," said Rebecca. "No, we're not. We need to move. You have to move. It's your turn now." She pulled a chunky satellite phone from the side pocket of her rucksack. "I think it's time to tell the cleaning teams they can move in, don't you? They've been standing by, waiting for the word. Waiting to see how things... turned out. When our boy... your boy sees that he's now in an alien and unsupportive environment, we... you'll be able to flush him out. If you haven't completely lost your skills. Where would he go though?"

"He'll run," said Flaws.

"He won't want to, but he'll retreat," said Murricane. "He'll have various options in his head. Avenues. Exit strategies. Road, foot."

"Water," said Rebecca.

*** *** ***

Jenks was sorry to abandon the ice house. He'd been happy there. But now, as he jogged painfully along his alternative path back to Creag Dhearg, one he'd marked with luminescent tritium pegs, he consciously put it into his store of pleasurable and useful memories. Another time, he'd meditate on it. Remember. And he had the photographs, stored away on Darknet. A pleasure for the future.

He felt a sickening twinge from his back. One stray bullet from that fool with the machine pistol, a Mac-10 or something equally inaccurate. And silenced. What was the point of that? The loss of Vance. Collateral. He had wanted it, wanted the kill, and it might have been all right. But no, it wasn't. And he protected himself. Whatever he owed Vance, he owed himself more.

There had been a set-up there, he was sure. He had been told he and Vance were being given the crippled SBS bastard as sport, as compensation for all their trouble. A gratuity. And then it had all begun to tip slowly but surely away from them. Awry. It had all gone awry. Faster and faster until suddenly, there they were. Fucked as a very fucked thing.

Coldstream. Put religion in the mix and you were always going to have trouble. And when the stupid jerk arrived at the ice house waving his ancient cowboy gun about, screaming about sin and redemption and the unity of death, he had realised that Vance's controllable madness, and his own, was being threatened by someone else's. He and Vance had stayed in the little hide he had created. The woman, the Brit woman, untouchable he'd been told, very seriously, was not in play. Do Not Touch. She was watching with them, all that superior, sardonic silence, ice-bitch solemnity. Inside, he realised now, she was laughing her guts out. He'd have her for that. In the end, someday, somewhere, he would have her. Bits of her. Pieces. He'd come back. And he'd come back for Murricane. That hapless, hopeless lucky prick.

She, Elmsworth, Rebecca, had watched as it all came undone. And why? Why would billions of dollars worth of investment and potential profit vanish on a religious asshole coming unhinged, over the tastes that he and Vance shared, that Vance had been afraid to indulge in until he, Jenks, had begun showing him the way?

Governments were involved, were teetering on the edge of great embarrassments, great losses. But Governments had always been dependent on human beings, fallible, sometimes strange human beings. Human beings with their little moral foibles, their ideas about right and wrong. That never seemed to apply to artists. They were allowed to be immoral. Weren't artists essentially peculiar, sometimes criminal people? What made him worse than an artist?

He remembered with a kind of dispassionate anger when it had all began to change. Not this project at all, but that business in Afghanistan. The heroin. That was the key to it all. The deals Vance had been doing took in all kinds of organisations, governments, armies. Vance had been too important to lose even then, too important not to appease. Even before this metal, this mineral. Varlindium. Ah well. The metal would always be there. Someone would mine it, and the governments would find a way. KokVan might break up, might be quietly taken over by less flamboyant, even better connected characters. Faceless men and women with conservative tastes. For now, it was time to go. It was time to get out.

He had the keys to the HiLux. He was hoping that the promised emergency service embargo was still in place. The woman had said it would last all night. But he had seen the glow through the trees. At first he'd thought Coldstream had set the whole lodge on fire, but after he'd trapped the bastard and left Vance and the woman on watch, he'd circled back and found it was only that oversized metallic womb, Vance's motorhome. More lost trophies. He'd come back to the ice house, sat in the hide, waited. Given Vance the opportunity he'd been pleading for. The chance to kill, up close and personal. Someone who was supposed to be crippled, unarmed, probably drunk. That Brit woman had lied. He'd have her. Even if it had to be quickly and unsatisfactorily, he'd have her someday.

Where would he go? He had contacts in Ireland. Getting there would be easy. If the worst came to worst, once he got to the south west of Scotland, he could steal a boat. Dinghy. Kayak. It was less than 20 miles. He felt calm at the prospect. That was enough of thinking so far into the future.

The motorhome was nothing but an oily, smoking slick on the car park's gravel, a carbonised pile of burnt framework, engine, wheels. A terrible smell of burnt plastic, flesh, oil. A body, crumpled and clearly shot. A woman, sitting on the Creag Dhearg steps, smoking. That woman, the one who'd always regarded him with such knowing contempt. Sister Melliflua. She looked straight at him. Fuck her. He raised the Glock he was carrying and shot her twice in the chest. White robe. Black blood. That would teach her. Looking at him. Patronising him. Smoking was bad for you anyway. Be the death of you. Raising the gun had hurt. It was just a graze on his back, but he could feel the cloaking stickiness, the stiffness. If he wasn't careful it would seize up. There was another pain, too, something deeper. Maybe he'd chipped a bone.

A distant sound. Somebody running. No sirens, though. If somebody had seen the flames, the block on any official response was working. Wait. That Subaru. That was the woman's. She'd been waiting in it at that Inverness mart when he and Vance had picked her up. There was no time to do a proper job, but what the hell. He put two bullets into the two front tyres, climbed into the Toyota and left, not revving like a mad thing, driving with the economy and care he'd been taught by his father, back in the great stillness of the past. A habit his dad had beaten into him, arms tied to the steering wheel. When they went on their hunting trips. Their collecting expeditions. Now, a burst of machine pistol fire clattered into the bodywork, smashed a back window. But they were too far away to be accurate or effective. Perhaps he didn't really care anymore. He wondered at that.

*** *** ***

"Shit," said Murricane. Did he shoot the Scooby's tyres out? Bastard."

"Not to mention Sister Melliflua," Flaws was panting. He really would have to do something about his lack of fitness, he thought. "Poor soul."

"She deserved what she got." Murricane was running his hand over the Subaru's offside front wheel, puzzled. "She could have stopped this if she'd just…"

"Nobody could have stopped this." Rebecca was stooped over Melliflua, feeling for a pulse. "It stops now, though. Or soon. Soonish." She straightened. "Have you been enjoying my little car?" She grinned at him. "If you have, then you should perhaps have taken a closer look at it. It's had the department's once-over. Basic upgrades. Those are Michelin PAX tyres, front and rear. Self-sealing. Ride flat. Hundred mile range. Nice shooting, by the way, Mr Flaws. I think you may have actually hit a tree."

"I don't," said Murricane. "He specialises in the spaces between them. Branching out. So. You're saying we can drive the fucker? Let's go."

"I'll drive," said Rebecca."

*** *** ***

Jenks saw blue lights flickering through the trees, heard the whoop of the sirens. His window of opportunity was being closed down. Lights off, he rammed the pickup down a narrow fire break and watched in the mirror as a fire engine and two police cars bumped past, heading fast for Creag Dhearg. He was about 20 metres from the tarmac road, but he was guessing the cops would seal the drive off. And his original plan, to head either for Inverness or Fort Augustus and one of the roads south, now seemed out of the question. The Elmsworth woman. She had turned on him. Correction: she had never been anything else but his enemy.

Foyers. If he could get to Foyers, to the pier. The *Baptist*? The submarine? No help to him. He couldn't cruise down the loch underwater and sneak through the locks. Besides, he had no idea how to make a submarine work, other than by waving a gun at the crew. Dive, dive, dive. Fuck that. There were boats, though. There was a fast RIB they were using as a tender for the sub. He could get to the other shore, that busy main road, stop a car... or hide, wait for daylight, get away in a camper van or something bigger... no. Tomorrow would be too late. Would his strength last? It was just a crease. Just a scratch. It would have to last. He would have to last. Survive. That was the thing. Survive. He climbed stiffly out of the pickup. Gun, backpack, handheld Garmin satnav. Night vision? He had Leitz infra-red binoculars. It should have been enough. Stupid. Those bastards had been using Cryes. That English fucking marine. So much unfinished business.

Still. There were paths through these woods. He'd spent a lot of time in them, a lot of valuable killing time. Crittirs. Deer, squirrel, rabbits, hare. Plenty of souvenirs. He'd find his way.

It took him an hour of steady, pain-defying military jogging. The occasional dead end, some badger paths into impenetrable barbed nets of thorns. Finally, he hit the old military road and jogged along it, diving into the bushes when lights indicated a car.

The power station pier was flooded with brutal industrial light, the steady pulse of police car blue rooflamps adding a weird epileptic flutter to the scene. The *Baptist*, carrying red and green riding lights and dimly lit, was moored to a buoy about 20 metres offshore. He wondered if anyone was aboard. It was impossible to tell from his prone position, on the very edge of the treeline. The RIB he was looking for was next to her. And he could see that Subaru, the Brit woman's car. But he'd shot the tyres. Fuck. Run flats. He should've thought of it.

There were police, two uniformed, maybe one plain clothes, and they were talking to the woman. A lot of movement, waving, hands going everywhere. This wasn't working for him. Pain in the back. Pain in the neck. He'd have to try somewhere else. Something else. A car in the village. Why hadn't he considered that? Steal a car and try to get past the inevitable road blocks. Might work.

Losing it. Maybe he was losing it. Decide. Act.

And then there were two muffled explosions, one a few seconds after the other. He knew immediately that the blasts were on the water, probably under it. Chemical timers, probably some kind of improvised mine. He'd heard that sound before. Practised responding, back in the day. There was even a company in the States that made replicas of every kind of improvised explosive device, for training purposes, they said. You could practise on anything. Roadside bombs, home-made underwater limpets. That's what this sounded like. Black powder stuff. Nitrogen fertiliser in a pipe. Crude but effective. There was no visual indication at first that anything had happened. Then he watched the *Baptist* begin to list away from her mooring buoy, tilting slowly.

After about 30 seconds, the hatch on top of the *Baptist* opened and a figure climbed jerkily out. One of the crew must have been sleeping on board. Security? Who's idea had that been? Vance's? Jesus, he was supposed to be his security advisor. Had been. Maybe they'd thought it up for themselves. He was going to get out, whoever he was. Just the one person. He disappeared as the vessel sank lower and lower in the water. Headlights from the cars on the pier were being turned out into the loch, catching the scene, the calm water in oily ripples, the pseudo-submarine. Its bright yellow hull was now a weird, sick near-green. Then the roar of an outboard. The RIB. The man who'd been on board, crew, guard, whatever, he was heading for the pier, slowly, as if he was out for a pleasure cruise, or a routine trip.

Then all the floodlights on the pier went out. The car headlights were left, beaming weirdly out in the loch. For a moment he thought he saw something, something low in the water, a strange pulse of movement. But by that time he was up and running.

*** *** ***

"Put out the headlights! Put them out!" Murricane was shouting, trying to raise his night-vision goggles, switching them on at the same time, peering out over the water. What had moved out there?

"Don't be an asshole, Murricane" said Peyronie. "I can see perfectly well. You bloody southerners with your city eyesight. There's a canoe. Somebody in a canoe."

The RIB's outboard faded to silence and suddenly they heard a voice echoing in over the water.

"The loch is innocent! The creature is innocent! The way of the sun and moon is innocent." The accent was distinctive.

"Davie," said Flaws. "Davie the Druid."

"Well, he is innocent," said Murricane. "You can tell that to your bought and sold superiors, Mr, ah, Peyronie. And to your wife, who I believe knows him. Innocent of nearly everything except blowing up a very expensive tourist submarine. And possibly attempted murder if you want to push it. But frankly, he's a very minor sinner indeed. What's an attempted murder between friends? Rebecca here will confirm this, if she has any authority left, or ever had any."

"I've been trying to explain to Mr Peyronie that I am here as departmental liaison," said Rebecca. "And as you have doubtless realised, to no great effect. Although the fact that Davie is here at all probably indicates that things are swinging in our direction, gentlemen. In yours."

"Which bloody department, though? The one that shut down the emergency services call-out network for the entire Highlands? And all of you armed to the teeth, totally without legality." Peyronie looked dazed. "Where would Davie learn about blowing up boats, anyway?" Flaws looked quizzically at Murricane. "The bloody internet, no doubt. Full of recipes for disaster and destruction." And at that moment there was a burst of gunfire from the northern edge of the pier. There was a splash and then the roar of the outboard.

"Jenks," said Flaws. "That has to be..." He raised the M11.

"Don't bother, Zander," said Murricane. "The range is..."

But the tinny chatter of the little gun had begun. Flaws was firing at phosphorescence, the glimmer of disturbance in the water. The engine note remained constant and all sign of the boat disappeared.

"Maybe Davie'll get him," said Peyronie. "Put that implement down, please, Mr Flaws. You might hurt someone."

"I believe that's what it was designed for," Flaws said, mildly. "But your wish is my command, Eric."

"Please don't call me that," said Peyronie. "The name is Richard."

*** *** ***

Jenks didn't see the canoe. Davie, in his camouflaged fishing Oceanwave kayak, neither saw nor heard him coming. He was dead, caught through the head and neck by two of Flaws's stray bullets. The RIB hit the kayak amidships, right where Davie's body was slumped. A little to the left or right and it would probably have surfed straight over the top of the little craft, but instead, as its momentum took the bow up into the air and over the kayak, the propeller of the big Mercury 50 horse power outboard caught Davie's Spraydeck, jammed, sheared its safety pins and the big inflatable flipped sideways, throwing Jenks into the water. The RIB continued to cartwheel, the engine now dead but its massive weight catching Jenks just above the left knee, shattering the femur but leaving the femoral artery intact.

The pain was excruciating. He had broken bones before, had suffered stab and bullet wounds, torn muscles, been kicked, punched and slashed, but nothing like this. He wondered if he'd lost his leg. All ability to move anything on his left side had gone. And he was sinking. Water filled his nose and mouth.

Cold. He was cold. Cold down one side, the right. What was happening to him? This wasn't right. Things weren't meant to end. Not like this. He was in control. He was the one who ended lives, who had proved his ability to end lives. Who displayed for his own satisfaction the trophies from those little existences he'd terminated. He shut his mouth, swallowed the cold water. Moved his right arm, right leg. His back was sore. And then he felt something beneath him. The bed of the loch? It was impossibly deep here, but he might have sunk more quickly than he'd... but no. This was something else. A log. A submerged tree? It felt... slimy. And organic. A sunken boat? It seemed to be moving. Something...

He came to in agony, coughing water, choking and with his head and shoulders resting on a tiny gravel beach. From the chest down he was still in the water, and unable to move. Where was he? How had he got here? He lay there, shock and cold and pain weaving through him. But he was alive. Somehow, he had survived. He was a survivor. Now all he had to do was move.

*** *** ***

"We'll call out the Lifeboat from Temple Pier," said Seoras. His uniform looked, as ever, slightly rumpled. So did his face. "In the morning. First light."

"What about Davie?" The Adderall was fading from Murricane's system. Flaws looked how he felt. Sick, old. A hangover from hell about to envelope both of them. He'd forgotten all about the drinking until now. His leg throbbed. They'd all heard the hollow glassfibre thump and the screeching howl of the RIB's engine; then silence. A borrowed rowing boat had revealed the upturned boat and the split remnants of a fishing kayak, readily identified as Davie's. No bodies. Nothing when they'd righted the capsized RIB.

"Why not just now?" Flaws was swaying with exhaustion. Even the eternally energetic Rebecca was preoccupied, crouched in a corner of the pier with her satphone, doubtless deciding their fates.

"Because," Seoras said, " there is a football match on. Just hitting half time. Scotland versus Luxembourg. Chance we could win it. Half time in about..." he pulled out his mobile, checked the screen. "Two minutes. Nil-nil."

"What's that got to do with it?" Murricane felt confused. Policemen didn't abandon a crucial part of the biggest murder inquiry in their career – how many dead up at Creag Dhearg? – for the sake of an international football match. Even one Scotland might just have a chance of winning.

"Because of this," said Seoras. "Listen."

The air began to tremble, to vibrate; there was a sound, a kind of slow, ragged humming. The floodlit power station seemed to shimmer and vibrate, like a body builder clenching his or her muscles in preparation for a lift.

In Luxembourg, with 30 seconds of injury time played at the end of the first half, Scotland had just scored a goal of such surpassing glory and wonder that the percentage of the nation's population watching on television had, as one, erupted in cheering and, for those with the physical strength or sobriety, physical movement. As the whistle was blown for the end of the half, family members were called, astonished football fans claiming that this was, just once, maybe, a game Scotland could win. Extra televisions were switched on as the news came through on Twitter and text. Kettles were filled and switches flicked. A nation stirred. The atmosphere became electric. And electricity, suddenly, was badly needed.

At Scottish and Southern Energy's Network Management Centre in Perth the spike in consumption was instantly picked up and the company's two functioning pumped-storage hydro power stations came on line immediately. In the hills above Loch Ness, a gigantic steel valve – actually a simple shuttering device – opened, and the shaft leading from Loch Mhor filled with water. Further west, towards Invermoriston, the network of pipes and tunnels leading from the artificial reservoir on the River Tarff began feeding high pressure water down into a cavern burrowed out of the rock. The 100 megawatt Glendoe power station, built in 2009 and carefully shrouded from potentially aggrieved tourists' attention by hundreds of metres of solid rock, began generating electricity within 90 seconds. At Foyers, where the basic technology stretched back more than half a century, it took a little longer. But in each case, millions of gallons of water previously pumped from Loch Ness met turbines. Water moving at up to 200 mph.

The two turbines at Foyers have blades 16 feet long, and each weighs 914 tonnes. The weight of the water, pressurised and moving so fast, hits them and for a microsecond stops, then begins to move the blades. Two enormous shafts in the main building next to the pier start to turn, with painful slowness at first, then faster, and faster still, a rumble gradually growing to a kind of elemental screech. Despite the advent of computer technology there are still old fashioned analogue gauges which show the power output of the turbines. They vibrate along with the rest of the building as a gigantic natural bathtub drains and kettles boil throughout the country, and 100 cubic metres of water per second rushes out into the loch.

Operating together, the two power stations can raise the level of Loch Ness by up to a metre. Normally, this is controlled by outflow systems integrated with the power stations, but there is an inevitable increase in level anyway. When the outflow systems aren't working, levels can be unexpectedly high.

On the pier, as the twin Foyers turbines reached peak operating capacity, the whole of Loch Ness and the surrounding hills seemed to shimmer in the blue near-darkness.

"The power station," said Rebecca.

"That thing there," said Flaws.

"I hope they've fixed the outflow pipes at Fort Augustus," said Seoras. "The Beastie doesn't like it when her habitat's disturbed. But that's the fitba' for you, eh?"

Murricane looked at him and said nothing.

*** *** ***

A WHISKY IN MONSTERVILLE

Jenks was moving. At least, he thought one side of him was moving. Centimetres at a time. Millimetres. Bits of millimetres. Fractions. Decimal points. Clenching, tensing muscles, tightening and loosening. The muscles were responding, the skin. Atoms. Flecks of blood and tissue. But his body stayed where it was, in and out of the water.

The pain was crushing. He laid his cheek on the wet shingle of the beach and found himself drifting. Back in time to childhood, to his father. Other nights lying on dirt and gravel, in agony, waiting for more of it to arrive from his father's boot, baseball bat, rifle butt.

Comfort. He sought comfort in the past, the same retreat he had found back then. The souvenirs. The birds' wings, heads, birds' entire bodies. Racoons, even a skunk. He laughed at the thought of the smell, that terrible aroma that would not come out of his clothes. Another beating. Another night with his cheek in the dirt.

Home schooling. No teacher to see what had been going on. His father's strange take on religion, fundamentalism lifted from every conceivable source he could obtain on the TV and through the mail. Internet? Not then, not for them, thank somebody's God. There would have been no end to his father's mad acquisition of beliefs.

Wet. Tears. Tears he had not shed for decades. No, not tears. He wasn't a weeper. The tide was coming in. But there was no tide on this lake, this loch. Landlocked. Rockbound. It was creeping slowly, icily past his ear now. He told his body to move, everything within him screaming for obedience from blood and bone. But the water crept higher and higher. Until he had to keep his mouth closed, breathing through his nose. Was his neck broken? Was he a tetraplegic, paralysed utterly? Not that it made any difference. He thought about prayer, to one of his father's fickle gods, to the God of Coldstream. To Vance's cynical collection of deities.

What was that? Was he feeling his feet float? Or was he flying, moving up through the water, up into the air? No. It was just a delusion. The water was at his nose now, and he had to breathe or die. Breathe and die. Breathe and die.

He smelt something then. Something familiar and comforting. Tasted it, too, in his last moments, as he inhaled water and shifting beach gravel. Burnt and rotting flesh filled him with its benediction, and he saw them, all his souvenirs, his collection, from childhood to the ice house, so close, so far away. Faces. All staring at him. All laughing. Fingers pointing.

Last supper

Raisins, damp linen, oak, beeswax, pork scratchings. peach juice and prickle of apricot skins on a hot Mallorcan night. Dark roasted spices, with a touch of cigar smoke.

AUCHENTOSHAN 1979 OLOROSO

A WHISKY IN MONSTERVILLE

He had started with *mousse de homard d'écosse en habit vert, sauce au Champagne*. Lobster mousse. Wrapped in green stuff. Spinach. Beware the lobster mousse, Popeye! That old Monty Python sketch. It was absolutely delicious, particularly with the half bottle of Réserve Mouton Cadet Graves Blanc. Enough for one. Moderation. It was a novelty. He'd have a glass of the Château D'Armailhac, AOC Pauillac 2006 that was open and sniffing the pleasantly garlic-scented air behind the bar. The Baron Philippe was hard to better.

Now he was on the French onion soup – *Soupe à L'oignon Gratinée*, as it was termed on the menu. Not *Soupe Francaise*, but then, why should it be? Lobster mousse and onion soup. Classic French country cooking. In Scotland. In Inverness. Courtesy of one of Albert Roux's many imitators. He felt the pulsing pain in his knee ease slightly.

Murricane was alone. He was giving himself a treat: early dinner for one at La Vielle Alliance, known locally as the VA. This small hotel on the fringes of Crown wasn't the Prebble. There was no raffish owner holding court in a pool of spilt single malt. It was owned by someone who went by the name of Gustave Flaubert, and, despite his fluent French and excellent culinary skills was almost certainly something like Billy Bloggs from Bermondsey. The head waiter was called Arthur, second name probably Rimbaud, though Murricane had never asked. Whatever, the food was fantastic and the French accents entertaining. It was good to be alone.

Flaws was busy, he'd said, with one of his supermarket widows. Maybe. Real or imaginary. Rebecca was in London. Really in London. Back in the bosom of her blessed department. Loyal to her adoptive family of faceless civil servants, or former soldiers with ugly scars. No ex-matelots with broken knees. She'd left the Subaru, with vague promises to come back and collect it. He suspected it was now some written-off asset, maybe even a drug deal confiscation. At any rate, he'd had new tyres fitted (colossally expensive VR rated Michelins, £250 each) and was enjoying driving it like a teenage hooligan. A late-life crisis of sorts. It was why he was in Inverness, to have the Scooby's turbo recalibrated. Its software tweaked. Something like that. Something he didn't pretend to understand. Perhaps he'd see if the VA had any rooms free. If the mood took him.

The massacre of Creag Dhearg, some papers had called it. *Bloody Cult of Monstrous Death*, one headline had read. Online speculation was even more lurid. The relatives of the cult members who had died had raged tearfully and incontinently on Twitter and Facebook. There was a Creag Dhearg Bereavement Forum. The few Nessatoreans who had survived were keeping a very low profile. Some were still in a form of what Rebecca called 'restorative custody'. Whatever that was.

It was as if Jenks had never existed. Coldstream was dead. It would have been a miracle if he'd pulled through, and if anyone didn't deserve a miracle, Murricane thought, it was Coldstream. He'd never gone back to look at the ice house, but if it hadn't been bulldozed it would have been clinically cleared, by Percy's eradication and extraction teams. Vance, well. Vance's body had – ostensibly – been found at Creag Dhearg, among *The Congregation of The Damned*, as one online magazine had put it. *Cowardly Poisoning Pastor of Hate Shot Those Who Ran*. Vance was identified as one of those, like the hapless Murder McGlone. He was portrayed as a deluded millionaire, a Howard Hughes figure, some said, rich beyond the dreams of avarice, swept up into funding Coldstream's madness. A submarine? Everyone knew the waters of Loch Ness were almost opaque, that no-one was really going to see anything. If there was anything to see, which most sensible people doubted. The masters of spin, disinformation and threat on both sides of the Atlantic had been hard at work

And Davie. Davie the Druid. Vindicated after death, environmental hero, saint. His spirit of course lives on, of course it does, in the trees, in the wind, in the bullshit. Poor Davie, thought Murricane. Unlucky in the end. Those home-made limpet mines. Effective. But then, Davie had learned by example. From Murricane. Had been with him that night, that fateful, stupid, drunken night, out to Muirtown and the bastarding gin palace

Sunseeker that had tipped him into the loch. Personal revenge. Uncool. And it had led, partly, to this.

Davie had a source of black powder, of course he did, from charcoal burners up in the high woodlands, one of the hippy communes up there. He got his black powder there for the little smoke and mirrors tricks your average post-Celtic shamanistic grand master had to perform sometimes to impress his followers. Of course he could get Murricane some. As long as he could tag along. As long as he could see what Murricane was up to.

And in those days Murricane had been prone to consuming a bottle of malt a day, plus whatever else he could get, Davie could get. Mushrooms, dope. Whatever. Not to mention the prescription stuff. The Tramadol and the jellies.

The claret. Murricane silently raised a glass, thinking of absent friends. And enemies.

"Do you mind? Any more of that red stuff? I wonder if there's a spare glass in the vicinity? I see they have a bottle of Baron Pip open behind the bar. Maybe we should just have it over, eh? Should we have it decanted? The divine Jancis Robinson always says decanting is the equivalent of four hours with the top off. And I presume she was talking about wine."

Percival sat himself down gently, carefully. He was looking, thought Murricane, very fit and well. The cat who had got, if not the cream, then a reasonable portion of salmon flavoured Whiskas. Sleekly dressed in a moleskin suit, open Gieves and Hawkes shirt. A tan.

"Been on holiday?"

"Los Angeles. California generally. A swift trip to Washington and then home. Soothing some ruffled feathers, laying on of hands, so to speak. Healing wounds. Knocking together a few heads. Kicking a few heads in, actually."

"Knives in a few backs? I see." One of the typically efficient VA waiters arrived with a glass, the bottle of Pauillac and a place setting. Crisp linen napkin. Everything easy, unobtrusive. Percival nodded his approval.

"Nice place, this. I believe the chef-proprietaire calls himself Gustave Flaubert these days. He used to have a bistro in Bristol. But he was calling himself Verlaine then. Tim Verlaine."

"Really? I hear Gustave is expanding. Opening a country house place at the other end of the Great Glen, near Fort William. La Nouvelle Alliance, it'll be called. More upmarket than this. You should try it when it opens. They're pitching it at celebrities, Americans, Hollywood types."

"Is there golf? Some of the Americans I have... been breaking bread with might very well be keen on a visit. Sounds like their kind of place."

"Golf? Maybe. Plenty of whisky. Mountains. Ben Nevis. Further west there are some interesting old mines, I believe."

"Yes. Well, anyway. Shall we bother asking for a decanter?"

"You paying? If so, you can do what you want. But I think it's fine as it is." He poured an inch of wine into Percival's glass. "See what you think."

Percy sipped the deep red Bordeaux, sucking it between his teeth as if it was mouthwash. "Hmmm. Not bad. All very much of a muchness, though, don't you think, clarets these days? Spoiled by all those Australians. Flying Winemakers with a taste for burnt toast, I shouldn't wonder. That's what all their wines are like. I favour Argentina, myself. Malbec. Terribly underrated grape variety."

"I'll stick with the Rothschilds, I think. Your health, anyway. Slainte! Not terribly nice to see you, even if you are paying."

"I haven't said I would, have I?" Their glasses chinked together. "Miss Elmsworth sends her... regards. That's, ah, one of the reasons I'm here. The car."

"The car?"

"That Subaru. It's on the department's books. Registered."

"I've just bought four new tyres for it. A thousand quid."

"I thought you had a vehicle. A Land Rover or something, Miss Elmsworth said. Surely more in keeping with your rural bohemian lifestyle?"

Murricane looked at him and said nothing. Eventually Percy sighed and reached inside his jacket.

"Registration document. Signed. I suppose we owe you something for your, ah, trouble."

"Indeed, you do. An explanation for a start."

"Oh, I rather thought you'd have worked things out for yourself. Now then." Percival peered at the menu, which had appeared in his hand as by some kind of voodoo. The waiter was imported. Polish and elderly, he had that appearance of dignity and ease which comes from long experience. London vowel sounds, eastern European consonants, French slang. Probably brought in by Gustave and Arthur to help train up the other, local staff. Young people who needed some of the servile magic to rub off on them.

"You've had the fish and the soup, haven't you? What are you doing about a main course?"

"*Daube de boeuf A l'ancienne.* Fish, soup, beef, why not? It's local."

"Indeed? Well, make that two. Goes with the claret I suppose." The waiter disappeared. "No apology, Murricane."

"None expected."

"Yes. No." A sigh. "You were under orders, and so was I. The Afghan thing. The idea was that you were to extract the evidence that would make Vance and his companies... unviable in American eyes. At least in territories where we had an interest."

"What about the so-called kidnapped charity worker? All that, what was it? The Islamic Centre for Agricultural Growth and Development. The plot to find a Sunni Aga Khan?"

"Smokescreen, I'm afraid. Connell, Bill Connell, our man. He would have been witness for the prosecution against KokVan, against Vance, against the Global Repentance and Redemption Trust. Well, I say prosecution. All under the radar. No *courts.*" Percival said the word as if it were some kind of ritual curse. "But Vance got to the Americans, who got to my superiors, and the next thing Jenks, or the man commonly known as Jenks, was in the mix. Mopping things up, taking out whomsoever he thought it necessary to take out. On Vance's behalf. And destroying the evidence. That heroin all vanished, you know. Though I expect it was made to reappear in pretty short order."

"And I was completely crocked, but not removed altogether from this mortal coil."

"Left as damaged goods. But of course, we kept an eye on you. Kept up with your welfare. You had Flaws."

" No, you had Flaws."

"We had Flaws. And then Rebecca... Miss Elmsworth. She came here to watch the Strontian aspects of things. And to see if your reactivation was a possibility, or if we should just use you as per orders from above. As meat to the grinder. Like poor Foster."

"Vance had everything sewn up. And he was completely and utterly bonkers. Mad and bad. And dangerous."

"Yes, but so very useful. So very rich. And then the Varlindium..."

"The Varlindium." Their beef arrived. It was so tender their forks cut through the meat as if it were butter, and yet there was still a slight resistance in the mouth and a near-perfect juiciness. "The Varlindium was, if you'll pardon the pun, the touchstone." Murricane swallowed. It was worth whatever it was costing Percy. He was determined now that the old man would pay.

"You saw all this as a chance to destroy Vance. There were probably people in the States seeing it the same way, the ones behind that undercover woman in Coldstream's church – Avril Anson. Yeah, she'd worked with Rebecca, hadn't she? And then there were Vance's supporters, some mad militarised evangelicals on nodding terms with Coldstream. Two factions in Whitehall too, the appeasers and the let's-fuck-the-bastards, let's act out of the moral righteousness we learned during the Eton fucking wall game. That sounds like you, Percy. That sounds just like you."

"This beef is really rather good. And the Bordeaux is almost on a par. But not quite. Argentine beef with a really good Malbec. In Buenes Aires. A collaboration made in heaven.

"Made in South America, actually. Am I right?"

"Touch and go, it was all pretty touch and go," said Percival. "Had to see if you were capable of dragging yourself into the fray with the verve I remember from yesteryear. And if you hadn't, if you didn't, well..." He waved a fork diffidently. "That would have been that. Vance would have remained a defence asset, the Varlindium would have been mined, Monsterville would have been built, and Coldstream might not have poisoned his hapless followers."

"Jenks?"

"No sign. Thought drowned after his little boating mishap. They found your, ah, acquaintance, the druidic Mr Lees, eventually. Washed up near, what do they call that place? Invermoriston. Shot, it appears, by bullets from an M11. But I expect you know all that. From Flaws. Or the Inspector with the unfortunate name."

"Peyronie?"

"I wonder if he's a descendent? Of Francois De La Peyronie, I mean."

"Who was?"

"Discovered the disease named after him. In the 18th century, I believe, at the French royal court. It's to do with penile plaques, scar tissue, following sexual trauma. Mostly found in middle-aged men. I'm surprised you don't have it yourself. Leads to deformity of the penis. Bending."

"That's why his colleagues call him Eric."

"Eric?"

"For 'erectile dysfunction'."

"Charming. Anyway, it was, apparently Flaws who was using the M11 during your little... adventure."

"I hope you haven't told Flaws this. And that Peyronie hasn't told him either."

"Mr Flaws has been reminded of his signature of the Official Secrets Act. No further information regarding armaments, forensics or ballistics has been passed his way. And he didn't ask. He did ask about money, and he is still on a retainer from our, ah, office. He'll keep an eye on you, should you decide to stay in the vicinity. Living your, if I may say so, rather self-indulgent lifestyle."

"I have a sore leg."

"You seem... to compensate for it. May I have your permission to call on you as, let us say, a consultant? Should the need arise."

Murricane ignored the question. "The Varlindium. If it's so valuable, and it's there, how are you going to...?"

"Ah. Have you seen the local newspaper today? The Highland, is it *Courier*?"

A WHISKY IN MONSTERVILLE

"*Inverness Courier* on a Friday, *Highland News* on a Thursday. Broadsheet and tabloid. Same company." Murricane watched with some astonishment as Percival removed an iPhone from his pocket, frowned at it and performed the range of finger-dabs and swipes that were necessary to make it reveal its wonders. Then he handed it across the table.

A miniaturised version of the *Highland News's* front page winked at him.

"If you sort of... snap your fingers, it will..."

"I know." He enlarged the text. *Third power station for Loch Ness* was the headline. Another, bigger pump storage facility, between Glendoe and Foyers. 'Massive investment', the story said. 'Two year project. Major underwater survey of the loch. Possible use of a commercial submersible from the North Sea.'

"Handy."

"Yes, convenient. Partnership between the ah, South of Scotland Electricity people – though technically this is the north – and an American company. An American company of... my acquaintance. Approved. Thoroughly approved. Vetted."

"No Monsterville, though."

"No. Are you a sweet sort of person? Cheese?"

*** *** ***

They moved into the VA's discreet little lounge-cum-bar, La Recherche. Espresso for both, Murricane kept it traditional and had the *Croustilliant aux Chocolate Noir, Glace Café*. It was Death by Chocolate only in French. Percival had *Tarte a la Frangipanes et Póire Pocheé*.

"Are you having a dram?" he asked Percival.

"Oh, I don't think so. Grain and grape, that kind of thing. You?"

"Driving. Half bottle of white doesn't count. What was it Pavarotti said? White wine is for women... begging the pardon of absent feminists. One glass of red. Or two. You had the bulk. I'll be all right. Besides, I know the road."

"Still popping the odd Adderall, are we?"

"No, just copper coins to take away the smell. In case you call the cops and have me stopped."

Percival smiled. "I wouldn't do that, Murricane. I have too much invested in you to play such a nasty trick. That would be terribly underhand. Now then," – he tapped the table – "that really was very good. Who's paying?"

Murricane gazed at the old man for perhaps ten seconds. Then he reached into a pocket and pulled out a small metal box. It was meant for holding rolling tobacco, and you could buy them in most of the tourist shops along Loch Ness. Its lid was adorned with a lurid picture of Nessie in full plesiosaur mode, not unlike the ones that had adorned the Creag Dhearg drawing room, Coldstream's church of death.

"Here you go." He handed it to Percival, who accepted it gingerly.

"Thank you. Thank you. And... may I open it? What..."

"It's... a souvenir." For a moment Percival looked genuinely shocked, and Murricane knew, delightedly, that he suspected he would find inside the little box an ear, a fingertip, even an eyeball. But he was too old a hand to flinch, and he popped the lid off the tin with one of those weirdly hardened thumbnails. He rummaged through the fine tissue paper, lifted the glittering, feathery object to the light.

"A lure," he said. "All your own work?"

"It's what I do, these days. I just thought I'd remind you. It's called the Columban Dragonbird. Good for salmon, when they're running. So I'm told."

"A lure," Percival said softly. "A suitable occupation. I take it you wish me to cover the bill. Do you think they take Coutts cheques here?"

Drumnadrochit time

A sweetie shop, candy, sweet-scented candles, mints, custard and woolly jumpers after a rainstorm. Aniseed in the mouth, gobstoppers, linseed oil, caramel and spearmint. A huge floral flourish to finish.

DRY FLY PORT FINISHED WHEAT WHISKEY

A WHISKY IN MONSTERVILLE

He drove back to Drumnadrochit sedately, parked at the Piper's Rest and went into the almost-deserted bar for a nightcap. Jan was clearing up after the fading custom of a Thursday night at the end of the season. He poured them both large Muckle Fluggas, a factory whisky apparently 'aged on a cliff face in the Shetland Island of Unst'.

"Brand fiddling," Jan said. "But it's actually all right. Cheap and cheerful. All you deserve, chucking away that young lass."

"Chucked by, actually. Chucked by."

"Och, women, eh? Can't live with 'em, can't shoot 'em! Families! Listen, we had a family in tonight," Jan said, "Americans. The dad was deaf, no hearing aid or anything, vanity I expect, and the boy, about 12, and his mum had obviously got used to shouting at the tops of their voices, all the time. Their entire dinner was conducted at just earsplitting volume. Everyone, me included, we're going, Americans, eh? What do you expect. So feckin' noisy. Shouting and bawling their bloody heads off." He paused. "Sorry. Bit insensitive. I know you found that... anyway. Finally the wifey comes up to me and she's whispering or what she thinks is whispering, except it's like the loudest stage whisper you've ever heard, and she's saying 'I'M REAL SORRY ABOUT THE VOLUME... THE OLD MAN'S A BIT HARD OF HEARING...'"

Murricane laughed, lifted his glass.

"Cheers."

"Cheers." The whisky was soft, creamy and about as island in character as Chipping Norton gin. As far as Murricane knew they didn't make whisky there. Or gin.

They spent an hour or so selecting increasingly rare malts. And drinking them. It wasn't the way to do it. Best to start expensive and then get cheap, as your taste buds grew more and more sedated. But they went from a 10-year-old Springbank through a Glen Scotia Distillery Select to a mighty Longrow 18-year-old single cask. And despite being in Drumnadrochit, they never left Campbeltown.

A WHISKY IN MONSTERVILLE

Still. Murricane didn't stumble, at least not much, as he made his way back to the *Gloria* through the twisted paths of the Cover, armed only with a customised Petzl head torch, one of the old focusable single-bulb versions, converted to use a halogen bulb and alkaline batteries. The night-vision sets had been whisked away along with the various forms of weaponry he and Flaws had been carrying. By Rebecca, accompanied by two large and lumbering members of Police Scotland Northern Division's firearms team, both of them in absolute thrall to Miss Elmsworth. He had decided not to contest their confiscation. There were always other guns available. There were always other guns available in Drumnadrochit. And these days, even with the kind of protection, such as it was, he enjoyed, you couldn't be too careful. Some poor ex-SAS bastard had been jailed for five years for keeping a Glock as a souvenir from the Big A. Let out after a public outcry, but still. Who needed that shit?

Souvenirs. He thought of Jenks. Body never found.

The wind was getting up, and the stunted trees whistled and creaked. It was cold too, though the alcohol in his bloodstream let him shrug that off. He had dressed relatively neatly for his visit to Inverness. Moleskin jacket, whipcord trousers, a Fair Isle sweater. Still, it would be good to get home. The icy halogen light caught the blazed tree-bark, the markers that signed his way. Roots curled beneath his feet, joined now by fallen leaves. Wet leaves. The loch had been abnormally high. Some kind of fault at the Fort Augustus outfall. They'd fixed it now. A shiver ran through his body. Autumn was on its way. After that, winter. The dying, the death... and then the rebirth of spring. Christ, he was starting to sound religious. Or mystical. He thought he heard Davie the Druid chuckling.

The darkness was profound, now, the white nights of summer gone. Beneath the shifting hiss of the trees he felt, suddenly, another presence. But it was the whisky whispering, he told himself.

It was too cold to sit outside, so he scrambled into bed clutching a last Highland Park, 25 years old, and a lump of strong artisan Wensleydale cheese he'd picked up at the new deli in Drum, Les Deliceuses. Cheese and whisky. Dreams and nightmares, or was it the other way round? He woke to a blue-grey dawn light, and the eerie howl of a gale, the old boat shifting slightly, uneasily. Winter was on its way. And what would he do with himself then? Wait for the call from Percy, if it ever came? Another free VA meal, old alliances patched up, an order to go and do some consultancy work far away? Azerbaijan? Jordan? Ireland? Edinburgh?

He pulled on some threadbare sweats, made coffee with the Aeropress. He'd picked it up years ago, seen one used by some of the US CIA guys, coffee fanatics. Apparently it was the only other thing designed by the guy who came up with the Frisbee. A kind of giant syringe. The coffee, pressed through a filter by sheer wrist-force, was particularly sludge-free. He wasn't in the mood for sludge.

He took the hot drink outside, staying in the shelter of the afterdeck. The loch and the sky were one, a grey, turbulent mass, pressing in on him, glowering and angry. It was when he looked over the side, feeling *Gloria* shift at her mud-locked moorings, that he saw the body.

The visible flesh was bleached white and blubbery by immersion, with one leg twisted unnaturally and clearly badly mashed above the knee. The eyes had gone, nibbled by birds, and it had been in the water about a week, he thought. It was tangled in the roots where the Cover's miniature Everglades met the loch. US camouflage fatigues. It moved with the lapping of the waves. It was, just, recognisable.

But Jenks could wait.

He gazed out at the loch, which was turning to a kind of greenish-white rotten milk colour as the wind got up. There were eddies and waves, strange shapes, shadows and half-smudges on the surface. They could be the effect of the weather, old bits of wood, seals, otters, anything. A giant sturgeon. Something shifting off the bottom, disturbed by the power station outfalls, the unusual levels of the water. The coming of winter. He raised his mug in tribute to the great mass of mystery that was Loch Ness.

A WHISKY IN MONSTERVILLE

The biggest single water mass in Britain. Depthless, enigmatic, unforgiving.

"Here's to you," he said. The coffee was smooth to the taste. Not bitter at all.

*** *** ***

Two days later, at the very end of the trout season, he was crewing once more for Ferg, one last set of clients before the *Happy Adventure* was moored up for a month so Ferg could go and visit his daughter in Tenerife. He went annually.

"Salt water. Black sand. Weird as fuck, man. But it's nice to get a wee bit of a tan. Keeps you warm all the way through until spring. Got to prepare for the winter."

Winter. Murricane found he was looking forward to it. Maybe some skiing at Aonach Mor or Cairngorm. Get fit, get well, hang around an ink well or a button tow. Be good to get higher up, away from the bottom of the valley, the glens. Away from the water.

The customers looked miserable. A young couple from Australia, huddled in Quiksilver Gore-Tex, from Darwin, apparently, and used to big game Barrier Reef fishing, sun on bronzed flesh, the elemental hot weather dangers of the southern seas. Sharks. Jellyfish. Now they shivered and sipped gratefully at coffee Murricane had laced with Famous Grouse. He remembered the day Avril Anson's body had bumped against this same boat. Ferg clonking Kevin from the Lifeboat with the Grouse bottle. He'd been admonished. The ice house. Dimly, Murricane remembered a head, a mere glimpse. He'd said hello to Avril twice. And now goodbye. Put it away. Leave it behind. Deal with it.

A nameless bore in a bar had once told him that Famous Grouse's Scottish popularity was due not to its taste, but to the sound of its name Grrrrouse: it reflected the Scot's basic irascibility. He took a slug. It tasted of anger.

They'd lowered the downriggers and were trolling for the last of the Ferox, the water choppy but the sky a wispy, autumnal blue, scattered with fast-moving clouds. Murricane looked up at the hills above Foyers, and then down to where the loch stretched away west,

A WHISKY IN MONSTERVILLE

narrowing at Fort Augustus. He felt his heart lift. Urquhart Castle looked like a bad giant's battered home. Over there was Dores, with the promise of great, simple food. Further to the east, Inverness. Great, complicated food. Ans everywhere in the Highlands, the best alcoholic drink in the world. A whisky in Monsterville. Really, why be anywhere else?

"Heard you found a body. Another one." Ferg was staring straight ahead, keeping the boat on a steady course. "Lucky, you, eh? Funny it came ashore right where you lived."

"Yeah. Well, the loch likes to provide its souvenirs, doesn't it?"

"Eh?" Ferg regarded him with momentary puzzlement. "Who was it anyway?"

"Oh, just one of those mad fuckers from Creag Dhearg. Religious type. Out of his depth, eh? Police took him away. No doubt they'll find some relatives and tell them." Or maybe not, he thought.

Just then the new sensor on the starboard rod, one of Ferg's recent and treasured gadgets, began to bleep, and both men heard the line began its steady whine into the depths.

"Ferox?"

"Maybe," said Murricane. He went to the stern and clapped the Australian husband on the shoulder. "Don't want to make any gender assumptions, mate, but are you wanting to play this fish?" His wife, seated in the shelter of the cabin with her coffee, gave a snort of laughter.

"Him? No, he's just your average marine biologist, mate. Just wants to see a, what's it called, a Ferox trout, the bloody legend, before the loch gets wiped out by all that construction work they're planning." Her husband sat down beside her, patted her knee.

"Yeah, she's right mate. Look, why don't you play the fish, eh? I just want to clap eyes on one of the things. Just once. Snap a couple of pictures, get them up on the old blog, on Facebook. Add to my collection. Take a picture. Put it back."

"Construction work? You mean the power station? The new one? There's two already and they haven't made that much of a difference to the fish. Not so's you'd notice."

A WHISKY IN MONSTERVILLE

"Ah well, how do you know that, mate?" The man look rueful. "I hear this

one's going to be three times the size of the last, the one at what do you call it, Glendoe? Work'll go on for years, they say. Divers going down, submarines, blasting. Jobs, though. Loads of jobs. Good for local economy." He gazed around. "Seems a shame. All of this."

"Nessie won't like it," his wife said.

"No," said Murricane. "No. She won't." Then he smiled. "Well, Let's see what we can do with the last of the Ferox for this year, then, shall we?" He hefted the rod, felt the reel for tension. "Feels big," he said. "Feels like a monster."

Author's note

This book was inspired by several enormously entertaining stays at Fiddler's Bar and Bistro in Drumnadrochit, run by the Beach family. Any resemblance between it and the Piper's Rest is completely coincidental. There is no Jan Beach. Although there is a Jon.

Rob Allanson of Whisky Magazine was responsible for some of the tasting notes used in this book, and has been a frequent motorcycling companion on some hair-raising adventures.

Jim Lister and Stephen Wright of Fairpley Ltd first introduced me to Fiddlers and Jon, and have, along with their colleague Fergus Weir, done splendid, long-suffering promotional work for my one-man show, The Malt and Barley Revue (drinkingforscotland.blogspot.com) and indeed for this publication. The Revue was first performed at the Verb Garden, which they promote at Belladrum.

Joe Gibbs and Rob Ellen introduced me to the Belladrum 'Tartan Heart' Festival, one of the greatest outdoor events in Scotland. None of this could have happened without them.

Many thanks to two Jennies: Jennie McFie provided absolutely crucial background information about Loch Ness and Drumnadrochit, but ALL the characters in the books are fictitious, apart from the ones that obviously and deliberately aren't! And Jenny Henry saved my textual bacon by proofreading and copy editing.

For the cooking, recipes and any reasonably believable foodstuffs mentioned, my apologies to Rocpool Reserve and The Mustard Seed, in Inverness, The Anderson in Fortrose, The Dores Inn, Fiddlers, The Barley Bree in Muthill, Inverlochy Castle, Au Bord de l'Eau in Wick, Hay's Dock Cafe and Monty's in Lerwick, Cail Bruich, Two Fat Ladies at The Buttery and the Ubiquitous Chip in Glasgow.

A WHISKY IN MONSTERVILLE

And finally thanks to two offspring for their comments, Sandy Nelson and James Morton. I have lengthened some sentences. And shortened others.

Love always to Susan.

Printed in Great Britain
by Amazon.co.uk, Ltd.,
Marston Gate.